# BODY PARTS

## JESSICA KAPP

## YA

**DIVERSIONBOOKS**

Diversion Books
A Division of Diversion Publishing Corp.
443 Park Avenue South, Suite 1008
New York, New York 10016
www.DiversionBooks.com

This is a work of fiction. Names, characters, places and incidents either are the
product of the author's imagination or are used fictitiously. Any resemblance to
actual persons, living or dead, events or locales is entirely coincidental.

For more information, email info@diversionbooks.com

First Diversion Books edition August 2017.
Print ISBN: 978-1-63576-166-5
eBook ISBN: 978-1-68230-381-8

To Matt, Soleil, Autry, and Tatum.
You make me whole.

# CHAPTER 1

Ten seconds. That's how much air I have left.

I peek at Paige, her body submerged next to me. Stray hairs float around her face. She looks peaceful like she found a way to sleep underwater. The chlorine stings my eyes so I shut them, letting my mind fill with fuzz until all I hear is the cadence of my heart—the sluggish beat coursing all the way to my fingertips.

Five seconds.

My chest burns.

Three.

Two.

A tap on my head tells me it's over.

I break the surface and take in shallow, painful gulps of air. The edges of my vision swim with black and someone grips my arm to keep me from slipping back under. Parker's blurry face comes into focus as he anchors my limp body on the side of the pool. "You did it. You won."

When I manage a smile through my fit of coughs he hoists me out and places me next to Paige so our legs are dangling in the water.

She kicks me playfully. "Show-off."

"You almost had me."

"Almost." Her eyes flit across the gymnasium to the exit door and her smile fades. "Almost isn't good enough for them."

A shiver creeps through me, shaking some of the strength out of my voice. "If a family can't see how great you are, they don't deserve you."

She nods as if she's trying to convince herself. I'm not sure

I believe me either. If we were good enough, why hasn't a family fostered us by now?

There's laughter behind us, producing boisterous energy that drowns out the thoughts in my head.

Paige's slightly purple lips curl. "You have a point, I *am* pretty great." She extends her hand. "But, so are you. Nice job." Our grip is weak and our handshake is soft like the bones have been removed from our fingers. We let go and I lean into her, content to sit here doing nothing. Days are so scheduled at the Center for Excellence, relaxing is a luxury.

Parker squats down next to me and holds out the stopwatch our trainer left on his chair—the one we're not supposed to touch. "Two minutes, thirteen seconds. That's your best time yet, Tabitha."

A personal best. I should be proud. I *am* proud. But without a trainer to witness it, to record it on my chart, it might as well read zero. My only hope is that I can do it again. Prove to potential parents that I take my health as seriously as my studies—that I'd be a productive and responsible addition to their family.

That I'm worth taking a chance on.

Paige's self-doubt is contagious. I don't know why we do this to ourselves, why we feel the need to compete when our trainers are on a break. They put enough pressure on us already. Tears prick my eyes and I push the stopwatch out of my face. "All right. Who's next?"

"Me!" exclaims Paige's identical twin. Her hand shoots into the air as she struts toward Parker. Meghan likes to claim she's older, but none of our trainers can confirm it. She's so different than Paige, I wouldn't even believe they shared DNA if it weren't for their looks: olive skin, high cheekbones, and plenty of curves. Their presence commands attention.

Meghan pokes Parker in the chest when he stands. "What d'ya say? We can swim laps if you don't want to hold your breath." She cocks her head to the side until her thick brown hair kisses her shoulders. Unlike Paige, she never wears it up. She says it makes her feel more girly, but I think she just wants to be normal, like girls on the television shows we get to watch—our only connection to the outside.

"You're the fish, not me." He waves Meghan away then helps Paige to her feet. He pulls me up next and our eyes lock long enough for me to see his dread. Parker struggles in the pool. He blames his muscle density, but I know it's really just fear. When he was younger, a trainer held him underwater because he wouldn't get in the pool. Parker thought he was going to die. If I had enough energy, I'd take his place against Meghan. I know he'd do the same for me. His confidence may dissolve in the water, but at the Center, he's my rock.

He points a thumb at the wall kitty-corner to us. "Rope climb?"

"Not a chance." Meghan dives in with a splash. She is just as motivated as the rest of us to prove she can be the best. Drive and discipline are two of the things the Center teaches us. It's why families agree to open their homes to us instead of kids at a traditional state facility.

I glance at the mantra above the rock wall. The letters are partially hidden behind three ropes connected to a metal beam in the ceiling, but I can still make out the words: "It's what's on the inside that counts." The phrase gives me hope that our hard work will pay off someday.

Before Parker and Meghan can decide on a new challenge, the exit door buzzes. Parker tucks the stopwatch behind his back. My breath catches when I notice it's not a trainer—it's Ms. Preen. And, she's holding a red file, which can only mean one thing.

One of us is getting out.

Her heels make quick, light clicks as she crosses the floor past the weight equipment and yoga mats. She crinkles her nose as she moves through the thick cloud of sweat. By the time she reaches us, Meghan's out of the pool. We stand, two-dozen bodies huddled together, anxious to hear the news. I scan my friends' faces, wondering whose turn it is to go. Parker wraps his free arm around me. I imagine this is how a gymnast feels after a routine, waiting for her scores. Did I perform well enough? Could I have done more?

Will I win the ultimate prize: a family?

Ms. Preen presses through to the pool area, but stands far from our group, as if she thinks we'll throw her in.

It's crossed our minds before.

The light shines off her blonde bob and her face is flawless. Freeze-dried, we like to say.

"Where is she?" Ms. Preen looks at our group as if she can't tell us apart, which is probably true. Even though she pops in at least once a month to check on our vitals, she isn't interested in getting to know us. She's the one in charge of pairing us with families, but all she knows is what we're good at. Meghan is the fast one; Paige climbs like she's part monkey; Parker's built like a brick house; and me, I have the lungs.

"The redhead, where is she?"

All eyes turn to me.

"We have names, you know," Paige says, her voice curt. "Hers is Tabitha. T-A-B…"

Ms. Preen pulls a piece of paper out of the file, holding it up toward the row of skylights to read it. "Yes. She's the one."

Parker tightens his hold on me and I clasp my hands together to stop them from shaking. Ms. Preen doesn't need to know I'm nervous. I'm supposed to be elated, ready to go. Maybe I've been fooling myself.

I wriggle out of Parker's grip to step forward. "That's me." Ms. Preen looks at me, then to the pool, with a trace of disgust. "We were getting in some extra laps."

Paige laughs and I dip my head to hide my smile.

Ms. Preen shoves the paper back into the file. "Get dressed. I'm taking you for your final screening. If you pass, you'll be out tomorrow." Her voice is hard and she turns to walk away.

I glance back at the group, at the faces I've known since childhood. They're excited for me, but I can see the disappointment in their eyes. I know the look, because up until today I've watched friends leave, waiting for my turn.

Now that it is, I can't move.

Paige gives me a weak smile and, for a moment, I thin..
going to lean in for a hug. Instead she crosses her arms, squeezing herself tight. "If you're not back by dinner, we'll save you
some broccoli."

I wonder if I'll be able to eat at all. Paige has always been good
at masking the pain with humor. It makes me sad to know she's
doing it for my sake. I don't want to be mourned. I keep my tone
light as I march toward the sleeping quarters on the opposite end
of the gym. "Don't do me any favors."

As I slip through the girls' door, it feels like the walls and low
ceiling immediately box me in. When I first transferred here, I
missed the bright colors and patterns. Brain noise. The facility for
younger kids felt more alive. Freer. Here, it's like being in a cage;
except right now it's almost comforting. I'm not sure I want to
leave. But isn't this what I wanted, the chance to have a family? I
curse myself for being such a coward and swallow my fear, pretending Ms. Preen's news doesn't affect me.

Water drips off me while I rummage through my dresser. I pull
out a sweatshirt that smells like sweat and perseverance. It's cold
where we sleep, but it feels especially uncomfortable today—like
the room has already forgotten me. Soon my bed will be occupied,
filled by someone else, someone still waiting to be fostered. I'll be
a record on the wall, a memory in the minds of those who trained
with me until they're gone too.

The crisp air fills my lungs as I peel off my bathing suit. I
change quickly because Ms. Preen has as much patience as she does
wrinkles. I can almost hear her call my name when I step back out
into the gymnasium. I know I'm imagining things though—Ms.
Preen wouldn't waste the energy to yell.

My heart speeds up when I see the train of people waiting
by the exit. On a normal day, everyone would be lining up to eat
lunch in the room that divides the boys' and girls' sleeping quarters. It's also where we feed our brains with books and homework.
But today is different. Everyone's waiting to wish me luck.

It's tradition.

Paige has her face pressed against the mirror near the exit, trying to look through it. We know visiting parents can see us because the last person that was fostered caught a glimpse of the one-way window when he came back from his screening. Ever since we learned that's how they watch us, like fish in an aquarium, our training has improved.

I've worked extra hard. I should be excited I've reached the end. Only, I'm not.

Parker hangs his head as I walk by, his black hair falls past his eyes. I want to push the locks back, tell him everything will be fine, but I resist the temptation. I don't have to see his eyes to know my leaving will be hardest on him.

The door opens as I reach for the handle. Ms. Preen is already on the other side and waves her hand for me to step through and it shuts behind me with a thud before I can look back.

I know I'll get to see them one last time, but my eyes well up. It already feels like goodbye.

• • •

The drive to the clinic took less than fifteen minutes, but we've been waiting to see the doctor for over an hour. Ms. Preen digs a fingernail into my back and I sit up straight.

"Did you take your medicine today?" She checks her manicure for any flaws before placing her hand back in her lap. I nod and squint at the clock on the wall to make sure it's moving. It is. Finally, a nurse at the reception area waves us over.

We walk toward the door that leads out of the waiting room. A woman with tight black curls is sitting at the door punching buttons on a keypad. When she notices I'm watching her, she shifts her body until the numbers are out of my line of sight.

"Is it going to hurt?" I ask her. I already know the answer is yes, but I want her to say something soothing, to ease my fear. Like a mother would.

Instead, she replies, "You'll get over it." There's a loud buzz and the door clicks open.

It's brighter in the hallway—white, but not a clean white. The walls look aged, like teeth that haven't been brushed for weeks. My nose burns from the mixture of rubbing alcohol and disinfectant in the air.

The nurse unlocks a six-paneled door with the name Doctor Morgan on the front. "Have a seat," she says to Ms. Preen.

I decide to stand until the offer is extended to me, but Ms. Preen grabs the side of my sweatshirt and yanks. "Tabitha. Sit." A thread snaps when she tugs again and I take a seat. It's an old sweatshirt anyway, more for warm-ups than meeting my new family. I wonder if Ms. Preen will give me something nicer to wear. If I pass the health screening.

"Fill this out. The doctor will be here shortly." The nurse hands Ms. Preen a clipboard with a pen dangling from a rubber band that's been made into a string.

When she leaves, Ms. Preen begins to fill out the form, repeating every question and answer while I gaze over.

NAME: Tabitha Rhodes

HEIGHT: 5'6"

AGE: 16

EYE COLOR: Green

HAIR COLOR: Red

"I'd say strawberry blonde," I correct her.
"You're a redhead."
"But in the summer my hair gets lighter."
"Well it's spring, so I picked red."
She fills out the last question in silence.

UNIQUE CHARACTERISTIC(S): Excellent vision and premium lung capacity. Check for 31 Processing.

She tilts the paper away from me when I point. I'm not sure what 31 means—maybe how many tests they'll run on me? I hope it's not the number of shots I'm going to get.

When she's finished, she slides the pen underneath the metal clip that holds the paper.

"That's it?" The questionnaire is so short it seems pointless. "Don't they want to know a little about me? Maybe you can write about foods I like or my favorite movies?"

"Why all the questions? Don't you want to be fostered?"

"Of course I do. It's just…what if they change their mind? Don't tell them I have freckles."

She lets out an exasperated sigh. "I'm sure they'll assume a redhead has freckles."

"You're right." I rub the back of my neck. I'm anxious about the skin sample and gigantic needle I've been told about.

Folding her hands on top of the clipboard in her lap, she adds, "They've reviewed your profile and you're a perfect match. That's how it works. End of story."

Her words do little to reassure me.

I grab one of the magazines in a wooden rack hanging on the wall. It's the *Gladstone Community Review*, and on the cover is a picture of a family sitting under a tree having a picnic. The mom is wearing a white dress with red polka dots while she feeds the dad a strawberry. Their kids are laughing and holding sandwiches that overflow with layers of meat and cheese. I feel a pang of jealousy, even though I know it's not real because the people in the picture probably don't even know each other. They most likely just have to sit there for a few clicks of the camera before going back to their real lives. Maybe they even get to keep the sandwiches. But I still want what they're portraying: a happy family.

I lean my head against the wall and close my eyes. Maybe I'll have a family like the ones in the movies and shows we get to watch. My personal favorite is a forty-year-old sitcom called *Growing Pains*. The Seavers adopted Luke, included him in every activity, and treated him like he belonged there the entire time.

Maybe that will happen for me. Maybe my family will sit around on a lazy Sunday playing board games. We could go on camping trips where my dad can teach me how to fish. It'll be perfect.

My dream fades when the door opens.

A man with hair like a Ken doll walks toward me. "Sorry to keep you waiting," he says with a wink.

Ms. Preen's bright red lips widen into a grin, exposing her veneers. I try to copy her, but when I smile, I feel like I'm just showing the doctor that my teeth are straight. It's hard to get excited when I know nothing about the family willing to foster me.

He reaches for the clipboard and pulls a tiny round stool out from under the desk. "I was just reviewing your file," he says as he sits down. His eyes shuttle from me to Ms. Preen and then back to my chart. "I noticed you're taking medication…"

"Just one, sir."

"For her heart condition," Ms. Preen says. "She takes Propannalean once a day."

"Ah yes, I remember the note now." The doctor scribbles something on the form. "How long has she been taking that?"

"We discovered the condition when we took her in."

"I understand." He gives her a sharp nod and turns to me. "Have you had any major injuries?"

"No."

"Any diseases?"

"Not that I know of."

He looks at Ms. Preen and she shakes her head. "We've cared for her since she was six. She was transferred to the Center for Excellence when she turned twelve."

"How many hours a day does she train?"

"Eight." Ms. Preen leans forward. "Even though she missed six years with us, I can assure you, Dr. Morgan, her physical condition is excellent." She pauses. "And since she's sixteen and her body has—how should I put it—matured, you can do *all* the tests, correct?"

I cringe as the doctor gives a knowing smile and jots down some notes on the paper. He should just use a marker and write it on my forehead: Tabitha is a woman now. Apparently, that means I qualify for the full range of tests. Lucky me.

When he's done, he puts the clipboard down and his eyes fix on mine. "I'm sure Ms. Preen has explained to you that we'll be drawing blood and running a series of tests to ensure you're in optimal health."

"She has."

"Then let's get to work."

I wipe my clammy hands on my jeans as we follow him down the hall and through a set of swinging doors. A handful of people wearing blue hospital caps and surgical masks are waiting inside. The weight of their stares feels as heavy as the air in my lungs, and I struggle to pull in my next breath. The man closest to the hospital bed taps it, clinking his nails on the metal side rail, a chime that says: *this is for you.*

I shuffle forward, studying the machine above the bed. It looks like a large eye with handles for ears. A robotic arm, with a needle that reminds me of a sharper version of Ms. Preen's finger, is attached to the metal tube that keeps the eye in place. A bead of sweat trickles down my back.

No matter how many times I've heard about what happens at health screenings, I feel unprepared. I fight the urge to look back at the door we came through because I'm afraid I might bolt.

As I reach the bed, a man says, "You'll need to strip down to your undergarments." I'm too nervous to look up to see who's talking, and my hands tremble as I fumble with the button on my jeans.

My pants drop to the floor and I pull off my sweatshirt, holding it over my bra until he hands me a stiff paper shirt. I keep my gaze level with the nametag hanging from a lanyard clipped to his shirt. The photo ID stares at me and I turn away from its eyes so I can change. I sit on the bed and a gloved hand brushes my hair over my shoulder. Someone wipes a moist cloth over the back of my neck. It's cold and I flinch. My nerves are on high alert, like I'm waiting for the horn to blast before the fifty-yard dash.

The skin sample is supposed to rule out any allergies. In the back of my mind, I've always wondered what would happen if the test showed an allergy to pets and the foster family had three dogs. Would the family revoke their paperwork?

"Now hold still," a man says.

A second later a blade pierces my skin and I bend forward, shrieking in pain. Two men immediately grab my arms and jerk me upright. I bite my lip as he cuts again. Blood rushes to the spot as he makes two more slices to complete the square. There's a pinch and a tug as the piece of skin is removed.

"Done," he says, blowing out a breath, as if he's the one who's been sliced.

My neck feels like it's on fire—like I've been branded.

The cutter reaches for gauze and presses it so hard into my neck it feels like his thumb is sinking into the wound. Tears streak my face as I pull in a shaky breath.

"Now the hard part," he says. His voice is so cold it makes me shiver.

Dr. Morgan chimes in next. "Lean back and keep your body still or we'll have to start over." I glance at the doctor as fresh tears start their descent. I want him to look up from his computer—to give a damn. A tiny part of me wishes he'd stop the tests. Or, at least give me something to dull the pain.

But he doesn't take his eyes off the screen.

I hear the sound of a keyboard. Then the needle starts to move.

"We'll begin with the body scan," the doctor says.

The needle looks like it will pierce right through me. I grip the sides of the bed to keep from screaming out. I close my eyes and try to picture the family from the magazine, the one with the sandwiches, but the hum of the machine makes it impossible.

"Shouldn't you put me to sleep or something?" My lungs can't pull in air fast enough.

Dr. Morgan ignores my question. "First, we'll scan your body. Then, you'll feel the needle."

There's no inflection in his voice. Not a lick of empathy. This procedure is obviously routine to him.

The eye above me, which must be the scanner, makes a whirring sound to warm up. The arm with the needle lifts until it's parallel with the bed. I exhale.

The scanner glows yellow with periodic flashes of red. It starts at my head and begins its way down my body. It feels warm, as if I'm inside a toaster. When it gets to my toes, the machine lifts back up and centers over my waist. The needle rotates to its position to impale me.

"Remember, stay perfectly still," says the man who cut my neck.

Keeping my head straight, I find his face; his light blue eyes are squinting, as if he's smiling behind his mask. I catch a glimpse of the name on his badge: Curtis R. He's standing close to my knee and I want to jerk my leg to kick some sense into him. Does he think this is funny? Maybe he'd like to swap places with me.

He catches me staring and steps out of view. "Don't move."

Easy for him to say. I wish they'd secured my arms and legs to the table because every inch it gets closer, the more certain I am that I'm going to roll out of the way.

My eyes close and I picture my new mom smiling at me. Hopefully, she is someone who understands that freckles multiply with each wink from the sun. My eyes fly open when the needle sinks into my skin. I bite back a whimper and clench my fists, reminding myself that when I'm done, when it's all over, it'll be worth it. I'll have a family.

# CHAPTER 2

An hour later, I'm being wheeled into an elevator. My stomach flips a little as we drop. I feel like the needle sapped my energy and took any hope and excitement with it. I'm not sure why the doctor needed so much blood, but at least it's over. I fight my way through the fog that has taken over my mind, trying to focus on something positive like what my new house will look like and whether or not I'll get my own room.

The elevator opens to a covered parking lot. The stench of oil and asphalt hits me immediately, and I take several slow breaths through my mouth to avoid losing whatever's in my stomach.

I use the little strength I have left to feel the bandage on my neck. The wound pulses in anger, and Ms. Preen bats my hand away. She walks next to the nurse who pushes the wheelchair out to the gray sedan.

"Thank you for your assistance. This is a big day for all of us," Ms. Preen says to the nurse when we reach our car. It's impossible to miss because it's the only one in the lot. I wish there were other cars, or even a person or two to look at. I'm about to become part of this community, yet I feel more disconnected than ever—like I'm in limbo. I don't belong at the Center anymore, but I can hardly say I belong with a family I know nothing about. Why haven't they told me anything yet? Did I fail the health screening?

Our driver gets out and comes around to help me into the car. He opens the back door before propping one of my arms around his neck. His body is warm, and I find myself wanting to curl into him when he lifts me. I don't even know him. Either I'm woozy, or the thought of having a dad is starting to sink in. I hope it's the latter.

"Here you go," he says as he eases me down behind the passenger's seat. I offer him what I think is a smile as he buckles me up, but the muscles in my face must not be working because he doesn't return it.

When he shuts the door, I faintly hear Ms. Preen talking with the nurse. The glass is tinted, and except for a few shadowed images, I can't see a thing.

The driver opens the other door for Ms. Preen, and she sits so softly that the leather seats don't make that crinkly sound like they did when I sat down. She digs through her purse and pulls out lipstick and a compact mirror. A thick coat of red goes over the layer she already has on.

"Congratulations," she says, tucking the lipstick and compact away and pulling out a chocolate chip cookie wrapped in plastic. One side is bent like it was sitting at the bottom of the cookie jar waiting for someone to pluck it out before it was tossed.

It's the nicest thing she's ever done for me.

"I take it I passed?" I ask, my mouth watering.

"Better than that! Your stats were perfect. Exactly what the family hoped for." She stretches her arm across the seat, holding the cookie away from her skin and clothes. "Your time at the Center is over after tonight."

I reach out cautiously, as if the treat might disappear. I can't remember the last time I had chocolate or anything sweet for that matter. My heart pounds like it's determined to break out and grab it before I do.

The chocolate chunks have melted from being trapped in her purse, and the middle of the cookie feels squishy in my fingers. Even before I take a bite, I anticipate the rush of sugar. I pull it out of the bag and bring it close to my nose, inhaling slowly. My real mom used to bake. I remember sitting on a counter and licking the spoon after she finished mixing the ingredients. The images are fuzzy, but they're mine. It's one of the few memories I have, but at least I retained some. No one else at the Center does because they were never raised on the outside. I feel a wave of guilt and smell the cookie again to trigger happier thoughts.

There's a hint of vanilla and brown sugar and a dozen other things I can't put my finger on. I lick the melted chocolate from my thumb, and Ms. Preen looks away as if I've done something dirty. Well, this is a rare treat, and I'm going to enjoy it.

I give her the best smile I can manage. "Thank you."

"You're welcome." She scoots her body closer to the window and stares at the dark glass even though we can't see what's on the other side. Like she'd rather look at nothing than at me.

When we start moving, Ms. Preen taps the headrest in front of her. "Don't forget the shield." The driver pushes a button near his visor and the barricade between the front and back seat goes up. "You were raised in the best conditions. People would kill to be as healthy as you are," she says, rummaging through her purse again. She grabs a green tube and pops the lid off, letting a pill that looks like a watermelon seed drop in her hand. It's glossy, and she slips it in her mouth and swallows it dry. "Now that we know how healthy you really are, delivering you safely is our top priority."

I try my best to sit up and remain alert. Our trainers warned us that there were people on the outside jealous of our health. In the past couple of years, there have been rumors about a group trying to kidnap anyone fostered from the Center so they can sell their organs on the black market. Once I'm released, I'll have to count on my self-defense training to keep me safe. I know how to fight. I know how to run. I hope I don't have to do either.

I eat my cookie slowly, savoring each morsel. The last bite hits my tongue when I hear the rattle of a gate, the same sound I heard when we left. The car pulls forward, over a speed bump, and turns to the right.

When we come to a stop, I feel a surge of power—like I could run a marathon. The driver opens my door, and I bring my arm up around his neck. I'm not sure I need him to help me get out, but I also don't trust this burst of sugar energy. Our trainers have warned us about the effects so I know a crash is minutes away.

He puts me down inside the garage, which could hold several cars, maybe even a small airplane. The evening light bleeds in through the large roll-up door we came in through, but because of the way the driveway curves into the garage after the gate, no one can see in—and we can't see out.

"I'll inform your instructors that you are leaving. You're dismissed from tonight's activities," Ms. Preen says.

"What if I want to participate?"

She stops in front of the door that leads from the garage to the Center's lobby. Her blue eyes flash like the flame of a blowtorch. "It's not up to you to decide. Don't you think you should focus on saying your goodbyes?"

The door buzzes open and she heads inside, leaving me momentarily stunned. I'm not ready for goodbyes, not when I don't even know where I'm going. I feel like I'm swinging from one rope to another, only my grip is slipping on both.

I snap out of my stupor and hurry after her. Hope pricks my heart as I scan the lobby, thinking maybe I'll see my new family. That maybe they're waiting inside, as anxious to meet me, as I am to meet them. The excitement in their eyes would be the reassurance I need.

But there's nothing to see. The lobby is empty, except for the girl behind the counter. She's about my age and has short blonde hair, a miniature version of Ms. Preen. She waves a pen as if she has a question, but Ms. Preen punches a keypad near the girl's desk, completely ignoring her like she's just another inanimate object in the room.

We enter the gymnasium, and my throat tightens when I hear the clank of weight machines and the high-pitched squeak of shoes against the varnished floor. It's a large room divided into training stations dedicated to strength, agility, and speed respectively. It smells of hard work and sacrifice, and I take in a deep breath.

"She's back!" Paige waves from the top of the rock-climbing wall and starts to rappel down.

Someone in the pool calls out my name and a barbell drops, making Ms. Preen jump. One by one, my friends gather around to hear the news. Paige stands next to me, her fingers reaching for mine. When she finds them, I squeeze, feeling my heart tighten as well. For the last decade, this is the only family I've known. We've lost baby teeth together and, here at the Center for Excellence, baby fat as well. I wish I could take everyone with me. Maybe I'll get lucky and end up in a home with a dozen kids, perhaps even a sister like Paige.

Parker wipes the sweat off his brow and marches over to Ms. Preen. He gets so close to her I'm certain his perspiration will drip onto her coat. "Are you ever going to get the rest of us out of here?" he says with a hostile tone.

Ms. Preen puts a flat hand against his chest and removes it almost immediately. She holds it against her side, fingers spanned like she's drying her nails.

"Easy, Parker." I use my body to wedge a gap between them. If Parker wants any chance at being fostered, getting on Ms. Preen's bad side isn't the way to do it.

His eyes cloud over in anger as he stares right through me, making it clear his words are for her. "I've been here the longest."

"You know that's not how it works," Ms. Preen says. She takes a step back and glances at the door we came through, probably gauging how fast she can get there in her heels.

Parker doesn't give her the chance to find out. He turns to leave, kicking one of the towels near a weight machine. I watch him cross the room until he disappears into the sleeping quarters. I face the group again, feeling like I need to defend Parker's actions, but the words stay glued to my tongue.

Paige is the one to break the silence. "Did you pass?"

I match her smile. "It's over. I passed."

She lets out a high-pitched squeal and throws her arms around me, the impact causing me to teeter.

She doesn't let go until Ms. Preen clears her throat. "I'll be back for you in the morning. You know the drill. Give your belongings away. Your family will provide everything you need."

"I get your running shoes!" Paige yells out.

"Hah! You wish," Meghan says, punching her in the arm.

"Are you afraid I'll beat you if I wear them?"

Paige puts her arm around me in an effort to seal the deal for the shoes. Someone else pipes in, begging for my red sweatshirt. The voices climb higher, everyone arguing over one another. Underneath all the noise, the click of heels fades away. Ms. Preen is gone. I still don't know anything about where I'm going tomorrow. All I have are questions and a stomachache—and I know it's not from the cookie.

• • •

My bed is right underneath a vent. Years ago, I tied a ribbon around one of the metal blades, and sometimes, when I can't sleep, I watch it flutter. Tonight, I'm also listening to the sounds of my friends for the last time: the deep breaths from Meghan in the bunk next to mine; the subtle snores from Paige, who sleeps on her stomach with one arm hanging over the edge of her bed.

Since the girls' sleeping quarters are separate from the boys', I can't talk to Parker. He stayed quiet all through dinner and sat as far away from me as possible. I can usually gauge how he's feeling by how tightly his eyebrows come together. Tonight, they practically kissed. He's angry, and although I doubt he'd admit it, I'm certain he thinks I'm abandoning him.

I picture the dream house he described: two-story with cathedral ceilings, a big front porch with a rocking chair, and a backyard that butts up to a park. I know he sees me in the house with him, that he envisions having children and a golden retriever together. He's told me at least a dozen times.

The idea makes me uneasy. I'm not sure if I could love him in that way, if the brotherly feelings I have for him could ever evolve into something more. But this isn't the time to imagine the future, because I know it'll lead nowhere. I just want to say goodbye.

As soon as I close my eyes, I feel something wet hit my forehead. I wipe it away and look up. There's a face hanging out of the open vent. It's Parker, and he's holding a water bottle.

"You coming?" he whispers.

I smile and sit up, catching the bottle when he drops it. I take a quick drink and set it on the ground so I can grab his hand. The bed doesn't squeak when I stand on it, and Parker pulls me up with ease.

"When's the last time we did this?" he asks.

The answer is easy. It was my fifteenth birthday. Parker thought it'd be fun to run through the sprinklers on the track to celebrate, but we got caught and had to do pushups until our arms turned to dough. I decide not to remind him.

He points the flashlight at his face and the light casts an eerie shadow, making him look dangerous.

"Turn that off!" I say, trying not to laugh.

"What? You can't get in trouble anymore; you're flying the coop."

To my relief, he dims the light, but just enough so we can still see where we're going. We crawl through the ventilation shaft to the end of the gym where there are some bleachers outside. We need to exit feet first in order to land on them, and I turn when we reach the flap at the end of the building. Parker has gained a few pounds since the last time we did this, and he struggles to get into position. His socks rub against my forehead as I shimmy out. I push the vent open with my feet and slide until my head and arms are the only parts left inside. The edge of the vent presses against my ribs while I feel around with my foot. Then, Parker's toe jabs me in the eye.

"Stop!"

He wiggles his toes in my face to be funny. I contemplate biting him, but chances are his socks aren't fresh. I stretch my foot to find the bleachers. I'm not quite long enough, so I keep sliding out and let go. My feet hit the metal bench with a clank and I freeze.

Parker drops down without much noise. "Are you trying to wake everyone?" He elbows me lightly in the side and motions for me to move down to the end of the bleachers.

We sit, and though my mouth opens, nothing comes out. I'm not quite sure how to say goodbye. Against my better judgment, I lean my head on his shoulder, and he immediately presses his chin into my crown.

The tightness in my chest eases as we take in the smells and sounds of the sea. On our left and right are concrete walls that stand for safety and security, but out in front of us, beyond the track, is the Pacific Ocean. There's a chain-link fence along the straightaway closest to the water—a window to the outside, even if we only see the occasional seal and distant boat.

On clear days I can see the California coastline during my laps, and on evenings like this, when the chain-link blends in with the night, it feels open and free.

The trainers want me to run to keep my heart and lungs strong. I run to be near the ocean. To be close to something that feels alive and inviting. I can always count on the ocean to be there.

A good five minutes pass before Parker speaks. "I'm sorry for how I acted tonight."

"I know."

"I can't help but think I'm not good enough or strong enough." There's a bite to his words. "I mean, what's it going to take? I can do two hundred crunches without breaking a sweat. What the hell do these parents want from us?"

I've asked myself the same questions a thousand times. Every time a kid leaves the Center it feels like someone else won the lottery, and all you can do is try to smile and be happy for them. But deep down you're not. You're dejected. Why wasn't it you? And each time someone else's name gets called, the rejection and loss start all over again.

Unlike Parker, I had a family once. My parents were killed in a car accident, but Parker was abandoned at birth. Rejection is all he knows. I try to remember that when I console him.

"Of course you're good enough. They don't know what they're missing." I rub his arm, noticing his bicep is bigger than my whole hand. All he seems to do these days is lift weights. I want to tell him to slow down, but I hold my tongue. The Center encourages him to build strength, and it keeps him busy while he waits. He's almost eighteen. The chances of anyone picking him now are as good as me bench pressing more than him.

"I don't even care if anyone fosters me, I really don't. But almost all of my friends are gone, and now you're leaving too." He reaches out and squeezes my fingers. I try not to cringe, but it feels like he's crushing me.

"You'll be out of here soon, and we'll go to all of the places we talked about," I say. He takes in a deep breath and I continue. "We'll go to the beach, and we'll see a real movie on one of those big screens—no more sitcom reruns. We'll go bowling and—"

He pulls me in for a sideways hug and my face presses against the armpit of his sweaty shirt. "I'm just a little emotional, that's all. It's your last day."

When he releases me from his grip, the feeling clings to me. I'm scared. I tell myself to be strong for Parker, but also because I don't want to blow my chance at having a *real* family.

"It's just…it seems stupid to foster someone so late," he says. "I know Ms. Preen says some families don't want to deal with toddlers, and everyone who's looking for older kids wants them to be healthy and disciplined, but do you ever find it odd?"

I don't want to. I want to believe it's a dream come true, that someone wants me to join their family. I hate that Parker is asking me right now. When I don't answer him, he keeps going. "And do you ever wonder why no one comes back to visit us?"

"Not really. They're probably just having a great time with their new family, playing board games, going fishing, that kind of thing. I'm sure that's what it is." I sound more certain than I am.

His head bobs up and down as if he accepts what I'm telling

him. When he looks at me, the whites of his eyes shine. "You won't do that, will you? You won't pretend we never existed. That *we* never mattered."

I force myself to hold his stare. "Of course not. I'll be back. I promise."

Why do I feel like that's a lie too?

A bright beam hits me in the eyes, and for a moment, I think Parker's flashlight is going haywire. Then, I hear a man's voice coming from the side of the track just a few feet from the bleachers.

"Get down here you two," says our lead trainer, Tony. He's big and bald, and the growl in his voice makes my body tense.

We follow Tony back inside. I'm somewhat relieved Parker and I don't need to climb back through the vent shaft, but when we stop in front of the pool, fear washes over me. My fingers tremble, and Parker grabs my hand as we stand by the edge of the deep end.

"Get in," Tony points. The gym lights are off and the water is so dark I can barely see the bottom.

Parker takes off his shirt and bends forward so he can sit. Tony gives him a shove and the splash douses my T-shirt and pajama bottoms.

I put my hands out to dive in but Tony grabs my shoulder.

"But I—"

"Not you," he says, yanking me back.

Parker clings to the edge of the pool. His fear is palpable.

"There's a time on my stopwatch. Two minutes and thirteen seconds. Let's see if you can beat it," Tony says. He puts a hand on Parker's head, like he's palming a basketball, and shoves his face down. "It's go time!"

My heart pounds, and my feet shift forward—ready to jump in.

"Let me take the punishment, it was my idea," I say. Tony stares at his stopwatch, and a mocking whistle escapes his lips.

Parker's hands grip the side of the pool as his pointer finger taps, counting the seconds. After one minute, Parker's tap—and my heartbeat—speed up. He's struggling. Tony pushes his head down farther, and Parker's hands come off the edge.

"That's enough!" I yell.

"Keep it down. I'd hate to have to start over." Tony says with a calm voice.

I scratch at my palms while I pace. Parker clutches Tony's arm, and Tony pushes down in response. Parker balls his hand into a fist and hits Tony's leg.

"Please be done. Please be done," I beg. The room blurs through my tears.

Tony pulls his arm back, and Parker comes up with a gasp.

I rush to the end of the pool to grab Parker's arms. I know he won't be able to get out on his own. He coughs, barely hanging onto the pool's edge. He rests his head on his forearm. His eyes close.

"A minute and a half," Tony says. "Time to get you off the dumbbells and back in the water. We've got to build your lungs up." He laughs to himself as he walks away. His shoes squeak when the water hits the glossy gym floor.

And for the first time since my final evaluation, I realize I could leave this place. I could let it go.

# CHAPTER 3

I've never handled goodbyes well, and now I'm on the receiving end. Paige is at the front of the line, which stretches along the gym wall and past the one-way mirror, ending at the door that leads to the lobby.

Ending with Parker.

My throat dries as I start the procession of hugs. By the time I reach him, my eyes must be as red as Parker's face.

"So this is goodbye," he says like he's been chewing on the words for hours, trying to make them softer, digestible.

I nod. "Only for a while."

A smile pulls at his lips a second before he envelops me. "I'm going to miss you."

"I'll miss you too." I squeeze him as hard as I can, knowing I can't hurt him. At least not physically.

"Don't forget about our pact," he whispers in my ear.

When he lets go, I stare at his chest, unable to meet his eyes. I know he thinks everything will change when we see each other on the outside, but there's this knot in my stomach that says it won't.

I muster the courage to look up, trying to memorize his features before I go: high forehead, sharp nose. It's not the face of someone who makes my heart swoon, but I promised him I'd give him a chance—give *us* a chance. I'm on the verge of opening my mouth when Ms. Preen taps her foot.

"Let's go. They're waiting," she says, shooting me an impatient glare. I give Parker one last hug and step into the hall that leads to the lobby.

His words follow me out. They permeate my brain. I even

catch a whiff of his smell on my fuchsia tank top. The blend of bar-bells and protein bars is embedded in the Hawaiian flower design as if he's determined to stay close to me.

If I'm being honest with myself, I wish he were coming. I could use a friend's hand to hold when I meet my parents in this ridiculous outfit. Sadly, it's the nicest one I own. The tank hasn't faded to a dull pinkish-purple yet, and the shorts smell more like lemon detergent than sweat. I thought Ms. Preen might surprise me with something new to wear, something more appropriate, but she doesn't seem to care how I look.

I slip off my vinyl backpack to get into the car. Ms. Preen scowls at the bag in my lap.

"What?"

"I told you not to bring anything."

"It's just undergarments and my heart medication." I stop there, omitting the fact that I also packed my toothbrush and my favorite sneakers. They're the only things I own; the contents of my life weigh no more than seven pounds.

She pokes at a lump with a tentative finger as if my stuff is contaminated.

"They're just shoes," I say, feeling guilty I didn't leave them for Paige.

"You have shoes on."

I want to tell her that my flip-flops don't count, but she's lost interest in the conversation. She reaches up to touch her forehead, and her fingers roll over the ridges. She must not have slept well. I know the feeling.

She takes some cream out of her purse. The jar is small, about the size of a coin, and the paste looks white and sticky. She dips two fingers in and rubs the lotion on her forehead until the lines vanish. When she goes to put it back, her cell phone rings. The ringtone is flirty, two beats serenading each other. She gets out of the car to answer.

The mouth of her purse is open. I shouldn't snoop, but I want to see what's inside—if the contents will reveal anything about my family, anything to fill the void that consumes me right now. There's a magazine called *Be Your Best* begging me to pick it up. I pull it out and skim through it quickly, taking in the smiling faces. That will be me soon. Happy. There are also dozens of ads for pills and creams. *Be smarter than your computer*, one ad reads. *Remember how it feels to be sixteen*, another says.

Ms. Preen's silhouette paces outside the door, and I strain to hear her conversation. The words are muffled, but I make out "military candidates" and "immune testing." Maybe she thinks the kids at the Center are army material. I wonder if that's what happens to those of us who aren't fostered.

I turn my attention back to her purse, surprised to see at least a dozen pill bottles inside. Is she sick? I pull a few out. The drug names are long, with letters jammed together, practically unpronounceable. I take out my medication, popping the top off my pill bottle. I spill some of mine on the seat and lay a few of hers beside them to compare.

Why does she have so many? Is she taking pills to dull the pain from an injury? Maybe that's why she's such a grouch.

It's quiet outside and I hitch a breath, shoving the bottles into her purse as the door cracks open. Before she ducks her head to sit, I slip my bottle into my bag and swipe the pills from the seat, clutching them in my palm so tight I am afraid they might crumble into white dust.

Ms. Preen seems oblivious when she sits. I flip my hair over my shoulder to hide the vein pulsating in my neck. I'll have to find a way to put her pills back later or dispose of them when she's not looking.

The car starts to move and I shift in my seat, putting my hand in my pocket so I can let go of the pills.

When she hasn't said anything for at least five minutes—I know because I've been counting in my head—I crack my knuckles.

"You shouldn't do that," she snaps. Almost immediately, her posture relaxes. "I guess it doesn't really matter anymore, does it?"

"No. I guess not." I finish cracking the last two, but I'm still fidgety.

Ms. Preen glances at me with suspicion and I spit out a question, one that should be simple for her to answer. "What are the names of my foster parents?"

She glares at me. "Don't worry about that right now."

"What am I supposed to call them when I see them?" It feels like I swallowed a gallon of pool water. I'm sick and confused at the same time. All I'm asking for are their names.

Ms. Preen flicks her hand at me like she's swatting at a fly. "Sir and ma'am." Then she looks away.

Maybe she doesn't know the answer. After all, she didn't know my name. To her, I was the redhead. Still, if it's Ms. Preen's job to connect foster kids to families, shouldn't the answer roll off her tongue?

I suppose I'm no better though. The names of my real parents faded from my memory years ago. I don't remember their faces or even the accident that took their lives.

"A drunk driver ran a stoplight," one of my trainers told me. "T-boned their car going eighty miles an hour."

They both died on impact. I was almost seven.

I jump in my seat when the driver taps the barricade between us.

"Are we there?" I ask, my heart speeding up.

"We need to stop by the hospital first," says Ms. Preen.

"What for?"

"Test results."

"Can't the hospital mail them?" Doesn't she realize how much I want to meet my new family?

Ms. Preen glares at me, her lips in a tight red line. The kind of slash our teachers made through incorrect answers. "One of the tests came back…"

"Came back what?"

Ms. Preen takes a breath and her eyes meet mine. "It came back abnormal after a second analysis. They just need to double check something."

"All right." I rub my nose. I used to think I could tell when someone was lying to me when my nose itched. Our nutritionist told me it meant I needed to eat more vegetables.

Ms. Preen reaches in her purse and holds out a piece of candy. "Eat this. You'll feel better."

I peel off the plastic wrapper, pop the candy in my mouth, and begin to chew. It's soft and delicious. I don't want to swallow, but Ms. Preen is watching.

The car stops, and I sit up and smile as if I'm about to go on display, which is not far from the truth. Maybe my foster parents will be waiting for me in the hospital lobby when the test is done.

"How do you feel?" she asks.

I try to move my lips, but my brain feels like it lost the connection with them. My eyelids feel heavy. So heavy. There are two Ms. Preens now. Both of them are grinning, but their eyes are narrow, devious.

The back seat beckons me to lie down, and I move her purse out of the way. My arm jerks and it falls onto the floor. I hear a clatter of pill bottles. I'm too tired to worry about picking up the contents right now. Instead, I press my head into the bend of my arm. The seat smells like Ms. Preen's perfume, a thousand flowers drowning in alcohol. It stings my nose.

Suddenly I'm on my back, and it feels like I'm drifting out of the car. I try to move my hands, but I've lost the ability to communicate with my body. I want to sleep, and yet I have this strange feeling that's a bad idea.

# CHAPTER 4

My eyes pop open and I awake in a panic. I'm lying in a hospital bed. Is the test over? How did I get here? Where are my foster parents and Ms. Preen?

There's a bank of fluorescent lights above me, spotlighting me like a canvas. I can see some medical equipment on my left. I can't move my neck, but the objects look shiny and sharp in my periphery.

Where the hell am I?

I try to yell for help, but my mouth doesn't cooperate. One of my fingers twitches and that's all I can do. I'm the living dead, only I know I'm not dead because I can feel my heart in my throat.

Why can't I move?

Voices murmur outside the door, and I shut my eyes when it opens. The agitated whispers belong to two males. I peek. They're standing at the foot of my bed and are too young to be doctors. One's wearing medical scrubs, the other a lab coat. They're grumbling about how many minutes they have left.

"Is she the one?" Lab Coat asks.

"Looks like it," Scrubs answers. "Why haven't they prepped her yet?" He tugs on the side of my tank.

"Not sure, but they probably will soon. Let's get her out of here," Lab Coat says.

Who are these guys and where are they taking me? A flood of instinct bubbles inside me, trapped with nowhere to go. My eyelids flutter when they start to wheel me out of the room. The gurney is headed toward the end of the hall, and my heart skips when I see the blurred red letters of an exit sign. Are these the people the Center warned us about? The ones who sell organs on the black market? Panic surges through my body.

They're kidnapping me.

I focus on my hands, bending my fingers. Good. Movement is coming back.

Lab Coat glances down and stares at me for a few seconds before looking forward again. He's taller than the blond on my right, who uses his hand to guide more than to help push.

The outside smells like decay, and when I peek again, I see a dumpster and a van parked in front of it, the rear door open like it's ready to devour me. My breath quickens.

"Load her up," a voice calls from inside the vehicle. He sounds excited—happy, even.

"Do you have the body?" Lab Coat asks.

*Body?* I can't wait any longer. I have to get out of here. I open my eyes all the way and try to sit up so I can jump off the gurney, but it's a bust. My neck barely moves.

Scrubs turns in shock. "What the hell?"

"They must not have given her enough anesthesia," says Lab Coat. "Redheads usually require more."

Scrubs presses down on my shoulders, and the guy in the van jumps out. He's short and thick, like a potato. "Come on! We've gotta get out of here!" He scoops me up, and Lab Coat takes something wrapped in a white blanket out of the van before I'm placed sideways on the floor behind the last row of seats.

The doors slam shut.

I'm cold and cramped, but I'm conscious. When the tires squeal, I try to wiggle my foot. I need to get up if I'm going to get away. If I'm going to live.

I'm fighting with my limbs when Lab Coat climbs over the back seat. He crouches down next to my head, careful not to step on my hair.

"It'll all be over soon," he says, clutching his knees to his chest and glancing out the back window nervously. I use this time to size him up. The Center trained us in case we were ever in danger. His jaw looks strong and would probably break my hand, but I might be able to strike him hard enough with my elbow. I try to muster the strength in my arms so I can be ready. Wherever we're going, it can't be good.

The van swerves sharply and my cheek connects with his shoe.

I groan and the guy lifts my head, placing it between his feet like they're bookends. "Sorry about that." He looks toward the front. "Adrian, try to be a little more careful, will ya?" Turning back to me, he says, "He just got his license."

My eyes grow wide and he laughs.

"That was a joke. At least I know you're coming to." We're looking at each other upside down, but he must see fear and confusion on my face. He presses his lips together, hard enough to make the pink fade. "You were drugged. They were about to slice you open."

"What?" Or at least, a garbled form of the word comes out. It's like there are rocks in my throat. I hardly recognize my own voice. The words *drugged* and *sliced* echo in my head, but they might as well be gibberish because nothing makes sense right now. My brain feels as useless as my limbs, fuzzy like a TV that can't find the signal.

One of my tests was abnormal. We stopped by the hospital to retake it. I don't know who these people are or why I'm in the back of a van.

All I want is to see the family who agreed to foster me.

"That's what happens at the Center," he says, his voice sympathetic. "You're raised for one purpose."

I try to shake my head, and my cheeks rub against his sneakers.

"Look, you don't need to hear the gory details right now. You've been through a lot. We were hoping you wouldn't wake up until we got to the safe house. I'm sure all this sounds terrifying."

My eyes sting. If he only knew.

He pats me on the head like a dog and climbs back over the seat. I want to grab his ankle, but my arm doesn't cooperate. *Don't leave! I need answers! What safe house? Where's my family?*

The second he's out of sight I start to cry. At least my tear ducts are working.

. . .

The rear door opens and I stay still, my eyes closed, waiting.

When someone reaches for my waist, I ram my palm into his face.

"What the—!" the guy says, stumbling back.

I sit up and whip my legs over the ledge of the van. My knees almost buckle when I hop out, but I manage to hold my stance, glowering at my captors. Intimidation might be my only weapon right now.

"I guess the medication wore off," Lab Coat says. Now, however, he's lost the white jacket, revealing jeans and a wrinkly navy T-shirt.

The driver he called Adrian curses and wipes his nose with his sleeve. There's a steady trickle of blood coming from his nostrils and his eyes are glossy. He walks toward a big red barn and slides one of the wooden doors open, pinching his nose.

Scrubs must not have ridden with us. That makes my job easier. One down, one to go.

My arms wobble as I bring my hands in front of my face.

"Easy there, tiger," Lab Coat says.

"Where the hell am I?" My voice sounds old and scratchy.

"You're safe now. They're not going to hurt you."

"*They?*"

"The doctors—" He rubs his mouth as if to wipe the rest of the words away. "Let's go inside and talk about this."

"I'm not going anywhere with you," I say. He steps toward me and I bounce on my heels, bracing for a fight. "I know what you want with me. You and your friends are sick."

His eyebrows mash together. "You have no idea what you're talking about."

"Then enlighten me."

"First of all," he says, stepping forward and extending a hand. "My name's Gavin Stiles." I give him a nod, but keep my fists tight. "Fine." He shrugs. "Have it your way."

"My way? Exactly how is being kidnapped *my* way?"

He folds his arms, the sleeves of his shirt tightening around his muscles. He catches me staring and there's a glint of amusement in his eyes. I refocus, adjusting my stance.

"You weren't kidnapped. You were rescued. And if you'd stop trying to fight me and listen," he says, uncrossing his arms to press down on my hands, "you'd see we're here to help."

When he lets go, my fists pop back up. I should hit him, but I don't. Ms. Preen's evil grin flashes in my memory. She gave me a caramel. It knocked me out. That's the last thing I remember before…

Is he telling the truth?

My hands start to drop as Gavin turns toward the barn. He waves without looking back. "Come on."

My first instinct is to run. I look around, but there's nothing but a field of tall grass and trees that barricade the land like the walls outside the Center. I've gone from one holding cell to another. But here I don't have any friends.

"You coming?" he hollers. He's in the barn now and I am on my own. Free to decide my fate.

Only I don't know where to go. And what if he's right?

Crap.

As I walk toward the barn, and possibly death, I realize I'm barefoot. The dirt is cool and mixed with bits of the gravel driveway. When I step inside the red building, hay cushions the floor.

Gavin holds onto a metal loop, propping open a hatch that leads underground.

"You want me to go down there?" I ask, pointing.

"I know this is overwhelming, but you'll be safe here. Trust me."

A car tears through the driveway, braking just before it hits the barn. A plume of dust surrounds us and Gavin drops the hatch with a clang. Before I can blink, he has a hand around my waist and one over my mouth. I open wide to get some skin between my teeth.

"I wouldn't do that if I were you," he whispers, his breath hot against my ear.

I hear the car doors shut, followed by the sound of laughter.

Gavin lets go and shoves me forward so he can step out. I have to catch myself from falling over.

"Are you trying to kill us?" Gavin says to the two guys approaching.

"Relax, we were just having a little fun," one of them says, putting a hand on Gavin's shoulder. I recognize him as Scrubs, the blond from the hospital who helped wheel me out. Or, at least pretended to help.

Gavin shrugs him off. "Rescue missions aren't a sport, Ry. We're not here to have *fun*."

"My bad," Ry says as he holds up his hands in defense. When he sees me, the apologetic face transforms. He swaggers over squinting as he assesses me. His blue eyes flicker with excitement.

"It's good to see you up and about." He leans on the same stall door my body is pressed against and crosses one leg over the other. I could easily kick his legs out from under him. His jeans are a deep blue and his hair is shiny. I want to touch it, to see if it's as soft as it looks. Everything about him screams that he belongs on the cover of *Gladstone Community Review*.

"I'm Reilly," he says, "but everyone calls me Ry." He extends a hand.

"Tabitha." I reach out, too late to remember I just shunned Gavin's handshake. I curse myself for falling for Ry's schmoozing charm, and out of the corner of my eye, I see Gavin smirk. I begin to wonder if I've been shaking Ry's hand too long when I hear a metal door creak open. The guy who drove is already on his way down through the hatch in the floor.

Ry lets go and bends to a bow, brushing the air with his hand. "Shall we?"

The ominous opening stares back at me, tempting me with its dark secrets. I guess there's only one way to find out what those secrets are.

I have to go down the hole.

# CHAPTER 5

I glance over the edge. A ladder leads down to a room with a cement floor, and the smell of rotting wood and rust wafts up through the hatch. I turn my face away and take a breath, filling my lungs with clean air before heading into the thick stench.

As I descend, something beeps and I glance over my shoulder. Equipment lines the wall above the counter where two guys are fiddling with a radio. The room is longer than it is wide, more of a hallway. At the far end, I spot a decaying door that looks like the entrance to a haunted house. Despite the creepy vibe, there's electricity, making the room feel much brighter than it should.

Ry comes down and stands next to me at the bottom. The hatch closes, and I look up as Gavin pushes Ry's head with his shoe, shoving him to the side so he has room to drop.

"This way," Gavin says, stepping in front of us. He stops for a moment to look back and says mockingly, "Tabitha, was it?" He puts a hand on the shoulder of one of the radio workers, the guy Ry rode with. "This is Craig."

Craig stands so tall his hair would probably sweep the ceiling if he had any. He has the upper body of a swimmer, and his skin is a deep brown, darker than Gavin's. Craig grins and gives me a quick wave. He has the same playful look as Ry—approachable and picture perfect.

"And you remember Adrian?" Gavin adds, patting the van driver's back. Adrian's nose is red, and there's a dried ring of blood around one of his nostrils.

"What happened to him?" Ry whispers to Gavin when we reach the door at the other end.

"He smelled a fist," Gavin says, the lilt in his voice reveals his amusement.

"Maybe I should apologize," I say.

"Give him some time to cool down," Gavin says. "He understands." He opens the door for me, and with a softer tone adds, "We all do. This is a lot to take in."

We enter a square room that feels moist and dirty. The lights are sparse, condensed mostly over the eating area, and there are bunk beds lining the walls. A few people are playing cards in the center, and they stop and stand when we approach, eyes wide with wonder. "They didn't sedate her?" a boy with shoulder-length hair asks.

"Apparently not enough," is all Gavin says before introducing me, rattling off their names as he points. Everyone's smiling except for the girl with frosty white hair. Her scowl says I'm not welcome, and my fists tighten involuntarily. I want to tell her I don't want to be here either. I want to be with my family. The one I was supposed to meet today.

The one Gavin claims doesn't exist.

Gavin leads me toward the bunks that share a wall with the hallway. The air is cold, and I shiver. I'm still wearing my Center clothes, and the hairs on my arms stand, searching for warmth. I guess I should be grateful I'm not in a hospital gown.

Next to the bed is a wooden cabinet with doors that don't quite line up, like a poorly buttoned shirt. Gavin opens it and grabs a pillow, blanket, clothes, and socks, tossing them at me without looking.

"Size seven shoe?" he asks. I throw the items on the bed to free my hands before he can launch the shoes.

"Eight."

"The closest I have is a seven." To my surprise, he hands them to me, a pair of beat up sneakers caked with dirt. I slap the shoes together and sit on the bottom bunk to put them on. The socks are too big and the shoes are tight, but they're broken in enough to the point where they don't pinch my toes. It's better than nothing.

I adjust my laces. One of the card players laughs and another swears as they continue their game. There's water running and the swooshing sound of broom bristles. It's too normal, too calm compared to what I'm feeling. All of my questions start to surface.

"You said I was saved…from *what* exactly?"

Gavin rubs the back of his neck and turns his face as he works a muscle in his jaw. He stares at Ry, who's poking around the kitchen. There's a small refrigerator on the floor and a long table holding a bucket full of dishes. Food lines the shelf above the sink, but the wood is bowed, like it will collapse if someone adds one more can of green beans. I can relate. I'm about to break as well.

"Well?" I say more forcefully.

"You weren't fostered. You were raised for parts," Gavin says. "The Centers are owned by PharmPerfect, the biggest drug company in the west, possibly the world. They use the Centers as a front, claiming to help foster kids. But they don't." He takes a deep breath, but his words sound muffled as he continues, like my ears are stuffed with cotton balls. "They kept you healthy and fit so you could be harvested for organs."

"No. That's absurd. Why would they—"

"Cloned organs are unreliable and lab-grown parts fail. People don't want to pay for lungs that will only last a year or two."

"What does that have to do with medicine?"

"PharmPerfect needs healthy livers, among other parts. If patients can't take pills, business drops."

I stand so the weight of his words don't break me, but I'm dizzy and have to grab the top bunk to brace myself.

"You all right?" Gavin asks, his hand quick to find my elbow.

"Of course not!" I jerk my arm away. "I think I'm going to be sick." My eyes flash to a bucket that's sitting next to the cabinet, and he hands it to me. I hug the pail between my thighs when I sit back down.

"They were minutes away from operating on you."

I shake my head. "It can't be true. It just can't."

"You think we brought you here to be our housekeeper?"

I lift my chin. "I think you have some sick plan to hold me for ransom. That's what I think." I try to slow my breathing so I can focus. "Where's my family?"

Gavin shuts the cabinet door, but it drifts back open and this time he holds it closed. "There is no family." He glares at the cabinet when he lets go. It creaks open an inch and stops. It must be as scared of him as I am. "We're here to help you. If you don't believe us, you can leave. But the moment you step off this property," he motions with his head, "you're on your own. PharmPerfect practically owns this island. They bought half the land and invested in most of the infrastructure. Beyond the records at the Center, you don't exist. They're the only ones who know who you are, and they'll be looking for you, but you'll be safe here."

He walks away, probably so I have time to absorb his words. I don't even know where to start, so it might be a while.

Is that what happened to Wes? Parker's lifting buddy was the last to be fostered. He never came back to visit. None of them did.

My stomach turns as I sit on the bed, contemplating how simple life seemed twenty-four hours ago. I bury my face in the pail as the bile creeps up my throat.

Parts. I was being raised for parts.

I stay with my head down until I hear feet shuffling toward me. Out of the corner of my eye, I see a small girl approaching. I try to remember what Gavin said her name was. Marcy? Mabel? She sits next to me, and her little hand rubs my back as I stare at the bottom of the pail.

"You're going to be all right now," she says. "They can't use you anymore."

I lift my head and stifle a gasp when I meet her eyes. They're pale blue, wide, and inquisitive, but something's off. The symmetry's been broken. I look closer at her right eye and notice there's no curvature, no peak—like it's been ironed flat.

She plays with a lock of hair, shielding her eye with it. I pull her hand down gently. "What happened? Did someone..." I can't even finish the sentence before my voice cracks.

She nods as she pulls the doll she's holding to her chest.

"They were trying to take your eye?"

"They don't actually need your eye. Just the cornea." She points and I lean closer, taking in the rest of her as well. Despite her fancy dress, she has long stringy hair that's in desperate need of a brush. Her face is dirty, but sweet.

"Can you...see out of it?"

"It's blurry, but yeah. Sort of." She gestures to her back. "They also took one of my kidneys." A chill runs through me, and she grabs my hand as if she can feel it too. "It could have been worse. At least I'm still alive. We both are."

Guilt settles in my stomach along with all the rest of my emotions. She must be half my age. If anything, I should be comforting her. I flip my hand over and give hers a quick squeeze. She hasn't just lost parts of her body; she's lost her childhood. At least I got to live with the illusion that there was a family waiting for me a little longer.

"I'm Mary," she reminds me.

"Tabitha," I say. "I like your dress." I run the fabric between my fingers. It's thick and there are little white flowers embroidered on the skirt. "It's very pretty."

"Gavin got it for me," she says, waving at him. Gavin stands in the kitchen next to Ry, who's eating fruit out of a can. Ry is doing all the talking. Gavin's arms are folded, but he finds a way to wave back. Our eyes meet and there's a moment of stillness. He offers a small smile that I would have thought was meant for Mary, but he's still looking at me. I avert my gaze. After I apologize to Adrian, I should tell Gavin I'm sorry for snapping at him.

"How long have you been here?" I ask Mary.

She strokes the head of yarn on her doll. "A few months."

"Do you like it?"

"Oh yes!" Her smile pops out but is gone almost immediately. "I mean, it's not the same as having a mom and dad, but at least we're safe."

We're safe. Does that mean we're only safe if we stay? I still have so many questions. How long do we have to be here? What's my role? Am I supposed to stay hidden beneath this barn until I'm eighteen? Or longer?

Mary's expression is so innocent that I stuff my questions back into my brain.

"What don't you like about this place?" I ask, keeping my tone light, but searching for any clues that I should run.

She stares at the doll as if it has the answer, then whispers, "The food isn't very good."

I put my hand on her back, feeling her spine straighten. When she grins again, I notice her teeth could use a good brushing too.

"Maybe we should put in a request for bacon," I say. "That's supposed to be pretty tasty."

Mary's tongue slides across her top lip. "Good idea!" She hops off the bed and makes her doll wave goodbye to me when she leaves.

I take a breath, psyching myself up for the reality of my new life. I'm used to mental pep talks—pushing myself on the last stretch of a run, holding my breath a few extra seconds until it burns so badly my lungs feel like they're going to explode. I have to get my head right, because it's not just Mary's or my life at stake. If the Centers are using kids for harvesting, my friends are next. The more I can assess what I'm up against, the better chance I'll have to save them.

There's a small bathroom in the back corner of the room, and I slip inside to change out of my shorts and tank. The T-shirt Gavin gave me is pink with a picture of a cat on the front and writing saying, *You're purrfect just the way you are.* Fitting, yet a little disturbing given the situation. The sweats are big, and I have to double knot the tie to keep them from falling down. My legs feel warmer, but my arms are covered in goose bumps as I wander out. I toss the clothes I got from the Center on the bunk and head for the kitchen to ask Gavin more questions, specifically how to help my friends. Except—he's gone.

I make a beeline for the exit and nearly collide with Ry as he comes back in.

"Where'ya going?" he asks, amused by the run-in.

"Is Gavin outside? I need to talk to him."

"He'll be right back." Ry rests his hand on the doorframe. Maybe Gavin put him in charge of keeping me confined down here.

I peek around him, but the hallway is empty. Darting under his arm, I sprint for the ladder. I climb fast and give the lid a hard shove. The metal clangs against the floor. When I reach the driveway, the van is there, but Gavin's nowhere to be found.

Ry pops up from the hole and joins me outside.

"I thought you said he left," I say.

"We only use the van for rescues. Gavin took his truck."

"Where'd he go?"

"To grab some food for lunch. Craig and Adrian went with him."

That means I'm stuck with Ry, Mary, the longhaired boy, and the girl with the spiky hair. Ry stands next to me, his face is open and inviting, like I could ask him anything. But something tells me Gavin has the information I'm looking for.

"They'll be back soon," he says as we walk back into the barn. "Gavin's never gone too long."

"Is he in charge or something?"

"You could say that. But for good reason. If it weren't for him, you'd be in the slaughterhouse by now."

A tremor rolls through me and I suck in a shaky breath. The air is stale and smells like hay. It's fresher than the oxygen below ground, but there's an ache in my chest, like my lungs are starving for something more. Something I can't get standing around in a barn. My legs twitch in agreement. "Do you run?" I ask.

"For fun?"

"For health."

"Give me a second." He reaches into his pocket and pulls out a small container. Popping off the cap, he takes a tiny white pill out and sets it on his tongue. "Now I'm ready."

"Are you sick?"

"It's an endurance pill."

"For running?"

"You'll see. Try to keep up."

We race out of the barn and head down the gravel driveway. When the road curves off to the left, Ry has us hop the fence that surrounds the field. The grass whips my pant legs until we hit the trees at the end of the property. The second we're in the evergreens, Ry takes off.

He's fast. Too fast. He tears through the path like a wild animal on the hunt, and my legs burn trying to keep pace. I didn't peg him for a runner.

He slows and turns, not a speck of moisture on his brow. "Ready for more?" he says, speeding back up.

I struggle to keep up, and when I round a corner where the trail bends like an elbow, he's gone.

I stop and lace my fingers above my head. "Ry?"

He jumps out from behind a tree and my leg jerks out to kick, stopping halfway when I see it's him.

He slaps his thighs and laughs.

"Sorry," I say. "It's instinct."

"Ah, so that's what happened to Adrian."

I shrug. Ry has speed, but I'm probably stronger. I wipe the sweat from my temple. "How'd you get so fast? You don't even look tired."

"I told you." He reaches into his pocket, pulling out the tube of pills. "Endurance."

"Oh crap."

"I've got more. You can have one." He pops the lid.

"No, it's not that. I just realized I haven't taken my heart medication. I'm supposed to take one every morning." I don't have my bag anymore, which means I don't have my pills. I shoved a few in the pocket of my shorts when I compared mine to Ms. Preen's. Hopefully, they're still there.

"Heart meds? I've got just what you need. Do you remember

what your pill looks like?" He pours the pills into his hand and separates them with his finger. They vary in size and color.

"It's a pale green tablet with a line through the center."

"Like this?" He holds up one that's exactly what I described.

"Yes! Do you have a heart condition too?"

"I need pills for a variety of ailments," he says with a wink.

"Like what?" I inch away from his outstretched hand. "What heart medication are you on?"

"I don't know the name, but this pill relaxes the blood vessels. That's what you need, right?"

"Yeah…"

"Look, it's not like I'm trying to poison you." He pops one of the green pills in his mouth and starts to pour the rest back in the tube. "We can wait if you want. I thought I could help, that's all."

It does look like mine. "You're sure it works like you say it does?"

"Your heart will thank me. I promise."

He hands me a pill and I swallow it. The chalky taste lingers after it slides down.

"Ready to head back?" he asks.

I nod, rubbing my throat as if I'll be able to wipe away the aftertaste.

Ry doesn't hold back as we retrace our steps. Nothing looks familiar, and I realize he could be taking me in an entirely different direction. The trees and ferns start to glimmer like they've been doused in sunshine and morning dew. Had it rained this morning?

Ry looks back and gives me a thumbs-up, and without realizing I'm doing it, I return his gesture. My feet feel like they're moving on their own while my upper body enjoys the ride.

We come to a clearing and he grabs my arm to keep me from stumbling into a tree when I try to stop.

"How're you feeling?"

"Good," I say. My cheeks feel flushed, but I'm not tired. Ry's face glows. "I think I have a runner's high."

"Is that bad?"

"No. I feel really good."

I start to sit, and Ry lunges forward to grab my arm. "There's no seat there," he laughs. "Let's get you back to the barn."

I try to concentrate. I know what a runner's high is. This feels too hazy. My mind is pushing the panic button, but I'm having a hard time hearing the signal.

"What did you give me?"

"Euphorium. It might look like your pill, but my mine's better." His smile is as broad as his shoulders. "Don't you agree?"

"Yes," I say before I can shut my mouth. "I mean no! Why would you do that?"

"Relax. My pills are harmless. Most of them just give you a mild high to take the edge off. I figured it'd at least hold you over 'til we can get your real medication."

He takes off before I can object again. I look down at my feet, forgetting how to make them move, but somehow they do.

I'm running to the music of birds and bugs. The plants wave at me when I glide by, and I can't help but smile at them. It's so peaceful.

We come through the clearing, and the barn has a halo of white around it as if I've arrived at heaven, only this gate is red and it slides open. We barrel through the grass. Bugs jump out of the way, and I laugh out loud. Everything feels like it's in slow motion.

Parked next to the barn is a gray truck. Gavin's leaning against it, and my grin widens. He's actually quite handsome, but not in a magazine way. He looks real. Rugged and tangible.

We stop in front of him and I brush a wisp of hair away from my face. My skin tingles, and I stare at my hands perplexed.

"Are you crazy, Ry?" Gavin says. He's mad. Very mad.

He needs a hug.

I walk toward him and wrap my arms around his neck, resting my head on his chest. He smells delicious—like apples. That sounds delightful right now. My mouth waters.

He pulls my arms down and pushes me back.

I cock my head to the side. He's glowing, but he's still angry.

He reaches out and grabs my chin. There's a surge of electricity where his fingers touch my skin. "Her eyes are dilated. What the hell did you give her, Ry?"

"She said she needed a pill."

Gavin lets out a low growl. "Get inside."

"Come on, Tabby." Ry puts an arm around me. "You've got green cat eyes and a cat shirt, so that's what I'm going to call you." I laugh and Ry meows, which makes me laugh more.

"I'm going to get the hiccups," I say as Ry leads us toward the barn.

"Tabitha stays." Gavin moves into our path, his arms folded like a genie. Maybe I should make a wish.

"Lighten up, Gavin." Ry unhooks his arm from my shoulder. "I could give you some Euphorium. It would do wonders for you." Gavin points at the barn and although Ry obeys, he lets out one last meow before sliding the doors shut. I can't help but smile. Gavin's eyes flash to me and the only thing I can do is cover my face with my hand. My grin feels permanently affixed.

"Come with me," he says, his brows furrowed.

We walk past the barn to an open shed with tools. Gavin doesn't join me when I decide to skip. Near the shed is an outdoor faucet. He turns on a hose, and we follow it across the gravel where it spits water into a metal trough that's already half full.

"Wait here." His face is tight. "I mean it."

He heads inside the barn, and once he's out of sight I play with the hose, watering the grass that lines the fence I'm leaning against, and spraying the air like the hose is a whale spout. The water tingles when it cascades down on me.

By the time Gavin returns, I've put the hose back in the trough and am lying on my stomach looking for four-leaf clovers. I roll to my side when I hear the gravel crunching beneath his shoes, and I pat the ground for him to join me. He doesn't take the hint. Maybe next time. He looks like he could use some good luck.

Instead, he flings a towel on the ground and scoops me up. His chest is warm and I rub my cheek against his shirt as he walks.

Then he drops me.

The cold water hits me like a thousand tiny slivers of ice. I come up gasping.

"You alert now?" Gavin asks when I try to stand.

"What the hell was that for?"

"To drag you out of la-la-land."

There's still a fuzzy white glow around everything, but my mind is racing. I'm so cold and there's not a happy thought in my brain.

He holds out the towel and I push his hand away. My teeth chatter when I step out.

"Leave me alone," I say, twisting my body away from him as he drapes the towel over my shoulders. One end drops to the ground and I drag it through the dirt back to the barn.

"I'm only trying to help," he says.

I stop in my tracks. Pulling the towel tight around my chest, I turn and glare. "If you want to help, figure out a way to get my friends out of the Center before it's too late. If you can't do that, stay away from me."

His face softens, but the lines on his forehead are deep like he's concentrating on forming the right words. "Then we're going to have to work together."

"Fine," I say, teeth chattering.

"Good." He crosses and uncrosses his arms like he's not sure what to do with himself. As I storm off, I hear him say, "Just remember, I'm not the enemy."

Right now, I'm not so sure I believe him.

# CHAPTER 6

---

Water trickles off me as I climb down the ladder. My shoes make a squishy sound when I drop from the fourth rung, and Adrian looks up from the electronic box he's taking apart. Except for the inch of black roots showing, his hair is golden brown and it's as greasy as the parts he has scattered around his workstation.

"Where's Gavin?" he asks with a chuckle.

"I drowned him."

He snorts and I walk past him without another word, heading for the windowless box of a room that, for now, is my home. The girl with the white hair, the one Gavin called Sasha, hollers at me, but I ignore her as I dig through the cabinet for some dry clothes. At the bottom of a box, I find a red sweatshirt like the one I used to wear on cold morning runs. It's hoodless, but it reminds me of my former life and the people I have to save.

I grit my teeth and hold back the tears. The Center may want me dead, but it also taught me how to fight, and that's exactly what I intend to do.

All the pants are oversized, so I grab the black shorts I left on the bed and change in the bathroom. Reaching into my pocket, I find the clump of pills and take my medication before coming out.

Gavin is in the kitchen and waves me over. I hope he can't hear my stomach growl. I walk up to where he's sitting and squeeze the wad of wet clothes over his shoe.

"I guess I deserve that," he says.

There are two plates of food in front of him with the exact same portions of corn, applesauce, tuna, and crackers. I drop the clothes on the table and grab the extra plate.

"Thanks for the food." I turn to walk away, leaving him with the laundry.

"Actually, that's for Mary."

Crap.

I spin around and put the plate back.

"But I think she already ate, so you might as well join me." He gestures toward the seat. "Please?"

"Tricky," I say, flipping the crate that serves as a chair so I can sit a little taller. Gavin and I are about the same height now. I twist my wet hair and ball it up at the nape of my neck. My finger jabs the spot where they took a skin sample, and Gavin shoots me a curious look when I wince. I force my face to relax and let my hair fall against my sweatshirt.

"You all right?"

"I'm fine."

He waits for me to take a bite before he picks up his spoon. The applesauce is runny, but there's a hint of cinnamon that makes it tolerable.

"I'm sorry for dunking you."

"I could have died of hypothermia."

He smiles at my exaggeration. "Cold *can* actually help. The shock temporarily speeds up blood flow, which helps you purge the drug faster. Think of it as an adrenaline shot."

"Yeah, well, you could have given me an ice cube instead."

His grin widens, then he looks down at my plate, where I've been making small circles with my spoon. "Not a fan?"

"Not of corn, but I'll eat it."

"Make a trade?" He taps his spoon near the glob of tuna.

"All right. It's a deal."

I hand him my plate and he slides the kernels off, careful not to let them mix with his applesauce.

"So how'd you figure out what was going on…that they were… you know…" I pretend to slice my stomach with my thumb.

He waits until he's finished wiping the tuna off his spoon,

making sure every speck is gone. The utensil looks cleaner than it was when I sat down.

"Research."

"Thank you for that in-depth answer."

He bites his lip. It gives him a boyish cuteness. Almost photo-ready. One of the guys they'd put in the background to give a picture depth.

He balls his hands and sets them on the table like gavels. "Are you sure you want to hear this while we're eating?"

I lean forward, pointing my spoon at his chest. "I want to know everything."

"Well, Tabitha," he sighs. "A few years ago I suspected Gladstone didn't live up to its slogan: The Perfect Paradise. And unfortunately, I was right."

I chew slowly, careful not to scrape the plate with my spoon. I don't want to miss a word.

"Nordic is a small island off the coast of California. PharmPerfect purchased it and cut down half the trees to create Gladstone for their scientists to live while they made super drugs: pills that can make you jump higher, lose weight, grow hair, you name it. There's a pill for everything except what the drugs do to your body after years of abuse." He fiddles with his place setting, centering the plate in front of him as if he can't think without symmetry. "That's why PharmPerfect started the two Centers. They use the Center for Growth to help with brain development. It's also where they start the propaganda—making you believe you're at some elite foster center—so when you're old enough to be transferred to the Center for Excellence for training, well…" Gavin glances at my hand. I'm gripping my spoon so hard the metal feels like it'll cut through my skin. "Maybe we should wait…"

"No. I need to hear this." I relax my hand and give him a nod to continue.

"They use the foster program as a front, selling kids' parts to clients who need a new liver, lung, kidneys—"

"How can people do that? How can they live with themselves knowing we're being slaughtered?"

"Because they don't know, or they refuse to believe the rumors." Gavin shakes his head in disgust. "Most people believe parts come from the cryopreservation unit or that they're buying parts from people who signed up for the Donor Program. People addicted to pills get pretty desperate. They'll sell a kidney or lung to buy more drugs. But their parts aren't in the best shape, and cloned parts don't last as long. Nothing beats healthy, live parts. Like yours."

The tuna sticks in my throat.

"Don't get me wrong, the Donor Program is a legitimate business, but there aren't enough healthy donors left on the island," he says. "Almost everyone is hooked on some kind of drug, which makes *you* so valuable."

"The health screenings they make us do, what are they for? To match us with buyers?"

Gavin's nod is almost imperceptible, but the entire room sways like the earth has rotated on its axis. I close my eyes for a moment to regain control.

"The doctors are just verifying what they already know," Gavin continues. "What your blood type is, what you're allergic to. They'll look more in-depth at the parts they need, and there are some tests they can't do until after puberty." I look down at my plate, afraid to ask what those tests are. Luckily, I don't have to. "Our bodies change with hormones, so they're looking at how your compatibility might be altered, if there's a better candidate on the waiting list."

"So no one at the Center can really *fail* the health screening?"
He shakes his head.

"And when the patients get new organs, they go back to buying their drugs. The cycle just keeps going."

"Precisely."

Parker was right to wonder about why no one came back. I

drop my spoon, my appetite gone. "What they're doing can't be legal. Why don't you just contact the police?"

"Who do you think paid for the police station and hired the chief? PharmPerfect is more powerful than a bunch of teens living under a barn. Until we can get some concrete evidence, it's our word against theirs."

"But aren't *we* evidence?"

"There are no records you ever existed. Sasha can tell you." He nods in her direction. "And I'm sure the local government is paid to look the other way."

"But people are dying!"

The room behind me falls quiet and I shove a cracker in my mouth. It's dry, and my throat hurts when I swallow.

"Drugs are a way of life here. And it's getting worse."

"Drugs like the one Ry gave me?"

"Euphorium? That's only the beginning."

"He took a pill before we went on a run; I couldn't keep up."

"Endurance. That's one of his favorites. Some habits are hard to break." Gavin scowls and takes a bite of corn. "It's easy to get hooked."

"I didn't know what I was taking." His head stays down, shoveling food in. "I was born with a heart condition. I told Ry what my medication looked like and he gave me a pill that looked identical."

He pulls the spoon out, but his mouth stays open. "Heart condition, huh?"

"You sound surprised."

"I am. Having a heart condition is like owning a puzzle with a missing piece."

I raise an eyebrow.

"What I mean is, it limits their profits. Once someone from the Center is sold, they harvest *all* the parts and keep them in the cryopreservation unit for future clients so nothing gets wasted." He waves his spoon at my chest. "The heart is worth almost as much as a liver."

Silence fills the air as I think about the amount of time my trainers made me spend in the pool. They must have been building up my heart's strength so it'd be worth something when the doctor carved it out.

"How do you know all of this?" I ask, shifting in my seat. "I mean, you sound like you work for them. Or used to…"

"Ry might not be the most responsible person in the world, but he knows the right people—even though some of them aren't worth knowing at all. A couple of his dealers work for PharmPerfect, and their info has helped us piece together what's going on inside, everything from prepping bodies to what meds are coming to market after being tested." Gavin clears his throat. "Speaking of medication, I take it you need more pills—or are you going to get your next pill from Ry?"

"I have some left, but I'll need more eventually," I say. He holds my gaze, his eyes narrowed. I don't like that he's judging me right out of the gate. Although in a way, I guess I judged him too. "So how'd you learn cold water would help when I took Ry's pill?"

I expect him to tell me a funny story about Ry falling into the trough, or that he read it in some textbook at school. But Gavin shifts in his seat like he has an itch he can't—or won't—scratch.

"Trial and error," he finally says, throwing in a smile. I don't buy it and when I wait for more, he relents with a sigh. "PharmPerfect uses the same base formula for most of their drugs. Cold doesn't always work. It depends on what else is in the pill. Plus, Euphorium is milder than most of the drugs they make." He looks away for a beat, then back at me. "I figured that's what you took when you hugged me."

My ears burn, and there's a flash of interest in Gavin's eyes. It's gone as soon as it appears, but it makes my heartbeat speed up.

"It helps that your body metabolizes things fairly quickly. Plus, you're an anomaly."

"Excuse me?"

"You're a redhead. One of only a handful I've seen on the island." He reaches for my arm but stops short of touching it. "Your skin, for instance, lets in more light to produce vitamin D. That means you're less likely to get certain diseases. You also need more drugs to knock you out. They obviously didn't give you enough at the hospital." He smirks.

The idea that I'm unique, that there's something rare and different about me, makes me sit up. I feel special, and even though it's nothing to brag about, it *is* something to hold onto. Something that makes me feel less like a body parts factory and more like a person.

But I also feel exposed, like Gavin knows too much about me. More than I know about myself.

I change the subject. "How'd you figure out how to get people like Mary and me out of the hospital without getting caught?"

"Don't forget Sasha," he says, glancing over at her. "She was the first."

"Are there any others?" My voice climbs too high, too hopeful.

"Lots of attempts…but no."

Even though I should have expected his answer, my stomach clenches like it absorbed a punch. "How many?" I ask.

"Six…before Adrian started helping me, I'd trail a car leaving the Center and go into the hospital like I was visiting a patient. It was luck more than anything." Gavin's eyes glaze over like he's lost in thought. Finally, he shakes his head. "Adrian can tap into the communication between the Centers and the hospital, which cuts through the guess work. Now we know when they're gearing up for a live transfer. He's one of the reasons your rescue was a success."

And I gave him a bloody nose. Way to go, Tabitha. "I guess I never told you guys thanks, did I?"

"You just did." We share a smile, and Gavin stands with renewed vigor. "Listen, I still have an errand to run. I know this is a lot to take in, but if you want to get out of here for a while, see what Nordic Island looks like, you can come with me."

"But…" I hesitate. "Isn't it dangerous? Aren't there people looking for me?"

"Yes, but I don't want you to feel like we're holding you

prisoner." His voice is comforting, but I see concern in his eyes. "Besides, I'm sure you're itching to see the island. I've got a hat in my truck that'll conceal your hair. You'll be safe. I promise." He gestures at the door.

I resist the urge to wipe my palms on my shorts when I stand. I'm nervous, but intrigued at seeing the outside world through older, wiser eyes.

He scoops up my plate and shakes the bits of food into the garbage before tossing it in the bucket of dirty dishes.

"Can you guess who missed dish duty?" he asks.

I follow his stare to Ry, who's playing a game of cards on the floor with the longhaired boy and Sasha. Gavin claims she's from the Center, but for whatever reason, she makes me feel like I'm not entirely safe here.

Gavin shakes his head at Ry and leads us through the hallway. "Any news, Adrian?" he asks.

The radio is assembled and Adrian wipes his forehead, leaving a black smudge mark. "Just static so far, but I'll get it working again, don't worry."

Gavin heads up the ladder first and leans down from the top with an arm extended. This time, I take his hand.

He lifts me effortlessly and puts me down beside him. His hand is rough like the track I used to run on. I would press my palms into it before I took off in a sprint, trying to beat my time in the one-hundred-meter dash. I miss that feeling, something I could control. Now life seems chaotic. No wonder Gavin likes things so neat.

His truck is unlocked and he reaches into the back seat. "It might be a little big," he says, pulling out a dark blue baseball cap. "But it'll hide the red." He slaps it against his leg before handing it to me.

I stuff my hair underneath, feeling calmer already. But the second I climb in and buckle the seatbelt, Gavin tears down the gravel road and my emotions jump back to the surface. I haven't been in a moving vehicle with a view since before I can remember, and I'm anxious to take everything in.

We're out of the trees in a matter of minutes and connect with a road that heads down a hill. Gavin follows the signs toward the Gladstone City Center. The ocean is in front of us, stretching across the entire view.

"Is that where the Center is?" I ask, my voice small. Gavin nods.

"You see that white dot in the water?" He leans into the steering wheel, narrowing his eyes at the image. "That's the ferry. It's the only way off the island."

My eyes drift from the ferry to the Nordic coastline. The buildings seem to be lumped together in sections.

"That's PharmPerfect's main lab," Gavin says, pointing at the building on the far left. "And the taller ones around it are offices for packaging and sales. The building on the right is the Testing Facility."

What the one on the right lacks in height it makes up for in length. "What kind of tests?"

"For any new pill they come up with. Speed, strength, you name it. They test them on people here before selling them to the rest of the world."

I don't want to know the answer, but I ask anyway. "Who do they test the drugs on?"

"Junkies looking for some money and a quick fix." There's a long pause. "And uh…anyone who isn't purchased for parts."

My chest tightens. That's where Parker will likely end up.

"Do they let Center kids go when they're done testing them?" I ask, clinging to hope.

"I'm not sure. We haven't been able to get very close to that building. The security's intense."

I ball my fists. "We have to try."

Gavin's eyes flash to my hands. He doesn't object.

I tear my eyes away from the building, searching for something to take my mind off the image I have of Parker being made to run for hours while he's force-fed pills. But I can't escape the reminders.

All around us are flashing billboards promoting pills. One touts it can give you larger breasts. Another promises sculpted abs with no exercise, while the billboard opposite claims it can darken your skin tone. The gold PharmPerfect logo is stamped in the corner of every sign—two Ps in a circle that looks like the world.

Then I see an ad that's different than the rest—one seeking military recruits. There's a muscular man pointing straight out. Under the waist of his green camouflage pants, it reads: *We're looking for American heroes! Big payout for those who qualify. Schedule your free lab test today.*

Again, there's the gold logo. Why would PharmPerfect be working with the military?

My body jerks to the side as Gavin cuts across a lane of traffic.

"Sorry," he says. "I almost missed our exit."

"Where are we headed?"

He clears his throat. "To the hospital to pick up the surgery schedule. We've got another mission soon."

# CHAPTER 7

I'm a ball of nerves and excitement as we head down a four-lane road. We're going to get the details on the surgery so we can rescue whoever's next. Maybe it'll be someone from the Center for Excellence, one of my friends. I put my hands on the dashboard and lean until the seatbelt won't give anymore.

Gavin glances at me and a smile takes over his face. I didn't know he was capable of that much cheerfulness.

"We're going to make a quick stop." He gives me a mischievous wink.

"What about the schedule?"

"Don't worry, we've got a few minutes. There's a place I want to take you first."

He pulls up to a black and white building that's painted to look like a cow. The roof is round and bumpy, resembling a scoop of ice cream, only it's covered in dirt instead of fudge, and there's an air conditioning unit coming out the side.

"Where are we?"

"Dairy Land," he says, still smiling. His attitude is contagious. "Consider it an apology for dunking you."

We park and hop out. It's warm, and I can smell salt in the air mixed with milk and chocolate. It's a funny combination, but I inhale deeply to take in all three at once. An entire store just for ice cream? I must be dreaming.

He holds the door and we walk up to the counter where a boy in a cowhide apron asks for our order. At the same moment, the bell above the door rings, and a couple with a young child get in line behind us. The boy swings on the metal rail used to keep the customers in line. He creeps closer. Eager to order, I'm sure.

"What kind do you want?" Gavin asks. He orders himself a strawberry shake while I stare at the options on the board above the employee's head. There are so many flavors, and I don't recognize half of them from any of the shows we were allowed to watch. These ones have funny names like Mud Pie and Candy Cove. It's overwhelming.

A loud crack startles me and I spin around, my hands balled, ready to protect myself.

I look down at the boy, whose feet have simply smacked against the tile floor. His eyes are full of fear as he pulls himself against his mother's leg. Silence coats the room like a layer of melted chocolate.

His parents glare at me and I drop my hands.

"She'll have a twist cone," Gavin says, putting money on the counter. We step to the side while we wait for our order, and Gavin shields me with his body.

Gavin doesn't move until the boy in the cowhide apron slides a tray toward us. Scooping up the shake and the cone, Gavin leads us toward the exit. There's a height chart against the doorframe, and when he leans back to hold the door open, I notice his head is just above the six-foot mark. But right now, he feels like a giant to me.

The truck starts with a thunderous roar. We roll through the stop sign and get back on the road.

"They must think I'm crazy," I say when we're a half mile away.

"Based on their gawking, I'd have to agree."

"I'm sorry." I stare at my cone. The ice cream is starting to trickle down the side.

"Don't be. They're assholes for pretending there's nothing wrong with this city."

"You think they know?"

"Probably not," Gavin concedes. "I didn't find out until Ry was high and kept babbling about surgeries and tests—"

"That's what tipped you off? He was on drugs and you believed him? Just like that?"

"Ry's a lot of things, but he's not a liar. He had nothing to gain by telling me what he'd learned over the years." Gavin chews on his lip while we wait for the stoplight to turn green. "But you're right. Most people aren't going to believe someone like Ry. PharmPerfect is good at keeping their image clean. That's why people trust them. Trust helps sell pills."

Gavin takes a big slurp of his shake and jams it into his cup holder.

The ice cream reaches my hand and I lick it off. *Pure bliss.* It's better than Euphorium. I try chocolate on its own, then vanilla, and finally a blend, savoring the ice cream on my tongue.

Gavin looks over with a satisfied smile.

I catch his gaze and the awkwardness melts away. I'm glad we stopped by Dairy Land, despite the scene I made. And I'm glad I was with Gavin. He's much softer than he first appeared, sweet like my ice cream.

"Why aren't you like the rest of them?" I ask.

His forehead scrunches. "What do you mean?"

"You're not from the Center, and you're not missing any body parts—that I know of."

He gives a deep, manly laugh and sits up.

"I just got tired of seeing what the drugs were doing to people around me."

"Like Ry?"

"Yeah, him. And other people I've known. Ry's a good guy, he's just addicted to what people around here call the *pill thrill.*"

"How did you guys become friends? You're so…"

"Different?"

I nod as I smooth off the top of my cone. I'm sure I look ridiculous right now, but I can't help it. Maybe we can stop by Dairy Land again on the way back.

"We went to school together. Played on the same little league team and eventually for our high school. But everyone was using, so it made the game less of a sport and more of a show. If you weren't taking Endurance or Power pills, you were one step up from the bat boy."

He takes a long drink—so long I get the impression he wants to move on from the topic of baseball.

"Did you graduate?" I ask.

"I decided I'd had enough of school. The girls all looked like plastic and guys like Ry, well, let's face it, he looks like a cologne model." He pantomimes spritzing me. "Care to try Eau de Ry?"

I laugh and push his hand away. But on the inside, there's a knot in my stomach. What happens when looking perfect isn't good enough? When everyone on the team hits home runs? Then what? More powerful pills? What if harvesting organs becomes acceptable and expands to the mainland? I imagine Centers popping up in every state, kids corralled into a slaughterhouse for mass liver transfers. The thought makes me queasy.

I consider Ms. Preen's flawless face and Tony's muscles, which bulged although I never actually saw him exercise. They took pills to perfect themselves, and someday one of them might need a new liver. I hope we can shut down the Center before that time comes, that none of my friends are used to keep either of them alive.

"You all right?" Gavin asks when I'm quiet for too long.

"I'm fine." I try to relax my jaw, but my thoughts drift to the twins. I'm sure Meghan's fixated on beating any records associated with my name, whereas Paige is probably welcoming the newbie they brought up from the Center for Growth to take my place. Paige will take the tween under her wing, helping her transition from brain growth to fitness, and Parker will keep benching as much weight as the instructors can fit on the barbell. All of them oblivious to the fact that the Center will never place them with a real family, no matter how old they are or how hard they train.

"What's going to happen with Mary?" I ask, the cold from the cone pressing into my palm.

"We haven't figured that out yet."

"She's just going to grow up at the barn?"

Gavin shakes his head. "I don't know. Right now she's safe.

That's what matters. And she's got a lot of people willing to do whatever it takes to look after her."

"But she needs to go to school, meet kids her age. And what about—"

"I'm working on it," he snaps.

The temperature in the truck feels much colder than it was a few minutes ago, and I shiver.

Gavin glances over and blows out a breath. "With a missing cornea, I don't know how safe Mary is out here."

"But she still has her eye."

"Only because cornea surgery is cleaner and faster."

"Can't she wear a patch?"

"Too obvious. If someone from the Center or the doctor who operated on her saw her, you can be sure they'd want to keep her quiet. She's safer at the barn. For now."

That makes sense, but there has to be another way. Something we could do to help her live a normal life.

"Maybe we could teach her," I say. Gavin quirks an eyebrow like I've asked him to teach her quantum physics. "What? Did you drop out?"

"No. I went to summer school and finished early."

"I'm sure there's something you could teach Mary." My voice is dry and mocking.

"You can teach the lesson in sarcasm." He pushes me lightly in the shoulder.

A tiny flutter starts in my stomach, and I change the subject before it can grow.

"When you left school did you miss your friends?" I ask.

"Just about everyone was hooked on Euphorium." He gestures with his milkshake for me to try it. "It makes it a little hard to get to know someone when they're floating in the clouds all day." He narrows his eyes, scolding me with his glare.

Guilt tunnels its way into my stomach. *Thanks a lot, Ry.*

I take a sip of Gavin's shake. The straw is blue and wide enough to let the real fruit bits climb out.

"You're seventeen then?" I ask, handing his drink back.

"I turned eighteen last month. What about you?"

"I'll be seventeen in October." Why am I trying to make myself sound older? "I've spent the last ten years at the Center."

"They didn't raise you from birth?" The truck sways just enough for me to notice. I glance at his grip, his hands tight around the wheel. "I've never heard of a kid who started at the Center late."

*Kid.* The word stings.

"Well, I did."

"Oh." His lips move, but he must be too afraid to ask. I let him stew for a while before I save him the trouble.

"My parents died; that's how I wound up there."

"I'm sorry to hear that." He looks at me, and I can see he means it. It doesn't make my heart hurt any less, though. Every time I talk about it, I feel like I'm checking the wound beneath a Band-Aid prematurely. The gash exposed—unable to seal itself, unable to create new skin.

"It was a car accident." My eyes burn and I look out the passenger window.

Gavin stays quiet and I have a chance to compose myself. When I turn back around his face is grim.

"What's going on?" I look straight ahead, but the traffic is moving, and a glance at the side mirror shows no one is following us.

"Nothing," he says.

I can't get a read on him. He seems so distant now. Cold. Like he was when I first met him. I take a deep breath and prop my feet up on the dashboard, leaning back in my seat for the rest of the ride to enjoy my soggy cone as we follow the signs to the hospital.

• • •

We pass several areas under construction. Subdivisions with massive homes, built with columns and brick, and wide enough to eat up the entire lot.

"The population's booming," Gavin says. "They can't build

homes fast enough. Pretty soon the houses will trickle further west, out toward the barn." He purses his lips.

The shops on Main Street are as neat and tidy as the people, a reflection of the flawlessness they're trying to project. Streetlights are polished and store windows gleam.

When we get to the medical district there are fewer people, but the glass buildings are just as grand. Workers in blue scrubs wander in and out with aimless expressions and hospital caps to cover what I can only assume is perfect hair.

Gavin's lips are still in a tight line as we drive past a grassy island with a concrete sign that reads *Gladstone Memorial Hospital* in blood-red letters. It's a curvy font, too whimsical for what goes on here, but the color seems appropriate.

We pull past the emergency entrance and head under a skywalk to the rear of the building. At the back, there's a dumpster stuffed with white drawstring bags and an ambulance that looks like it's been retired. It's the ugly side of the hospital, hidden from view, just like the truth about the Centers.

"Here he comes," Gavin says.

I look over my shoulder and my heart seizes. The guy runs a hand through his honey-blond hair, and without thinking I dive behind Gavin's seat.

Gavin's window is already halfway down, and he doesn't question me as the footsteps approach.

"How's it going?" the guy says.

The wound on my neck seems to throb at the sound of his voice.

"Good," Gavin says. "Thanks for meeting me."

"Last mission go okay?"

"Damn near perfect."

"That's what I'd hoped," the guy says. "We make a good team." I hear the crumpling sound of a paper being wadded up. "The schedule is at the bottom of the bag. Mostly routine stuff, but there's a surgery on there that fits what you're looking for. Same doctor being called in, so I assume it's a transfer."

"Thanks." Gavin puts the brown bag on the passenger seat.

"You're bringing the same crew out next time, right?" the guy asks.

"That's the plan."

"Good. They should be able to get in and out in no time."

They exchange goodbyes before Gavin brings the window up and pulls away. He waits until we're back on the road before he lets me have it. "What the hell was that?" Gavin tosses the bag in the back after I climb into my seat. I search for the man in the side mirror, but he's long gone.

"I think I know him."

"That's impossible."

"He was at my health screening. He's the one who sliced my neck."

"You don't know what you're talking about. He never finished med school; there's no way he'd be cutting people." Gavin shakes his head; like that should be enough to appease me.

"I remember seeing his badge. His name is Curtis."

"Wrong. That guy,"—Gavin points a thumb over his shoulder—"is Kenny."

"His last name starts with an R."

"No. His last name is—" Gavin squeezes into the left lane. "It doesn't matter. What matters is he's on our side."

"I recognize his face, that voice—"

"From a truck window?"

"I know it's him." I fold my arms, squeezing myself tight. At least *I* believe me.

"You're wrong." Gavin shakes his head and pounds the accelerator when the car in front of him changes lanes. "Kenny works in scheduling. He's behind a computer all day. He wants to help us stop what they're doing to innocent kids."

There's that word again. *Kids.*

"I was going to introduce you since he helped spring you, but then you freaked out." Gavin scratches his head like he's trying to scrape the last thirty seconds from his memory. "He's already paranoid someone will turn him in for helping us. He even eyed the backseat like he knew someone was hiding. He's probably worried we're setting him up."

"I'm telling you, it was him. I know what I saw—"

"Just drop it." His voice softens, but his arm muscles stay tight as he grips the wheel like it's the only thing keeping him steady. "We need Kenny. He can get us exact surgery dates and times, not to mention badges and scrubs. He's putting a lot on the line to help us, and if you spook him, I guarantee he won't help us get your friends out."

I stare out the window as I answer, my eyes stinging. "Well, I don't trust him."

"You'll take a random pill from Ry, but you don't trust Kenny?"

"It looked just like mine. I thought—" I didn't think, though, I realize. I let my guard down too quickly.

"Maybe you should rethink your instincts," says Gavin. He pauses then throws one last jab. "I'm just glad you didn't break Adrian's nose."

My face feels as red as my hair. I want to hit something. Preferably Gavin. Of course, that would only strengthen the argument that I am a kid—too immature to control my emotions.

We spend the rest of the ride in silence.

# CHAPTER 8

Sasha is outside with some of the others when we pull up. They're tossing a disc back and forth, and Craig flings the saucer toward Gavin when he gets out.

Gavin tosses it back and looks at me. "You coming?"

I leave the hat on the seat and shake out my hair. "I'm gonna go for a walk." Regardless of what Gavin thinks about Kenny, trust isn't going to be that easy for me. Not when everything I've ever trusted has been a lie.

"Suit yourself." He shakes his head and carries the bag with scrubs and badges toward the barn.

Gavin hasn't been raised like a fish in a bowl to be chopped up like sushi. Still, he's trying to help us. I should trust him. And maybe, I should trust he knows more about the people he's chosen to help than I do. I stare at his back, and the disc hits me in the leg. Sasha laughs and waits for me to return it, but when I toss it the disc ends up in the trough Gavin dunked me in.

"Nice one," she says, her sarcasm as thick as whatever she uses to make her hair stick up. Probably paste, based on how white it is.

"Oops." I flash a false smile and start for the woods.

I hear gravel crunching behind me before I make it to the bend in the drive, but when I turn, it's not Gavin.

"Wait up," Ry says, jogging up to me.

"Where'd you come from?" I look past him. The disc throwers are still outside. "I didn't see you out tossing that pancake thing… what's it called again?"

"A Frisbee." He smiles like Gavin did when we pulled up to Dairy Land. It must be interesting to watch someone experience so many things outsiders have taken for granted—except right now I feel like someone's science experiment. "When Gavin came in without you, I figured you were hitting the trail."

"How perceptive."

"Can I join you?" When I shrug, he pulls out a pill bottle. "Want some Euphorium for the run?"

"No thanks." I push the pills away and he pops one in his mouth as we start to jog.

Without Endurance, he's not as fast. I have to keep a slower pace so I don't lose him. He spends most of the time peering up at the trees like he's seeing something that's not really there. Gavin must have thought I looked like a fool when I took Euphorium. I catch myself grinning as Ry shrieks with joy when a ladybug lands on his finger.

I stay on the widest route, glancing back at Ry each time we pass a split in the trail, to make sure he doesn't wander off without me. Luckily my red sweatshirt is easy to spot because he seems to have no sense of direction.

We don't make it too far before Ry wants to sit and play with some flowers that look like miniature bells. I'm glad, because I'm overheating and in desperate need of my tank top.

"How do you guys do laundry?" I ask.

"Usually we use the trough, but there's a waterfall not too far from here. Makes the chore much funner if you ask me."

It's not the fun that perks my interest in the waterfall. It's the privacy. I could really use a bath. "How do I sign up for laundry duty?"

"There's a board on the back wall. Just put your name down."

"No one will mind?"

"Not. One. Bit." Ry's face is so close to the ground he could snort the dirt. He's following a ladybug and trying to balance one of the flowers on its back, but he's not having much luck.

"Thanks, Ry."

"That's what I'm here for," he says, smiling at the bug. "Sasha will be happy to give up laundry duty."

"So Gavin busted her out, huh?"

"Yep. 'Bout a year ago."

"Last year? Then how come I don't recognize her?"

"You probably wouldn't. She had black hair and was about fifteen pounds thinner. She was fit and fast. She made the Endurance pills look worthless."

A memory surfaces of a girl with long hair and a valance of bangs that framed her face—a face that never scowled.

"There was a girl…but her name wasn't Sasha," I say, although I can't recall what it was. "She left right after I transferred from the Center for Growth. But that had to have been three or four years ago, not a year."

"That's how long she was in isolation. The patient died right before the operation was scheduled. They hadn't cut Sasha open, so they just locked her away until they could redo the tests and match her with a new patient."

"Why not just send her back to the Center?"

"She knew too much, had started to question what was going on when she woke up from the anesthesia. Didn't you?"

He doesn't look up, but I nod anyway.

"The day of her surgery finally came, and they took her uterus. She'll never have kids."

I gasp. "That's awful." The look she gave me when Gavin introduced us makes sense now. They took away her ability to create life. I was lucky enough to get away with everything intact.

"Surgeries can take hours, so they space them apart to give the doctors a break. Before they could cut up the rest of her, Gavin got her out. She doesn't want to remember her old life. When she cleaned herself up, she renamed herself Sasha. A rebirth if you will."

"Cleaned herself up?"

"She got hooked on pills trying to numb the pain. It's a trip what they do to you guys if you really think about it."

I'm trying not to, but it will happen again, to people who need me. It's the one thing that keeps me from dwelling on the reality of it all. I need to save my foster friends. The only family I have.

I draw in the dirt with the toe of my shoe. It's odd knowing Sasha once succumbed to pills. She seems anything but weak now.

"So after they removed her uterus, they kept her alive to take the rest of her organs?"

"Yep. Just like Mary with her cornea and kidney," Ry says. "Some parts need to be used immediately. Others can be stored. That's what the top floor at the hospital is for. It's the cryopreservation unit. You never know when someone might need a lung or heart. With today's technology, parts can keep for a couple of years."

He sounds proud. I want to step on his fingers. But Ry is so focused on the ladybug I have to believe the drugs mask his real emotions.

I dig out some of the pills from my pocket. I have less than a week's worth of my heart medication. I'll need to space them out to make them last until I can get more. The handful I have left are mixed in with the ones I took from Ms. Preen. "Any idea what these do?"

Ry looks up, and his eyes grow wide. He stands so smoothly it's like strings are lifting him. His mouth quivers for a moment. "That's the holy grail," he says, pointing a flower stem at the big red pill.

I put the rest of the pills away and hold the red one out, pressing it between my fingers. It's squishy, like there's liquid inside. I move it to the right and left, and his eyes follow. They're so dilated the black sucks up most of the blue. He doesn't blink until I tuck my hand behind my back.

"What's so special about this pill, Ry?"

"That's a Fireball."

"But what's it do?"

"I've never taken one." He takes a step and I scoot back. "It's supposed to be some sort of love pill. Better than Euphorium and Lust put together."

"Like a love potion?"

"More like…ecstasy. You lose self-control. All that's left is desire." I wait for him to start to drool but he manages to pull himself together. "You gonna take it?"

"I was just curious."

"What *are* you going to do with it?"

"I'm not sure." It's the truth. But I have a feeling it might come in handy. I stuff the pill back in my pocket. "Let's head back." I run past him, listening for his feet. He must like the ladybug-red sweatshirt I'm wearing because he doesn't lag too far behind.

• • •

No one is outside throwing the Frisbee around when we get back. I'm glad because all the information I have about Sasha is eating me alive. I hate that I can't remember her name and I wonder if she feels slighted I don't recognize someone I looked up to at the Center. She made me want to be a better swimmer. Then again, she's probably glad I haven't said anything. If she's trying to escape her past I don't want to be the one to dig it up.

I help Ry down the ladder, but he manages to fall when his foot slips on the second to last rung, and he bursts into a fit of laughter.

Adrian shoots us both a look and I step over Ry.

"He took Euphorium," I say. "Don't worry, I'm not on anything."

Adrian makes a noise that sounds like a chuckle.

"What are you working on?" I ask.

He glares at me apprehensively.

"Look, I'm sorry about your nose. Self-defense was a priority at the Center."

He makes a clicking noise with his tongue and nods. "Yeah, I heard they really stepped up the training after Sasha got out."

"You think we were trained to fight off people trying to save us?"

"Yes and no." Adrian fiddles with the knobs on the radio.

It looks ancient, like something out of a retro scene in the *Gladstone Community Review*. The magazine devoted an entire issue to the 1970s. It was in the stacks Ms. Preen brought to the Center for us to read. Some of the pages were torn out—probably ads for drugs they didn't want us to know about—but there were plenty of pictures left for a group of us to create a game. We spent the evening pretending to pick out our perfect moms and dads, the cars they drove, the furniture we'd have. We kept going until we had our ideal family. It seems like a stupid game now.

"There actually *is* a group that kidnaps young, healthy kids to try to sell on the black market. Heard it happens near St. Vincent's in the north end. It's the hospital in junkie territory." His eyes are serious. "They perform alleyway surgery, and I can't imagine it's pretty. You don't want to go under the knife with those guys."

I swallow the image as I nod. "Our trainers talked about it." In great detail, unfortunately. "We were taught to trust no one."

"With the exception of Center employees, of course," he says with a smile.

I roll my eyes. "Of course."

Ry laughs and I glance over. He's still staring up at the hatch, but now he's tracing the shape in the air with his finger. He must have taken a larger dose than before.

"So," I say, turning my attention back to Adrian. "Did you go to school with Gavin too?"

"No, I was homeschooled. But I've known Gavin since he was in diapers."

"Really?" The image makes me laugh.

"Our moms did the whole playdate thing when we were kids, but they eventually lost touch. Gavin and I hadn't seen each other since the fifth grade, then one day I found him stranded on the side of the road. His truck had broken down, and I got it running well enough for him to make it back here. We spent the next four hours catching up while we gave it a tune-up. Then Mary came wandering out of the barn…" There's pain in his eyes. "When I learned what happened, I wanted to help."

Gavin's voice startles me. "I knew it was a risk telling Adrian," he says from the doorway of the main room. In three big strides, he's by Adrian's side. "But we had a history, and I thought his technical expertise could be helpful. Plus, he didn't use drugs."

"Why would I want to alter this physique?" Adrian pats his belly and smiles.

"What about the others? How'd they join the team?" What I'd really like to know is how Gavin met Kenny.

Gavin shoots Adrian a look. "I think that's enough of a history lesson for one day."

"Why can't he talk to me about this?" Heat rushes to my face. "What? You don't trust me?"

"Not when we almost lost our new contact because of your paranoia." My fingernails dig into my palms. I want to snap back, but the words feel like they're jammed in my throat. Gavin's eyes dart to the ladder. "What the hell happened to Ry?"

"Euphorium," Adrian says.

Gavin's gaze immediately comes back to me. "Decided not to join him this time?"

"If you expect me to trust people, perhaps you'd better take your own advice."

Adrian drops one of his tools and it pings against the floor. Gavin bends down to pick it up, and when he hands it to Adrian, he's almost smiling.

"All right. Tell her whatever she wants to know, Adrian." He looks me in the eyes. "I trust her."

The tension in my body starts to fade. I wish I could say it back, but I can't yet, and I'm glad he doesn't wait for me to.

"But," he turns back to the main room, "if you'd rather learn about the rescue mission, you can take a rain check and follow me."

Adrian must see my eyes widen because he waves me away. I hurry behind Gavin to the kitchen table where Mary is eating applesauce like it's ice cream from Dairy Land. There's a blob on her dress and I think some is in her hair, although it's hard to tell because her hair is so messy. Is it possible it's rattier than it was earlier?

"Hi, Tabitha!" Mary shrieks, holding up a heaping spoonful. "Want some?"

I smile. "No thanks, Mary. But before I forget..." I turn to Gavin who's already sitting, unfolding a piece of paper he pulled from his pocket. "Can I sign up for laundry duty?"

He stares at me like I've asked to cut out my own lung.

"That's a lot of work. Have you seen the pile?" He points to the far corner of the room. To the right of the signup sheet, there's an overflowing mountain of clothes. Mary is small enough to climb to the top and use it as a slide.

"It has to get done sometime," I say. "Ry said there's a waterfall not far from here..."

"Yeah, well, good luck. You're going to need help."

"I'll go! I'll go!" Mary says, rapping her spoon repeatedly on the table.

"No, I need you to help Reilly with the dishes, Mary. You're the only one who can keep him focused."

Mary gives him a big juicy smile. He reaches across the table and wipes some of the sauce from the side of her mouth with a napkin.

I take a seat next to her and Gavin turns the paper around so I'm not reading it upside down. It's a spreadsheet with dates and times, like my former workout schedule, only this one shows when my friends are going to die. There's a tight squeeze in my chest. The Center acts like our hearts are for selling and nothing more, like our only value is the price of our parts. Who are they to decide our fate? I blink back angry tears before they can escape.

"There's a surgery scheduled for May 31," Gavin says, pointing at the first column.

The paper has some marks I don't understand. I tap one on the page.

"That symbol means they need a live donor," he says, "not a part from the cryopreservation unit."

"Do we know who the buyer is?" Maybe if we told them, if we explained to them what was going on...

"All we have are initials."

"Do we know who's next? Who's being *fostered out*?" The words roll off my tongue with bitterness.

"Now that Kenny's on our side, we'll have a better idea."

"How do you know this guy, anyway?"

He wipes Mary's chin again and takes the time to fold the napkin when he's done. "A friend of a friend."

"Hmm." I nod as if I'm satisfied, but it does little to build my trust for Kenny. Who would their go-between be? I scan through a list of names in my head—trainers, mostly. It can't be Ms. Preen. She'd probably volunteer to cut us open if she could. I draw a blank, and my eyes shift to Mary as I word my next question. "Now that we have an idea about the next surgery, how do you… prepare? I mean…the people…what you unloaded at the hospital…how do you, um…?"

A flash of understanding crosses Gavin's face. "Mary, can you check and see if I left the keys in my truck?"

Applesauce flecks splatter when she drops her spoon and scurries off. I blow out a breath of relief. "Thanks," I say.

"No problem. I wouldn't have told you with her here."

"So what are the bodies for? You don't, you know…kill, do you?"

I can tell my question amuses him. "They're replacements. That way the room isn't empty if someone pops in before the surgery. But no. They're already dead."

"Where do you…get them?"

"Ry's in charge of that." Gavin bounces his pencil on the table. The eraser is surprisingly springy. "People overdose on pills all the time. The pharmaceutical companies can still use the bodies for a while, to test skin and hair products, stuff like that. They pay for dead junkies. It's disgusting."

"So we buy bodies before they can?"

"More or less."

"Where do we get the money?"

"We have an account. Well, I do, that is." Gavin hesitates, scratching a thin layer of hair on his chin. "Needless to say, my college savings aren't going toward tuition."

My jaw drops. Gavin has given up his education to stop the Center. He's funding this operation. I want to reach across the table and hug him.

He gives a small shrug, and I realize I'm gazing at him with a smile that's not appropriate for talking about dead bodies.

"Anyway," he says, clearing his throat, "sometimes we don't use money. Ry trades pills for them before the bodies are sold to companies for testing. We save the sellers a trip and they get what they really want—drugs."

"Isn't that dangerous?"

"Ry says it's perfectly safe." Gavin's gaze drops to the table as he traces a knothole. "But I'm starting to think he's been around that crowd too long."

I look over my shoulder at Ry, who wanders around the room listening to music. He's having a hard time keeping the earphones in, but to him, it's the funniest thing in the world.

"The hospital doesn't realize you're replacing the bodies with ones that are already dead?"

"Eventually, but it buys us some time to get away. It's not like the body we replaced yours with had your hair color. I'm sure the doctor noticed as soon as he looked at the chart. That reminds me…" Gavin scribbles a note about hair dye on the paper. "You need to lose the red."

"Of course. If you think that'll help. I don't want anyone to recognize me at the hospital."

"Whoa whoa whoa." Gavin's hand goes up. "You're not going on a rescue mission. I'm just filling you in so you're in the loop. Sasha will tell you where to hide if we're not back within a couple of hours."

I make my voice as firm as my fist. "I want to go."

"What makes you think I'd let you?"

Does he think I'm going to twiddle my thumbs while one of my friends lies waiting? "I'm fast. I'm strong…" I lean forward. "And you need me."

His face twitches just enough to let me know I'm right. His team is small, and they don't have a lot of successes under their belts.

Gavin doesn't nod, but he does sigh, and that's better than a no. "I'll think about it. If—and that's a big if—I say yes, you have to follow my orders."

"I can do that."

"And be a team player."

"Done."

"That means you need to get along with everyone." He gives me a stern look, one eyebrow raised and lips tight. "Kenny confirms the surgery room and time so we can get there before it happens."

I force myself to smile and I nod. I understand how important Kenny's role is, but I still don't trust the guy. If I run into him again, I can't guarantee I won't give him a swift knee to the groin.

"Let me get this straight," I say. "You and Adrian take the rescue van, and Ry and Craig haul in the body double." Gavin nods. "What's the other guy do? The one with the long hair?"

"Burk? He helps when he can. He's got a regular job at a grocery store, but he'll ask for days off if we have a mission. Everyone makes it a priority."

"So what happens when donors like me go missing after a mission? Do the buyers just wait for another match?"

"In some cases." Gavin fills in the letters on the paper. His hands seem to always need to stay busy. He notices I'm watching and stops, but it's only a few seconds before he has to straighten it so the pencil and paper are perfectly aligned.

I like this about him. It makes him seem normal, not quite so perfect.

"The buyer might settle for frozen parts," he says. "It depends on how sick they are and what they need."

"But don't be surprised if they head back to the Center for fresh meat," says Sasha from behind me. Her arm grazes my hair as she walks around the table and sits next to Gavin. I try not to meet her eyes. I don't think I can hide my sympathy for her, and I suspect she doesn't like pity.

Gavin drums his fingers on the wood, staring at the paper for more answers. The table is waxy, and his nails make soft clicks. "I'm gonna see what else I can find out." There's urgency in his voice. Determination.

He meets Mary at the door when he gets to the hallway. Of course the keys have been in Gavin's pocket the entire time, but he thanks her profusely for looking and asks her to walk him out.

I feel Sasha's stare and meet her eyes. A lump forms in my throat.

"I don't like you," she says.

"I figured that much." I stand to leave, unwilling to be her verbal punching bag.

When my back is to her she calls out, "I've got my eye on you."

Despite my every intention, I can't help myself. I turn around. "What did I do to piss you off?"

"You got out."

"*That* makes you mad?"

"Mary's just a kid. But you." She points at my heart. "You're a liability. I can see it in your eyes. You insist on going to the hospital, but you have no idea the danger you're putting everyone in by going inside that place."

"I just want to help. What's wrong with that?" My hands are shaking and I curl my fingers to stop them. "Do you think we should leave everyone to die? Don't you care about your friends?"

Sasha's cheeks redden like she's about to explode. Her fist pounds the table. "All my Center friends are dead by now. I have to protect what I can. And that's here."

I take a deep breath, forcing my emotions to recede. Sasha is terrified of losing the only family she has left. How can I be angry with her when I feel the same way? I give her a nod to show her I understand. But if I can help in any way, I want to be there.

"I know it's risky. I'll keep a low profile. Trust me, I don't want anyone to…to get hurt." Then I turn and head for my bunk before she can see the fear in my eyes, the fear that maybe she's right. What if her friends are caught because someone recognizes me?

# CHAPTER 9

———

"You don't want a heart," Craig says, playing a diamond. "Hearts are points."

"And points are bad, right?" I play a diamond too, even though I'm still not sure what I'm doing. "Can't we just play Old Maid?" It's a game we played at the Center, one I'm pretty good at. Only Parker could tell when I had the Old Maid card. He said he could read it in my eyes.

"That's a kid game," Sasha says with a laugh.

I clamp my mouth shut before something snappy can come out. Gavin is still wary about me going on the next mission, but if I can prove I'm a team player—that I can play nice with others—I'm hoping it'll seal the deal.

Mary sits next to me on the floor while we play, leaning in like a puppy with her head on my thigh. Her hair is smooth, and she can't keep her hands off the strands that fall over her shoulders.

I asked Sasha if I could borrow a brush the day after our heated argument. She hesitated, but once she knew what it was for, she said I could keep it.

"I don't need it anyway," she'd said. "I can style my hair with my fingers." Then she asked if I wanted to play cards when I was done. For the last week, it's become a routine.

We've been playing for an hour, and my stomach growls at the spicy smell of whatever Ry's cooking. Gavin puts away groceries while Adrian sits on the table with headphones on, shoulders hunched as he fiddles with a dial.

"It'll be a miracle if he gets that thing working again," Sasha says, following my eyes to the kitchen. She lays down a four of hearts.

We all have to play a heart now, and I have the ace, which means I'll win the hand and collect four points. At least I'll have control of the next round.

"How'd the radio break?" I ask.

"It didn't. They must have scrambled the signal," she says. "Reception went fuzzy around the same time Gavin got you out. But if anyone can tap in, Adrian can. He's a tech wiz."

"Maybe he should try breaking into the network again," Burk says. He sits with his legs crossed and his back straight—it's a meditative pose, which seems to fit his hippy hair and goatee. It's like he's on a low-dose of Euphorium all the time, but Gavin says he's a Nordic native—here before PharmPerfect moved in—and the only drug he takes comes from a plant.

"He might have to." Sasha gestures for Craig to play a card.

"It'd help if we had a better signal out here," says Craig, dropping the Jack of spades.

"If reception's so bad, can't he just listen in from another city?" I ask.

Everyone laughs but Mary and me.

"There *are* no other cities on this island," Craig says when it's quiet. "We'd have to go to the mainland, and to get a signal from that far away, we'd need better equipment than what we have now."

"Ferry tickets aren't cheap either," says Sasha. "They're the only way on and off this island. And I'll give you one guess who owns the ferry system."

I collect my points and start the next round.

"You're making a commitment to the lifestyle when you move here. There's little incentive to leave," says Burk. "The doctors get fat checks and the people get skinny."

"PharmPerfect gives people the life they've always wanted," Craig says. "Problems can be solved with a pill. It's the perfect place…"

"With perfect people," Sasha and Burk finish.

Craig drops the dreaded queen of spades and Sasha slugs him in the leg. "Asshole."

Mary gasps.

"Sorry!" Sasha hits Craig again, this time in the shoulder.

"Ow! That's my pitching arm." He massages the spot. "You're lucky I don't play anymore."

"Gavin told me you had quite an arm," I say. The group stops talking and my voice sounds louder than I intended.

"I did." Craig bobs his chin. "There was a time when I took more than twenty pills a day. My synapses were working overtime. My body was a machine. I scored off the charts in tests and threw hundred-mile-an-hour pitches. Everything was going my way until my liver started to fail."

Sasha rubs his back and Mary sits up as if she hasn't heard this story either.

"I had a new one put in," Craig says, sucking in a breath. "I didn't know where it came from until Ry told me." Ry keeps his eyes on the ground. "That's when I came here. Started helping Gavin, Burk, and Ry." He nudges Sasha with his elbow. "I needed to make it right."

I nod, afraid my voice will crack if I speak.

"All right," Sasha says, touching her Mohawk. "Let's finish this game before Burk has to go back to his *real* home."

"Does your family own this farm?" I ask Burk.

Burk and Sasha exchange a look.

"He's a Nordic native," I say, "so I just figured…"

"Close. But wrong family." Sasha gestures in the direction of the kitchen.

"You mean *Gavin's* family owns this property?" I glance at the kitchen and catch Gavin's eyes, his playful smile. My cheeks flush and I turn back to the game.

"His grandparents moved out here when his folks did and bought the land from my family. That's how Gav and I became friends," Burk says, playing a card.

"There used to be more farms and trees until PharmPerfect

threw money at people so they'd give up their land," says Sasha. "But not Gavin's grandparents. They didn't want to sell. They preferred the country life."

"Does Gavin?" I ask.

Sasha shuffles her cards around. She only has three, so I know she's just buying time. I don't like the way her lips curl. The sly smile can't be because of her stellar hand.

"Never mind. It doesn't matter," I say.

She looks at me over the top of her cards and I'm trapped in her gaze. Her eyes say she knows it *does* matter—that I want to know more about Gavin. My heart jumps a little.

Craig slaps his card down and Sasha plays a heart. He throws the rest of his cards at her. "Damn you, Sasha!"

Mary presses an ear into my thigh and covers the other one with her hand.

"Dinner's ready," Ry calls out.

Everyone rushes for the table. There's salsa and ground beef in bowls with tortillas on a plate next to some shredded cheese. Gavin sits across from me. We've established a regular seating pattern, but this time I notice my crate is turned on its side when I go to sit. Just how I like it. He smiles and I mouth *thank you*.

We've worked so well together this past week, sharing information about the Center and the mission to save whoever's next, I feel like we've developed a trust—an appreciation for each other.

Underneath the sound of chatter and people pouring drinks and scraping food, Gavin leans forward to whisper something to me. "You still up for doing all that laundry?" He gestures to the massive pile behind me.

"I thought you said it was too much for one person to handle."

"It is. But we're running out of clean clothes."

"Does that mean you're volunteering to help me?" My heart pounds and I can't decide if I want him to say yes. Does he want to be alone with me too? What if he says no? The silence seems to last forever.

"I guess so," he finally says, his voice indifferent. When he looks down at his food, my excitement fizzles like a firecracker in the rain.

• • •

After dinner, Mary stands on a crate next to Ry and they sing while washing dishes together. They're actually pretty good, and I'm kind of sad to miss the rest of the show. But Gavin's right. We need clothes, more than just the bare essentials. We've been washing our undergarments with the hose outside, and using the trough to clean our faces. I'd be tempted to give up my big toe for a bath right now.

Next to the pyramid of fabric, I find a stack of duffle bags and fill one completely. I don't know whose clothes I'll be washing, but I make sure to include my tank top and a pair of jeans in my size. Hopefully, they're not Sasha's, but I'm prepared to fight for them either way.

There's a shelf by the laundry sign-up sheet with soap and a scrub board. We had washing machines in a supply closet at the Center. This feels so primitive, but I kind of like the idea of simplicity these days.

I decide to make a break for it before Gavin notices. Craig drew me a map to get to the waterfall, so while Gavin's busy talking to Adrian and Burk, I slip out the door and down the hallway. I don't want him to feel obligated to help me. Especially when I'm not sure I want to be alone with him. The idea makes me feel nervous and sweaty. One more reason I need fresh clothes. After climbing the ladder, I ease the hatch back in place, making sure it doesn't clang.

It's hard to run with the extra weight on my back, but I sprint as long as I can until my thigh muscles feel like melted cheese. The burn helps me work through the backlog of thoughts pecking at my brain. I'm angry I let my heart get caught up in the idea of having a foster family, for believing in the people who raised me.

Nothing would satisfy me more than making the Center trainers—and Ms. Preen—suffer.

I imagine my friends sitting on the bleachers, watching our trainers run around the track with laundry strapped to their backs. Meghan, always the control freak, would be in charge of the stopwatch. Parker would bark out orders for them to run faster, and Paige and I would sit back with the others and enjoy watching them gasp for breath.

It's at least twenty minutes before I make it to the waterfall, but when I finally do it's worth each second and every ache. The water flows over a ledge that looks higher than the rock-climbing wall at the Center and there is a small meadow on the other side. The trail winds under the boulder where the spill starts, and I reach out to touch the waterfall as I pass through. The cold mist tickles my cheeks, waking every nerve in my face.

I drop the duffle bag to undress. I leave on my panties and slip into my crusty tank top so I can wash it while I swim. Ry claimed the waterfall made laundry more fun. I decide to test his theory and jump through the curtain of water streaming down from the rocks.

My knees curl to my chest in a cannonball. When I hit the water, cold jolts through my body like I've been awakened from a deep slumber. I swim to the edge and grab the bar of soap I'd set out. It smells like apples.

It smells like Gavin.

Rolling the bar around in my hands, I make a thick lather for my face and hair. Then I rub the bar all over my body and tank top before tossing it onto the land. The water is frothy around me, and I dive under, making sure all the bubbles rinse away.

Under the surface, the waterfall sounds like thunder, yet it's too peaceful to elicit fear.

When I pop up, I swim toward the bag of laundry, which should be an arm's length from the shore—only it's gone.

# CHAPTER 10

I swim back toward the middle of the water and wait. Whoever took the laundry has no idea how long I can tread.

In a burst, a body flies through the waterfall and lands inches from my head.

Gavin pops up, laughing. "Decided to do laundry on your own?"

The water coats his bare chest in a glossy sheen, sliding off the lean muscles of his arms as he wipes his face. I swim to shore; suddenly very aware I'm in my panties. And we're alone. Is he here to do laundry, or is this weird fluttering in my stomach mutual?

"You didn't sound too excited to help," I say, keeping my voice even.

He swims up next to me, holding the rocky ledge. I can see his breath as it steams against the surface of the water. He shivers, probably from the cold, but it makes him look as nervous as I feel, and I smile.

"What's not to like? Who wouldn't want to wash dirty clothes in cold water?" he jokes.

"No one forced you to come."

"I know." He drifts a little closer. "I wanted to."

I watch a trickle of water roll down the side of his face, clinging to his skin, unwilling to let go.

The rush of the waterfall seems to fade away. All I hear is Gavin breathing.

"You don't need to babysit me," I say.

Our legs bump underwater. The fabric of his boxers feels soft against my thigh.

"If you want," his eyes flash to the bank, "I can leave."

We're so close to each other that I'm scared he can hear my heart pounding against my sternum. His eyes shift back to me, wide and inviting with a soft golden hue. The color of sand you sink into.

And I'm sinking.

I know I should say something, but I'm afraid to break this moment, especially if he's going to kiss me. I've only ever kissed Parker—a quick peck that caught me by surprise. What would this kiss be like? His lips are parted, just enough for me to see a thin black line as if he's thinking the same thing.

Neither of us speaks. Our bodies turn slowly until we're facing one another.

He inches my way and I catch the smell of mint on his breath.

Then, someone shouts and Gavin flinches. I glance back just in time to see spray erupt. By the time the faces emerge, Gavin and I are several feet apart.

Sasha, Burk, Craig, and Ry bob in the water.

"Wait for us!" Adrian calls out, jumping in with Mary in his arms.

Did they see what almost happened? *Did* anything almost happen? I look to Gavin, but his hands are up, preparing to fight off Ry's advance.

"I don't see any laundry getting done," Ry says, trying to dunk Gavin, but he's too quick and buries Ry's face in the water with one hand.

For the next hour, we play in the water between loads of laundry. Gavin stays as far away as possible, and I scrub clothes to work out my frustration. Maybe I just imagined we had a moment. I wish I could wash away my doubt. What if it was nothing?

"Everybody out!" Craig hollers from the bank, breaking my thoughts. "Let's see who can make the biggest splash!"

It's the kind of thing we'd do when our trainers were away, and it makes me homesick—not for the Center, but for my friends. I climb out and force myself to smile, even though my face muscles are fighting me.

Adrian goes last, and everyone cheers when he comes up for air.

"We have a winner!" Burk says, clapping. All eyes are on Adrian, and I use the moment to steal a glance at Gavin and am surprised when I catch him staring back.

For a few seconds, it's just us. Like we were never interrupted. A silent admittance that we had a moment…something.

"Who's up for Marco Polo?" Ry hollers.

It's a game I actually know, and I raise my hand. "I'll be it first."

"Take it easy on us," Ry says, and I can tell by his tone he means it. I move swiftly, and even with my eyes closed, I can feel the ripple of Gavin's movements. I sense him lingering close by, just out of reach.

I want to grab him, to let my arms slip around his waist, but not here. Not now.

Instead, I snag Ry's arm.

"Craig blocked me from getting by!" He whines until I agree to go again.

After a few rounds, Sasha puts an end to the fun. "It's getting dark, guys." She motions for us to finish the last load and we begrudgingly swim to the edge. She pulls herself out of the water and pushes her hair back up, like it will make her bigger and scarier if it looks like a shark's fin.

"Adrian." She tosses him a few items and continues down the line as we stand around the rim. When everyone has a handful, she walks the last bunch of clothes over to me.

She bends down, whispering as she holds them out. "We didn't interrupt anything, did we?" She has that same look she did when we were playing cards.

My breath quickens. "I don't know what you're talking about."

"Just be careful," she says. Craig calls out for soap and she's gone before I have a chance to ask if she meant to be careful of Gavin or of her. I hope it's the latter. My fists are stronger than my heart.

• • •

Mary leads the way while the rest of us haul wet laundry back to the barn.

"Believe it or not, we didn't finish," says Craig. He's got a bag on his back and a smaller duffle in his arms.

"I'll volunteer to do the rest if no one else wants to," says Gavin. He's walking in front of me, and he looks back, glancing past me first to see if anyone objects, and then pausing to catch my eyes. I'm glad it's too dark for him to see me blush.

By the time we reach the barn, black has settled over the sky and my body is exhausted.

Sasha, Craig, and Ry offer to hang the clothes on lines that stretch the length of the barn while I take Mary down below.

"Good night," I say, kissing her forehead. She sleeps on the bunk next to mine, her head only a body length away from my feet. I crawl under my covers and fall asleep before the blanket reaches my chin.

• • •

I dream about my mother.

She pedals leisurely so I can keep up. "You're doing great!" she says, sticking her feet out to the side. I squeal with delight and try to copy her, but my bike wobbles, and I grip the handlebars tight to steady myself.

Her hair waves behind her like a red flag. "Hang in there, Tabitha, we're almost home."

She holds up her hand to make a right turn signal and I look at the sign, the name registering slowly as I put the letters together: Jamison Street. When I finally turn my attention back to the sidewalk, I have to jerk the wheel to keep from hitting a white fence. A little dog yips at me from behind the slats and I shriek. I want to pedal faster to reach my mom. But I can't.

It's like a TV show, and I'm powerless to do anything but live through the episode.

Out of the corner of my eye, an SUV approaches, rolling along at the same speed we are. I try to look inside, but the windows are too dark. The engine revs and the car speeds up the road before stopping in front of our house.

Mom hits her brakes when a man gets out, and I almost run my bike into hers. "Who's that man, Mommy?" I ask, pointing.

"You need to leave," she whispers, narrowing her eyes at the man coming toward us.

I tug at her pants and she pushes my hand away when the man starts jogging. "Now, Tabitha!"

She turns my bike around and gives me a push. My heart races and I glance back to see if she's coming, if she's right behind me, but the air around her turns black.

I wake with a gasp.

For a moment, I'm not sure where I am. I look up, but there's no ribbon fluttering softly overhead, just coils from the bunk above. I take in the smell of dirt and musk and sink back into the bed.

I'm not home. Wherever that is.

Aside from the squeak of a bedspring, the room is silent. I wish I could go back to sleep, but the dream felt so real, closing my eyes seems pointless.

I slip out of bed and tread lightly across the floor and into the hallway. Once outside, I sit on the fence, kicking at the long grass, wondering if I will be resigned to this. If my fascination for the perfect family will consume my life, consume my dreams. Will this unattainable goal haunt me forever? My eyes gloss over.

Gravel crunches behind me. I wipe my eyes with the heel of my palm.

"Can't sleep?" the voice says.

I turn, barely glancing up. Gavin's hands are in his pockets. He looks relaxed in flannel pajama pants and a white T-shirt.

"Just a bad dream, that's all."

"Care to talk about it?"

"Not really," I say. But it's a lie. The images from my sleep rattled me and I want help sorting them out. Still, my instincts warn me not to open up when Gavin's around. How can he possibly understand how it feels to have your dream turn into a nightmare?

He leans on the fence, staring out past the field as if he can see through the trees. In the dark, the forest looks like a black wall, big and impenetrable. It's strangely comforting. Walls are what I'm used to.

"Can I ask you something, Gavin?"

"Shoot."

"Is this really your grandparents' farm?"

"Did Sasha tell you that?"

"Yes."

He stands straight, and his hands go back in his pockets. "It's true."

"Do they know you're here?"

"They died shortly after my mom passed away." He kicks a fence post as if he's checking its stability.

"I'm sorry," I say, my voice small.

"It's just my dad now. And he thinks Ry and I got an apartment somewhere."

"Do Ry's parents know he stays here?"

"They wrote Ry off when he got hooked on pills. They probably think he's on the street, living in the Junkie District."

He stretches, and I think he's going to reach out and put a hand on my shoulder, but he laces his fingers over his head. I can't help but feel disappointed.

"I know this isn't what you expected when you left the Center," he says. "I didn't realize what I was up against until I freed Sasha. But I don't intend for us to hide out forever."

He sounds confident, like he has a plan, but when I glance up at him, the details of his face are hard to see underneath the night sky. I want to believe him. I guess at this point, I really don't have a choice.

"Didn't sleep well?" Sasha asks, tearing apart a croissant and dipping the bread in some coffee that, if any clearer, would be tea.

My head is in my hands, my elbows up on the table. Not only is last night's dream plaguing me, I have an equal desire to throw up and drill a hole in my skull.

"Headache," I mutter.

"Euphorium might help." Ry drops a plate of food next to me. It smacks the table and I wince.

"Her head hurts, moron," Sasha says.

I lift my eyes as she throws a piece of bread at Ry's face.

"Good morning," says Gavin, his voice chipper as he sits. It makes my head hurt worse knowing I can't enjoy his mood with him.

Sasha and Ry answer back, and I release a hand and wave a little to let him know I heard him.

"What's wrong with her?" Gavin asks.

"Headache," Sasha says.

I hear a bottle pop open and the clicks of pills as they fall on the varnished tabletop. "I've got you covered," Ry says.

"She doesn't need drugs, Ry," Gavin says with a gruff tone. I can't tell if he's concerned for my well-being, or if he's worried about my ability to resist pills.

Then I realize Ry is right.

"Yes. I do." I lift my head and the room sways until my eyes find a focal point.

Gavin stares at me, his mouth open like he wants to object. I notice he has two plates of food. Breakfast for both of us. His lips flatten out to a firm line, a look of disappointment that makes my stomach twist.

"I don't want Euphorium," I say quickly. "I started getting headaches when I stopped taking my medication."

"I thought you needed them for your heart?" Ry asks.

"I—I do. I've been spacing them out. We've been planning a

rescue mission. I didn't want to bother anyone about getting me more." I rub my temples. "It's just a headache."

Only it's not. It's like someone's taking a jackhammer to the inside of my skull. I stand slowly.

I buried the pills in my pillowcase so I wouldn't lose them, and my fingers tremble as I walk to my bed to sort through the hodgepodge of medication. The red pill is easy to spot, but the light-colored ones hide in the creases until I find them and dig them out. I can almost feel my headache subside from the residue of pills on my hand.

An invisible vice-grip presses against my temples, telling me to hurry up as I search for mine. They're mixed in with Ms. Preen's drugs, and some of them look the same. Without being able to focus clearly, I'm not sure which ones belong to me.

I find two that look alike, and hold one in each hand. One is flatter. But not by much. They could be the same. But what if they're not? I'm on my knees, shaking, unsure what to do but ready to take whatever I can to make this headache go away.

Flat pill or thick?

I peer over my shoulder. Gavin is watching, his face slack. Ry talks wildly with his hands. Mary has joined them, her face alive with wonder.

Right hand or left?

Right. No, left. I swallow the pill in my left hand and choke it down. I hurry to pick up the rest of the pills and toss them back in my pillowcase.

The room pulsates. My headache comes with me when I rejoin the table. I'm not sure how long I'm supposed to wait to see results. I've never gone this long without taking my medication. My chest hurts, and I hope that's not a bad sign. I need to stay alive long enough to get my friends out of the Center.

I fake a smile and Gavin pushes a plate of food under my nose. His eyes lack any spark of interest. He turns his attention toward whoever's talking, and I focus on my meal.

It's difficult to chew. My headache should be going away. If it's not, then I must have taken the wrong pill. I try to think of what kind of medication Ms. Preen would take, but my brain hurts, and all I want to do is reach into my head and massage it.

I stand without finishing my food and make a beeline for the door. I'm hoping fresh air will at least keep me from passing out. Adrian has a new piece of equipment dismantled when I stumble through the hallway, and I grunt when he acknowledges me.

My vision is fuzzy, and I struggle to get up the ladder. By the time I reach the top, the ringing in my ears has grown louder. I crawl into one of the open horse stalls and curl into a ball in the corner, begging the pressure in my head to stop.

After a few minutes, the ringing is replaced by the sound of Ry and Gavin talking. They must have followed me. I try to listen to what they're saying, and when I focus, it sounds like they're right outside the stall. I hold my breath so they don't hear me. Their voices are so clear.

"She hasn't been getting them from me," Ry says.

"How do you explain what's going on?" Gavin says. There's a thump and a vibration that echoes like a metal prong humming inside my ear canal.

They're walking now, their footsteps heavy. I flinch and press my hand against the stall door. It's as if they're walking on the walls that surround me. Everything sounds so close.

"Keep away from her, Ry, I mean it."

"I'm telling you, I haven't given her anything else."

"She's not a client of yours. Stay. Away."

The pain rolls behind my eyes. I grip the stall ledge, mustering the strength to pull myself up. I'm compelled to stand through an insatiable urge to defend Ry—and more importantly, to defend myself. But I'm surprised to find the barn is empty.

Bewildered, I make my way toward the hole and glance down. I can hear Adrian tinkering. More than that, I can hear him push buttons, the buzz and crackle of electricity, the turn of a dial as he searches for a signal. Tiny clicks that I know I've never heard before, even when I've stood next to him to watch him work. But that's impossible. Unless…

Unless my hearing has been intensified.

I press my back against the wall. A mouse scurries out of my way, and as soon as I focus on it, I pick up the sound of little footpads against the dirt and hay. It's incredible, and I shudder in nervous excitement.

I look out at the forest, past the field. A flood of sounds pours in: birds in flight, nuts being cracked, a thousand bugs marching. I turn my attention back toward the barn. I hear Mary's voice as she plays with her doll. Someone flips the page of a book. A utensil scrapes a bowl. A sneeze.

Gavin's voice emerges, and I try to block it out. It feels wrong to listen, but I'm not sure how to control what I hear. It's impossible not to focus on him when he's the person I want to hear most of all.

He's with Sasha, and they're whispering.

A bed creaks and I hear him sigh. It sinks into my brain as if Gavin's mouth was pressed against my ear.

"If that's what she told you, then why don't you believe her?" Sasha asks.

"I do."

"Then why are you acting like you don't?"

Sasha has my back. I'm impressed.

"You didn't see how she looked when she came out of the forest with Ry. I've lost too many people to *pill thrill*. And she says she has a heart condition? That's unheard of for a Center kid."

"You think she's hooked on what Ry gave her?"

"It was Euphorium, Sasha. I've seen what it can do to people."

"Then talk to Ry. He won't lie to you. He loves you like a brother. A better brother than the one he has."

"I already did."

"So you either have to trust her, or move on."

Gavin huffs. "There's nothing to move on from." My body stiffens.

"You can pretend all you want," Sasha says, "but she's getting to you."

"You don't know what you're talking about." The bed squeaks and two sets of footsteps clomp across the room below me.

Her voice is louder and there's a hiss in her tone. "Stop punishing yourself for my mistakes."

"I'm not." The footsteps stop. He makes a low growl, and Sasha laughs through her nose. "All right, I'll talk to her." Only one person moves now, and by the sound of the rhythm, I'm sure it's Gavin.

The door to the hallway creaks, and my heart races. He's coming to find me, and I'm on something that's *not* my medication. A knot forms in my throat. I can't let him see me like this.

I dive back into the stall, bringing my knees to my chest while I hold my breath—and pray he doesn't find me.

# CHAPTER 11

I press my hands over my ears and wait, but even layers of skin and bone can't block the sound of Gavin's booming footsteps.

"Tabitha!" He's right outside the stall, and I grit my teeth as my eardrums throb. Finally, he clomps outside, calling out toward the trees.

I want so desperately to answer, but fear paralyzes my mouth.

After several minutes, he comes back inside and calls down to Adrian. "I'm heading to town to run errands. Keep an eye out for Tabitha."

I want him to know I'm okay, but if he sees me like this he'll know I'm on something, and he'll assume I got it from Ry.

Car tires grind through the gravel, and I wait until the rubber connects with the smooth asphalt before sneaking out of my hiding spot.

I need to stay away from the barn until this drug wears off. I wish I knew how long it'd take.

There's only one place I can think to go to speed up the process without being seen, so I head for the trail.

I sprint as if someone is chasing me, running so hard it feels like my brain is bouncing around my skull. The pain proves to be too much and the headache forces me to slow. As I do, the forest sounds amplify: whistles and caws, crunches and burrowing. It's like a symphony conducted by Mother Nature, something no one with normal hearing will ever get to enjoy. It's a tragedy, really.

It takes me twice as long to get to the waterfall as last time, but I can hear the roar of the water as soon as I focus on my destination.

When I get to the meadow, I ignore the painful pounding of

the waterfall and strip down. No one followed me. I would have heard them. I position my hands in front of me and dive in.

The shock of the cold jolts my body, and I gasp when I resurface, taking in long pulls of oxygen before settling in a spot where I'm submerged up to my neck. The temperature seeps into my pores, penetrating my bones. I recall what Gavin said about the cold, how it makes the blood flow speed up, protecting the organs first. I close my eyes and wait for the drug to release me from its grip.

When my teeth start to chatter, I pull myself onto the bank and wring out my hair. The drug hasn't left my system entirely, but the cold water had an impact, like someone turned down the volume.

My head still throbs, as does the wound on my neck. I touch the scab tenderly and wince at how sore it is. It shouldn't hurt so bad, unless I scraped it unknowingly. It's hard to say because it feels like someone's been throwing rocks at my head most of the morning.

I get dressed and hit the trail. When I reach the field, I see Gavin's truck. I strain to hear, but I can't pick up on any conversations. The world feels right again, as unsettling as it might be.

The barn is quiet until I lift the hatch. Laughter billows up from the hallway. Gavin's is deep, hearty, like he's been holding it in for weeks. It has a substance that I've never heard before.

I climb down the ladder and find everyone standing around the kitchen, plus someone new. She's standing next to Gavin. No, she's leaning into Gavin. Sasha catches my eye, and I bolt for the clothing cabinet as if it's the sole reason I came inside.

I pull out a box of clothes and rifle through it. Maybe I'll find something warmer, comforting. I see movement in my periphery, and I dig deeper. But what I need isn't in here. We don't have an invisibility robe. I'm cold. I'm wet. And I feel like an idiot for being excited to see him.

"You okay?" Sasha stands behind me. She's far enough away from the group no one can hear her. I pretend I can't, either.

"Tabitha?" There's an edge of irritation in her voice.

"What? I'm fine." I continue to pick up useless articles of clothing.

Did I think he'd replace the void in my heart? The longing to be close to someone, since I don't have my Center friends or the loving family I thought I was joining? I don't need anyone to fill that place, including Gavin. So I turn and push up my cheeks into a broad smile. It's a fleeting effort, and Sasha eyes me suspiciously.

"Do you want to meet our guest?"

"Absolutely!" It comes out more enthusiastically than I intended and she steps back, brows arched.

"Yeah, right. Well, come on then."

I try to put a bounce in my step; as if I don't mind the way the girl presses her slim frame into Gavin's body. As if I'm not unnerved by her perfect posture and radiant skin. She has a glow, and I'm not on Euphorium. Sasha glances back and rakes me over with her eyes. I walk normally.

Mary breaks away from the group to greet me, wrapping her hands around my waist and walking to the table with me. What I wouldn't give to carry Mary around in my pocket. I could take her with me everywhere I go, and anytime I felt an ache in my chest, Mary would be there to make my heart sing again. Maybe it's better this way. Gavin is a distraction. My friends' lives are at stake. Kids' lives, Gavin would say. That's what I need to focus on.

When Mary lets go, she sits on the crate next to Ry. I move between them and lean across the table to shake the blonde's hand, cutting the laughter with my body.

"I'm Tabitha."

The girl's eyes, blue and as big as walnuts, flash to me. Our hands touch and I gasp, retracting my arm as if I were about to pet a poisonous snake.

Ry elbows me in the thigh. "That was rude."

I see Gavin glare in my periphery, but I can't tear my eyes away from her.

"You work at the Center." My voice comes out like an accusation. I'm almost certain she's the receptionist Ms. Preen snubbed.

The room is quiet.

"That's right…" She keeps her hand out, waiting for me to shake it. Gavin shifts his stance.

I suppress a scowl and take her hand. My grip is tight, and her nose scrunches when I squeeze her fingers.

"So you two have met before?" Sasha asks. She makes no effort to hide her amusement.

"Something like that," I say.

"Cherry is one of our inside sources," Gavin beams.

*She's named after a fruit?*

Cherry puts her hands on Gavin's chest like she's embarrassed, but her eyes tell a different story. I don't trust her. Not. One. Bit.

"Cherry played a role in getting you out," Gavin says to me.

I want to crawl under the table. This girl, whose beauty is so captivating I want to throw mud on her just to level the playing field, is supposed to be my savior?

Her smile widens. "I was just doing what I could to help."

Mary's chin is propped in her hands, basking in Cherry's glow, entranced by the living doll in front of her. For a moment, I think about covering Mary's undamaged eye, letting her see Cherry as a smeared image instead. I'm being petty and I know it. I have to figure out how to tuck my jealousy down deep and lock it away.

"Thank you," I say, making sure to smile. I mean it. I am grateful. But when the words come out, there's a bitter aftertaste. I don't think saving me was her main objective.

As if he can still feel the tension, Gavin offers to show her around.

"Show me where you sleep," she says in a low voice. She struts past me in a tight blue top that accentuates her eyes—among other things—and strappy heels that make my feet hurt when I look at them.

I'm still staring when Adrian pokes me in the shoulder. "Want a donut?" he asks when I turn to him. He licks a bit of white powder from his fingers. "Cherry brought them."

Of course she did. I refrain from hinting they might be laced and instead shake my head. It's only now I realize everyone else has left the table. In fact, Adrian and I are the only two in the room beside Cherry and Gavin. Behind me, I hear her laugh and the hair on the back of my neck stands up. It's a sound that doesn't belong here. Don't they realize they're harboring an intruder?

Adrian closes the box of donuts and gets up.

"Can I help you with anything?" I ask, trying to sound nonchalant as I stand in his path. "Do you have something that needs to be put together, or maybe you just want some company?"

He looks up at me with surprise then shrugs. "Sure. Grab some rags and meet me in the hall."

Gavin and Cherry are walking the perimeter of the room, and I hurry to the cabinet to grab what I need. I estimate I have twenty seconds to get the rags and get out of the room before they reach me.

But I'm wrong.

I block my face with the cabinet door when they approach. There's a knock on the wood, and when I glance down I see Gavin's shoes—ragged sneakers, just like mine.

I peek around the door. Gavin stands with his hands on his hips, smiling. He's so relaxed it's disheartening.

"Cherry says you had the fastest sprints at the Center." He opens his body so that the three of us are in an awkward triangle. Cherry brings her perky breasts closer to him, and it's clear I'm the odd angle in the isosceles. I can't help but think she's doing it on purpose. "And that you held your breath underwater for more than two minutes? That's impressive."

How do I respond? I can't think of the right words, so I nod and turn my face toward the inside of the cabinet. I grab a sock that will have to double as a rag and shut the door. "Gotta go help Adrian."

Cherry grabs Gavin's shoulder and almost purrs, "Have fun, then."

He wiggles away, and a crease forms between his eyes. Was he expecting me to entertain Cherry with him? I'd rather busy my brain with other things. Life. Freedom. Friends. Dare I say, family? I'm not going to compete with a doll for the interest of someone who might not be interested in me at all.

Adrian waits for me in the hallway with an extra set of tools. He stutters a little at first, trying to explain how phone signals can be intercepted and how he can boost the strength with some wires and other items. Most of what he says goes over my head, either because he talks too fast or explains things far beyond lessons they taught at the Center. They didn't want us to learn. They just wanted to strengthen our brains and eyes so they could sell them.

What I do understand is fascinating, and I try to take it all in, interrupting him when I need him to repeat or reword things. I must be his first pupil, because his face lights up when I ask questions.

"The Centers send out a signal that's locked to prevent mainland cities from accidentally intercepting the transmission," Adrian says.

"But you managed to break in?"

His chest puffs. "Yeah, well, electronics are kind of a hobby of mine. And it's not just the Centers; I can tap into hospital chatter too."

"To find out when they need a donor?"

"Or when there's an unwanted baby." Adrian shifts his weight uneasily. "St. Vincent's lets the Center for Growth know there's been a birth, and there's a flurry of conversation after that about weight, length, gender, all that stuff."

"Not Gladstone Memorial?"

"Sometimes, but most of the babies come from the hospital in the Junkie District. Nurses convince families to give up their kids, and PharmPerfect gives them a kickback."

"So, the parents and nurses are making money selling babies?"

It feels like someone cinched a rope around my waist. That must be where Paige, Meghan, and Parker came from.

"Sick, isn't it?" Adrian says. "But, to be fair, the parents are told their kids will be fostered out to loving homes, not dissected."

"Does St. Vincent's know?"

"I'm sure there are a few who don't mind a bonus check, if you know what I mean."

I nod, wishing I didn't.

"St. Vincent's started out doing blood drives, selling extra blood to Gladstone Memorial for transfusions. Somehow, that transitioned to selling babies," he says, his eyes serious. "And wouldn't you know it, five years ago, S.V. built a new medical wing."

Adrian fumbles around for a spiral notebook hidden in a drawer underneath his workstation. "I've been trying to keep track of how many have been sold. This year alone, I've counted eleven." He flips the page. "And here are the deals the Centers made for parts."

I look at the notebook. There are no names, but there are prices, ranging upwards of twenty thousand dollars. At the bottom of the page is a zero with a star next to it. I lean closer to try to read the details, but Adrian shuts it.

"Is it true, what Gavin said about you?" he asks. "That you weren't sold as an infant? He said the Center for Growth took you in when you were six."

"Yeah, it's true."

"But how is that possible?"

"What do you mean?"

"I'm just shocked they allowed you to be around other kids. Weren't they afraid of what you'd tell them? At the Center, you're taught health and fitness. They don't give you ice cream or fast food. But you would have known about all that, maybe even told kids about the outside world."

"I guess I was too little." My voice is weak and unsure. Why don't I remember the simple things? Have I really blocked out that much? Would the Center have gone so far as to mess with our minds? It seems unlikely since they need our brains in tip-top shape, but an uneasy feeling settles in my stomach.

I think hard, and a memory cracks open from my first few weeks at the Center. I'm sitting by myself inside a room, staring out the window. Kids are running around, playing hopscotch and tag, laughing with delight. I'm angry. My hands are wrapped in towels, and I can see blood stains where my knuckles peak. I don't want to be there.

The memory is fuzzy, and I don't know what it means. Of course I was angry; my parents had died. But the anger didn't feel like it emanated from grief. It was brought on by something else. Why can't I remember the accident? And why didn't another family member adopt me?

The sound of heels clicking against the concrete makes my body tense.

"Thanks for bringing me out here," Cherry says as she and Gavin enter the hallway. Adrian's eyes trace her legs and pause on her breasts before finally resting on her face. I want to sock him in the arm. Cherry smiles as if she didn't notice, and I consider socking her too. Just because of where she works.

Gavin stops next to Adrian and me. "I'm taking Cherry back to town," he says.

"Oh, you're leaving so soon?" I cock my head at Cherry and smile.

Gavin's mouth crooks, and there's a glint of amusement in his eyes. I might as well wear a sign in bold green letters that reads: I'm jealous.

"You should join us," he says to me. Cherry's head snaps to look at him, and a small frown grazes her lips.

"I can't," I blurt out. "I'm helping Adrian with—"

"I've got it. Go ahead." Adrian pushes me away from the table and I step on the manicured toes peeking out of Cherry's shoes.

"Ow!"

"Sorry!" I glare at Adrian. He's lucky I don't give him a fat lip.

Cherry bends down to clean her shoe, and Gavin catches my

eye. I feel like I'm treading water to keep from sinking again. And I'm losing.

He claps his hands together and grins. "Then it's settled. You're coming with us."

Crap.

Cherry's mouth pops open like she wants to object, but Gavin motions for us to head out before she can. Somehow I end up first on the ladder, so pretending I'm being called back to the main room isn't an option. Cherry scales the ladder as if she were clinging to a skyscraper, and out of impatience, I extend my hand and haul her up the last few rungs.

"My goodness, you're as strong as a man," she says. Gavin chuckles when he emerges, and I scowl at him.

"You would know, Cherry. You seem to have all my stats," I shoot back.

She looks hurt, and Gavin gives a slight shake of his head behind her.

As we walk to the truck, Cherry suddenly has a surge of energy and makes it to the passenger door before me. Gavin moves to open the door for her, but before he does, he pulls out two bandanas.

"Time to put these on. Cherry, I'll put yours on first."

I watch as he positions it over her eyes. When he pulls the knot tight, she grimaces.

"Now her, right?" Cherry's voice lacks the confidence it had inside.

"Yes, Tabitha's next." He puts his finger up to his lips and hands me the bandana. When he opens the door, he motions at the hat on the seat. I grab it and tuck my hair safely away as he helps a blind Cherry load up.

"Can you help me buckle?" she asks, lifting her arms to the roof.

I go around and squeeze into the back seat, sliding in behind Cherry. Gavin talks to us both while he drives, but he's beaming at me. Proud of his deception and, if I'm not mistaken, glad to have me witness it.

"You know the rules. Blindfolds stay on until I tell you it's safe to remove them." Gavin steals looks at me every so often, and my stomach flutters.

"Are we still going to see a movie soon, Gavin?" Cherry asks.

The flutter turns to a twist.

"We'll figure something out," he says.

"We don't have to see a show. You could come for dinner? My mother hasn't seen you in a while. Maybe you can swing by this weekend?"

"We'll see."

His answers are short, but not cold. I wish I knew what the story was between them. Her hand floats across the seat, and she reaches out to touch his arm. He doesn't scoot away. The way her finger traces his skin, I can tell there's history there.

I lean in and yell in the gap by the window and her seat. "So, Cherry, how's the job going?" She jumps a little, and I swallow a laugh.

Her hand is back in her lap. Mission accomplished.

Gavin smirks.

"The job is fine, Tabitha. It breaks my heart that I can't do more to help, but at least I'm in a position to do *something*."

That felt like a dig.

"I know what you mean," I say, gripping the back of her seat with both hands. I could stick a finger out and poke her face if I wanted to. Cherry doesn't move. "The problem I had," I continue, "was that the position I was in, being locked up at the Center for ten years, made it hard to do anything. But now that I'm out—thanks to you—that shouldn't be a problem."

A smile tugs at Gavin's lips. Cherry won't intimidate me, and I have no intention of sitting by idly while my friends die. We sit in silence for a few miles, and after some pretend detours where Gavin exits, makes a few turns and gets back on the same road we were on, he tells us to remove our blindfolds. Cherry glances around her seat, and I quickly rub my eyes as if I've been wearing the bandana the entire time.

"Did I tie it too tight?" Gavin asks me.

"A little," I say. Gavin drums the steering wheel and kicks on some music. The musician sounds like he's yelling to be heard over the guitar.

Cherry turns the knob until some upbeat love song comes on. A girl, slightly off key, sings about a boy she's crazy for and the million ways she's going to let him know. Gavin sticks his finger in his throat and pretends to gag. I laugh and Cherry hits him with a weak fist.

"I love this song, Gav." She rubs his shoulder, as if she hurt him, then leans in with her lips inches from his ear to add, "It reminds me of our first date."

Now it's my turn to gag.

Luckily, I don't have to endure Cherry much longer. We pull into a parking lot full of shiny cars with fancy hood ornaments. Cherry unbuckles and waits for Gavin to come open the door for her.

Gavin doesn't disappoint, lifting her down as if she might twist an ankle when she plummets twelve inches. She shuts the truck door and they stand outside her car, a red convertible with the top down, showcasing the white leather seats. Jewel-encrusted cherries hang from her rearview mirror by a silver chain.

I have a clear shot of the back of Gavin's head and a nice view of Cherry's chest. She says something as she points to the building. A car goes by, and a large gate slides open. The hum is faint, but I recognize it immediately and my heart flips. A gray sedan passes through and curls around to the hidden enclosure.

I slap a hand over my mouth to keep from screaming.

How could I be so stupid? We're at Cherry's work. We're at the Center.

Gavin seems oblivious to the car that went by. Cherry hugs him close, pushing her breasts into him. She glances at the truck, and when she sees I'm watching, she kisses him on the cheek.

Why did he bring me here?

She removes a piece of paper from her glove box and hands it to Gavin before she follows a path around the side of the building, heading back to her desk.

I play with the bandana in my hand, twisting the fabric tight; thinking about how good it's going to feel when I shut the Center down.

# CHAPTER 12

Gavin hops in the truck and I'm grateful for the roar of the engine. He can't hear me sigh.

"Are you going to join me up here?" He taps the vacant seat.

I'd rather be alone with my thoughts, but I unbuckle and move to the front. The seat smells like cherries. How fitting.

At least I have an open view from up here. It's easy to lose myself in the world around me; it moves along without worry. Everything seems so organized—the way the crowds glide along the sidewalk, the flow of traffic. Plus, the colors are a nice reprieve from the drab basement I've been hiding in.

"Why are you so quiet?" he asks.

"You just took me back to the place that raised me for parts. How am I supposed to be?" I can tell by the way his mouth twitches that he hadn't really considered how being near the Center would make my anxiety spike.

"I'm sorry," he says. I turn my eyes back toward the road. "I thought you'd want to come along, it didn't dawn on me—"

"Why *did* you bring me?"

"Because I wanted to take you through tomorrow's rescue plan." Gavin pinches his nose and takes a deep breath. "Sasha's never wanted to go near the hospital again, and there's no way I'd let Mary go." He drops his hand and locks eyes with me. "I thought you'd be okay, but maybe this wasn't such a good idea."

"It is! I'm fine." He eyes me suspiciously and I shut my mouth, remembering I need to control my emotions if I'm going to prove I'm ready. But after my talk with Sasha about putting everyone at risk, maybe I'm *not* ready. What if something goes wrong? The air feels like it's been sucked out of the van, and I crack the window. "I'm okay. I promise."

"You don't have to come—"

"I want to."

He flicks on the blinker and changes lanes. "We could always use more eyes and ears, but…" There's trepidation in his voice. "I'm not going to lie, it's dangerous. The only reason our mission to save you went smoothly was because we had inside help from Kenny."

"I can do this. Trust me."

He looks in his rearview mirror as if he can still see the Center. "Just so you know, Cherry connected us with Kenny. That's the *only* reason I keep in touch with her." He gives me a sideways smile.

When we reach the hospital, Gavin points out the surgical floors from the car. "That's where they take the kids as soon as they're sedated—we think they're given something to knock them out once they get here."

"Caramels," I say under my breath.

"Candy?"

"That's what they gave me."

"Candy." Gavin shakes his head and turns down the next street. "So the sick bastards use sugar to knock kids out before sedating them for surgery."

"Wait. Their organs are harvested while they're *alive*?"

He shifts in his seat, his eyes on the road when he answers. "Well, yeah. They want the organs to be as fresh as possible."

"Unbelievable." My stomach twists. I tap him on the shoulder when I feel like I'm about to throw up. "Get me out of here."

Gavin reaches over and grabs my hand.

"We've built a good team," he says. "We got you out, didn't we?" He keeps glancing over, like he can't relax unless he knows I believe him.

I squeeze his fingers and nod. But the thought of heading into the hospital to rescue someone makes my heart speed up like I've stepped onto the track. We're racing to save a life, and there's no second chance if we fail.

Gavin pulls his hand away and turns down a street. "We're going to take a detour. A *real* detour." He wiggles his eyebrows. "But this time I want you to close your eyes."

I hold up the bandana. "Do you want me to put this on?"

"No. I trust you."

My ears warm, and I cover my face.

He drives slowly, turning a few times, which makes my stomach swish without a horizon to focus on. Then the truck stops, and Gavin kills the engine.

I can smell the salt and sand before I open my eyes. We're at the waterfront. Without a gate. Without any walls. It's the first time I've seen the ocean up close without a chain-link fence in the way.

And it's incredible.

I fumble with the door handle, but Gavin is outside my window before I can get my hand to cooperate with the lever. He opens the door and helps me out. A few cars are scattered in the parking lot. They're much older than the ones at the Center, with bumper stickers and fender dings.

Gavin convinces me to leave my shoes and socks in the truck. I'm giddy with excitement, and he has to run after me when I hurry down the path that leads to the beach.

I stop when I hit the sand, my feet sinking into the warm grains. It's soft, but gritty, and tickles when I curl my toes.

"This is amazing," I say when he catches up. I take a step toward the water, marveling at how the sand molds itself to my foot. I let the waves roll over the tops of my feet and suck in a breath when the cold courses through my body. When my toes are numb, I wade up to my calves, but it's like someone is vacuuming the sand out from under me.

"Undertow," Gavin says, as if he knows what I'm about to ask.

"Are you coming in?"

"Maybe in a minute." He grins from the safety of the shore and I kick water at him, missing his shorts, but not by much. His legs are well defined, but a shade lighter than his arms.

I block the sun with my hand. "I'm going to break out in freckles after today."

"Good." He comes a little closer, his hands in his pockets. "I like your freckles."

My cheeks feel flushed, and I look down the shoreline.

"It goes on for miles," he says, following my gaze. "Let's take a walk." When he removes his hands from his pockets our fingers brush, and there's a flutter in my chest. Then he slips his hand into mine.

"Thank you for bringing me here," I say.

"I figured you needed something like this."

"It's exactly what I needed."

A woman running along the beach smiles as she passes us and a couple tossing a Frisbee says hello. No one stares at me like I don't fit in. I'm just a person enjoying life. Like I belong in this world.

"You don't like the water?" I ask, watching him sidestep any waves that try to kiss his feet.

"Not seawater." He cringes, and I wait for him to explain. "My grandpa and I used to fish a lot. He was always talking about omega oils and how great fish were for the body, so we'd stay out all day trying to catch our fill. My dad even made him fish oil vitamins to take in the winter."

I turn to give him a smile, but Gavin's staring at the sand, the lines in his face tight.

"This one time he fell asleep while we were at sea—well, I thought he had. I was only twelve at the time. He'd had a heart attack and we were stuck out in the middle of the water. I called out to a nearby boat, but they couldn't hear me, and when I tried to start ours, the engine kept stalling.

"He was dying and I couldn't save him, so I dove in the water to get help, only the closest boat was too far for me to swim."

"Did they see you?"

"Yeah, but by the time they got to me my lips were blue. We were both rushed to the hospital." He squeezes my hand. "My grandpa died in the room down the hall from me. I didn't even get to say goodbye."

"I-I'm so sorry…"

He takes a breath like he's refueling his soul. "I haven't been back in the ocean since. I haven't forgiven it. Or myself, really."

"But you didn't do anything wrong…"

"Maybe not. But I'll always wonder what would've happened if I'd stayed, maybe kept trying to get the boat to start. At least I could've said goodbye…"

We walk in silence for a quarter mile, until a bird flies over Gavin's head and he flinches. "That's another reason I hate the ocean. Seagulls. They're like rats with wings." He lets out a laugh, and I take a risk while the topic of family is fresh.

"Is that why you don't stay with your dad? Is it hard to be around him after…after what happened?" I'm almost certain his grip tightens, but he stays calm as he answers.

"No. No. It's not that…" Gavin's pace slows. "We, uh, never really saw eye to eye on things. My dad spent a lot of time at work, and after my grandpa passed, I thought he'd slow down." He tries to shrug it off, but his shoulders sag like the impact is still there. "My mom was great, though, she could always tell when I needed to talk or had a crappy day. She'd throw the dishtowel in the sink and say, 'Let's go to Dairy Land!' We'd share a bowl of strawberry ice cream and sit in one of the booths where we could watch people come and go. It was our thing, and it always made me feel better."

Gavin has a far-off smile I don't recognize. I'm still not sure why he left home, but I don't want to spoil his fond memories by pushing the issue. His hand is warm, and I lean my head against his shoulder. He lets go and puts his arm around me. It feels good to be close to someone, to let him in.

We find a bench facing the water and talk until the beach is almost empty. The sun hovers over the ocean, ready to call it a night. I wish I could reach out with my foot and kick the orange ball back into the sky. I don't want this day to end.

"What were your parents like, before they died?" His voice

floats along the ocean breeze, and I take it in, looking up to let him know I don't mind that he asked.

"I don't remember much," I say. "It was so long ago."

"Nothing?"

"A few blips here and there. I remember baking with my mom, being pushed on a swing. My mom was pretty—so pretty—but my dad's face escapes me. I know I loved to climb trees and would go as high as the branches would take me."

"A daredevil. Good to know." He gives me a smile that suggests he wants to learn more, and it makes me both nervous and thrilled. Then his arm is around me, pulling me closer. He whispers into my hair, overpowering the sound of the waves crashing against the shore, "But even daredevils need someone to look out for them."

• • •

We stumble through the dark hallway and into the main room when we get back. We're guided by a ragged snore that Gavin claims belongs to Ry. Tiptoeing over to Mary's bunk, Gavin adjusts her blanket, then he walks me to my bed, his hand on my elbow to guide me. When we reach my bunk, he turns to face me. I can smell the ocean on his skin and feel the heat from his body. It's like we're at the waterfall all over again. I lift my chin to hint that it's okay to kiss me.

"Thank you for taking me to the beach today," I say, leaning in.

"Anytime." He squeezes my fingers and lets go, walking backward like he's being pulled by some invisible force—one that doesn't want me to know what his lips feel like against mine.

I feel weighted down by disappointment as I watch him leave. I force my feet to move and crawl into bed, mumbling "good night" as he climbs into the bunk above Adrian.

• • •

I wake to voices in the kitchen and sit up, turning toward the smell of eggs and something I don't recognize. My mouth waters.

Gavin sees me and waves me over. He looks rested. Happy. Is he glad he didn't make the mistake of kissing me?

I push my confusion away and walk toward the table where Ry's holding a bottle of mustard over Sasha's eggs. "Just try it," he says to her. "You're gonna love it. I promise."

"That's disgusting." She wrinkles her nose and moves her plate to the side, shielding it with her shoulder.

I start to sit but a jolt of pain rips through my head. *Not now. Not on the day of the rescue.* I hurry back to my bed, digging out the pills from my pillowcase to find my heart medication. I already took the wrong one which gave me ultrasonic hearing, so the two remaining pale green pills should be mine. Hopefully. I need to remind Gavin to get me more. Maybe we can steal some from the hospital today.

With my pill in my hand, I head back to the kitchen. This time there's a plate with eggs and three strips of bacon waiting for me. I feel like I'm in one of the TV diners where the actor waltzes in and nods at the waitress, and she's already got a plate ready to go. It makes my insides warm to think I'm starting to belong here.

When I sit, Sasha gives me a subtle grin. "Feeling okay?"

Gavin looks from Sasha to me like he missed something.

"Yeah," I say, smiling through the throb that's building in my head. "I'm fine."

"Good. Because today's the big day," Gavin says.

I fake a cough and pop the pill in my mouth, taking a swig of water.

A few bites into breakfast, my headache subsides. I can even enjoy the bacon, the toasted meat packed with deliciousness. No one should be denied bacon.

Burk arrives and immediately goes for the coffee machine.

"Burk'll try it!" hollers Ry. "He'll eat anything!" Ry dishes up a plate of mustard and eggs, and in true form, Burk takes a bite.

"It's good," Burk says just before he swallows.

"You'd eat a worm if it had enough seasoning," Sasha says, rolling her eyes.

Ry snatches the plate out of Burk's hand and sets it in front of Sasha. "I'll bet you dish duty for a month you'll like it."

They're about to shake when Adrian bursts into the room.

"We've got a problem." His eyebrows are raised like he shocked himself. Gavin rockets out of his seat, and I follow them into the hallway.

Adrian picks up his notepad and points at the information he's gotten from the radio and Kenny. Notes about the room, time, and parts purchased. I hear a soft rattle of papers and notice Adrian's hand is shaking.

"There's more than one," he says. "It's the only thing that makes sense."

"More than one *what*?" Gavin's voice is stern. He grabs the paper and squints at it, flipping back to previous notes to read the communication log from the beginning. He waves the notes in Adrian's face. "Are you sure about this?"

"Sure about what?" I ask.

Gavin's eyes flit from side to side as he reads. His jaw clenches. "They're operating on twins today."

The room sways, and I grab Gavin's arm to brace myself.

"At first I thought it was a mistake, that they just changed the room number," says Adrian, "then I heard the Center say twins."

I glance at the notes, and in small writing scribbled beside the room numbers I see a P and M. It's all the confirmation I need. My breathing stalls. "Paige and Meghan," I mumble. Gavin slumps against the counter, and I bite my lip when it quivers, trying to sound stronger than I feel. "We have to save them both."

Adrian's eyes are big and afraid. He shakes his head and Gavin puts a hand on his shoulder, squeezing until Adrian stops.

"We will," Gavin says before he turns to me. I wish he hadn't. All I can see is false hope in his eyes.

"Are they on the same floor?" I ask.

"Yes," says Adrian. "But they're at opposite ends of the building."

A throat clears, and we turn toward the doorway. Sasha, Ry, and Burk are standing in the room; Craig stands behind them holding Mary.

"How do you expect us to pull this off?" Sasha asks, her arms folded. I see what I'm feeling in her taut expression. "We only have a replacement double for one of them."

"We have to try," says Gavin. "They're being prepped for surgery at the same time. They'll be knocked unconscious, probably operated on an hour apart if they use the same doctor."

"Why both of them?" asks Burk. "They never do two in one day."

Craig disappears with Mary into the main room.

"Because the buyer probably wants a backup," Gavin says. "If they're matched with one twin, they'd match the other. And if the buyer has taken a lot of pills, the Center could have convinced them to buy extra organs to be kept in the hospital's cryopreservation unit."

"Security for the future," Adrian adds. "The buyer might not need another liver for ten years, but the number of surgeries keeps growing, so who's to say they'll find a match as easily when they need another one?"

"Why didn't we know earlier?" I ask everyone—and no one at the same time. Shouldn't Kenny have given us a heads up? Isn't that his job?

"It's the first I've heard of it," says Adrian. I don't miss how his eyes flit to Gavin's. "It must have been a last-minute decision."

"Whatever it is, we'll never pull this off," Sasha says.

Gavin claps his hands together. "We need a plan. Focus everyone."

We gather around the counter where he spreads out Adrian's notes and pulls a map of the hospital from the drawer by his hip. "The surgery units are staggered on the fifth floor, divided by prep rooms and computer docking stations for nurses and doctors.

Tabitha and I will go after Paige. If our information is correct, she'll be in room two when she's knocked out." He points at Craig. "You and Ry will go after Meghan. She'll be in room six."

Gavin shoots Ry a pleading look. "Is there any chance you can get us another body?"

"I—I dunno," Ry says, rubbing the back of his neck. "Maybe."

Craig tosses Ry his keys and says, "Take my car."

Ry heads up the ladder without another word.

"How much time do we have?" Sasha asks.

Gavin eyes the clock on the wall. "They'll be transported to the hospital in less than three hours."

# CHAPTER 13

Everyone is jittery as we prepare for the rescue. Except for Ry. He returns with Craig's car a half hour before we're supposed to be at the hospital. We're waiting, ready to go as Gavin hollers out the van window. "Did you get a body?"

Ry salutes him with a big smile plastered on his face.

"Not now, Ry," Gavin mutters. "He better not be on Euphorium."

Adrian spins around in his seat before we pull onto the road. "Keep your eyes forward. Act like you have somewhere you need to be, and don't stop to talk to anyone."

I nod with each point, feeling my face lose a little color every time my chin dips. My lungs fight for air that can't seem to come in fast enough and my stomach feels like it's being trampled on. This is it. My friends' lives are on the line.

We're dressed in scrubs, and I twist my newly brown ponytail into a bun, pulling the skin at my temples. I miss the red, but in less than thirty minutes, I'll be back at the same hospital where I was about to be hacked up, and I know I can't be recognized. I put on my hospital cap and sit on my hands to keep them from trembling.

There's a buzz from Gavin's seat and I jump. "What was that?" I ask.

Gavin pulls out a phone. "It's just Ry answering my message." Other than the clicks his fingers make as he types a response, the van is eerily quiet.

When I see the hospital sign, my heart sputters. Adrian parks behind a strip mall a block away.

"We'll cross the street like we're walking to work," Gavin says.

"I'll get the body from Ry and I'll meet you at the exit," Adrian says when we climb out. "It'll take me ten minutes, tops."

"Not on Ry's watch," Gavin says, his voice tense. "They won't have much time to get Meghan wheeled out if they don't hurry."

When Adrian pulls away, Gavin sucks in a breath.

"We'll get Paige first," he says, exhaling. "Once we wheel her out safely, we'll come back to help Ry and Craig with Meghan." I nod and start to march around the building. Gavin grabs my hand to stop me.

"What's on your neck?"

My fingers find the wound. The scab is thick and tender when I touch it.

"I told you. They took a skin sample from me." *Your buddy Kenny's the one who cut me*, I want to add.

He brings his face close to my neck. I feel his heat, the warmth of his breath as he traces the cut.

"It looks swollen." He tugs on the back of my hair cap, pulling the elastic down until it covers the scab. Unless I walk without moving my neck, it's not going to stay. "We'll need to keep an eye on it."

"I'm sure it's nothing," I say, but when I turn back around, his face is etched with concern. "I'm not the one we need to worry about right now."

"Let me be the judge of that."

His eyes are serious, and I realize this might be the last time I stand face-to-face with him. What if something goes wrong?

Before I can stop myself, I lean in to kiss him. His mouth is soft and my lips tingle as I pull away.

"What was that for?" he asks, his eyes still closed.

"F-for…for everything." I look down, afraid when he opens his eyes they'll reveal the kiss meant more to me than him. "For saving my friends."

"We haven't saved them yet," he says, his voice low. He grabs my hand and leads us around the building. He lets go before we pass the blood-red hospital sign and walks a few feet ahead of me. I slow my pace to give us distance.

I'm dressed exactly like the nurse sitting on the bench outside, but I feel like the cameras on the building are zooming in on me— like security knows I'm here. I reach for my hair cover but drop my hand when I realize it might look suspicious.

The entry doors slide open for Gavin. He steps inside and stops to fix his shoelace as I go through. Before I can pass him, he stands.

I want to reach out and grab his hand, overwhelmed by the bright and busy room. A nurse at the front desk is on the phone, and her eyes shift to me as I turn down the hall that leads to the elevators. I imagine she's glaring at my neck, and I press my back against the wall to let a man on crutches hobble by me.

Just then, the intercom above my head blares: "Security, please dial 3-4-4."

My stomach climbs into my throat. Do they know we're here? Did Adrian get caught? I want to race down the hallway, but Gavin keeps his composure and shoots me a look that says *stay cool*.

I play with my lanyard to keep my hands busy, staring at an image that's not me. The girl's hair is a lighter shade of brown, her face round with small features. If anyone stops us, they'll know immediately I don't belong here.

Gavin nods at the elevator, and panic seizes me when he cuts away to take the stairs. Splitting up seemed like a good idea in the van, but now that I'm alone, I feel exposed without Gavin by my side.

After what feels like forever, the elevator bings. My breath catches when I see Ms. Preen on the other side of the open doors.

I wait for her to look up from her phone, to call out for security, but she doesn't. I force my shoulders to relax and slip inside.

For a split second, I consider giving her a fat lip to go with her full hair. I quickly shove the idea away. An idiotic move like that would put us all in danger—especially Paige and Meghan. I push the number five and wedge myself in the corner, as far out of her view as possible.

Her nose wrinkles as a female voice echoes through the receiver. "He doesn't even have a job," she says to the person on the line. "I'd much rather see you with that Murphy boy you've been spending time with. At least you'd have security."

Just before the door slides shut, she sticks out her hand to stop it. Her heels make that familiar click as she marches off. The elevator closes and I exhale. My relief is short-lived when the door bings again and a man gets on from the second floor.

He's wearing scrubs like mine, and I fold my hands over my name badge when he glances at it.

"I don't think I've seen you around…"

The elevator climbs to three, and I force myself to smile. "You haven't. I'm new here. It's my first day."

"I'm pretty new myself." He taps on his name badge. "The name's Curtis."

I do a double take when I notice the letter tacked on after his name: Curtis R. It's the same name badge I saw the day of my screening. But Kenny was wearing it. Are they friends? Enemies?

I swallow my questions and smile.

To my relief, the elevator stops on four and the doors open. "Good luck today," he says as he steps off.

The doors shut and I blow out a breath. Before I can dwell any further, I reach my floor. My anxiety lifts when I spot Gavin a few feet down the hall. He's writing something in a notepad, and his eyes light up when he sees me. He tucks the pad away and starts to move. I follow him. We pass exam room four, then three. Two is locked, but Gavin has a universal keycard that Kenny slipped into our supply bag.

I continue past Gavin to a docking station. The computer screen has a few details about a patient's symptoms and I rub my chin, pretending to care about what I'm reading. The patient is waiting for a kidney transplant. She's twenty-eight and there's a list of drugs she's currently taking. I count seventeen, but there's an arrow at the bottom indicating more on the next page. How many more?

Gavin rattles the door but it doesn't open. I look away while he tries the keycard again. The computer screen has gone black, and I touch the keyboard. There's a flash of white and the page reloads, but the content has changed. I read the name at the top of the screen. Meghan Collins. Only she's not in room six, she's on floor six.

And she's in surgery.

"Oh my God!" My hand flies to my mouth. A nurse walking by glances at me and I fake a cough, turning my body away from her.

I hear a click and look up. Gavin waves me over. We slip into Paige's room and he shuts the door.

"We're too late." I stagger and he grabs my shoulders to hold me up, his face wrenched with confusion. "I saw it on the computer. It's Meghan. She's already in surgery. We need to do something!"

"That can't be right." Gavin rubs his temples, pacing in the small room. He walks behind Paige's head and brings his hands down to his sides, balled like he needs to hit something. "Let me think."

I step toward Paige, unnerved by the hospital gown she's wearing and her shallow breaths. I stroke her hair. A section of it is pulled back with a string, tied into a tiny bow. It's something I've never seen her do. She wanted to look perfect for her new family. My eyes burn, and I fight back tears.

"There must be something we can do for Meghan," I plead.

Gavin removes his hospital cap, wiping his brow before he yanks it back on. "Ry will be too late. And we need to get out of here. The longer we're here—"

"We can't leave her!" My voice booms and Gavin's eyes grow wide. He presses a finger against his lips.

"Take Paige to the freight elevator and head to the basement." He grabs the sidebars on the bed and kicks the wheel locks loose with his foot. "Get her loaded up and head back to the barn with Adrian. I'll try to save Meghan."

*Try.* The word never felt so small to me. So hopeless.

He moves toward the foot of the bed and opens the door to peek out. "It's clear."

It takes every bit of strength I have to push the gurney out. Paige is light and the wheels roll along as if they've been greased up, but it feels like I'm wading through a hallway filled with oatmeal. Two doctors absorbed in conversation hurry by, and a nurse bolts past me, speaking into a walkie-talkie. This can't be happening. My heart gets heavier with each step. We can't lose Meghan.

The freight elevator opens and a man gets out, holding a device that fits in his palm. I slip in and keep my back to the door.

"Hey," he says. "Don't I know you?"

I spin around. It's Kenny, and I know without a doubt he was in the room during my final screening. If he's kept this secret from Gavin, what else is he hiding?

"What are you—" he says before the door shuts. A wave of panic hits me. Why didn't he tell us Meghan would be on a different floor? And what if he gets in the way of saving her? My eyes flash to the number panel. Do I hit the reopen button? I jerk my hand back. No. I have to get Paige out of here first.

I reach my floor and race to the exit door. The gurney slams against it as I burst through, and Adrian looks up, startled.

"Where's Gavin?" he asks.

"There's been a mix-up. I need to help him. He said you should leave, take Paige back to the barn."

Adrian doesn't move.

"Help me," I say, grunting as I struggle to lift Paige. He hustles over and I thrust her into his arms. "Where's the replacement?"

"Side door."

I pick up a young girl wrapped in white sheets. She's lighter than Paige, and her face is exposed. She can't be more than thirteen. She looks like a dead doll when I set her on the gurney.

"Don't wait for us," I say, yanking the sheet up to her chin.

"But I thought—"

"Just go!"

I barrel down the hallway and press the freight elevator button, but it doesn't light up. I stab the button again and kick the door. "Come on!"

When the door finally opens, Kenny is standing in the middle with his arms folded. "Going up?"

My stomach drops. *What do I do?* I don't have a weapon. I know I can get away from him, just not in an elevator. But I need to get to Meghan and Gavin. I push the gurney inside, creating a barricade between us. Kenny is on the side with buttons. The door closes but he doesn't move.

"Gavin said it'd be the usual crew." He tilts his head, and a smile tugs at the corner of his mouth. His features are stunning, but he lacks charm. He's like one of the bad boy models you want to look at, but never want to be around. *Gladstone Community Review* only used those guys in motorcycle ads. They didn't run very often.

I lift my chin. "I told him I wanted to come."

"You shouldn't have," he snaps, then relaxes his mouth and softens his voice. "I see you dyed your hair." He eyes the strands that have slipped out of my hospital cap. When he tries to touch one, I back away. He reroutes his hand, caressing the corpse's face. Her skin is still peach—freshly dead.

"Aren't we supposed to be on same side?"

Kenny gasps as if he's offended. "Of course. What would make you think we weren't?"

"Then how come Gavin doesn't know you were at my health screening, *Curtis?*" I eye the panel, my hand itching to jab the button. I'm stuck with a dead body and someone I want to hurt. It won't end pretty.

"I work in scheduling. It allows me...certain privileges. Freedom to move around the hospital." He weaves his thumb over the panel, failing to push a number. "With so many new hires, I can go anywhere I want."

"Well, you're not much help," I say, anger tainting my words. "They're operating on two people today, and we weren't ready."

"Oh dear." He shakes his head, but his eyes don't reveal any remorse. "They've been watching the employees so closely since you got away. It's hard to keep up with schedule changes." He shrugs like it's nothing. Like there's no reason to get worked up. It's just someone's life, after all.

Finally his thumb sinks into the number six. I start to object. "First I have to take the body to five—" Six is where Meghan is. My stomach knots. Is his office up there? Or did he know Meghan's room was switched earlier? And if that's the case, why didn't he tell us?

The elevator movement throws me off balance and I grab the gurney. Kenny's hand is over mine in an instant.

He follows my stare. "I'm sorry, what floor did you need?"

"The body needs to go to room two, on five."

"I'll go with you." He smiles as he presses the number. "We're on the same team. We should stick together." He doesn't let go until I nod.

The elevator opens and he steps off, towing the gurney. I wait until his face turns to step back in and push the elevator button.

"I think it'll be safer if we separate," I say as the door shuts.

Kenny's head whips back with a glare that could burn through the steel.

Blowing out a shaky breath, I wipe the hand he touched on my scrubs and hit the number six repeatedly, but the elevator still doesn't go fast enough. The door finally opens and I step into a busy hall. I pretend to rush after a nurse, but I'm trying so hard to not look anyone in the face, my shoulder bumps a doctor going the opposite direction.

"Excuse me, I'm sorry," I say, bending down to get the papers that have scattered around his polished shoes. When I stand to hand him the stack, my eyes widen. Doctor Morgan frowns like he recognizes me but is unsure why.

I step around him, feeling his eyes on my back and the cool air on the exposed part of my scab. I move in front of another nurse, cutting her off without apologizing.

At the end of the hall I catch a glimpse of Gavin carrying a tray into a room. Did we make it in time? I speed up until I'm practically running toward the room, but Gavin comes out before I reach the door.

And Meghan isn't with him.

My breath hitches, and my words come out ragged. "W-what's going on? Where is she?"

His eyes are blank, almost deadened as he grabs my shoulder.

"What happened?" I shrug him off to hold my ground.

"We need to go." His voice is low and urgent, and he pushes me toward the elevator.

I wriggle away and dart for the door, but he slams his hand against it before I can open it. I elbow him in the gut and swing it open as he groans.

And then I scream.

Meghan's body is laid out on a table. A doctor holds a knife that is dripping blood, over her stomach.

It's too late...

My knees threaten to buckle, and my mouth quivers as the tears build.

"What's the meaning of this?" the doctor barks, waving the scalpel at me. "Are you supposed to be in here?"

I shake my head and back away from Meghan's body. My eyes drift to the lines marked across her breastbone, the incision across her abdomen.

The door behind me opens and a hand yanks me out.

Gavin leads me into the stairwell. He starts down the steps and pulls at my arm to follow, but my legs are shaking beneath my weight, and I can't get a firm grasp on the railing.

My emotions erupt. "Sh-she's dead—"

He slides a hand over my mouth. My tears stream into his fingers as he holds me against the wall. His eyes are red and pained. Confirmation we failed.

Meghan is gone.

Several flights below us, a door opens, slamming against the wall. A walkie-talkie crackles to life: "Security, be advised for a possible code 43."

They know our group is here.

Gavin drops his hand and I wipe my eyes. I want to ask him if he thinks Adrian is safe, if Paige and the rest of the team got away, but Gavin's face is wild with fear. I swallow my questions, but the dread stays.

"Let's go," he says, gesturing for us to head back up the stairs, past the floor we came from.

He uses the skeleton key to open the rooftop door, then grabs my arm and practically throws me through the opening. I stumble forward as the door closes behind us.

"What the hell was that?" Gavin kicks the air and pulls off his blue cap.

"I was trying to save Meghan."

"What the hell did you think *I* was doing?" The veins in his arms bulge as he grips his head like he's trying to keep it from bursting. "I told you to go with Adrian. To safety."

"What if you needed my help?"

"With what? Getting caught?"

"I didn't mean to scream," I say, taking in a jerky breath. "But there was all that blood on the blade, on the doctor's hands, all over Meghan." Meghan…oh God, Meghan is dead. And now we're all in danger because of me.

Gavin puts his hospital cap back on and his face goes slack. "I'm sorry about your friend," he says, voice sincere. "But we're in a lot of trouble now." He takes a step toward me as if he wants to console me but stops short. I want to bury my face in my hands, but now is not the time to cry.

Not when we need to escape.

I sniff back my tears and follow Gavin to the edge of the building. He leans against the concrete wall that encloses the rooftop. I take a spot several feet away from him and glance down. The parking lot is below us. I see the abandoned building where Adrian dropped us off. There are a few police cars driving with their lights on but no sirens.

"Are they looking for us?"

"Probably." His voice is flat and his eyes are fixed on the horizon.

"I'm sorry I put the team in danger," I say.

Before he can reply, he gasps, jerking his body away from the ledge and dropping to the floor. I follow suit. Our backs are against the wall, and Gavin's breathing is heavy.

"I think someone spotted us," he says. "We have to get out of here. Now."

"Do you think the stairs are clear?"

He shakes his head. I stay low as I dart to the other side of the building. There's another rooftop about ten feet away. With enough speed, we could make it across.

"Over here," I say, waving him to join me.

Gavin hustles across and assesses the jump. His brows slant. "Even if you make it, you'll break a leg."

I ignore him and climb onto the ledge. There's a slight breeze, but it's favorable. All I need is a running start. Gavin hovers near my legs. His hands twitch like he might need to catch me at any moment. I eye my target. *I know I can make it.*

But maybe Gavin won't. He's strong, but is he fast? Can he jump? Would he?

No. This won't work. And I won't leave him. Not when I'm to blame for our entrapment.

I canvass the rooftop, taking inventory. We can't jump. We can't use the stairs. Then I see the ventilation system. It's larger than the one Parker and I used to sneak out of at the Center. Maybe this system leads out too.

"This way." I hop off the ledge, and Gavin follows me to the intake unit. We pull on the wire grate, and when it detaches, he rams it into the fan. The motor makes a high-pitched wheeze as it stops. Who knows how long it will hold.

Gavin leans back on his hands, kicking two fan blades to make a hole for us to squeeze through.

"You first," he says, keeping a tight grip on the grate.

I duck under his arm. The machine rumbles when I'm halfway in. I wince, expecting the blade to turn and rip my torso in half.

Gavin groans. "Hurry!"

I fall forward and spin my body around.

"Your turn," I say, locking my hands around the grate that's shoved through the blades. Gavin lets go of his end and waits a beat to make sure the fan doesn't move. I brace my feet on the metal tube and lean back. If my grip slips, Gavin's as good as dead.

His shoulders are broad and it takes him twice as long to shimmy through the opening. The metal grate digs into my fingers. I'm fighting a machine. I need Gavin to move faster.

His face strains and he drops through, pushing the blades back into place with his feet before helping me pull the grate inside. The fan makes a loud cah-thunk and starts to whirl. My blue cap is sucked off, slapping Gavin in the face. He hands it back to me, and I see his faint smile through the brown hair tickling my face.

"Now," he says, the hint of relief gone, "let's see where this goes."

# CHAPTER 14

Dust stings my eyes as we crawl through the metal tunnel. It's warm and feels like I'm inhaling a plume of death with every breath. We reach the elevator shaft and climb down the maintenance ladder to the sixth floor.

"The elevator should have an escape hatch," says Gavin. "Our best chance is to get back inside and walk out the front door. They won't expect it, so it's probably the safest exit."

Logically, it makes sense, but my heart disagrees. I'm terrified. Jumping from one rooftop to another sounds more appealing right now. I keep my mouth shut, as the hum of the elevator grows louder. Gavin signals with his head when it reaches us and we drop on top. The elevator sways slightly. We stay still, listening for voices or the crackle of a walkie-talkie. Finally, Gavin leans down and peels back the escape hatch just enough to peek in.

"Empty." He rips it open and extends his hand. I take it and he lowers me into the hole. When he lets go, I land with a soft whomp.

Gavin lowers his body, hanging on with one hand so he can flip the escape hatch shut before dropping to the floor. I press one and the elevator begins its descent.

"Are you sure we should walk out the front door?" I point to my knees. Our scrubs are stained black from the dirty ventilation ducts. At floor three, the elevator slows and Gavin's eyes dart to the door. My heart freezes mid-pump. "What do we do?" I spin around, searching his face for answers.

The door slides open and Gavin lets out a breath of relief, the warm air grazing my forehead. I glance over my shoulder as Kenny steps inside.

"I'm glad I found you," Kenny says urgently. He presses the close button and holds it. "What the hell happened up there?"

Images of Meghan flash in my head. The slash across her stomach. The bloody knife. I want to hurl. I want to hurt Kenny. I blame him, if for no other reason than I think he knows more than he's letting on.

"We walked in on the surgery," Gavin says, his head hanging.

"Well, you guys have gotta get the hell out of here," Kenny says. "Do you need a ride?"

"We'll get a ride from a guy on our team. Thanks anyway," I say, keeping my back to him. My tone is as cold as the trough water, and Gavin gives me a sharp look.

"Let me help. I feel awful about what happened today." Kenny lets go of the button and pats me on the shoulder. "We'll take my car."

"Thanks, man." The worry lines on Gavin's face soften and he gestures to me. "I don't think you two have met. Tabitha, this is—"

"Kenny. I know." I turn around, but I don't extend a hand.

"We met earlier," Kenny says, showing off his perfect white teeth. His smile suggests we go way back. My skin crawls and I lean closer to Gavin.

"So how bad is it out there?" Gavin asks.

"They know you went into the stairwell, and some guy said he saw people on the roof." Kenny points at me. "Someone in the surgery room noticed a scab on your neck. Better keep that thing covered up."

I adjust my hospital cap with shaky hands. Maybe I shouldn't have come. What if we don't make it out? What will happen to everyone else at the Center? To Gavin? To the people back at the barn? To me?

The elevator pings and Kenny waves us out. "This way."

I walk between them and keep my eyes forward. Gavin stays close to my heels to block my scab from any onlookers.

We pick up our pace when we reach the front door and head for the prettiest car in the lot. How does someone in scheduling afford such a fancy vehicle?

Gavin opens the door for me to climb in the back, and I slide across the leather seat to sit in the middle.

"Where to?" Kenny asks as Gavin gets in.

"Our safe house," Gavin says. My heart knocks against my chest like a warning. We can't exactly blindfold the driver, but is it safe to bring him back to the barn?

Kenny follows Gavin's directions toward the main drag that connects with the highway. My stomach flips a little as he talks about the landmarks we pass; it's as if he's trying to memorize the route.

"Ah, you're out in the sticks," Kenny says. "You must get terrible reception."

He looks in the rearview mirror and we lock eyes. When he winks, I look away.

I try to convince myself that I'm jumping to conclusions about Kenny, that it's just my anxiety about the day catching up with me—that Meghan's death has coated my mind with vengeful thoughts. I don't believe myself at all.

• • •

Mary and Sasha jump off the fence when we pull up, running toward the car with expressions of relief and surprise.

"What happened?" Sasha asks, clinging to the side of the convertible as we roll to a stop. She uses her arm to keep Mary from coming too close. When Kenny turns off the ignition, Sasha drops her hand, and Mary leans over the side of the car to hug me before sprinting to the passenger door to greet Gavin.

"Meghan was already in surgery," says Gavin, climbing out. He lifts Mary up into an embrace. Mary is the best drug for both of us, it seems. When he puts her down, it's as if he's let go of some of his tension, but not all of it. His body is more rigid than usual as he moves toward Sasha. "We tried to get her out," he tucks his chin, "but we couldn't save them both."

Sasha nods, her face solemn. A teary-eyed Mary returns to Sasha's side and grabs her hand.

Kenny holds his seat forward for me to get out, and as I do, his hand grazes my hip. I jump forward, and he steps to the side, his expression blank. The hairs on the back of my neck stand up.

"The hospital sent security after us," Gavin says, careful not to meet my eyes when he glances around the group.

I swallow the lump that's formed in my throat as I turn to Sasha. "Are Craig and Ry okay?"

"Yeah. They bolted when workers tried to corner them. Craig wanted to get some air, but Ry's inside with Paige."

I start for the barn door as Gavin introduces Kenny to Mary and Sasha. I don't want Paige to wake up without a familiar face. My stomach coils when I think about how I'm going to tell her about Meghan. *Your sister was murdered. We couldn't save her. And thanks to me, we probably won't be able to rescue anyone else. Welcome to your new life.*

As I climb down the ladder, a terrible thought enters my mind. I'm glad it wasn't Paige. Guilt crushes my heart. What kind of person am I to choose favorites? I hate myself for thinking any less of Meghan and bury the notion in the recesses of my brain. I love them both, they're family. Still…I don't know what I'd do if I knew I'd never see Paige again.

The basement smells vaguely like disinfectant and rubbing alcohol, scents from the hospital that must have traveled with her. When I round the corner into the main room, Paige is in Ry's bed. He doesn't see me approach.

"How is she?" I ask.

He looks up, startled. His eyes are heavy. I've never seen Ry so tired. Even in the low lights of the basement I can make out dark circles.

"No Meghan?" He sounds like he might cry. I squat next

to him, fighting back tears of my own. "I should have stayed focused…it's all my fault…"

I put my hand on his knee. "They switched Meghan's surgery time. There's no way we could have known."

Ry pinches the bridge of his nose and I sit, putting an arm around his waist. His emotions are contagious. My breath shudders, and I choke on a wave of tears.

Meghan is gone forever.

Every time I look at Paige, I'll be reminded that PharmPerfect won. That my friend was taken. I want to break the mirror against the far wall so that Paige doesn't have to be reminded too. For the rest of her life, she'll see Meghan's face staring back at her. And when she looks at us, she'll remember no one could save her sister.

We failed.

My chest heaves and Ry pulls me into a hug. I cry into his shoulder, squeezing his frail frame. Every bone feels like it's on display. When he releases me, I notice his pupils are slightly dilated. He must be coming down from whatever he took.

He squeezes his eyes shut as if he knows what I'm thinking.

"It was only half a pill," he whispers. "I thought it would keep me calm, but I couldn't focus. I shouldn't have taken it…"

"No. You shouldn't have. But that's not why she died, Ry. PharmPerfect did this." He opens his eyes.

"I wasn't in the right mindset. It *is* my fault." He wipes his face with the back of his hand. "Gavin asked me to call the hospital since my number wouldn't look suspicious."

"Who were you supposed to call?"

"Me," says a voice an octave lower than Ry's.

Kenny walks toward us and Gavin and Sasha follow him like he's their leader. There's a stabbing pain in my chest, and I grit my teeth. The room seems darker as Kenny towers over us and his head blocks the kitchen light.

I stand, scowling back at him. Ry pops up too.

"Hey…" Ry's voice is wrought with emotion. "I-I wasn't sure if you'd pick up." Then he practically falls into Kenny's arms, his muffled sobs echoing in an otherwise quiet room. "I'm sorry. I'm so sorry."

"Of course I would've answered." Kenny pats his back, his arms stiff. "We all make mistakes. But hey, at least we got one of them out." Kenny pushes Ry away, ruffling his hair when he notices me glaring. "It's good to see you again."

Ry turns and the resemblance slaps me in the face. He's younger, more delicate. A boy with a pinch of athleticism—more of a soccer player than a football star.

Kenny is quite the opposite. He's taller, thicker—more intimidating.

"Is he...?" I point at Kenny. "Are you...?"

"Brothers," Ry says, his voice as weak as his smile.

Gavin gives me an expectant nod, as if being related to Ry makes Kenny an instant member of the team. As if I should be excited about the revelation.

Hardly.

Paige stirs and I drop down to her side. I grab her hand and whisper her name, coaxing her to look at me. Her eyes flutter open a few seconds later.

"Where am I?" she asks.

Gavin kneels next to me. His body feels warm. There's a bubble of safety whenever he's around. It's comforting, but it also terrifies me. I don't like the idea of having to count on him, believe in him. I can't even trust my own thoughts right now.

I smooth Paige's hair. Her head rolls and she scans my face. "Tabitha?" She musters a grin and reaches out, but her hand flops on the bed like it's weighted. "What's wrong with me?"

My lip quivers. How do I start to explain what happened?

"The—the Center...they took you t-to...it's not what you think..."

"There's no foster family," Gavin says, his hand finding mine. "The Center used you. And Tabitha helped you escape."

I nod at Paige. Her eyes widen as I explain how the Center

trained us to keep our organs healthy and how PharmPerfect sold us for parts.

She takes in a jerky breath. "What about Meghan?"

I glance at Gavin. My throat suddenly aches like it's been stuffed with rocks. I can barely force out the words: "She didn't make it."

Paige wails something inaudible. She rolls to her side, away from the crowd, pulling her hand away as she does. Her chest heaves with sobs, and all I can do is rub her back until she cries herself to sleep.

Eventually, the room empties. Only Gavin and I stay. We sit on the floor, our backs against the bed. Paige hasn't asked for anything, even water, and it's been more than an hour.

Aside from the occasional throat clearing, Gavin and I have stayed quiet. I'm alone in my head. My body tenses as thoughts swirl. I need to talk to someone, even if Gavin is still mad at me for jeopardizing the mission.

"I'm sorry for what happened back there. At the hospital." I play with my shoelace. "And for elbowing you in the gut."

"I'm sorry for yelling at you. I freaked." He nudges me with his knee. "But you got us out. And Paige is safe."

But not Meghan.

My heart tightens. "You should go," I say. "Get something to eat. Check on everyone. Make sure they're okay. Ry seemed pretty upset."

He stares at me and I give him my best smile, which feels more like a broken frown. "Are you sure?" He looks unconvinced.

"Yeah, I'm sure." My emotions must be messing with my mind because I can't help but tell him what's really plaguing me. "Besides, someone should keep an eye on Kenny."

"You still don't trust him? Come on, he's Ry's brother." Gavin stands and extends a hand. "You should take a break too. Paige will need you to be strong when she wakes up." I take his hand. He pulls me up fast and with enough force to bring me against his body. Our paper-thin scrubs do little to block the heat. I step back so I can think straight.

I should let the issue of Kenny go. Part of me wants to go outside, clear my head, but my mouth disagrees. "He was at my screening. Ask him yourself."

Gavin smirks. Is he humoring me?

My jaw tightens. "You don't believe me?"

"Of course I do. Before we came in to see Paige, Kenny told me." He puts a hand on my shoulder. "You were right. He was in the room, but only so he could get information about what goes on when someone leaves the Center. He even thought about warning you then but didn't want you to screw up our mission."

"You buy that? That Kenny'd be a one-man show, warning Center kids so they could what—climb the twenty-foot wall and dive into the ocean?"

"No, but I could see how he'd want to try." Gavin pauses like he's considering the idea. "It would have saved us the trouble of dealing with the hospital. When Kenny asked if he could help us—"

"Wait. He came to *you?*"

Gavin sighs. "He kept bugging Cherry about Ry, asking what he'd been up, who he was spending all his time with. Kenny claimed he wanted to turn his life around and do something good for a change. Cherry said she didn't tell him much, but he put two and two together. Then he offered to work from the inside. He got us the information we needed to get you out, but he thought the security would be a problem. Don't blame the guy for trying to rescue you on his own."

My arms are crossed and I hold myself tight. It's the only thing I have to hold onto right now. I know Kenny's lying. I can feel it in my core. I just can't prove it. And Gavin has no interest in assumptions. Not when Kenny's so valuable to our team.

"He was only trying to help." Gavin rubs my arm, but it feels like he's placating me. I shrug him off and turn my attention back to Paige. "Take a break," he says. "She needs you to be strong."

Paige hasn't moved. Her breaths are slow, and she might be asleep, but I can't be sure. Gavin's hand slips over my shoulder, pulling gently.

Maybe fresh air will help clear my head. Strengthen my crippled spirit.

"I'll be right back, Paige," I say.

She doesn't stir. We walk toward the exit, and I glance back when we reach the hallway.

"Don't worry, I'm thinking the same thing," Gavin says. "We'll send Ry or Sasha in. I don't want her left alone either."

It's a small relief, but part of me feels like I'm abandoning her. He's right though. I need to be strong for her. Strong for all of my friends at the Center. Stronger than I was for Meghan.

Outside, Kenny and Craig are playing Frisbee. Kenny tosses it toward Gavin when we step out of the barn, and I walk away before they can pull me into the game.

I head toward Ry and Sasha, who are talking by the fence. They appear to be alone until Mary's head pops up in the field. She looks like a rabbit hopping through the tall grass.

"She's picking wildflowers for Paige," Ry says as I walk over. "She thought they might cheer her up."

"I love that girl," I say. "If anyone can make this day brighter, it's Mary."

They nod.

"How's Paige?" Sasha asks.

"Resting," I say. "Hoping to wake up from a bad dream, I'm sure."

"Give me a minute, guys," Gavin says, tossing the Frisbee to Craig before jogging toward us. "Ry, do you think you could keep an eye on Paige for a while?"

"Sure thing." Ry looks grateful to be on patient duty. There's urgency in his eyes, like he has to right a wrong. He hustles to the barn and disappears down the hole.

I see a disc fly at my face and deflect it with my forearm. When I glance in the direction it came, Craig's arm still hangs in the air.

"I told you," says Kenny.

Craig drops his throwing hand and shakes his head. "You were right."

"What's the big idea?" I pick the Frisbee off the ground and launch it at Kenny. My aim is better this time, but not direct. Still, he's able to catch it and in one motion toss it to Craig.

"Kenny said you had mad reflexes, that's all." Craig shrugs and resumes his game.

"Don't take it personally," Gavin says. "We review notes before every mission. It also said you had premium lungs."

The words jar a memory loose. I cringe, thinking about Ms. Preen filling out the form during my health screening, noting my lung capacity.

"What's 31 Processing mean?" I ask. "I saw it on some paperwork about me."

Gavin rubs his throat like it hurts. "Formula 31 is the base of most PharmPerfect drugs. It has to be diluted, though, otherwise it can cause liver failure." He scans my face, my hair, my eyes, like he's processing something too. "Your form had 31 on it?"

I nod as Kenny and Craig trot over to us. I shift my body toward Sasha, but she puts an elbow out when I crowd her.

"This is quite the setup you've got here," says Kenny. His eyes are intense.

"So does that mean you're willing to help us?" Gavin asks.

"I thought he already was?" I blurt out. I wish I hadn't. Kenny puts an arm on my shoulder like we're pals.

"Even with my help, you'll never make it past hospital security now. But I can get you in somewhere else." Kenny's eyes flicker with excitement. He looks like a madman with a devious plan. Everyone else smiles. "How about a rescue at the Flat House?"

"What's the Flat House?" I ask.

"The Testing Facility. Locals call it the Flat House," says Craig. "It's where they send anyone who isn't fostered out."

I nod as I remember the long, low building Gavin had pointed out on our way to Dairy Land. A face flashes in my head. "Parker." All eyes turn to me. Kenny is the first to look away. His eyes dart toward Gavin, whose brow is creased. "He turns eighteen soon. He'll be sent there for tests."

"Well then, I guess you're going to need my help to get him

out," says Kenny, squeezing my shoulder. "Aren't you glad I'm on the team now?"

I feel sick all over. "I need some air." I pull away from his grip and head for the trail. I hear footsteps behind me and start to run for the trees. Gavin calls out for me to stop, but I wait until we're in the woods before I turn around.

"What's going on with you?" he asks.

The words pour out—everything I've held back since I got here.

"Imagine what it's like to want a family. To dream of the perfect family. Not even perfect, just a family who loves you." My eyes well up, but I fight through it. "Then one day you wake up, and you learn no one wanted you. You were going to be cut up. And that your friends are next." The dam breaks and hot tears roll down my cheeks. "And you want to know what's going on with me? Why I don't trust anyone?"

I turn to leave, but he hooks my arm and pulls me close. My hands are sandwiched between our bodies. I don't want to feel close to him. I don't want to feel vulnerable. I don't want to lose anyone else. I can't. I don't have the strength.

"You can trust me." He wraps his arms around me and rests his chin on my head. I struggle to break free, but Gavin won't let go, holding me until I lose the energy to fight. He presses me deeper into his chest. I feel his breath, hear his heartbeat.

I try to let go of my inhibitions. Of the fear.

His voice is calm and confident. "You can push me away, but until you can look me in the eyes and tell me you don't trust me, that you want me out of your life, I'm not going anywhere."

He pulls back and lifts my chin. I can't look away. I'm lost in his eyes. In this moment. In this feeling. All I want to do is climb into his skin. To feel safe.

"Do you want me to leave you alone?" he asks.

My heart stalls as if it's afraid I'll betray it. I don't. "No," I say, holding his stare.

He kisses me, slowly at first, and my arms wrap around his neck. He slides a hand down to the small of my back. A flood of warmth drowns the fear and pain inside of me. His kiss is like a drug, the only drug I need to keep from going mad.

We're interrupted by a cough.

Gavin lets go and spins around and my body tightens when I see it's Kenny.

"Sorry," he says, but his smile says he's not. "Paige is asking for Tabitha."

I sprint away without another word, barreling through the barn door and down the hatch. Ry meets me at the entrance to the main room. His hands are up in defense. "Don't be mad," he says.

"What's going on?"

"I gave her something to help her feel better."

I peek in. There's a glass full of flowers by the bed, the ones Mary picked. Paige is sitting up. She has a smile on her face.

I stifle a gasp. "You *drugged* her!"

"It's just to get her through today," Ry says.

"Euphorium?"

He nods. "The pill's supposed to help people with grief." He averts his eyes. "It wasn't just made to help people calm down. It numbs your pain."

"What about Gavin?" I ask. "Don't you think he'll be livid?"

"I was hoping you wouldn't tell him."

"Why wouldn't I?"

"Because you know what it's like."

I have no words for Ry. For as careless as he is, he understands in a way no one else seems to. Her life will never be the same. She lost everything in a matter of hours. The Center she thought wanted the best for her is now the enemy, and the family she hoped for doesn't exist. Worse than that, the family she did have, her flesh and blood, is gone.

"Okay, Ry. You have my word," I say. "But how do you expect no one to notice? Meghan is dead and she's *smiling*."

"Yeah, I probably should've given her only half a pill."

"Or none at all."

I glance over as Paige giggles. She smells the flowers and lets them tickle her nose again like it's the most amusing game in the world.

"Good luck fooling Gavin," I say.

"She won't be like this for long. I gave her a sleeping pill too."

I slap my forehead. "Ry!"

"I didn't know what else to do." He squirms, his back bumping against the doorframe.

"How much time do we have?"

"Considering this is her first time taking anything, the sleeping pill will put her under in about ten minutes."

Paige rips off her blanket and stands when I cross the room, her hospital gown hanging off her shoulder haphazardly. We embrace and she hugs me hard, her nose buried in my neck as she rocks my body back and forth. Even if she's high on Euphorium, she's still Paige. And I've missed her.

She plays with my hair when we let go.

"What happened to the red?" She studies it, her eyes lost in wonder.

"I had to change it." I pull the strands out of her hands. "Speaking of changing, how about we get you into something more comfortable?"

Paige looks down at the thin blue material as if she's seeing it for the first time.

"Okay!" She follows me to the supply closet. I don't know what to say to her in the state she's in, and she seems so entranced with the bland room, I wonder if she even remembers what we told her an hour ago. Her eyes look like they've been taped open, and the black takes over most of the brown. She's in her own world right now. A happy, numb place that won't last forever.

I pull out a pair of shorts and a yellow T-shirt with a smiley face. As expected, Paige shrieks with glee. I figured a euphoric person would appreciate a happy shirt.

Before I can stop her, she peels off her gown and crumples it into a tight ball.

"Look away!" I say to Ry as Paige tosses the wad in the direction of the kitchen.

Despite the snap in my voice, Ry's eyes stay fixed on her body. Paige's skin is a beautiful bronze. A natural pigment that I could never achieve no matter how much I baked in the sun. She's wearing a pushup bra judging by how much her breasts protrude. I try to shield Paige with my body when Ry's mouth falls open.

"Are these my clothes?" she asks after she pulls up her shorts.

"They are now." I give her a wink. "Now let's get you to the bed so you can lie down."

As we move, she keeps her eyes on the ground, trying not to step on a crack. The floor is riddled with them.

"Paige?" I say.

She looks up and her head sways. The sleeping pill must be kicking in.

I tug on her arm. "I need you to move faster."

"Oh. Okay."

This time she keeps her eyes on me. We make it across the room, and I get her to the bed and under the covers.

"I've missed you so much," she says.

"I've missed you too." I brush back her hair.

"Parker misses you the most. Do you miss him too? I bet you do." Paige's words slur as her eyelids droop.

"Of course. I've missed all of you."

I hear voices. Gavin and the rest of the gang are in the basement. I look over my shoulder, glad to see Kenny's not with them. I hope he's gone for good.

"He loves you, did you know that?" Paige says. "Maybe you can give him a chance now that you're out?"

Footsteps approach. "Shhhh…go to sleep Paige, we'll talk in the morning."

"*Sweethearts forever*," she says, her voice fading out. When I stand and turn, Gavin is right behind me.

# CHAPTER 15

"What'd she say?" Gavin asks, as Paige starts to snore.

"I'll ask her when she wakes up. She needs to rest right now." I distance myself from the bed and grab his forearm, pulling him away while I change the subject. "Did Kenny leave?"

"Don't get too excited. We'll be working with him again, I'm sure."

"Oh, joy."

Gavin shoots me a look. "He's doing damage control for us."

My pace slows as we head for the kitchen table. It feels like someone's cut the blood supply to my heart. I screwed up. And who knows when we'll be able to resume rescue missions? How many lives did I put in jeopardy? Lightheaded, I slump onto my crate.

"Does this mean we can't save the others?" I ask Gavin as he takes his seat. The table talk fades, and eyes shift in his direction, but Gavin doesn't answer right away. The sound of paper towels being ripped in half echoes in the silence. Mary's setting the table, oblivious to the mood. She hands Ry a thick section and gives Adrian the sliver that's left.

"Thanks, Mary," Adrian says, tucking his napkin into his collar like a tie. A few chuckles follow and the tension breaks.

"It's risky, but there are other ways to stop surgeries," Gavin finally says.

Before I can ask what he means, Craig puts ground beef and mashed potatoes on the table. Hands immediately dart out. I keep mine in my lap and lock eyes with Gavin. Food can wait. Besides, I'm not sure I'll be able to keep anything down tonight. Not with the impending blood on my hands.

Gavin takes a spoonful of potatoes and nods at my dish. I hold it out and he loads my plate. It's as if there's an unspoken agreement that he'll explain as long as I eat.

"There's always Plan B," Gavin says, waiting for me to stuff a bite in my mouth. The potatoes are drowning in butter and my stomach tries to reject them. I count to five silently before I think it's safe to open my mouth.

"What's Plan B?" I ask, taking a swig of water.

"We rescue them *before* they get to the hospital," Gavin says. "But it's dangerous."

"We'll need to know when the car leaves the Center, what route they'll be driving," Adrian chimes in. "Then we'll have to stop the car."

"And hope the driver doesn't have a gun," Ry adds.

"What if they do?" I ask.

"They'll shoot." Adrian shrugs like it's a no-brainer. "Technically, we'd be a threat and they'd have every right. They can just say we were trying to steal their car."

The conversation dies along with my hope. I wish I hadn't gone into the operating room, hadn't screamed. Now I have the image of Meghan's bloody body in my head and a layer of guilt coating my heart. As hard as I try, I can't finish my meal. After several minutes, I glance at Gavin's plate and notice he can't either. We exchange feeble smiles, and I gesture toward the garbage. He gives me an understanding nod. Today isn't an easy day to digest anything.

When the table clears, Sasha and Craig volunteer for dish duty. There's still some laundry left, and I load up a duffel bag and put it on like a backpack. Gavin stands as I head out. I want to be alone right now and don't look back to see if he follows. I need this little reprieve, a chance to collect my thoughts. Plan B sounds impossible. There must be a better way to get my friends out. At least we have access to the Flat House, but that means working with Kenny. And if we get Parker out, I face a different problem. I promised to give Parker a chance once we left the Center. We were young, and I didn't think Parker would hold onto an old pact. Clearly I was wrong.

Images of my kiss with Parker surface. We were on the track, and it was his sixteenth birthday. I let him beat me in a five-mile run. We were sweaty, and he leaned on me as we walked back to the gym. He put his hands on his knees, and we waited for everyone else to pass by. That was when he confessed he had a crush on me. I stood in shock, and he made his move, his lips brushing mine before I pushed him away. I'd made him tear up. It was the first of many rejections he would face. Girlfriend. Family. Health. I wince at the memory.

I avoided him for a while, but it's hard not to make amends when you live with someone day in and day out. I figured he'd move on, that his feelings for me would fade in my absence. According to Paige, that hasn't happened.

And now there's Gavin.

As thoughts of Gavin fill my brain, the duffle bag feels heavier and my body slows. There's a rhythmic beat behind me, a steady pace that will catch up with me soon. But when Gavin closes the gap, he doesn't stop.

"Let's go, slowpoke." He flashes a smile as he passes me.

The weight lifts and I chase after him, letting the fresh air tunnel down my throat. My mind calms when we reach the waterfall. Gavin throws his duffel in the meadow and helps me slip mine off. He tosses it aside and runs his fingers down my arms, bringing goose bumps to the surface. I turn slowly, and he cups my face, his thumbs caressing my cheeks as he leans to kiss me. He tastes like mint.

He pulls my face back, his mouth still partly open. His eyes flit from side to side, like he's searching for words. "I'm not giving up. We'll do what we have to do to get your friends out." His mouth settles in a spot behind my ear. Then he kisses my lobe and whispers, "I need you to trust me."

His mouth follows my jawline and his lips are so light against my cheek they tickle. Gavin's hands move to my waist. I want to tell him I do, that the world doesn't seem as dark with him in it, that my heart does backflips whenever he's near me.

"I'll try," I say before he kisses me again.

The laundry can wait.

I've never been in love with a boy. I don't know if that's what this is, but Gavin makes my heart work in ways I don't understand, speeding up with just the brush of his arm or sound of his voice. I didn't know a person could make me feel the exhilaration of running without setting foot on a track.

We swim around, talking until I can barely see his features. My fingers have pruned, and I can't feel my toes, but I don't want to leave.

"There's no way I'd make it two minutes," he says, "but I bet I can hold my breath for one." He disappears below the surface, and I start to count. At thirty seconds, I feel a ripple underwater and a hand grabs my waist. I shriek with laughter when he emerges.

"You weren't even close," I say, breathless because his hand is still on my waist.

"Is this better?" He leans in until our mouths are inches apart. I nod, and he slides his hand to my back, pressing my body into his chest. His lips are warm, enough to melt me, and for a moment I forget about how cold I am, how awful the day was. But when we pull apart I shiver, and Gavin eyes the laundry bag.

"We need to get you into some warm clothes." He climbs out and pulls me onto the bank, wrapping an arm around me as my teeth chatter.

He lets go to sift through the bag. "Here. This will warm you up." He pulls out a sweatshirt that's far too big. It smells like him, and I smile.

"Is this yours?" I ask.

"It's my old high school sweatshirt."

I look closely at the yellow emblem, an eagle holding a bat in its talons. Memorabilia from his baseball days.

"Do you ever miss your old life?"

"Nah," he says as we slip the dry clothes over our wet undergarments.

We huddle close for the walk back to the barn, his arm sliding around my shoulder.

"What about your dad? Do you miss him?"

"He's always working," he says. "It's hard to miss someone who was never there." Gavin sighs and his feet slow. "He believed science was more important than sports. Still does."

"Does he work for PharmPerfect?"

His arm tenses at my question.

"Yes," he says through a breath. "You can imagine we don't see eye-to-eye on a lot of things."

I shiver again, and Gavin holds me closer.

"He develops new drugs. He's been working on finding *the next big thing* for years." Gavin cracks off a branch that reaches into the trail, swatting the air with it. "Sometimes the family you have isn't the family you want. As much as I loved my mom, she loved what drugs could do for her, how they would make her feel, more than she loved me. When I found out people were being killed for body parts, my parents didn't believe me. My mom at least listened, but she was too scared to get involved." The twig makes a whooshing noise as he cuts the dark space in front of us. "They didn't want to help me, so I left home."

"That's when you came here?"

"Not initially." Gavin slaps a fern with the twig. "At first, I moved in with my girlfriend." He pauses for a second. "That was back when Cherry and I used to date." Another whack at a fern and the awkward moment is gone. "Then my mom found out she was sick and needed a liver transplant. She died without trying to get a donor. That was her gift to me. She didn't want to risk getting a part from someone at the Center. She wanted me to forgive her."

"Did you?"

"I had to." He tosses the stick into the brush. "But my dad didn't. He was angry she didn't use a donor, and he blamed me. Said I made my mom feel so guilty she chose death."

I'm glad it's dark, because I don't want to see Gavin's face, which I'm sure is twisted in pain.

"I moved back home with him for a while, but we fought the entire time. We both said some things that we probably shouldn't have. Finally, I decided we needed to part ways."

"When's the last time you saw him?"

"About six months ago, but nothing's changed. He's too absorbed in his science."

I lean into him and close my eyes as he guides us. In my head, I watch the magazine clippings blow away. Maybe there isn't such a thing as a perfect family after all.

• • •

I expect to have sweet dreams, ones with Gavin, preferably. But I don't.

My mom is trying to pry my little fingers off her leg. She's strong, but I don't want to let go. She finally manages to break my hands free and starts to run. The man from the SUV chases her. His tie flaps over his shoulder and I hurry after them.

She turns down a side street, but he's gaining on her, and soon they're out of sight. I hear her scream as I try to catch up, crying and calling out for her. When I round the corner, she's in the man's arms, her body limp. She's missing a shoe and her hair is over her face. The man looks up.

"Stay where you are," he says in a voice that tells me I'm in trouble. But he's not my father, and my mom isn't moving.

Now I understand what she meant. I spin around, running toward my bike. My legs are short, but I run faster than I ever have. I reach my bike and glance back as I pick it up. He's less than a block away, running with my mother in his arms. I'm so stunned it takes me a second to get going. The street colors blur as I pedal as fast as I can.

• • •

I sit up with a jolt and whack my head on the bunk above me. A male voice makes me jump again.

"Are you okay?" Gavin asks in a whisper, his mouth just inches from my face. The lights are off and the silence is deafening. It must be the middle of the night. He kneels next to the bed, stroking my hair back. I can feel the moisture pull away with the strands. Have I been crying?

"Was I…talking in my sleep?"

"A little."

"What did you hear?"

"It sounded like you were trying to get away from someone. Was it the same dream?"

"Slightly different. More like the second act."

"What happens in the next act?"

"I don't know, and I'm not sure I want to find out."

"Want to tell me about it this time?" He pulls his hand back and sits next to me.

I shake my head.

It's hard to see his face, but his head drops a little. "Well if you change your mind…"

"I won't." I just want to forget the fear.

"Try to get some sleep," he says, kissing my forehead.

When he stands to leave, my voice squeaks out his name, but I'm too afraid to tell him I don't want to be alone right now, and too proud to ask him to stay. My hands do the work for me, pulling back the covers and patting the mattress.

"Are you sure?" he asks.

I nod and shimmy over to make room.

"Don't try anything funny," he says as he climbs in. I laugh and nuzzle my face against his T-shirt. I imagine his breath against my forehead blowing out the bad dreams. It feels safe here, wrapped in his arms, and when I fall asleep, the nightmare doesn't return.

• • •

Gavin sits on the side of the bed with a cup in his hand. Steam rises and I recognize the smell of coffee. I prop myself up on an elbow.

"Caffeine?" he asks, bending down to pick up a blue mug with snowflakes. "It's the only substance I allow in my body."

I adjust myself so I can sit next to him, letting the coffee warm my face like a steam bath. It's the closest I'll get now that I don't have access to one. The Center, of course, was all about detoxifying, making us as healthy as possible.

Almost everyone is up. Mary is in the kitchen helping Sasha who looks over with an *I-told-you-so* smile.

"Aren't you going to drink that?" he asks.

I stare into my cup. My coffee is much lighter than Gavin's, but the smell makes me squeamish, like the acids will eat away the lining of my stomach.

"Not a fan?"

I scrunch my nose. "We weren't allowed to have coffee, but if it tastes anything close to what it smells like, I can't say I'm disappointed."

He takes my cup. "Then we can't be friends," he says with a playful smile. "Hungry?"

"I can definitely eat."

We join the others at the table. Paige is the only one still in bed.

"How'd you sleep?" Sasha asks me. Adrian nudges Ry, and Mary rocks back and forth on her crate as if I'm about to launch into an exciting story about princesses and dragons.

"Good," I say as Gavin slips a bowl of cereal in front of me. I grab my spoon and put a bite in my mouth. It tastes like cardboard. Old, wet, cardboard. I fake a smile and force myself to chew.

"You looked pretty cozy," Sasha says, her eyes moving from me to Gavin, fast enough for Mary to miss, but obvious enough for the rest to notice.

My cheeks burn. Gavin sits next to me and slings an arm around my shoulder. "The only thing that would have made the night better would have been a set of earplugs. I could hear you snore from across the room, Sasha," he says.

Adrian and Ry laugh, and it's Sasha's turn to blush.

Halfway through my cereal, my vision blurs and my headache is back—this time worse than before. I've been spacing my pills out, saving them for a chest ache, figuring my heart will tell me when I need my meds. But right now my brain feels like it's on fire. I groan and Gavin stands to check the wound in the back of my neck, babbling about a possible infection, but his voice becomes garbled and the room starts to tilt.

I stumble when I try to stand. Gavin catches my arm, holding me steady. He mouths a question that sounds like white noise. I think he's asking me what's wrong, but I can't get my lips to move. Mary is crying, and Sasha's face is so pale it matches the white of her hair. Adrian rushes out of the room as Gavin scoops me up. He puts me on the kitchen table and pulls the hair back from my face. Everything hurts. My head feels like it's swelling—a bike tire that's been overinflated, ready to burst.

Someone puts a cold rag on my forehead and I lie still, letting the muffled noises disappear. I close my eyes and I see my mom. Her face is radiant, her eyes as green as snow peas. She's caressing my face. Maybe I'm dying. I don't want to. I have more to do, people to save. People who need me.

And I need them…

•  •  •

Sasha is the first person I see when I open my eyes. She holds the rag against my head and smiles when I blink.

"How'ya feeling?"

"Better," I say. "What happened?"

"I was hoping you could tell me," she grunts. "Whatever it was, you passed out for a while."

"How long?"

"It's after lunch."

I look around the empty room.

"Where's Paige?"

"Ry is showing her around. Took her away from here to get something to eat. She needed some fresh air."

I understand the feeling and nod when I sit up.

"And in case you're wondering about anyone else…he went to get help."

"Gavin?"

"No, Burk," she says, snapping me in the arm with the rag. "Yes, Gavin. He knows someone who might be able to figure out what's wrong with your head."

"Cherry?"

Sasha smirks. "Don't worry, little miss prissy pants knows squat about medicine. She can tell you what the pills she takes do for her, but she can't tell you how they work."

"Who then? A doctor?" My voice escalates an octave. "What if they ask questions? What if he gets caught?"

"He's not seeing a doctor." She helps me down. "He went to see his dad."

I grimace. "I thought they didn't talk."

"They do now."

When I see white dots in my vision, I lean back against the table. Sasha joins me.

"So what happened with you two last night?" she asks.

"With Gavin? We just…talked. That's all."

"And then decided to share a bed."

"We didn't…you know…"

"I know." She throws her head back and laughs. I squirm in my seat, feeling as young as Mary. I half expect Sasha to give me the birds and the bees talk. "But you guys kissed, right?"

I don't answer her, but my face must be red because her chin bounces like I've told her.

"I'm glad." She knocks her knee against mine. "What I said about not liking you, well, you're not so bad."

"Thanks, I think." I rub my head.

"What I mean is, Gavin's like a big brother, despite the fact that I'm older than him. He helped me get my shit together. He didn't turn his back on me when I needed him, even though I let him down." She scratches her thighs and keeps her eyes on the floor. "I guess what I'm saying is, it's good to see him smile again."

I've never seen her look so vulnerable. The white spikes on her head contradict her expression. I look away in case she needs to cry.

"When Gavin saved me, I was pretty depressed," she goes on.

"Because he didn't save you in time?"

She nods in my periphery. "I was kept in isolation, then they ripped out my uterus." Her voice is shaky. I debate whether I should put my arm around her, whether she'd let me. "When Gavin brought me here, I started using any pills Ry would give me to numb the pain. Gavin helped me get sober so I could deal with my anger, but I don't know if I'll ever really get over it. The past is one thing…but I'll never get to start my own family. They stole that from me too."

I don't realize I'm crying until a drop hits my hand. I wipe my face because Sasha doesn't seem like the type of person who cares much for sympathy, but I'm not stealthy enough, and I hear her chuckle. Soon we're laughing through thick lenses of tears. When it fades out, Sasha lets out a sigh and I stand. I have a strong urge to give her space.

"I'm going to stretch my legs."

"You should really take it easy." She wipes her nose. "At least until we figure out what's going on with you."

"I'm just going to walk. The air might be good for me…do you want to come?"

"No thanks. I told Ry I'd do dishes for him. He seemed pretty eager to take Paige out. He wants to be the one to cheer her up."

"Can I ask you something?"

She tilts her head like she's unsure.

"What do you think about Ry's brother?"

"I dunno. Kenny's been helpful. He's kind of bossy, but we need him right now."

I don't know what I expect her to say, so I purse my lips and turn to leave.

"Craig doesn't trust him," she blurts out.

That makes me freeze. When I look back, her feet dance in place like she's nervous. She revealed too much. She trusts me with Craig's feelings. I'm both honored and worried about what she's about to tell me.

"What do you mean?"

"Kenny's tight with his dad. He's the son every father wants. Ry's the black sheep. He pops pills. The family's pretty much disowned him. Craig doesn't understand why Kenny suddenly changed sides."

"You don't think he's a do-gooder trying to reconnect with his brother while helping our clan of misfits?"

"The thing is…" Sasha sharpens her spiky peaks with her fingers, twirling them into points that remind me of Ms. Preen's nails. "Their dad is the CEO of PharmPerfect."

"W—what? You mean, Ry's dad?" I grip my stomach as a wave of nausea rolls over me. "Should we be worried?"

"With Ry? No. Never. That guy hates his dad."

"What about Kenny? Why would he help us?"

"He told Gavin he wants to make things right with Ry. Maybe that's why Kenny dropped out of med school."

"Do you believe that?"

"Dunno," she says. "Craig was a grade between them. He said Kenny would be the first to badmouth his brother if it worked to his benefit, especially if it made him look like the better son. He even tried to get Ry kicked off the baseball team." I grunt my displeasure. "But like Gavin said, he's useful to us."

She clasps her hands together and turns toward the sink. I leave her alone and slip into the bathroom to change my clothes, mulling over the new information.

Why hadn't anyone told me Kenny's dad runs PharmPerfect?

Do they think it doesn't matter? Does Gavin believe Kenny's changed? I certainly don't. Which leads to the question that's bugging me most: what's the *real* reason he's helping us?

• • •

By the time I return from my walk, the sky is gray, and it smells like it's about to rain. Gavin's truck is parked near the barn, and he's sitting on a bale of straw, waiting for me. His smile is timid, like he's afraid to be happy in case I'm still in pain. He stands and I inch closer until there's no space left between us. His arms slide around my waist.

"You okay?"

"Much better."

"Is your headache gone?"

"For now."

He lets go and we sit on the straw, watching the first flecks of rainfall. It doesn't take long for the cool air to circulate through the room, and I lean into Gavin, craving his warmth.

"Where did you go?" I ask, pretending not to know. I want to keep the thread of trust I have with Sasha intact.

"At first, I planned to see my dad," he admits. "Then I realized Cherry might have the answer."

"Cherry?" My tone is a little snarky. Too late to take it back.

He gives me a wry smile. "I thought she might be able to access some old files, figure out what medication you need. Looks like you need Propannalean."

"But how am I supposed to get a prescription without a doctor? I thought people at the Center didn't exist to the rest of the world."

"I'm working on that." He reaches into his jacket pocket and pulls out a bottle with a half dozen pills. "For now, she got some to tide you over."

He shakes one into my hand. Immediately, I notice there's no groove down the middle.

"Are you sure these are mine? They don't look the same."

He squints at the bottle then reaches in his other pocket. "She gave me a fact sheet. I told her you didn't need it, but she insisted I take it."

I read it out loud. "Take them with a full glass of water. Avoid heavy lifting, driving, and physical activities that might significantly increase your heart rate for at least an hour after ingesting." I shake my head. "That's odd."

"What's odd?"

"I've never followed these instructions. I would take my pill in the morning right before my first run of the day. The training never slowed down, never stopped. This doesn't make sense."

Gavin scans the paper. "It says it's for heart conditions, and this is the drug you took, right?"

Propannalean. I say the name in my head, replaying the conversation between Ms. Preen and the doctor. "Yes. I'm certain of it."

"There must be some mistake. I'll have it tested." He puts the instructions down and reaches for the pill in my hand. I close my fist. The thought of having another headache scares me more than what this pill might do to me.

"Test the other ones if you want to, but let me take this. Please. I don't know if I can handle having my brain spontaneously combust like it did this morning."

Gavin's forehead creases. He stuffs the instructions in his pocket. "I trust Cherry, but I don't trust her supplier. They could have given her bunk pills, trying to pass off Tylenol as your meds. Whatever it is, you're not getting the rest of these," he rattles the bottle, "until we know for sure what's in them."

"Deal," I say, swallowing the pill.

"You'll tell me if you feel funny?"

"I don't think I could hide it from you." I try to smile, but now that the drug is traveling through my system, I'm worried about my rash decision. He might trust Cherry, but I don't think she trusts me. What if she gave him something to harm me? I shake the thought out of my head.

He takes out his keys.

"You're leaving again?"

"I want to make sure what you're taking is safe," he says. "Stay close to Sasha in case you have a reaction." I follow him to the door. The sky is full of black, ominous clouds, and the rain is coming down by the cup-full now. I'm not sure what lab he plans to use, but I imagine a scientist's son will have access to one. I don't want him to have to face his father alone.

"I'll go with you." He has one foot outside the barn, just out of reach from the rain. "Paige is still with Ry and I'd like to see how you test it."

He looks up at the sky and then at his truck. Taking off his jacket, he wraps it around me. "All right. Let's go."

We run through the rain and he opens my door. By the time he hops in, he looks like he just climbed out of a pool.

"I dropped my keys," he says, wiping the rain off his face. I try to give him back his jacket so he can have a layer of warmth, but he waves it off. "Cover your legs with it, you must be freezing."

His T-shirt sticks to his body and he pulls it away from his skin over and over again as if the puff of air that gets sucked in each time will dry it. When he catches me smirking at his efforts, he stops. The shirt forms to his torso and my eyes can't help but drift to his arms. He's muscular, naturally strong, not from a machine or pill. Not as thick as Parker, but close.

Parker. As soon as he enters my mind, I look away.

I know I have to save him, but I don't want to face him. Not like this. I want my friend to be happy for me. My chest tightens. Somehow, I don't think that's going to be the case.

# CHAPTER 16

———

"Are we going to your dad's work?"

Gavin doesn't answer at first. "No. We can't go there. It's too risky."

"Where to, then?"

"We'll go to my house. My dad has a lab in the basement."

"You don't need his help?"

He laughs and turns on the radio. After a few stations, he finds one he likes, but keeps it low enough for us to talk without having to raise our voices.

"My dad always thought I'd follow in his footsteps. I could have. I have a knack for science." The last part comes out stiff. "I took my first steps in his lab. I don't need his help."

He starts to fidget, drumming his fingers, fiddling with the tuner. He seems uncomfortable, and if I had to guess, unsure of himself.

He takes me to Dairy Land, but instead of going inside this time, Gavin pulls into the drive thru and gets me a twist cone. I stare out the window while I eat, reading the glowing billboards that light up the dark sky. I count fourteen ads for drugs and one sign for the ferry.

"How long have you been taking Propannalean?" he asks.

I let the ice cream roll over my tongue while I think. "I've needed it for as long as I can remember."

Gavin juts out his jaw like he's considering the possibilities, but there's a sick feeling in my stomach, like a poison has entered my system. If the Center lied about foster families, could they have lied about my medication, too? Would they risk damaging my liver?

We pull off a busy road, disappearing under a canopy of trees that wind toward Gavin's childhood home. It looks like a cottage. The cedar roof has a few slats missing and the yard is overgrown. If he told me his father had moved out, abandoned the home after his mother died, I would have believed him.

The rain is barely a drizzle when we park, but we run to the porch anyway. He lifts a gnome near the doormat and picks up a silver key. His fingers shake as he sticks it in the lock.

"You know how I like order?" he says.

I smile. "I might have noticed."

"Well, you're about to see why."

He turns the handle and I stifle a gasp. The living room is cluttered with stacks of books, papers, boxes, and garbage. There are sticky notes on the walls, even pen marks where someone—I presume his dad—needed to write down a formula and couldn't be bothered to sort through the plethora of papers. He chose to share his thoughts with the house instead.

Gavin grabs my hand to pull me across the threshold, and I step over the stacks of scientific journals and books in the foyer. They're everywhere, suffocating every inch of space. I cringe, thinking about Gavin growing up here.

We move as quickly as we can through the living room, but I stop in front of an upright piano against the wall, submerged in clutter. It's dusty and covered with things that make it more of a table than a musical instrument.

Notes sound in my head. My fingers move as if I know how to play the tune. Gavin glances back at me, brows mashed together.

"Are you all right?" he asks.

I can't explain why the piano bothers me, so I lie. "I'm fine."

We press on through the kitchen where the smell of rotten food assaults my nostrils. I have to hold my breath until he can unlock the basement door. The wood creaks with each step. Halfway down, Gavin pulls on a cord and the basement lights up.

The stairwell is cold, and when we reach the bottom I see why. Along the walls there are coolers with see-through glass filled with beakers and test tubes.

Unlike the rest of the house, this room is spotless. Even the large workstation in the middle looks like it's been freshly wiped down. The smell of bleach lingers in the air. I'm grateful to be in a room where I can touch the surfaces without worrying about contaminants, but I'm also disgusted. Gavin's father clearly cares more about his workspace than his living space. What does that say about his priorities?

I sit on a round stool next to the workstation. Gavin grabs some equipment from one of the cupboards behind him and a beaker from the dishwasher by his knees.

"This is incredible," I say in awe.

"What can I say? My dad's obsessed with his work." His tone drips with sarcasm.

Gavin searches through drawers, plucking out gloves and an empty container to pour the pills into.

"Did they teach you science at the Center?" he asks.

"Only if Nutritional Science counts."

Gavin pulls out some tongs and some colored liquid. It looks like he's about to create something dangerous not extract ingredients. The truth is, I have no idea what he's about to do, and I sink into my stool, feeling helpless. Gavin seems to notice.

"Everyone in Gladstone should be required to take the class you took," he says. "They could use it." I give him a small smile and he motions toward a shelf behind me. "Why don't you grab one of those petri dishes?"

After I return with the dish, there's not much for me to do but watch him work, admiring how he furrows his eyebrows when he measures. He seems to enjoy the thrill of the test. Gavin has science in his blood—there's no denying it.

I search the room for signs of Gavin's childhood, pictures or notes for his father, but there's nothing that resembles warmth or family.

"Did your dad ever go to your baseball games?" I ask.

Gavin doesn't answer. He's carefully setting the test tube inside a container. When he closes the lid, he pushes a button and watches it spin. "After this mixes, I'll run some tests."

"There's more you need to do?"

He grabs some bottled water from one of the coolers while we wait.

"A little bit. It won't take too long."

I push the question again. "So, your dad...did he go?"

"He came for an inning once or twice." He takes a long drink. "Most of the time he'd get caught up in his work and miss the entire game. He said he was close to a breakthrough."

"What was he trying to discover?"

"He was hired to make a drug to prolong the liver. That way people could take that pill along with whatever other pills they wanted. The project was doomed to fail." He sets his water down. "At home, he works on natural drugs, things that can replace pills like this." He holds up one of my pills. "Something that won't harm the body. Like the fish oil pills he made my grandpa."

"That has to count for something."

"It would, if he didn't have the pharmaceutical companies working against him. They couldn't care less about what's in the drugs they pump out as long as they do what they're supposed to do."

"Don't people want safer pills?"

"Of course. But not when they have to pay ten times more for holistic ones. They want a quick fix, and they can get instant results with a synthetic drug."

"Why are the healthy drugs more expensive?"

The machine chimes and the whir slows. Gavin pops open the lid when it stops and pulls out the tube. The crushed powder and ingredients he added have turned the liquid an electric blue.

"Because pharmaceutical companies have their hands in a lot of pockets, they influence regulations. Organic farmers go broke trying to keep up." He flicks the tube he's holding. "Drug companies will do whatever it takes to make sure their prices are better so customers have no reason to consider an alternative."

"Let's hope your dad succeeds."

A dry laugh escapes him. "We'll see." He flips open a book full of long drug names and what looks like serial codes. More science I don't understand.

I hop off the stool. "Do you mind if I use the bathroom?"

"Down the hall. First door on your left," he calls out when I hit the stairs.

I forget to hold my breath when I enter the kitchen and hurry through to the living room. The hallway is bleak, but the temptation is too hard to ignore. I want to look around.

I push the door across from the bathroom open. It's an office, although the computer is caked with dust. A little further down, I find a door on the left. It's hard to open, blocked by something I can't see. There's a big bed taking up most of the space, along with furniture that belongs in a cabin. It smells like a laboratory in here too, and I decide it must be his dad's room.

Across from that door is the only one I haven't looked in. Unless Gavin slept in the bathroom, this has to be his.

The door handle twists with ease, and aside from the stagnant air, the room is clean and tidy. Definitely Gavin's.

There's a twin bed in the corner and a poster of a baseball stadium on the wall. A few pennants, perfectly spaced, line the room. There are trophies on a shelf above a desk and some pictures—Gavin in his glory days. He's wearing a blue baseball cap, and his smile reaches his eyes as he poses with a few players from the team. One of them is Ry, whose face and body look thicker, more natural.

I put the picture back and grab the next one, tucked away and linked to a cobweb. The velvet frame holds a photo of a formal dance. Gavin's wearing a tux and holds onto a girl with blonde hair. I recognize Cherry immediately. She looks magnificent, and I can't help but feel jealous, not because she's so stunning, but because she got to experience this with him.

All the events I've seen on shows and movies: playing sports, going to proms, attending public school. None of it will happen to me. I shouldn't feel sorry for myself, but there's a hole in my heart, an absence that will never be filled.

Cherry and Gavin go back to their spot on the shelf and I rummage through the old papers and schoolwork on his desk. They're neatly stacked with notes, as if he was in the process of filing them away. I pick up the paper on the top. It's a science test. Gavin scored ninety-nine percent, and there's a note that reads: *Your dad would be proud, nice job!* I wonder if his dad ever saw it. Based on how neat the room stayed, it didn't appear he'd been in here.

I walk over to Gavin's bed. The corner of the comforter is folded back as if it's waiting for someone. I take the hint and flop backward. The bed is firmer than I expected and it spits out a puff of dust when I land. There's a musty odor, but Gavin's scent overpowers it, like it's been woven into the fabric. I close my eyes and try to imagine what it'd be like to go to a high school dance with him. I'd wear a long, shimmery dress—maybe green to match my eyes. We'd slow dance and stay out late. He'd walk me to my door and try to steal a kiss before I had to be in for my curfew.

"Knock, knock."

I sit up, a little embarrassed, as if my daydream had been projected on the wall for him to see.

"I thought you had to use the bathroom?" He folds his arms and walks across the room, admiring some of the items he's probably forgotten about before sitting on the bed next to me.

"I got distracted."

He puts his hand on my thigh, just above the knee, but it's enough to make me blush. "Sorry about the mess out there."

"What mess?"

He laughs. "My dad can be a little extreme."

"Has he always been that way?"

He has to think about it, but he answers with conviction. "Yes, but his life kind of exploded all over the house after my mom died."

I lie back, sad that my question reminded him about his mom, but relieved Gavin didn't have to grow up in a house this messy. He stretches his body out next to me, propping his head on his hand. He traces my cheek, my jaw, my lips.

"I wish you could have met her."

"Me too," I say.

"She would have liked you." I feel a surge of heat rush to my face from his touch.

"You think so?"

"Of course. You're resilient and feisty."

I frown a little, and he continues, "You're opinionated and outspoken."

"Is there a compliment in there somewhere?"

The corners of his mouth curl. "And you're caring and optimistic. Strong, but sweet. I've never met anyone like you. You're a mixture of everything I've ever wanted. It's like you were created just for me." His hand drifts to the back of my head. "But what I like best is that you're not trying to be anything but you."

I look down for a moment, not sure how to take it all in. I try not to mumble. "That's because I'm still trying to figure out who I am."

He waits until my eyes meet his. "I think you already know. You're just trying to figure out the world around you."

It's the perfect answer, and I kiss him. Hard. His fingers tug gently on my hair and then suddenly he pulls away.

"Did you hear that?" Gavin whispers, his breath shaky.

"Gavin? Are you here?" a man calls out.

Gavin is on his feet in seconds. "Get under the bed."

"What?"

"It's my dad. Quick, hide!"

I do as I'm told, although I'm not sure why. I try to ignore the knot in my stomach that says it might be because his dad works for the company we're fighting against.

"Gavin?"

My head faces the door. When it cracks open, I see his dad's feet—they're smaller than Gavin's. His brown shoes are worn, his khakis too long and the bottoms dirty and frayed.

"Dad. You're home."

"I came home to get some files…what are *you* doing here?" He sounds timid, hopeful.

Gavin is monotone in his response. "Getting some clothes. I was just leaving."

"C-can't you stay a little longer? I'll make dinner for us."

"I'm not eating anything out of that kitchen."

"I'll order takeout." There's desperation in his voice, and I want to roll out from under the bed and push them together for a hug.

"I'm sure you have work to do. I don't want to be in your way."

"Actually, there's been a breakthrough. The project's on again. Sit with me, let's talk. I'll take the night off."

"I can't; I have to go." Gavin paces in his room like he's trapped. His dad stays in the doorway, blocking his path. Finally, Gavin concedes. "Five minutes," he says in a gruff tone. "But if you want to talk, can we do it somewhere else? Like the living room?"

"I thought you didn't like the mess."

"That's putting it mildly."

Why is Gavin being so cold? His dad is trying. And why would he not just talk in here? Is Gavin really that worried his dad will find me? Or does he not want me to hear their conversation?

"We can talk wherever you want. I can't wait to tell you about the receptor gene we've analyzed, and the LFTs—this one's strong enough for 31."

What's an LFT? And why is he excited about 31? Gavin pushes past his dad before I can find out. The door clicks shut. What am I supposed to do now?

As if he knows what I'm thinking, the door pops back open. "I just need to grab my bag, Dad," Gavin calls out. "I'll be right there. Make some room on the couch for me." He bends down and extends his hand to me. "Are you all right?"

"Why did I have to hide? And what was your dad talking about?" He pulls me out, and I notice his breathing is rapid.

"It's a long story." He grabs a bag from his closet and fills it with clothes. When he turns back, he won't look at me, and an icy prickle creeps up my spine. "I need you to climb out the window." He hands me the keys to the truck. "I'll be out there as soon as possible. Don't worry about closing the window behind you, I'll take care of it."

He kisses me on the forehead and leaves. It doesn't take a scientist to know there's something he's not telling me. I count out ten *Mississippis* before I crack the bedroom door so I can listen.

"This is what we've been waiting for!"

"What *you've* been waiting for, not me," Gavin says.

"They've even started recruiting people for the tests. Of course they have to have the right immune system—"

"Can we talk about something else?"

"Sorry, I'm just…I mean, it's been almost a decade. And now it looks like all my work has been for something."

"I suppose they have you working long nights again?"

"Well, not yet…the body hasn't been delivered to the lab."

Gavin doesn't respond immediately, and I open the door a little further to keep from missing his answer. What body?

I hear someone exhale and stand. Gavin's voice follows. "That's what I was afraid of. I have to go."

I pull the door closed and rush to the window, opening it far enough to wiggle through so I can drop to the ground. The high grass and weeds hide me as I run, keeping my body low. The truck is parked sideways, and I'm able to dart around to the passenger side and climb onto the floor behind the seat.

Before I can get comfortable, Gavin opens the driver's side door. He extends his hand for the keys, and when I hold them out, he snatches them away. I don't say anything until we make a few turns and the truck has settled into a straight path.

"Can I come out now?"

"What?" Gavin sounds startled. "Yes. Sorry."

"Did you forget I was in here?"

"No, I, uh, was just thinking."

"Care to talk about it?"

He shakes his head as he stares at the road, and I realize I don't know Gavin as well as I probably should.

# CHAPTER 17

Aside from Gavin confirming the pills are for my heart condition, we hardly speak on the drive back. It's like there's an invisible wall between us.

At least the rain clouds have moved on.

When we pull in, I see Craig's car and excitement courses through me. Ry borrowed it, which means he's back with Paige. A moment later, I see they're outside playing Frisbee with Craig and Sasha. Paige waves at me, her face fixed in a smile.

I growl inside when I consider why and rush over to her, saying hello to everyone before spinning Paige around so her back faces Gavin. "How are you holding up?"

"Great!"

I give her my *let's be serious* face, but Paige is all smiles. "Are you on something?"

Ry leaves his spot and jogs over to us. The game has stopped, and I relax when I glance over to see Sasha and Craig have Gavin trapped in conversation.

"She just needed a little more, that's all," Ry says, his pupils dilated.

"You're on Euphorium too," I say, shaking my head. Paige mumbles something about missing the red as she plays with my hair, and I swat her hand away.

"Let's go for a walk." I lead Paige by the arm. We climb the fence by the trough and cut through the field to avoid Gavin.

"Wait for me." Ry chases after us, and I can't say no because I don't want him to get in trouble either.

I ask Paige to race me to get her to stop frolicking through the tall grass. She's faster than Ry, but her competitive edge has slowed on the drug, and she loses to me by several feet.

"That was fun," she says. "It's much better than running on the track."

"I have a surprise for you guys," I say.

"What is it?" Ry claps his hands repeatedly.

"You'll see." I wave them forward and have to remind them about the surprise every so often to keep them moving. Ry thinks it's imperative to point out every flower and bug on the way, and Paige is much too willing to engage him.

There is no surprise, of course, and I'm glad Ry's not disappointed when we reach the waterfall. Both he and Paige start to strip off their clothes, and I have to beg them to keep a little bit covered. Paige leaves her shirt and underwear on. Ry sticks to his boxers. I know when they hit the water, they'll be glad they did. Or at least I will.

Their reaction to the cold isn't as quick as it was for me. Does being a redhead really make my processing speed faster? I wait on the bank in the sun that shines an oversized rock. It takes Paige a shorter amount of time to come around, and she climbs out and sits next to me. I put an arm around her to control her shivering.

"Are you back to normal, Paige?"

Her lip quivers, but I don't think it's just from the cold. "For now."

We hug and I feel her shudder. "I'm so sorry about Meghan."

"Yeah. Me too." She breathes into my hair. Her body's so cold I'm reluctant to let go. "I never thought I'd miss the Center, but at least I wasn't afraid before."

"I know what you mean."

"Did they cut you?" She pulls back, examining me with lucid eyes for the first time since she's been here.

"No. Gavin and Ry got me out in time."

"And you helped save me."

I nod. "We tried to go back for Meghan, but we were too late."

I dry my eyes, and she hugs me again. "I'm glad you're here. It's not as scary having you by my side."

Ry splashes us, and Paige lets herself laugh through the tears.

"Where'd you and Ry go today?"

"He took me to a pizza place." She smiles at the memory. "I think I'm in love."

My breath catches in my throat. "With Ry?"

"No." She socks me playfully in the arm. "With pizza."

"Thank goodness."

"He's not so bad." Her eyes drift back to the water. Ry is floating on his back.

"He's a good guy. Just…go easy on the Euphorium."

"We didn't spend the entire day high. This morning we found a spot overlooking the city center and talked for a while. We watched the ferry come in and he took me to lunch. It was really nice, actually."

I shake my head to recover from the shock. "Ry did all that?"

"Let's just say, he knows what it's like to feel disconnected from things." She wipes her eyes. There's a hardened maturity to her expression. "Ry's been a good friend so far, but I can't promise you I won't need more drugs to stop the pain. My heart's been ripped in half."

"I just don't want to see you zoned out all the time, you know? I like being able to talk to you. Like this." I bump her with my shoulder. "Besides, it's not fun to race you when you're not really trying."

That makes her laugh, a deep laugh, enough to bring Ry out of the water to join us.

I toss his clothes at him and watch him give Paige a flirty show as he puts his shirt on. She tears her eyes from Ry when he struggles to get his pants on over his wet boxers. "Ry says you guys are going to save Parker next," she says.

"When he turns eighteen, they'll move him to the Flat House," I say. "That's where they test new drugs. The security will be tight, but we're working on a plan."

"The day before I left, Parker was talking to some guy about a job doing clinical trials once he got out." She squeezes my hand. "Since no families seemed interested in him, he agreed."

"I don't think he really had a choice," I mutter.

"They made it sound like he'd make a ton of money. He thought it would be good to have some security, start a new life. Meet up with some old friends." Another squeeze, although she might as well have her hand around my stomach.

One night when Parker and I were forced to run extra laps for doing cannon balls near our trainer, he told me he'd prove his feelings were genuine. "I'll get a job and take you on a real date—the fanciest restaurant in Gladstone."

I don't know which thought makes me more uncomfortable: telling Gavin about Parker's feelings for me or telling Parker about my relationship with Gavin.

"We should get back." I stand abruptly, but Paige doesn't let go of my hand.

"Don't worry, I've already told Ry."

My heart plunges into my gut. "Told him *what*?"

Ry looks at me without judgment. "She said he's in love with you."

I pull my hand away from Paige's and cross my arms. It's as if Ry can see right into my heart, that he can tell there's a part of me that does care for Parker. The guilt is unsettling. "No, Parker just thinks he is." I shrug and hold myself tighter.

"Look, I'm not going to say anything to Gavin," Ry says.

Paige's mouth drops open. "Gavin? The guy with the truck?"

"Yes." I move out of the sun's spotlight, suddenly feeling very exposed.

"I didn't know—I'm sorry." She glances back at Ry with a scowl. "Why didn't you tell me?"

"I figured they were just having a little fun."

"Are you?" Paige asks.

"No. I mean, I don't know." I want to jump into the water,

drown out this entire conversation. "I like him…a lot." Too much, I might add.

"And Parker?"

"You know how I feel about him, Paige." I bite my lip. Parker is like warm soup after a cold run. It's comforting, but you're still hungry for something more. "It's Parker. He's one of my best friends."

"I just thought with the pact—"

"He told you about that?" I snap.

"What pact?" asks Ry, tugging on his pants.

"They agreed that once they got to the outside they'd try dating," says Paige. "Tabitha wanted to make sure it was real, that Parker didn't just have feelings for her because they were confined to the Center."

I bury my head in my hands. I feel like a cheater, only I haven't done anything wrong.

Except not tell Gavin.

"Please don't breathe a word of this," I say. "Gavin needs to hear it from me first."

"Are you going to give Parker a chance?" Paige asks.

"No." It comes out strong, but it doesn't sound like I mean it. Gavin feels new and exciting. Parker is safe. There's a kinship and years of trust. I know Parker's secrets. Gavin has mystery, which, to be honest, scares me a little. The unknown makes me afraid to get close.

Ry pretends to lock his lips with a key. "It's none of our business. We'll stay out of it."

He holds out a hand for Paige. She takes it, and I feel a prick of unease. Paige accepts Ry's hand without question. She barely knows him, but she doesn't hold back. How can I ask her to work through her issues when I haven't?

"I'm going to head out." Before they can object, I slip behind the waterfall's curtain. My legs speed up, and soon I'm running— far away from my feelings and any secrets that I'm afraid will pull me under.

• • •

My emotions are still festering when I reach the barn. I'm not ready to face Gavin, so I head toward the van where Adrian is tinkering with the motor, his face buried in the open hood.

"Car trouble?" I ask.

"It's always something." He shoots me a sideways glance. "Can you hand me the spark plug by my foot?"

I grab what he needs and reach into the hole. His face strains as he works the plug into place.

"There! Got it."

Once he's upright, I decide to pry. "Are you any good at science, Adrian?"

"Not according to my mom."

"Well, do you know what an LFT is?"

He wipes his hand on his shirt while he thinks—although it's so greased up, it's hard to tell where the new marks are. "Liver Function Test, I think. Why? Do you need one?"

"No, no. I just heard someone at the hospital talking about LFTs." I hate lying to Adrian, but I don't want Gavin to know I was listening to him and his dad. "It must be painful."

"Not really, they just need to draw some blood."

"That's it?"

"Yep. They can figure out the enzyme levels and a bunch of other stuff. The high school did a blood drive, and I remember seeing something about it on the pamphlet near the cookie table." He raises an eyebrow. "Now a biopsy, that's the painful one, or so I've been told."

"I'll steer clear of that one. Thanks, Adrian," I say, walking away.

"If you have any more questions, just ask Gavin. He's the resident science geek around here."

I give him a reticent smile as I head inside the barn.

Mary's in the kitchen helping Gavin pack some food. "Where're you going?" I ask her.

"We're having a campfire tonight."

Gavin's mood seems to have lifted. He smiles and it's hard not to return it. My body feels a gravitational pull when he's near, with my heart leading the way.

"We thought everyone could use a little cheering up," he says. "We'll have hotdogs, chips, cantaloupe…and some watery lemonade."

"Hey! I made that," Mary says, although she looks only slightly offended.

"And I promise to drink at least one cup," Gavin says. "Or maybe half."

Mary's giggle warms the room, and I gather my courage. "Gavin, do you have a minute?" I want to come clean about Parker, but I also want to ask him what happened at his dad's house. I'm still a little unnerved by how he needed to hide me and how he stayed clamped shut for most of the ride here.

He takes out half of the napkins Mary has put in the bin and holds up a finger. "Can it wait? I promised Mary I'd take her to get the makings for s'mores."

"Sure." I try to sound aloof, but I must not have pulled it off because he stops what he's doing and looks up.

"If it can't wait—"

"No. It's fine. It's nothing."

"I figured you'd want to spend some time with Paige, so I asked Mary to go with me."

"Absolutely." I whisper in Mary's ear, "Make sure you get a lot of chocolate." She winks at me as she grabs Gavin's hand.

I watch them leave, wondering if I should have pressed more. I hear the hatch clang and know it's too late. I've missed my chance.

# CHAPTER 18

Paige and Ry take another Euphorium pill as soon as they learn Gavin is gone. If Burk, Sasha, and Craig notice, they don't say anything. We play cards on the floor, and Paige laughs her way through, tilting her hand way too often. At least she doesn't mind losing.

Ry plays just as badly, only it's because he's staring at her with a drug-crazed fascination. I wonder about his tolerance and how he gets his pills. Unless he steals them, it doesn't seem like he'd have much to sell or give. Not when he's spending his days in a barn rather than at a paying job.

At the start of the next shuffle, the door opens. Ry's eyes light up, and I turn to see his brother standing in the doorway.

"Kenny," Ry says, throwing down his cards and hustling over to greet him.

They exchange a few words and Kenny slips something in Ry's hand. Ry puts it in his pocket and my body clenches. Kenny is feeding Ry's addiction. As Kenny walks over to join us, the uneasy feeling grows, like a balloon of distrust inflating in my chest. Ry wanders toward the kitchen to get a glass of water.

"How's it going?" Kenny asks, introducing himself to Paige and plopping down next to me. His knee touches mine and I scoot over. "Don't worry, I won't bite," he says.

"Gavin's not here," I say.

"I didn't come to see Gavin."

The game has stopped, but my cards are fanned, covering my nose and mouth. I realize how cowardly I look and lower them, posturing up, but still falling several inches short of being equal in size to Kenny.

"I came to check on Paige." He stares at her with admiration, and Paige can't help but react with delight. Kenny is attractive and she's drugged up. "How're you doing?" he asks her.

"I'm hanging in there," Paige says.

Ry takes the seat on Kenny's left. Seeing them side by side is almost too much for me to bear. It's as if Kenny has absorbed all the beauty out of Ry, whose frame is frail and cheeks are hollow. The model-like looks Ry has fade now that Kenny has joined the circle. Approachability is the only category where Ry is winning.

"We're having a campfire tonight. You should come," Ry says.

"Are you sure?" Kenny looks around. No one in the group seems irritated but me. Even Craig, who told Sasha he didn't trust the guy, grins at the idea.

Kenny's eyes stop on mine.

I shrug. "It's not my call."

"If you have a problem with it…"

"I don't want to make the decision for everyone else." He's put me on the spot and he waits for me to hang myself. He's here to help; I'm sure that's all anyone else sees. "Whatever." I tap the floor with my finger. "Are we playing or what?"

Craig picks up his cards.

"Great. Over dinner I can tell you how we're going to save your friend Parker." Kenny pats me on the back and I grit my teeth. "What are we playing?" he asks Craig.

"Hearts."

"One of my favorites. Deal me in."

• • •

I try to keep myself busy in the kitchen after cards, but Kenny lingers, shadowing my every move. He stands next to me with a dishtowel so he can dry the lunch dishes that have been sitting for hours. We're going to need them to eat tonight, but the food is caked on and the scrubber is worn down to the plastic handle, making it nearly impossible to clean them. Now I understand why Ry avoids dish duty.

"Your friend Paige seems to be doing all right," Kenny says.

"That's because she's masking the pain." I push a washed plate into his hands and take my aggression out on the next dish.

"Give her time. The medicine will help absorb the shock of it all. Euphorium was created to help people grieve. It's a wonderful drug for those who need it."

"What happens when she can't stop taking it?"

"Who's to say that's going to happen?"

Out of the corner of my eye, I see his hands move in slow, methodical circles as he dries the plate.

"Your brother seems to enjoy it," I say. "Is he grieving?"

"You could say that." Kenny snorts a laugh. "He's grieving the loss of himself." I cringe at how cold his voice sounds. "Besides, rumor has it you're on something. Am I right?"

"That's different. I need it for my heart." The water sloshes out of the bin I'm hunched over and Kenny places a hand on my hip as he wipes it up. He doesn't let go right away, and I count to five in my head. That's how long he has until I break his arm.

I hear Mary's laugh and unclench my hand. She doesn't need to see violence when she's already been through so much. Luckily, Kenny lets go and turns his attention back to the dishes before Gavin and Mary come in. Mary runs over to join Ry and Paige in a game where they try to toss cards into a bowl. Gavin looks surprised to see Kenny but pushes out a smile.

"What are you doing here?" he asks, setting the groceries on the table.

"I thought I'd check on the newest member of your crew." Kenny gestures toward Paige.

Gavin's lips are pursed, and I can't help but wonder if he's bothered by the unexpected visit. He carries on as if he's not, unpacking the supplies and setting the marshmallows, graham crackers, and chocolate in a dry bin for our campfire.

"Are you staying for dinner?" Gavin asks Kenny. The question is monotone, too difficult for me to get a read on how Gavin really feels.

"Of course. I couldn't turn down Tabitha's invitation."

My fingers coil around the dish and my mouth drops open to object. I snap it shut when I see Gavin's face. He's smiling, and it washes away any uneasiness I thought I noticed.

Gavin walks around me to put something on the shelf, and when he's done, he kisses the side of my head. He leaves Kenny and me to finish the last few cups in the bin.

"I never thought I'd see that happen," Kenny says when Gavin is out of earshot. "He hasn't dated since high school, and then, there was only one girl that could capture his heart."

Cherry.

"You must have done something right," he adds. His words don't sound reassuring. They sound seductive. Vile. A ceramic mug slips out of my grip and shatters on the floor.

Kenny puts his hand on my shoulder like I need consoling. "Don't worry. I'll clean this up." He grabs the broom in the corner of the kitchen while I pick up the large pieces, slicing my finger on one in my rush to clean the floor with as little help from Kenny as possible.

Why am I letting him get to me? What is it about him that makes me so angry? Before I can unclench my jaw, Gavin rushes over and squats down to examine my hand.

"You're bleeding. There's some antiseptic in my truck."

I start to shrug it off but realize it would get me away from Kenny, and that's something I don't want to turn down.

• • •

The stars aren't as bright as they are near the ocean. At least not tonight.

Gavin pokes the logs as we sit around the fire pit Burk and

Craig built between the shed and the barn. Sasha insisted we have the hose ready, just in case the fire got out of control.

"With Ry on drugs," she said, "anything's possible."

Paige and Mary gorge themselves on marshmallows. Ry drowns his bun in mustard before slapping a burnt hotdog on it. Kenny doesn't eat. From where I'm sitting, his face looks like it's being licked by the flames. He's as far away from me as possible, but it's a direct line of sight. I'm forced to either stare back or look to the side. I finally let him command my attention when he starts to explain the plan to rescue Parker, although my stomach churns in disgust at the notion of taking orders from Kenny.

"They've already started giving Parker the trial drug. They wanted to measure the short-term effects, and now that they have, they'll move him to the Flat House in a couple of weeks to undergo the *real* tests. He's agreed to go because they've promised him an absurd amount of money."

I think back to what Gavin told me, how people volunteer to be test subjects to make some quick cash—as well as try new drugs. They're not the ideal candidates, but since no surgeries are being performed, what goes on there is common knowledge.

"But won't people question Parker about his background?" I ask.

"During the trial, Parker will only be allowed to talk to doctors and testers," says Kenny, the fire reflecting in his eyes. "Even if he did talk about the Center, he'll be too drugged to make much sense. The doctors will push him to the point where his body shuts down. That way, they can assess how much a person can handle. It helps the drug companies evaluate dosage."

"Shut down? Don't they want to keep him intact?" I say. "I mean he's from the Center. They'll send him to the hospital when they're done with him, right?" I thought we'd have more time in case we weren't able to get him out of the Flat House. At least we're familiar with hospital missions, even if my scream made them bulk up security.

"That's not how it works," Kenny says. "The scientists like his vitals. They want a full report on the drug's effects in order to get approval to market it to the public. They've been given orders to push him to the limit."

It feels like an ember has wedged its way inside my skin, burning a hole in my chest. I clench and unclench my hands at my sides. I won't let the Center take another friend from me.

"What kind of drug are they giving him?" Burk asks. His voice squeaks like mine would had I asked the question.

"It gives you energy. And power."

"Don't they already have drugs like that on the market?" Sasha asks.

"Not like this one." Kenny's voice falters for a split second, but any trepidation fades when he continues. "This drug can be used to help cancer patients that are weak from chemotherapy."

Heads nod in approval—all but Gavin's and mine.

"Tell them what else it's for," Gavin says, jabbing his stoker into the fire.

Kenny's sitting next to him, and he gives Gavin a faint scowl. "It can also be used for soldiers in combat."

"For war?" Sasha asks. Craig puts his arm around her as if the concept threatens her.

"That's one possible use," Kenny says.

The pieces from my past fall into place. Parker being forced to work out, to build his muscles; being led to believe no one wanted him. I doubt the Center even looked to match his organs with a donor. He's been groomed for this experimental combat drug. To be their lab rat. I shudder.

"So what's the plan?" Gavin asks. "It needs to be foolproof." He pulls the stoker out of the flame, pointing it toward Kenny.

"It's your lucky day then, 'cause I've got one." Kenny's voice is smug as he leans back in his chair. "I took the liberty of looking at the Flat House schedule. The Wednesday after Parker's sent there, a new staffer is scheduled to start. I'll call the guy the morning of his shift and tell him he's not needed. Then I'll take his place."

"Wednesday? What if it's too late?" I sit up. "What if Parker doesn't last that long?"

"He will," Kenny says. "On Monday he'll get a mild injection of the drug, right into his bloodstream. Tuesday they'll increase the dosage and will have him do some minor tests. The third day is when the action happens. That's when he'll have enough of the drug in him to really do some damage. I'm going to convince him to break down one of the exit doors, and I'll chase after him. Adrian, Burk, and Gavin can wait out back in the van."

I hate how much he seems to salivate about watching the drug's effects on Parker, but I have to admit, his plan might work.

Adrian sounds wary. "The Flat House will sound an alarm if Parker escapes. They'll be on high alert. There's no way the van will get out of the lot without being searched." He stuffs another marshmallow in his mouth and holds it in his cheek.

All eyes shift back to Kenny. "That's a good point, Adrian. We'll need a second vehicle." He looks around as if he's waiting for volunteers.

"We can use my car as a decoy," says Craig. "I'll squeal my tires and drive in circles to distract them."

Gavin nods. "With eyes on the car, the van should be able to get away."

"Ry can ride with me," Craig adds. "Hell, I might even have him drive."

"Mary, you stay back and protect the girls," says Kenny. She giggles when he winks at her. As dangerous as this mission is, I want to be there when Parker gets out. Part of me doesn't think I deserve to go, but I hate the idea of staying behind. I try to catch Gavin's eye, but he's fixated on the fire.

"We'll need a signal," says Adrian. "Something that lets us know they've surrounded the car so we can leave."

"Easy. We'll honk the horn." Craig says.

"What will they do to Ry and Craig if they're caught?" I ask.

"They can just say they were messing around. The back lot is for deliveries," says Gavin. "It's pretty open, perfect for figure eights. Kids have been caught racing there, so it won't look too suspicious."

"What if they stop the van?" Paige asks. She looks petrified. Any Euphorium in her system has metabolized.

"That's one reason we need to keep anyone from the Center away from the Flat House," Kenny says. "They'll be safe here."

Gavin looks at Sasha and Mary first, then his eyes drift to me. "Kenny has a point," he says. "Adrian and I have IDs. The worst that can happen is they haul us to jail." He holds my gaze long enough to make heat rush to my face. "I'm not going to risk losing any of you."

For a moment it's just us, but when I look away, I see Kenny staring at me, and my body tenses again.

"It sounds simple enough," says Sasha. "But Kenny, how are you going to convince Parker to break the door? Tell him it's a strength test?"

"No. I've got a better idea." He stands, and from my angle, it's like he's rising out of the fire. "We'll tell him she's waiting for him outside." He points at me. Gavin looks confused, and Paige and Ry turn to each other. Their bodies seem to shrink into one. Kenny's grin is devilish. "He won't be able to resist seeing the love of his life. Will he, Tabitha?"

There's a pop as one of the logs releases a pocket of trapped air. As much as I don't want to look up, I do. Gavin's face is taut. His head stays down as he tosses the stoker in the fire and walks away. Ry and Paige are huddled into one another, avoiding my eyes.

So much for keeping secrets.

It's too quiet for me to leave without anyone noticing. I feel eyes on my back as I get up to search for Gavin. He's leaning against one of the horse stalls. The light is dim, but it's brighter than the campfire. All the questions he's collected on his walk into the barn show on his face.

I don't know where to begin. Gavin starts the conversation for me. "When were you going to tell me?"

"I was waiting for the right time, but then…I just…" Guilt

needles my insides, and my shoulders sag. "I'm sorry. I should have told you earlier. Parker and I…we were good friends, then there was this kiss." Gavin's eyebrow shoots up. "It's not what you think. He caught me off guard. I don't think of him like that."

"But he thinks of you in that way." I can see he's not mad, but his body is tight, his arms folded.

"Yeah, but last I checked I was in charge of my emotions."

He doesn't smile, but the corner of his mouth twitches like it wants to.

"So we're not going to save him because he cares about me?"

"That's not what I'm saying." Gavin holds up his hands in defense. "Look, maybe we moved too fast. I don't want to get in the way of anything."

"Or maybe you're overreacting." Still no smile. "Parker and I are friends. When we lived at the Center, he wanted something more."

"Did you?"

"Yes and no." It feels like a lame answer, but it's the truth.

His eyebrows push together.

"It felt like I didn't have a choice, that we were only interested in each other because we were both there. I told him when we were on the outside I'd reconsider. If there was anything there, I wanted it to be real, not forced. I wanted to find someone based on compatibility, not circumstance." Gavin's guard is down and I seize the opportunity to press my body into his. "And I did, Gavin. I found you."

He embraces me and lets out a sigh. The air filters through my hair, warming my neck.

"I don't want to get in the way. Are you sure this is what you want?"

The answer comes out easier than I expected. "I'm sure."

# CHAPTER 19

That night, my dream is so vivid even the pain feels real. My shins are covered in scratches, and the bush I'm hiding behind claws at me every time I shift. I hear the sprinklers kick on and I try to shield my body with leaves. The spray hits me anyway.

I'm wet and uncomfortable. Even though the SUV is gone, I don't want to move.

My body tenses when the front door creaks open. I catch a glimpse of a girl skipping down the porch steps. She looks a little older than me, maybe seven. She spots my bike leaning casually next to the stair rail. I wanted it to look like it belonged here.

"Mommy!" she squeals. "Did you buy me a new bike?"

Her mom shouts back a sharp "no" from inside the house, but the girl isn't deterred. She examines the bike, running her hands along the seat and peering into the basket. She rings the bell, and I want to call out for her to leave it alone, but I'm paralyzed with fear. My mouth opens. Instead of speaking, I start to cry.

"Who's there?" The girl looks around. Her hair is thick and frizzy, and she wipes a clump away from her eyes.

I shift in my hiding spot and the bush rustles, sending my heart into a panic.

Footsteps approach. "Hello?"

I tuck myself back into the house, but she moves the leaves aside, peering in with big blue eyes.

"What are you doing in our bushes?"

I have no choice but to crawl out. I wipe any remaining tears before I stand, only to realize my hands are dirty, which means now my face is too. My eyes drop to my dress, fiddling with the tear in the hemline from where I snagged it.

Ashamed and embarrassed, I don't answer her.

"What are you doing in there?" There's a hint of excitement in her voice. "Playing hide-and-go-seek?" When I look up, she's smiling and I feel my mouth twitch like it wants to as well.

Our heads turn in unison when her mom comes onto the porch.

"Mommy, look! I found a girl in our bushes."

"What on earth!" The woman storms down the stairs, grabbing my chin and turning my head from side to side. Her breath smells like sour milk. "Get inside. Both of you." She pushes me up the stairs when I don't move fast enough.

She slams the door behind me and I freeze in the middle of the room. The lock clicks.

"What's your name?" she says, her voice noticeably calmer than before. My hands tremble as I turn to face her.

"Tabitha. Tabitha Jane Rhodes."

"Are you lost?"

"N-no. M-my mom. She was taken."

"Taken?" The woman reaches for my hair, sliding the red strands between her fingers. "Do you know why?"

"A man came out of a car. She told me to run."

The lines on her forehead stack up like she's filing information into the creases. Then, her eyes flicker with life, and she smiles. "Would you like something to eat?" She ushers me into the kitchen along with her daughter and rips open the tops of two chocolate puddings. My mouth waters when she drops spoons on the table. "Eat this while I make a few calls."

"This is the best day ever," the girl says, taking a gigantic bite. "I made a new friend *and* I get chocolate."

We laugh, and I forget my fear for a moment.

Her mom talks excitedly to whoever is on the phone. "How much did you say?" When I glance over, she steps out of the room.

I'm halfway done with my pudding when she reemerges. She

grabs something from the cupboard and washes it down with a glass of water. Then she walks over to the table and squeezes my hand. Her fingers are cold.

Our eyes meet. "Did you find my mom?"

"No." She pushes her lip out apologetically. "But, uh, do you happen to know if your father is home?"

I shake my head. "But my mom says he'll be back in three weeks."

"Maybe she can stay with us!" the little girl says, scraping out the last bit of pudding.

"Not tonight, dear. She has somewhere to be." Her finger runs down my jawline. The nail is sharp, but I force myself to smile. Maybe we're going to the police station, where they can track down my mother and the mean man who took her.

She hurries us outside and into her car, humming a happy tune while she drives. But when we park in front of a plain gray building, my heart sinks.

There are no police cars in the parking lot and no officers inside.

The mom whispers to someone at the front desk, and a man in a lab coat comes out.

"Per our agreement," he says to the woman. He gives her an envelope, and she clutches it against her chest like it's a bandage she's been waiting for—something to stop the bleeding.

The man extends a hand to me, and I take it. At the same time, the mother grabs her daughter by the wrist. The little girl tries to wave but is yanked out of the room before I can say goodbye. The doctor tugs and I obediently follow. We go through a set of double doors, and he asks me to stick out my finger. He pricks it and sends a drop of blood through a machine. A paper spits out the other side, and he examines it with a smile.

He gets me a glass of water before handing me a pill. "Take this," he says.

"What for?"

"It'll help you feel better."

My mother taught me to respect adults, so I do as he says.

• • •

I don't wake up afraid, just perplexed.

The dreams come in sequences, and I'm always six. They play out through my eyes, like a recording, or a memory. My head hurts and I press my temples as I sit up in bed. The room is dark, and as my eyes adjust, I see bunk beds and hear the snores of heavy sleepers.

I grab the medication Gavin got me, and head to the kitchen for some water. I take one of the pills, but instead of crawling back into bed, I tuck the bottle in my pocket and sneak out of the room. I'm too alert to sleep, and if my headache progresses, I'm not going to want to be around anyone—not even Gavin.

The cool morning air bleeds through the barn doors, and I walk out to the driveway to breathe it in. The sky has a thin veil of light. It must be dawn.

I find myself walking toward the trail where I can sort out the haunting images from my dreams. Is this my mind's way of processing everything that's been going on? The reality of my life? The uncertainty of my future? And if so, what do they mean? Are the bushes symbolic of me hiding from those around me? Am I keeping myself hidden from Gavin?

I pause to answer my own question and realize I've made it halfway to the waterfall. I keep going, assured that the movement is helping my mental state, although the headache shows no sign of letting up.

I want to trust Gavin. He hasn't given me any reason not to. He's secretive at times, but I'm no better. I didn't tell him about Parker as soon as I should have.

Thinking about Parker makes my head throb even more. Am I rushing into things with Gavin? Should I give Parker a chance? Refusing to let myself start down another emotional path, I press on. This isn't about Gavin or Parker. It's about me. But when I try to look inside myself, it's like I'm peering through a window with an obstructed view. I just don't know what's in the way.

The waterfall booms in the still of the morning. I didn't intend to swim, but now I want to jump in and wash away the bad dreams.

The water is so cold it burns. My head pulses with pain, but I force myself to stay submerged until I'm too numb to feel much of anything. My arms are pale and my hairs stand on end. I pull myself onto the bank, dressing quickly. Just as I'm about to leave, the chatter of birds stops. I wring out my hair and look up. Wings flap as the birds abandon their branches, either ready for breakfast or spooked by something in the forest.

Then I see a familiar face emerge from behind the waterfall.

Kenny stayed the night at the barn, and he followed me here.

"What are you doing?"

"I wanted to apologize." He comes closer. "For outing you last night."

"I don't know what you're talking about." I rub my arm to erase the gooseflesh.

"About Parker. Ry tells me you two were close."

"He doesn't know what he's talking about." Water drips from my nose, and Kenny takes off his jacket. It's thin but dry. I want to put it on, to feel some sense of warmth right now, but I won't give him the satisfaction of making me feel better.

"I don't need your coat," I say with more venom than necessary.

"Yes, you do." He throws it at my face and I catch it. My hands shake, betraying my words. When I try to get around him, he blocks my way and I zero in on his jaw, imagining the sound of it cracking.

"Just hear me out. Five minutes, that's all I need," he says.

I wouldn't be so cold if I could run back to the barn. If he's going to make me listen, I might as well be warm. I put on the jacket with disgust on my face. But on the inside, I'm terribly grateful. My shiver slows and I sit on the rock, wishing the sun would hurry up and do its job.

He tries to sit next to me, but I don't move until it's obvious he's going to sit regardless. I slide to the very edge of the rock, as far from Kenny as possible.

His shoulders sag. "Why don't you like me?"

"I don't trust you." My teeth clatter when I speak. "Now what do you want? I'd like to get back to the barn."

"Is this because I cut your neck?" He tries to lift my hair, and I tuck my head into my body like a turtle. "Look, Tabitha, I'm sorry I followed you. I didn't know you were going for a swim. I'm not trying to make you feel uneasy." He sighs. "I know you've been through a lot—and I know my dad's to blame—but don't hate me because of his choices. I just want to help. Honest." He stands and my body relaxes. I shift toward the center of the rock. He points in the direction of the barn. "I saw you leave this morning and thought if I got you alone, then maybe you'd hear me out. For what it's worth, I'm sorry about what happened to you."

Kenny turns to walk away and part of me feels guilty—a very small part, but enough to make me question my own judgment. Have I been wrong about Kenny? What if he's the only chance we have to get the rest of my friends out?

"I wasn't going for a swim." He stops and looks back at me. "I came here because of my headache." The admission feels like a small token. Not worth much, but enough to let him know I'm not full of hatred all the time.

"Headache?" It comes out as more of a statement than a question. I think I see the corner of his mouth twitch, and I look away, ashamed I'm judging him again.

"The headaches started when I ran out of my heart medication."

"You ran out?" I glance up to read his face. His eyes are lit up with concern. "Why didn't you say something? I can get you more."

"Gavin already did…only my headaches aren't going away."

Kenny runs his hand under his chin. "Let me guess, he got them from Cherry?"

How did he know that?

"Yes," I say, my voice small. He chuckles to himself. "What's so funny?"

"Cherry can be…how should I put it? Conniving."

Kenny comes back to the rock and extends a hand, and while I don't like the way my stomach curls in on itself at his touch, I don't trust Cherry anymore. He helps me up and explains while we walk.

"Cherry has one goal in life: to win Gavin back. She'll stop at nothing to get what she wants. It's a way of life for her. She wants flawless skin: she takes a pill. She wants her hair to grow: she takes a pill. She can't take a pill to get Gavin back—but she can give you pills, can't she?"

I have an urge to throw up, rid myself of whatever it was I took this morning.

"What do you think she gave me?"

"Who knows, but I'm sure it's not to make you prettier."

"But Gavin tested them. He made sure the pills were legit."

"I don't mean to knock your boyfriend down a notch, but he doesn't have much of an education. His science skills are limited. I'm sure Cherry has contacts that could get certain things to show up so the pills you're taking match the ones you really need."

My fingers curl, but I decide to sidestep his comment about Gavin, at least until I know if Cherry is trying to kill me. I relax my hands. "You think she'd do that?"

"You're her biggest obstacle, the one thing that stands between her and Gavin."

"How does she even know we're…together?" I'm not sure if that's the word I should use, but it feels awkward to refer to Gavin as my boyfriend in front of Kenny when I haven't even said it to Gavin yet.

"I didn't want to tell you this, but I ran into Cherry at the mall the other day. She said she could tell there were sparks between you two, and I didn't deny I saw the same thing."

Part of me is elated. It's validation that there's chemistry. Proof, as if I don't know my own heart. My instincts about Cherry must have been spot on. It's either trust Kenny, or trust Cherry. Which one is the lesser evil?

"So, what are you suggesting?" I ask.

"Do you have the pills she gave you?"

I reach into my pocket and hand him the plastic tube. He

takes a pill out and holds it up, examining it while we navigate the trail.

"I don't recognize this one. I can ask one of the guys in our lab. You could come with me to see for yourself how we analyze it."

My eyes grow wide.

"No, no! The lab's completely safe. No one will be looking for you. Besides, you'll be with me," he says. "We could start over. Pretend I didn't cut your neck." He bumps me with his shoulder like we're chums.

I can't believe I'm actually considering it. But I have to know. Is Cherry trying to hurt me?

He keeps the pill and hands the bottle back to me.

"They won't ask for ID or anything?"

"I'll scan my badge and we'll both walk in. Everything will be fine."

He juts out his elbow so we can link arms as we break through the trees. Instead, I pat him on the shoulder. "All right. Let's make it quick."

"Don't worry, my car's fast." He winks. "Maybe we'll bring everyone back some breakfast. What does Gavin like?"

"He likes coffee." I'm excited about the idea of surprising Gavin with a treat. It's not Dairy Land, but he did say it was the one thing he indulged in. Kenny opens the passenger door and I hesitate, looking toward the barn. "I should let them know I'm heading out."

"Relax. I'll go tell them." His eyes are full of promise. He nudges me to sit, and as I do, panic washes over me.

Kenny doesn't get a chance to tell anyone, though.

I hear the clang of the hatch and the rough morning voice of Gavin calling out for me. My panic dissipates.

"Gavin." Kenny sounds startled. "I was just coming to find you. Thought we'd grab everyone hotcakes."

"Then it's a good thing I found you first." He walks past Kenny and opens the car door. "Breakfast is ready." Gavin's face is blank. The only feeling I get from him is the gentle grip of his hand as he helps me out. He presses against the small of my back to lead me to the barn door. Gavin's hospitable but not warm as he asks Kenny if he wants to join us.

Kenny pulls out his phone and grimaces at the screen. "Maybe next time. Something important just came up." He gives me a subtle nod as he pats the pocket the pill is in.

"Funny. I thought you were going to get food." Gavin flicks his hand in a wave and we head into the barn. He lifts the latch for me to go down but hooks my arm as I dip my foot. "Wait."

Gavin motions toward my clothes. I look at my sleeves and realize I'm still wearing Kenny's jacket. I take it off, but by the time Gavin walks out to the drive, Kenny is gone.

"He'll be back." When he turns, it's obvious he's forcing himself to smile, maybe to quell the uncertainty I have about what just happened. "You two are friends now?"

Is he jealous, or is he starting to question Kenny's intentions?

"I wouldn't go that far. He caught up with me this morning when I was leaving the falls. He wanted to start over with a clean slate."

Gavin tosses the jacket toward the stall, and we start down the hole.

"Where was he taking you?"

The question trips off an alarm in my brain; the way it's worded bothers me. He didn't want to know where we were going to get food, but rather where Kenny was *taking* me. Maybe Gavin's trust for Kenny isn't as deep as I imagined. Still, I can't be sure, and I decide to leave out the part about retesting the medication. I don't want Gavin to think I don't appreciate his help or that I think he's not capable of getting the right results. The problem is that I'm not sure he did.

"Like he said, we were going to get everyone breakfast."

"Why go anywhere else when we have the best breakfast menu in town?" He grins, and I let out a small sigh of relief.

The smell of breakfast pours down the hall, and we join the others in the main room. Although almost all the food has been picked over, there's at least two of everything on the table—including bacon.

"You can have mine," Gavin says as my eyes zero in on it.

He drops the slices on my plate with a smile that warms me all the way to my toes. I'm glad I didn't go with Kenny. I wouldn't have wanted to miss this.

"Oh my God! This is so good," Paige says to Ry, her mouth stuffed full.

"You should try it on a sandwich," says Ry, leaning closer. "Before lunch, maybe we could take a drive. Clear our heads?"

Paige nods through another bite, and while they're not high yet, I can see the anticipation in their eyes as they finish quickly and rocket from their seats.

"Ready?" Ry asks Paige, his hand twitching as he reaches out for Craig's keys.

Sasha takes Mary to bathe at the falls, and everyone else disappears until it's just Gavin and me.

"You had another headache this morning, didn't you?"

"How'd you know?"

"I can see it on your face. You still have one."

"It's almost gone." I push the last clump of eggs around on my plate. "They come every time I have a dream. Not just any dream. Ones where I'm little, younger than Mary."

Gavin sits up, and I'm grateful. I want to tell him and he appears eager to listen.

"The first couple of dreams were about my mom. We were riding bikes and a man stopped his car and started to chase her." Gavin doesn't look surprised as I keep going. "In last night's dream, I was at some stranger's house."

"Do you remember where?"

It's not the question I expected him to ask, but I try my best to answer.

I sift through the remnants of my dreams until I recall the sign. "There was a Jamison Street…"

Gavin leans back, his face solemn.

"Do you think they're real?"

"Yes. I think pieces of your past are coming back to you."

Hearing him say that hits me like I've had the wind knocked out of me. I have to force myself to breathe again. "What makes you say that?"

"Because I know exactly where Jamison Street is."

# CHAPTER 20

After a week of headaches, Kenny comes back to the barn, just as Gavin predicted. He waltzes into the room just in time for breakfast. Only this time, I'm happy to see him.

When Kenny heads to the coffee pot for a refill, I slide away from my seat, pretending to need more paper towels.

I tear a sheet from the roll. "Well?" I say, my voice a whisper. He glances behind me then pulls a pill out of his pocket. There's a thin line down the center, different from the ones Cherry got for me, more like the ones I've taken for years. When he presses it into my palm, I squeeze my hand tight. My head pounds as if it knows what I'm hiding: salvation.

I head back to the table just as Gavin stands.

"Everyone about done?" he asks, his plate empty. I shake my head and slip back into my seat, shuffling around bits of food. "Join us when you're finished. We need to go over the details for Wednesday's mission."

"I'll be quick," I say, watching him stuff his plate in the dish tub before heading toward the middle of the room with the others. Adrian and Ry look weary and Sasha's spike isn't as high today. We're still recovering from the last mission, but in two days we're heading to the Flat House. Parker will be free.

Parker will be here.

When Paige and I are the only ones left at the table, I wash Kenny's pill down.

"Was that your heart medication?" she asks, tracing the rim of her cup.

I nod at my eggs.

"Really?" Paige raises an eyebrow when I meet her gaze. "Because I saw Kenny give you something…"

My shoulders straighten and I peek back to make sure Gavin's not listening. She leans in as I start to explain. "What Gavin got me isn't working, so I asked Kenny for help." I stab a clump of eggs. "What was I supposed to do? My headaches are getting worse."

Paige gives me an empathetic nod. The pain has been so bad it's been almost impossible for me to hold a conversation with her or anyone lately.

"Kenny said the pills Gavin got me didn't look like heart medication."

"What are they, then?"

"I don't know." I take my last bite and stand. The room doesn't tilt and I feel a rush of relief as the pressure in my head starts to dissolve. "But whatever Kenny gave me," I say in a whisper as we walk over to join the others, "it seems to be working."

• • •

After the meeting, I head outside with Sasha and Paige, grateful I can actually engage in conversation. We sit in the field of yellowing grass. A car starts and we all look over at Kenny. He leans against the door and motions with his hand.

"Tabitha! Come here."

The three of us exchange an uneasy look as I stand. Now that I'm of sound mind, my muscles tighten the closer I get to Kenny. I have to remind myself that he's responsible for my clear head.

I stop a body length away from him. "Thanks for the pill. My headache's gone."

He gives a slow nod, pleased with himself. "Glad I could help."

"So…I was taking the wrong stuff?" I can't help but glance over my shoulder, checking to see if Gavin is listening, as if I'm betraying his trust. I guess I am, sort of.

"The ones you took weren't strong enough, that's all." A wave of relief washes over me. That means Gavin wasn't wrong and

Cherry wasn't trying to kill me. "Now that I know they work, I'll get you more."

I walk backward, not sure what else to say. There's a feeling of debt, that I owe him something. I consider whether this feeling is worse than the headache. I lift my hand in a wave. "Okay then, drive safe."

"Wait." I freeze, and he reaches into his jacket pocket, pulling out a tube of medicine. I let out a breath, and he smirks. "What did you think I wanted?" I force my shoulders to relax as he shakes pills into my outstretched hand. "See you in a couple of days."

It's only when his car's out of sight that I look down. Two pills. Why two? I thought he said getting it wouldn't be a problem? I don't like having to depend on Kenny, and if he only gives me pills in small doses, I'll have to see him more often.

• • •

Ever since Kenny stopped my headaches, I've had a hard time looking Gavin in the eye. We've become magnets, but instead of being drawn to each other, I've flipped. The closer he gets to me, the further I push away. I turn him down when he asks me to join him for laundry duty and try not to sit directly in front of him at meals.

While a small part of me questions his alliance to Cherry, I'm mostly disappointed in myself. Kenny has weaseled his way off my enemy list and even made me doubt Gavin's ability to help me. I need to sort out the chaos in my head. I turn to the only person I can trust. The only person I truly know. Paige.

After a lot of begging, Gavin agrees to drop us off for ice cream while he runs an errand.

"This one's never busy," he says when we pull into the Dairy Land furthest from the city center. There are only three cars in the parking lot, but he stares at every license plate as if he's memorizing each letter and number.

Paige practically pushes me out of the truck and into the

building, eager to get to the counter. Gavin doesn't drive away until we have our ice cream in hand and are safely seated at a table outdoors. We're the only customers eating on the patio, but I feel like there are eyes watching us from the neighboring woods.

Paige snaps her fingers. "Hello? Did you hear me?"

"Sorry, Paige. What'd you say?"

She shields her eyes from the sun and takes another bite. Her eyelids flutter in ecstasy. "I said I think he's nervous."

"About the mission?"

"No." She waits for me to take another bite. "About Parker."

A wave of uneasiness hits me. "That can't be it. I told him he had nothing to worry about."

Paige tilts her head back and talks to me with her eyes closed, soaking in the sun. "Sorry we told Kenny. He caught us at a bad time, you know? He kept asking questions and giving us pills to try."

The thought of Kenny using drugs to get them to talk makes the ice cream in my stomach curdle. "What kinds of questions?"

"About you mostly." As Paige says this, she brings her chin down, eye level with me. "Come to think of it, that's all he asked about."

An icy chill runs through me. Why would Kenny be focused on me? What do I have that he wants? I take another lick, but my stomach is twisting so hard I can't eat it. I toss it in the garbage and Paige shakes her head.

"Well that was a waste," she says with a smile. "I would've eaten it, you know."

I play with my napkin. "Paige, don't tell Gavin, but I think I made a big mistake."

"Did you fool around with Kenny?" Her eyes are wide. Paige has always enjoyed gossip, what little there was at the Center always made it to her ears.

"Are you trying to make me throw up?"

"What's the mistake then?"

Paige won't judge me, but I hate admitting it out loud. "I trusted Kenny."

"Is this about the pills he gave you?"

I nod. "It's stupid, I know, but he doesn't seem to be helping us just to save lives. It's like he wants something. Control, maybe?" I want to ask Gavin what he thinks, but then I'd have to admit I questioned the pills he went out of his way to get me.

Paige tenses and angles her head.

"Are you all right?"

She brings a spoonful to her mouth and a bit of ice cream drops on her shirt. She grabs a napkin to wipe it, but not before pointing behind me.

In the window, standing in line at the counter, is Kenny. He gives us a quick wave. There's not a trace of shock on his face. Of all the places, of all the people, Kenny is at Dairy Land.

My blood runs cold. Is this a coincidence? Or did he know we'd be here?

"Now's your chance to ask him if he's up to no good," Paige says, taking a big bite of ice cream.

Despite her joke, I want to confront him. Not here, though. Not in public. And not until we get Parker out. I need to play this cool. Keep my enemy close. But what if he doesn't plan to get Parker out at all? A trickle of sweat rolls down my back.

"Pretend you're excited to see him," I say as he heads our way.

A bell chimes when he opens the door to the patio. "What a surprise, ladies. Mind if I join you?"

He sits without waiting for approval, wearing swim trunks and a sleeveless white T-shirt. His skin has darkened a couple of shades and I swear his eyes are bluer. Probably some pill he took to look approachable and alluring. I want to kick myself for trusting him, but I grin like he's as delightful as ice cream.

"You're not getting anything?" he asks me.

"I just finished. In fact, we were about to leave. It was nice to see you though." I stand and Paige furiously scrapes the bottom of her plastic bowl, shoveling the last bite in her mouth.

"Would you like another one?" Kenny takes out his wallet.

"No, we have to go," Paige says, popping up.

"Are you walking back to the barn?" Kenny's eyes flicker mischievously like he knows we're trapped.

Just then, the truck pulls into the parking lot and Gavin gives the horn a quick blast. My heart lifts. "Here's our ride."

Gavin parks at an angle, taking up two spots. He jogs over to the fence that surrounds the eating space and hops over, his feet slapping the concrete next to me when he lands.

"Fancy seeing you here," Gavin says with deadpan delivery. His hand finds the back of my chair.

"Just keeping the girls company." Kenny pulls down his glasses and glares into the sun. "It's a hot day. Looks like we all had the same idea. Maybe we should make this our new meeting place."

"Maybe." Gavin looks at me, and some of the tension between us melts away. "Are you guys ready to go?" He continues to hold my gaze.

The magnet in me flips over and I slip my hand into his. I forgot how much I like the way his fingers feel woven through mine. I don't want to let go again.

"We'll see you tomorrow then," Gavin says to Kenny.

"Later."

Paige and I climb in the truck and share a look of relief. "Good timing," she says, taking a seat behind me.

"Was it?" Gavin starts the engine and tears out of the parking lot. Once we're on the road, his arm muscles relax. He flicks on the radio and finds a station that has music Paige and I have heard before. The songs are old, from singers Gavin says are dead. He calls the music *folk*, but he taps the steering wheel as if he's enjoying himself.

Paige belts out all the words. Her voice is better than the singer's. The same can't be said about me, so while she sings, I pick up the manila envelope that sits precariously on the lip of the dashboard. Gavin reaches over, pinching it closed when I start to open it.

"Don't," he says loud enough to make Paige falter. She starts singing again on the next verse. "It's for my dad." Gavin's voice is calm but his jaw looks as hard as steel.

I hand him the folder, not sure if this means they're talking regularly again. "Is that where you went while we had ice cream? To see your dad?"

"Not exactly." He puts the folder in his door panel and waits for me to look at him before he speaks again. His face has softened. "It's something I need to talk to him about."

I'm disappointed he doesn't elaborate, but I respect that he's at least trying to forge some kind of relationship with the man who reared him. Maybe he doesn't want to talk about it in front of Paige.

We pull up to the barn, and Paige bails before I have my seat-belt off. Someone has mowed the field, and there's a soccer game she's anxious to be part of. Burk pumps his fist in the air, happy to have a teammate to face Craig and Sasha. Paige could probably take everyone on by herself and win.

I start to open my door, and Gavin touches my leg. "Whatever happens tomorrow, stay with Sasha. She'll know what to do." I don't like the intensity in his eyes.

"I will."

"If we get caught," he starts, "if they catch you…"

"We'll be fine." I manage a small smile.

He reaches for my face. I lean into his hand, wondering if this will be the last time I'll get to. I push the thought away and lose myself in the warmth of his kiss.

• • •

Adrian agrees to play as long as Paige and I are on his team. We play three against five until it's so dark we kick each other's shins more than the ball. It's late, and Mary lies down in the grass, signaling the end of the game.

The fatigue will at least help us sleep. In the morning, we'll load up to save Parker.

It's not until I crawl into bed that I start to think about what it will be like to see him. How he'll adjust to the real world—the one that used us—and if the nature of the situation will overshadow any part of our old life, like our pact.

Gavin tosses in his bunk, and I debate wandering over to his side of the room to lie next to him. I replay what Paige said at Dairy Land and consider that Gavin might be worried about Parker more than he let on. And then there's Kenny. What does he *really* get out of helping us? The way Sasha described him, Kenny would do anything to please his father, and hurting his dad's company is the exact opposite. Questions swirl in my head as I drift off.

When I open my eyes, someone's rustling around in the kitchen. Ry is making a sandwich, coating the bread with a week's supply of peanut butter and banana slices.

"Want one?" he asks when I join him. No one else is awake yet.

I shrug. "Why not?"

He hands me the one he's already made and starts another. I take a bite but have to drink a cup of water in order to unstick my mouth so I can talk.

"Interesting choice for breakfast," I say, before taking a much, much smaller bite.

"Groceries are dwindling. You make do with what you have 'til the next food run."

"Kind of like your eggs and mustard?"

"Yep."

Ry and I sit at the table, both facing the room of sleepers, but Ry's having a hard time looking at anything but his sandwich.

"Are you okay?" I ask.

"Just a little nervous, that's all."

Ry devours his breakfast, although I don't know how he can swallow. I hand him my water and he chugs it.

"I'm sorry about what happened to you guys," he says. "The Center is an awful place."

"It's not your fault, Ry. At least you're doing something about it."

"Yeah." Ry finally looks out at the room, his eyes glossy.

I want to ask how he can be related to Kenny, who sends prickles up my spine, but I stop myself. He is, after all, Ry's family. I choose a gentler approach. "Why don't you live at home with your brother?"

The question is enough to pull him away from his trance. He shakes the last few drops in his mouth before he answers.

"If you look closely at my skin, you can see yellow undertones." He tilts his face toward the light as if I need proof. "When I was born, I was jaundiced. It took a week to clear up. Now I'm yellow again because of the drugs."

I'm not sure where he's going with this or how to answer. "Your jaundice must've been pretty serious."

"Sort of." Ry speaks softly and dips his head, flicking crumbs off the table. "I kept getting sick, random illnesses when I was three, four, five. I've never been healthy. Not naturally, like you and Paige."

I want to tell him that it's as simple as keeping the drugs out of his mouth. But it doesn't feel appropriate right now, and since he was just a kid, I know it's not the right thing to say.

"My brother doesn't need pills. He'll take a few for his appearance, but he's smart. Scary smart. Our parents were always comparing us. I started taking pills so I could keep up with him. I used Clarity to whiz through tests until the teachers started testing our urine before each exam. When I couldn't excel at school, I started taking Power on the field. Unlike my math teacher, the baseball coach looked the other way. We'd play well enough to win, but hold back enough to keep mainlanders from asking questions." Ry chuckles to himself. "I was finally good at something."

"Did your parents know?"

"I'm sure they did. But it didn't matter. Kenny was their star child. That's when Gavin and I became closer. We cheered for each other when no one else showed up. His mom was ill and his dad…

well…you know." I nod as he continues. "No matter what I did, I would always be the sick kid or the drug-crazed teen in my dad's eyes. Kenny was the smart one. And he's the one who showed interest in the family business."

"What about your mom? Wasn't she there for you?"

"Put a wig on Kenny. That's my mom."

I shudder. Kenny would make an ugly girl. "That bad, huh?"

Ry smirks, as if he knows what I'm thinking. "Personality. Not looks."

I seize my chance, keeping any irritation out of my voice. "Why is Kenny helping us? If he's supposed to be a daddy's boy or the next CEO, why is he here?"

His face morphs back to a trance, as if his body shut down from the inside out.

"College wasn't his thing. I bet that pissed my dad off." At the sound of footsteps, Ry blinks. A grin tugs at his lips as Gavin approach. "I'm sure Kenny has his reasons."

"You guys are up early." Gavin rubs my head on the way to the coffee machine.

"Burk's text woke me," Ry says.

"Yeah, I got it too." There's disappointment in Gavin's voice.

"What's wrong?" I ask.

"Burk can't make it today. Family emergency." Gavin reaches for a cup, the back of his shirt wrinkly. "But I've been thinking about what we talked about, Ry." He puts the grounds in the machine. "You're right. Tabitha should ride along with me and Adrian."

Out of the corner of my eye, Ry flashes a smile and stands to leave. "Good idea."

Gavin flips the coffee pot on. When he spins around, I realize my mouth is hanging open. It takes me a second to get my thoughts together.

"You said it wasn't safe for me to get that close to the Flat House." I make sure to keep my voice light and cheery. The last thing I want is for him to think I'm afraid, that I'm not ready for another mission. What I can't handle is being on the sidelines. Waiting without knowing.

"It's not the best scenario, but I think Parker needs to see someone he's familiar with when he gets in the van. Especially since we don't know what this super drug will do to him." He shrugs. "And I'd like to keep my arms in their sockets. I doubt he'll trust me without you there."

• • •

Adrian and Gavin are quiet on the drive to the Flat House. When Gavin gives me the signal to get down, I crawl behind the second row of seats and cover myself with a blanket that matches the blue vinyl. The van slows and passes over two speed bumps before it stops.

We don't have to wait long. An alarm goes off, and someone calls for help. It sounds like Kenny, and he's screaming so loudly I wonder if something's gone wrong.

I'm about to peek when the van door opens, and I hear a new voice. It's Parker's, but it sounds thick and distorted, like a recording played at the wrong speed.

"Where is she?" Parker yells.

"Get in," Gavin snaps. "We'll explain on the way."

"What the hell did you do to her?"

"Nothing!"

"Then where is she?"

"If you want to see her, get in and stay low."

My fingers grip tightly around the blanket. I thought Gavin wanted Parker to know I was here, that my presence would help. I want to call out to Parker, knowing he must be terrified right now, but since I can't see what's going on outside, I don't question Gavin's judgment.

The van floor vibrates as Parker lies down. I picture his sleeves stretched around his muscles, protruding like grapefruits stuffed in nylons.

The van starts to move. There's shouting in the distance. I want to tell Gavin to punch the gas.

I want to be safe at the barn.

Tires squeal outside, tipping me off that Ry and Craig are doing their job. They're causing chaos, so we should be heading for the exit.

"Shit," Gavin says. My heart catches in my throat. *What's going on?*

"Step on it!" Adrian says.

"I can't! There's too many, I'll run them over."

"Just do it!"

He brakes, and I roll into the metal bar that keeps the seat in place.

"Get out of the vehicle!" a man screams.

"Is there a problem?" Gavin's voice is anything but calm.

A hand reaches for my leg. I'm about to kick whatever's touching me when I hear someone whisper my name. I pull the blanket down just enough to glance out. For the first time since I left the Center, I see Parker. He's looking back at me from under the seat with a wild mixture of rage and happiness. His smile is the only thing that convinces me he's sane.

The van door opens and I hear the shift of metal and a click that makes my already taut muscles grip my bones even tighter. "Let's go. All of you," a man says.

In an instant, Parker's face morphs into an expression that terrifies me.

He pops up from the floor, and I scramble to my knees, peering over the seat to see what he's going to do. The man points his gun at Parker, who's hunched over to keep his head from hitting the roof. Parker rips the gun out of his hand, bends the barrel, and drops it. It clatters on the cement and the man stands, frozen in fear. Parker grips his throat and lifts him off the ground. After dropping him next to his gun, Parker slams the door shut.

"Go," he barks. "Now."

Gavin doesn't hesitate.

I climb into the seat as the van flies through the lot. Gavin swerves just as two workers jump out of the way to avoid being steamrolled.

When we barrel through the gate, Parker changes rows and slides in next to me. He looks the same size, not bulky as I imagined. His veins are more prominent and his skin is speckled with a red rash. But he's alive. A sob of relief builds in my chest, and I throw my arms around his neck before it can escape. Burying my face in his shoulder, I breathe in his familiar smell of protein bars.

"Are you okay?" he asks when we let go.

"Of course I am." He looks me over like he's trying to find an open wound.

"Then why are you in trouble?"

"Me?"

"I was told you were in danger, that someone was trying to hurt you." He reaches for my hair, frowning at the brown. Strands slide through his fingers as he pulls his hand away. "One of the workers said you needed help."

"I did." I recount my rescue, trying to catch Gavin's eye in the rearview mirror. But he's talking to Adrian, his voice full of anger and curse words. I turn my attention back to Parker. "The Center was using you too, testing some military drug on you. They were going to pump you full of it until you died."

Parker grips the seat in front of him, the skin on his knuckles so tight his bones threaten to break through his skin. I rub his back, not knowing what else to say.

The wheel jerks and Parker's body slams into me.

When I sit up, I see a sign that reads: Off Road Vehicles Only. Parker and I exchange a glance as we bump along in our seats. Gavin parks behind a group of trees and unbuckles. There's something shiny in his hand. A knife.

Parker grabs my leg. The muscles in his arms twitch, and his fingers press down so hard I wince.

Gavin moves toward us.

"What's going on?" I ask.

"I'll explain in a minute. Step aside," Gavin says to Parker.

"You'll explain now." Parker lets go of my leg and stands, hunched like Gavin. His eyes look more red than blue. He's going to rip Gavin's head off, and although there's a knife pointed at me, I don't want him to.

"I need to check Tabitha's neck."

"What?" Parker and I say in unison.

"We were ambushed back there," Gavin says, pointing with the knife. "They had to have known we were coming. And I think I know who told them." He eyes shift from me to the weapon he's waving around, and he drops his hand down to his side. "Kenny called Ry when we left this morning. He wanted to know why we changed the plan—except I never told him we did. I think he put a tracking device in your neck."

I reach up and feel the scab.

"There's no other way he could have known you were in the van," says Gavin, his chin dropping slightly.

A small part of me feels vindicated. I knew it wasn't just a coincidence that he showed up at the same Dairy Land the other day. But why is he tracking me when he helped free me to begin with?

"We have to cut it out. Fast," Gavin says. Parker's face pales as Gavin leans over the seat, blade pointed at my throat. I turn and lift my hair. "Are you ready?"

"Make it quick."

"I can't watch," says Parker, taking my hand. I squeeze hard, but it's not enough to brace me for the pain. The blade pierces, reopening the wound. I manage to hold in an agonizing wail until the second pass.

"Give her this," Adrian says. Parker reaches for something with his free hand. "Have her put it between her teeth."

Parker holds a pen in front of my mouth and I bite down. My nails dig into his skin.

"You okay?" Gavin asks. I grunt, giving him a quick nod. "The next part is going to hurt more. But we're almost done. Stay with me."

When Gavin uses the end of the knife to dig out the tracker, the edges of my vision flicker with white spots. My stomach heaves, and just when I think I'm about to pass out, Gavin is done.

"Got it."

Hot tears roll down my cheeks. I turn around as Gavin tosses it out the window. "There," he says. "The tracker's gone."

Adrian hands Parker a cloth to stop the bleeding, then hops into the driver's seat. The van lurches when he throws it in reverse. In the sudden movement, Parker presses harder against my neck and I gasp. "Sorry."

I try to concentrate on the hum of the motor, but the throbbing in my neck makes it impossible. Gavin is watching me, and we lock eyes.

"I'm sorry I had to do that. How're you holding up?"

Parker interjects. "We need to take her to the hospital before the wound gets infected."

Gavin gives him a throaty laugh. "That's not an option. PharmPerfect controls Gladstone Memorial too. They have people there who'll be looking for us. We're on our own."

# CHAPTER 21

---

"A barn?"

Parker's disappointed, and he hasn't even smelled the mildew-laden basement yet.

"It's worked so far," Gavin says when we roll to a stop.

Sasha, Paige, and Mary step outside warily, crossing the drive as if they're avoiding landmines.

Sitting up makes me dizzy, but I'm focused enough to read the fear on their faces. I grab Gavin's arm. "Do they know?"

"I had Ry call Sasha, just in case something happened. They needed to be prepared to leave without us."

"Leave?"

His jaw tightens. "It's not safe here." He slides the van door open.

Fresh air floods the vehicle, but it doesn't wash away the anxiety. Did Kenny pretend to help us so he could find out where our hideout was? To stop the group working against his dad's company?

Paige lunges herself into Parker's arms when he emerges from the van, and I can't help but smile. We were lucky to get him out.

She eyes my neck when they release. "You okay?" she asks, touching the trail of dried blood. I nod, but when she hugs me, it's with much more restraint, as if the wound might start gushing if she squeezes me too hard.

When Paige lets go to introduce Parker to Mary, Sasha grabs a first aid kit. She pulls out a container and unscrews the cap, revealing a pearly pink cream. "This will help with the pain," she says, dipping her finger.

The cream is cold and tingly as it coats my skin. The wound is numb in a matter of seconds.

"And take this." She holds out a pill and I lean away.

"What is it?"

"It's for infections." She thrusts her hand out farther.

I take it, reluctantly. The pill leaves a chalky taste in my throat and I shudder as it descends.

"How long have they been tagging us?" I ask. Sasha puts the cream back without answering.

"Did you or Mary get one?"

Still no answer.

"Well, did they put one in Paige?"

Sasha shifts her eyes to Gavin and then the ground. "No. You're the only one with a tracking device. Kenny's only after you."

I spin around. Gavin's arms are folded high on his chest like a safety barrier. In my periphery Sasha scoots away, quicker this time, as if *I'm* the landmine. My heart thunders in my chest.

"It's true," Gavin says.

"W-why?" Questions flood my brain faster than my mouth can move.

"The most popular drugs are made with Chemical 31." Gavin turns to me. "You said it was on your form, so I looked into it. Turns out you have a mutated gene that allows you to process it. Something only redheads have." His throat clicks when he swallows. "Kenny put a tracker in you because he knew PharmPerfect would want you back. They can replace Paige and Mary. Even Parker." When Gavin glances at him, Parker widens his stance. His eyes come back to me, landing so heavily my chest hurts. "But you're different. Pills go in and your body keeps functioning."

"I-I don't understand…" I step back, distancing myself from what Gavin is saying.

Sasha, Mary, and Adrian have disappeared to the basement. Paige is off to the side, her hand over her mouth. I have to fight to keep my knees from buckling.

"Your body reacts differently. That's why they took you to the hospital and not the Flat House. They don't just want to put drugs in you. They need a sterile environment to replicate what your body creates naturally," Gavin says.

"Why didn't you tell me?" My anger surges and blood roars in my ears.

"I wanted to be sure." His eyes lock with mine, and for the first time today, I notice the dark circles underneath. I hope guilt's been keeping him awake. "Kenny is looking for a way to be the golden boy again. I'm sure he's covered his trail so we take the fall. All he wants is to make his dad proud by bringing you back."

That must be why he acted so weird at Paige's rescue. He didn't want someone else to catch me first. I clutch my side.

Gavin steps closer. "You're a drug company's dream come true."

"Whose side are you on?" Parker yells from behind me.

"Hers, of course!" Gavin looks crushed, but I don't care right now. He reaches for my hand, and I jerk it away. "I would have told you sooner, but I had to be certain."

"It's my life, Gavin. Don't you think I had a right to know what was going on, even if it's just a hunch?" I turn on my heels and head for the forest before my tears can escape.

Parker calls out to me, and I run faster. He isn't as quick and doesn't know these woods yet. There are plenty of paths that jut off the main trail, so it's easy to throw him off course. I find a tree and climb until I'm a good twenty feet off the ground. In the distance, I hear Parker calling out for me. Eventually his voice fades, and I know he's moved farther down the trail or left the woods completely.

The silence helps me clear my head. I think about Kenny and what I want to do to his face, and how awful this new world must seem to Parker. But my thoughts drift back to Gavin again and again.

How long has he known my genes made me a target? I cringe when I think about what would've happened if I'd gone with Kenny to test my pills. I would have walked right into PharmPerfect's lab wearing a tracker. Kenny could have handed me over on a silver platter. Gavin had stopped me. Had he known then? I was foolish to trust Kenny, and if Gavin's tests were right, what pills did Kenny give me?

Every dot I connect leads to more questions, and soon my head is a jumbled constellation.

"Tabitha?"

The bark grates against my back as I shift in the tree to hide from view. Gavin is several feet away, drawing closer. Just when I think he won't look up, he does.

"There you are." He gives me an impish smile, and my traitorous stomach flutters.

"How'd you find me?"

"You said you liked to climb when you were little. I figured it was worth a shot to look in the trees."

"Go away. I don't want to talk to you."

"Good, because I want you to listen."

"There's no way to get rid of you, is there?"

"I'm afraid not." Gavin scoots around until he has a clear shot of my face. "I didn't tell you what I knew because I didn't want to scare you. I hoped it wasn't true, but the more I looked into it there was no denying they weren't going to forget about you like they did Mary and Sasha."

"When did you figure it out?"

"When you didn't have a price. That was my first clue you were special." He holds onto the last word, and I avert my eyes.

"Is that why you got me out? Because of how *special* I was?"

"Of course not. But I wondered why we never heard details about a buyer. And the cut Kenny gave you at the screening didn't look like a normal skin sample. It was too red and inflamed. When he showed up at Dairy Land, I knew he must have done something. I suspected it was a tracking device."

"That morning we were going to get breakfast...he tried to get me to go to the lab with him," I confess. "He made me think..." Guilt settles in my gut, and I push out what I've been holding back from Gavin. "He convinced me that the pills you gave me were wrong."

"Is that why you two got chummy?" He scowls when I nod.

"My headaches weren't going away."

"When I see him again—" Gavin sucks in a deep breath. His face is still taut after he exhales.

"Why didn't you confront him if you suspected he was tracking me? What if something had happened today? What if Parker had died, like Meghan?"

"I needed to keep him close until I could figure out why they wanted you so badly."

"So you treated me like bait?"

"No. Leaving you here at the barn would've been worse. The rest of us would have been miles away. But Kenny knew you weren't here. The tracker tipped him off that you were in the van. I wanted to keep Kenny close, but I also wanted to keep you close. To protect you. I wasn't going to let them take you without a fight."

My throat feels raw, like I've been chewing bark. I want to smile and cry at the same time. Life was so much easier when I was at the Center. Prior to knowing I was going to be harvested, and before Gavin had yet to take my stomach on a rollercoaster ride of emotional ups and downs.

"Can you come down here? You're making me nervous."

I'm still slightly angry, but I don't want to spend the rest of the afternoon in the air, away from my friends whose lives are in danger because of me. I start to climb down. My foot touches the branch below, and there's a crack.

"Tabitha!"

My fingers tighten around the branch, and I struggle to keep my grip. My feet dangle, and I glance down. The next limb that's thick enough to hold me is through a cluster of smaller branches.

"Hold on!" Gavin starts to climb.

"What are you doing?" My fingers slide against the rough bark.

"You're going to have to drop."

"Are you crazy?"

"Drop straight down. The other branches will slow your fall and I'll grab you."

"That's insane!"

"There's no other choice."

I duck my chin, trying to gauge where I need to land, counting the seconds until Gavin makes it to the branch that I'm supposed to hit. I can't hold on much longer.

"Ready?"

I'm not. But I let go.

My shoulder bumps against one of the smaller limbs and I hit the branch with one foot. I'm off balance. My arms flail. He catches my wrist and pulls me upright. My heart races, and I steady myself against the only solid mass available. Gavin.

He leans back against the tree, holding me in place. It feels good to have his arms around me, but I won't let myself enjoy it. It's too tempting to forgive him completely, and I ease myself out of his arms.

"I'm so sorry, Tabitha. I was only trying to protect you."

"I don't need anyone to protect me."

"That's what you do when you care about someone."

"I don't need that, either."

It's such an obvious lie he doesn't hide his doubtful expression. "Well, it's too late."

He reaches an arm behind my waist and slides his other hand behind my head. I can't fight against his kiss without risking us falling. Once our lips touch, the urge to resist drops away like a pinecone released from its branch. I hope I'm not a fool for forgiving him.

"Promise me you won't keep things from me," I say, pulling back slowly.

Our foreheads touch and he sighs.

"What aren't you saying?"

"I will tell you everything I know, I promise—but you have to give me time."

"Time?" Maybe I am a fool, because at this point I don't know how much time I have left.

"Trust me, please?"

I bite my lip. No matter how hard I try, my heart won't allow me to say no.

"Give me a few days and I'll explain everything. But it can't be here. We have to leave the barn. They'll come after us."

"Kenny will bring them right to us, won't he?"

Gavin nods and my ears burn. I wish I'd drowned him when I had the chance.

"Where will we go?" I ask.

"You and I will go to my house. Ry's told him I don't talk to my father, so he won't expect it."

"What about everyone else?"

"It's safer if we separate. Adrian and Craig will make the arrangements."

It's amazing how much the barn already feels like a sanctuary, and how the idea of leaving it makes me ill. In such a short time, this has become my home.

By the time we make it down the tree, my hands are chafed and red. But my heart throbs even worse. Leaving tonight means I'll be abandoning Parker and Paige when they need family the most. After all, isn't that what we are? What we'll always be?

I just didn't realize it until now.

# CHAPTER 22

---

Ry and Craig are in the kitchen, surrounded by the rest of our team. Ry's talking like he's jacked up on adrenaline. "And as we're leaving the Flat House, Craig clips a guy." He gives Craig a slap on the back, the kind you'd give a teammate when they made you proud.

Gavin's hand feels clammy in mine, and his grip tightens when he clears his throat. "I have an announcement." The group quiets down, but their expressions say they aren't sure they can handle any more stress today.

Parker sits on the edge of the table, and his eyes form tight slits as he zeros in on Gavin's hand linked with mine.

"They will come looking for Tabitha, so it's best if I get her out of here tonight. I won't tell you where we're going in case they use drugs to try to get info out of you."

"Who put you in charge of her?" Parker says, hopping down. I don't know if it's the injections they've given him or that he doesn't like the idea of Gavin taking me away, but his chest seems to puff as he walks aggressively toward us.

Gavin stays calm. My hand tightens, yet part of me wants to pull away. The last thing I want to do is make Parker feel worse today.

"It's the only way to keep everyone safe. Ask her yourself," Gavin says.

Parker waits for me to stand my ground, but I know Gavin is right. Leaving the group is the best thing I can do right now. I lower my chin. "I have to go."

"Then I'm going with you." Parker startles me when he slings his arm over my shoulder.

"It's better if you're not involved," Gavin says, his voice sharp.

"I've known her a lot longer than you, buddy."

I'm being sandwiched by egos and testosterone. This is not what this group needs. Anger. Blame. I pull away and turn to face them. "That's enough," I snap.

They stop glaring at each other long enough for their brows to relax.

"Fine. If it's all right with Tabitha," Gavin waves his hand at Parker, "you're welcome to come."

As much as I want to keep Parker safe, I don't want to leave him again. "I'm okay with it," I say, my voice softer this time.

Parker grins. Gavin acts like he doesn't mind, but I can tell by the way his body tightens, he does.

We grab blankets and pillows and say our goodbyes. Leaving Paige is harder this time because I know we're being hunted, and that any of us could get caught. That I might never get to hug her again.

I hold on as long as I can before we head for the truck.

"Stay safe," I say to her.

"Stay alive," she whispers back.

I climb in the back so Parker can ride next to Gavin. I don't want him to have to sit by himself, and until I can address the pact, it seems like the right thing to do. But when he and Gavin start talking, I wonder if I've made a mistake.

"So, you think you know what's best for her?" Parker says to Gavin when we hit the paved road.

Gavin looks at me in the rearview mirror. Our eyes catch, and he has a mischievous look about him. I hope he's delicate with his answer.

"You could say that."

Parker grunts. It's clear he doesn't think the short time I've known Gavin could contend with our years at the Center. I can't blame him. He does know me, just in a different way. Parker knows my habits, my routines. Gavin knows my desires. It helps that he's one of them.

I'm thankful Parker doesn't comment about the yard when we pull up to Gavin's house. The door creaks when we enter, and Parker nudges me from behind. I glance back, and he wrinkles his nose. It smells like ink and dust, and somehow the papers seem to have multiplied as we wade through the clutter to Gavin's room.

"Make yourself at home," Gavin says, tossing my pillow on his bed. "Tabitha, you know your way around."

Parker's jaw clenches, and I see a thick blue line in his neck—a vein ready to burst.

"We came here to test my heart medication," I explain. "There's a lab in the basement."

The answer is a Band-Aid solution to the situation, and I shoot Gavin a scolding look. He smiles defiantly.

"Who's sleeping where?" Parker asks.

"Tabitha can have my bed, and you and I can take the floor."

Parker nods, satisfied with the plan.

"What do we do when your dad gets home from work?" I ask.

"He won't be back 'til Sunday. He's at a conference."

I don't ask him how he knows, but it strikes me as odd. For someone who hasn't been close to his father in recent years, knowing his schedule seems a bit unusual. Have they been talking more? Based on the way Gavin shifts his jaw, I doubt the discussions have been good.

Parker picks up the picture of Cherry from Gavin's dresser. "Is this your girlfriend?"

"Used to be."

"Isn't this the girl—"

"From the Center," Gavin finishes.

"How convenient."

Gavin rolls his eyes. "Cherry's mom got her the job, but even she was kept in the dark. And after I told her, she only stayed there so she could help us."

"We're supposed to believe that?" Parker says, joining me on the bed. He lifts the picture for me to see, holding it so close I'd be able to smell the corsage on her wrist if photos were scented. Cherry's smile mocks me. I'm glad I've already had practice blocking it out.

Gavin rips it out of Parker's hand and puts it face down on his dresser. "I got Sasha out on my own, but I almost got caught. Cherry lied for me, said I was with her so PharmPerfect would back off. I let Cherry know what was going on and told her if she gave me the name of the next person fostered out, I'd prove it. That was Mary, and if you noticed, she had her cornea lopped off for someone else to use. I didn't have Adrian listening for surgeries being scheduled then—or Kenny giving me exact room numbers." Gavin's voice drops an octave, sounding less defensive. "Mary's basically blind in one eye and short a kidney. That was all the evidence Cherry needed. She was happy to help after that. Plus, her mom looked like a jackass every time one of the kids she was supposed to deliver went missing."

"Wait. Her mom...so she's Cherry Preen?" I ask, piecing it together.

Gavin nods, and Parker lets out a small gasp. "That little—"

"Cherry's not like her mom," Gavin says, shaking his head. "Nadia would spit and crawl her way to the top. She started out running PharmPerfect's blood drives and now she runs the organ harvesting scheme." Gavin grunts in disgust. "Nadia would sell her soul for a life of privilege. Not Cherry. She might be prissy, but she's not evil."

It feels as though the room has been divided into teams: the Center kids versus the Preens. Although Gavin sounds so sure of his assessment of Cherry, it makes me pause to reconsider. I may not like the way she looks at him, but she didn't poison me when she had the chance.

"I believe you," I say. Gavin looks just as surprised as Parker.

"Once I had a crew," Gavin continues, his face softening, "we were able to get Tabitha and Paige out."

"Paige told me what happened to Meghan," says Parker with bite. "Doesn't sound like Cherry was that helpful."

"What happened to Meghan wasn't Cherry's fault," Gavin says. "I think Kenny knew the surgery rooms were changed. Hell, he might have changed them himself for all I know." Gavin shakes his head.

There's a sharp pain in my chest as I picture Meghan's lifeless body on the operating table. Parker has no idea how guilt-ridden we are.

"We tried, Parker," I say. Gavin jerks his head in my direction, looking relieved I've come to his defense. "The hospital staff even came looking for us after I walked in on Meghan's surgery. Gavin and I had to hide out on the rooftop and climb through the ventilation shaft to get out."

Parker's face turns a fiery red. "You took him through the ventilation shaft, huh? Must be a habit of yours."

He gets up, shaking his body like he's loosening his limbs, ready to box something. Or someone. Instead, he flicks one of Gavin's baseball pendants, making it askew. "So, Gavin...got anything to eat around here?"

"Nothing you'll want to eat out of our kitchen..." Gavin stands, hesitating at the door. "I'll call for pizza."

When we hear Gavin on the phone, Parker's tongue unleashes. "How can you trust this guy?"

"You've got him all wrong. He risks his life to save people like you and me."

"What's in it for him?" He plops down on the bed. "A pretty redhead?"

I slug him in the leg. "The satisfaction of doing the right thing."

"Is that what he told you?"

"Do you think he *wants* to live in the basement of a barn?"

"I just have a hard time believing he's just being friendly." Parker's forearm presses against my back, a little too close for friends to sit. I lean forward, but Parker notices. "What's going on between you two?"

"Nothing." Immediately regretting the hole I've put myself in, I backtrack. "I mean, we're getting to know each other, hanging out."

"I noticed you're also holding hands. Have you kissed?"

I rub my hands together, a reaction that probably makes me look guilty. My palms are moist. This is not how I wanted to break the news to Parker, not through an interrogation.

"Is it hot in here?" I stand to crack the window.

"I guess that means you have."

I pull the window up and let the fresh air envelop me. I need to compartmentalize my thoughts so I can talk about the pact, how silly it was to commit to something without knowing where life would take us—or whom it would bring into our lives.

I turn and Parker is on his feet. He takes two steps and kisses me before I can get my hands up to hold him back. His lips are plump and forceful, like he's trying to infuse me with all the memories of our time together.

"What are you doing?" I push him away, covering my mouth.

"I just thought—"

Parker stops when we hear footsteps in the hallway. I lean against the windowsill. Gavin enters the room and looks from Parker to me with concern.

"What's wrong with your mouth?" Gavin asks.

I drop my hand.

"We were just reconnecting," Parker says, keeping his back to Gavin.

Gavin's mouth is in a firm line, his voice sharp. "The delivery driver called in sick. If we want pizza, we have to go get it."

I look at Parker, who has probably been kept on a strict diet of healthy foods at the Flat House. I struggle to keep my voice steady as he stares back with a smug expression. "You'll love pizza. It's worth the drive."

"Let's go, then," Gavin says.

"Why don't you two go?" I blurt out.

"Us?" Parker says.

Gavin's face tightens like he's been slapped.

"I need to freshen up." I keep my head down so I don't reveal the truth. I don't want to be around either of them right now. Maybe if they get to know one another, it'll be easier for Parker to understand Gavin is a good guy, and perhaps Gavin will see there's more to Parker than anger and muscles.

"I'm not leaving her here alone. Not when they're after her," Parker says. "I'll stay here and nap while Tabitha showers." A sly grin pulls at his lips. "You go ahead."

Gavin walks up to Parker, putting a hand on his shoulder. "Nah. Come with me." He shakes him lightly, like they're teammates on the baseball field. "It'll be fun. Tabitha will be safe." Gavin turns to me. "If anyone comes by, head to the lab. It locks from the inside as well. Bolt it and stay quiet." He hesitates for a moment. I wonder if he's going to change his mind, but he pulls Parker out the door.

I stay in the room, pretending to busy myself by airing out the blanket. When I hear the truck pull away, I squeeze my pillow in relief. A small, red pill falls out and hits the floor. The Fireball. It must have been trapped in the corner of the pillowcase. Why would Ms. Preen need some love pill anyway? A picture of her in a scantily clad outfit with a burly man flashes in my head. It's disturbing, and I shudder. Isn't natural passion good enough?

I put it in my pocket with the one pill I have left from Kenny, the one I refused to take when my instincts about him crept back to the surface. If Cherry gave me the right medication, then what did Kenny give me? Do I even have a heart condition? If not, what have I been taking for the last decade?

I wander toward the basement, wanting to look at the book Gavin paged through when we came to test my pill. But when I reach the kitchen, a bag on the counter moves on its own. I scurry out to the living room. There has to be another medical book around here I can use.

I find a small patch of unused space on the couch and begin to rummage through the piles.

Gavin's dad must be brilliant. The formulas look like hieroglyphics, and there are stacks and stacks of them. When I compare a few, I notice they're slight variations of the same problem. A number or letter changed here or there, a few notes about diluting some chemical or changing the mixture. I wonder if this is what his father has spent his career working on.

I notice there are a few books on top of the piano, and I gravitate toward them. My fingers are more interested in the keys at first, and I let myself play a few notes, amazed at how easily a song pours out.

Do I know it?

I do. My mother taught me to play.

I sit on the bench and let my fingers stumble through a broken rendition of a nursery rhyme. Each time I strike a chord, it feels like something is cracking open inside my head, pieces of an eggshell falling away. A thick yolk of memories floods my mind. My hands tingle as if my mother's fingers are helping me hit the right keys. Her hair smells like lavender. I close my eyes and I'm transported back to my childhood.

She lets go of my fingers and stands to the side, beaming in her white polo and khaki shorts. Her hair hangs over her shoulder, the red tips grazing a sticker on her shirt that reads *I Give*. I want to stop playing so I can throw my arms around her, but I'm afraid she'll fade if the music stops.

When I finish the song, I look down at my fingers and see that I'm trembling. I hop up and back away from the piano, keeping my eye on it as if my mom will miraculously appear. This wasn't a dream. This was a memory.

Memories I haven't had until I left the Center and ran out of pills.

I swipe the books off the piano and run back to Gavin's room, scouring them for information. The first one covers Alzheimer's, a disease that deprived the elderly of memories, stripping them of their connection to loved ones. It sounds horrible, but thankfully it's been eradicated.

The next book is more of a medical journal with information on something called the hippocampus. It's an overview of how the tube-shaped structure in the brain is responsible for forming and processing memories.

The last book proves most useful. In the index, I find information on medication to help patients with mental trauma. I flip through the chapter and find a picture of a pale green pill with a line through the center. I pull the pill Kenny gave me out of my pocket and hold it up to the page.

They're identical.

I read the first paragraph: *Memoritum may be used to help suppress memories in patients who have undergone a traumatic, life-altering event. Taken regularly, the patient will be able to prohibit any negative memories from resurfacing so that they may maintain an adequate state of well-being. Patients may experience headaches if they stop taking this medication without a doctor's supervision. Taking a pain medication in conjunction with a reduced Memoritum dosage may help alleviate migraines.*

My heart is pounding when I reach the end. This is why I have no memories. Was there even an accident? Is my mom alive? And where's my dad? I scour the page, trying to find information on whether the memories will return. There's nothing that says they will, but if my dreams are any indication, they might.

I hear the truck pull up and hurry to the living room, using my finger to bookmark the page.

Parker comes in first, kicking the door back with his heel as he carries one pizza. Gavin stops it with the box he's holding and glares at Parker like he's trying to burn a hole through him with his eyes.

My idea to bring them together must have backfired, but I'm too excited to worry about that right now. "Look what I found!"

Parker grabs the book before Gavin can put his pizza box on the coffee table. "An old book?" He scowls at the pages.

I point to the section about Memoritum. "This is what the Center made me take."

Gavin reads over Parker's shoulder. "Propannalean was just a cover," Gavin says with relief. "You don't have a heart condition. They just wanted to wipe out your memory."

"Why?" Parker clutches the book, blocking Gavin from reading any further.

"Do you remember when they brought me to the Center?" I ask Parker.

A flirtatious grin expands across his face. "I'll never forget it."

Gavin proceeds to clear the couch off as if he doesn't want to listen, but he's careful not to rustle papers, so I know he is.

"You had bandages on your hands, and they kept you away from the rest of us at first. You'd watch us play, frowning the entire time. Then, one day you were ready to join in. Your hair was in pigtails and you wore a white dress, and you skipped over to me and the twins and asked if you could play. They'd given you a nametag to wear, but you had it on upside down. I had to tilt my head to read it."

My heart expands as he retells the story, sharing details I don't even recall. Parker has always had a way of making me feel important enough not to forget.

Somewhere in the midst of Parker's story, Gavin disappeared. "Dinner's ready," he says, coming back from the kitchen with paper plates.

I sit next to Gavin, smelling the pepperoni longer than necessary. Parker sits across from us in a lounge chair and seems at odds with the cheese that stretches between his mouth and the slice before snapping. But when he bites down, his face lights up like the moon on a clear night.

"This is incredible."

"Glad you like it," Gavin responds. They share a smile, and my body relaxes.

"I'm starting to remember my past," I say to Parker. "I saw my hands in bandages, like you described, and dreamed my mom was kidnapped. Only it wasn't a dream. I got away and a woman brought me to a building where they started giving me pills. That must be how I ended up at the Center."

"Did they ever tell you anything about Tabitha?" Gavin asks.

Parker looks annoyed he has to stop chewing in order to answer. "They told us she had some head trauma from the car accident her parents died in. We were told not to ask her about it because it might make her cry." Parker shifts uncomfortably. "Every morning at breakfast they'd give her a little pill, and someone would stand next to her to make sure she took it." Parker squeezes in another bite. "Until it became routine, and she took it on her own."

We chew in silence while the cloud of uncertainty hangs over us. Parker finishes four slices and wipes his hands on his shorts. "Mind if I shower?"

Gavin grabs him a towel from the hall closet, and when the bathroom door opens, I crane my neck to peek in. It's the one room I haven't actually seen, and it's clean. It must not be the one his father uses.

Parker shuts the door and Gavin flashes me a dubious grin.

"I thought you needed to freshen up earlier?"

"I did," I lie.

"Then how come nothing's been touched, not even the hand towel?"

I shrug. "Did you get to know each other on the drive?"

"Parker's a good guy. I can see that. You don't need to force us into a friendship."

He sits next to me on the couch and I snuggle close. His arm slips around me as he talks into my hair. "Parker's in love with you." My heart kicks into a nervous speed. "You can't expect him to like me. And I can't expect you to forget any feelings you might have for him."

I look at Gavin and his expression makes my chest ache. I know I'm holding back because I don't want to get hurt. Parker is familiar, someone I can trust. I care about them both. It's not fair to either of them.

Gavin kisses my forehead then whispers in my ear, "He's not the only one in love with you."

My heart feels like it doubles in size, but I don't answer. Instead, I let myself melt into him, enjoying the few minutes we have where I can be in his arms without hurting anyone.

# CHAPTER 23

---

Gavin's bedroom seems to trap the heat of three bodies as we lie, listening to each other breathe. My lids are heavy, and I'm drifting off to sleep when someone pokes my arm. I look down from the bed and Gavin has a finger to his mouth, signaling me to keep quiet.

I glance across the room at Parker. His image is dark in the moonlight that bleeds through the curtains. I can't tell if he's asleep, but Gavin speaks so softly I can barely hear him, which means Parker can't unless he took an ultrasonic hearing pill.

"I've been thinking about where we could go to keep you safe, and I keep coming back to the same answer. We can't stay in Gladstone."

"I can't just leave," I whisper. "What about my friends? Not just Paige and Parker, but the ones still at the Center—the ones who will die if we don't get them out."

"Even if we stay there's not much we can do. Hospital security has been beefed up and we've lost our inside guy. There's no way we're getting anyone else out without help." Gavin reaches for my hand. "We can either keep hiding and spend the rest of our lives looking over our shoulders, or find someone who can help."

I shake my head. "Who's going to believe us?"

"Not the local cops, that's for sure." His fingers trace my skin, sending a tingle down my arm. "I imagine PharmPerfect could slip them enough drugs or money to buy their silence. We'll need to go higher up, find some Feds."

"Some what?"

"Government investigators."

"What makes you think they'll listen?" My eyes are starting to adjust and I can see a wry smile on Gavin's face.

"Because unlike the others, you had a life before the Center. You had a family, a birth certificate, and a past. They can test your DNA and confirm you never died in a car accident. That's a place to start, a way to pique their interest."

"But how? I can't just walk onto the ferry. Sasha told me no one leaves without ID."

Gavin moves his hand to my cheek, stroking it with his thumb. "Let me worry about that." He sits up and kisses me. I can't help but look at Parker when Gavin pulls away. Even in the dark, I can see the confidence fade from Gavin's face. "Are you sure this is what you want?"

I read through his words: *Are you sure about us?*

"Of course I'm sure." I lean forward and kiss him again.

"Then all you need to worry about is picking a new hair color." He lies back and puts his hands behind his head like he's gazing up at the stars. "Since Kenny may have tipped them off about the brown, what do you think about dyeing it black?"

I flip my pillow to feel the cool fabric against my cheek and whisper, "I'll be any color but blonde."

• • •

My dreams are vivid, a replay of all of the past dreams merged into one. I sit up with a headache, but the throbbing is duller than it used to be. Perhaps knowing they're real makes the pain manageable. Parker is standing, fidgeting by the closet. I can sense he's about to burst if he doesn't get out of the room. He keeps lifting his knees, stretching like he's preparing for a run. I remember that feeling, the need to expel energy when I first left the Center. Gavin looks relaxed in his position on the floor until we hear a car slow outside. In a flash, Gavin and I are on our feet, all of us glancing at each other in trepidation.

"How did they find me?" I ask.

"They didn't," Gavin says when he peeks through the curtain. "It's my dad. Stay quiet."

Parker and I don't have time to ask questions. Gavin leaves the room, shutting us in with the lights off.

"Why are we hiding?" Parker asks.

"I'm not sure. I had to hide last time too."

"That's a little suspicious, don't you think?"

I remind myself that Parker isn't being objective. He has ulterior motives. *A pact that needs to be addressed.*

"We need to talk." I pull him toward the only place to sit in the room—the bed. Not ideal, but my options are limited. I put a foot of space between us. Parker's shoulders are so broad it seems pointless to distance myself. "Were you always this big?" I ask in a whisper.

"I worked a little harder after you got out." Parker puts a hand on my thigh. "I had to keep my mind busy."

I go to lift his hand, but he moves it quickly, trapping mine underneath. A tight ball forms in my stomach.

"Parker...I need you to know how much I care about you."

"I care about you too, Tabitha." His voice is soft and sultry, not the right tone for where I'm going. He leans forward and I pull back.

"I know we've been friends for a long time, that we had a pact, but everything has been a whirlwind since I got out. Gavin and I are...together." I feel my fingers being squeezed as Parker struggles to keep his smile. "I know we agreed to try dating on the outside, but I didn't know when you'd get out. I didn't plan on falling for Gavin."

He retracts his arm like I've bitten him, and the muscles in his jaw work overtime. "Oh. I get it," he finally says. "He's got you brainwashed into trusting him." He waves his hand flippantly over his head. "Funny how you think he's genuine yet he can't even introduce you to his dad."

"His dad's a scientist at PharmPerfect, so they aren't on the best terms. I'm sure Gavin's just trying to keep me safe. I know what I'm doing, Parker. I can think for myself." Parker's scowl tells me he's not convinced. He's lucky I'm trying to consider his feelings; otherwise I'd wallop him right now. "I care about him, and Gavin cares about me."

"He doesn't know anything about you." Parker stands abruptly, poking at the trophies and pendants around the room. "Ten years, Tabitha. That's a long time to get to know someone." He folds his hands behind his back while he paces from wall to wall. "I bet he doesn't know your favorite color, what your dream house looks like, or what kind of wedding dress you want to wear."

"That's not fair, you got to see all of that from magazine clippings."

Parker paces faster, but he might as well be stomping on my dreams.

"He's known you a fraction of the time I have. So he got you out? What happens when he gets tired of running? He has a family and friends, Tabitha. Hell, he can drive and get a job. Is he really going to stick around?" Parker stops in front of me. His eyes are intense, and I can't look away. He squats down and lifts my chin; our noses almost touch. "The people out here don't understand what it feels like to be us. You're the closest thing I've ever had to family and I'd do anything to protect you."

The kiss starts and ends so fast I don't even have time to blink.

"Right now, it's us against them," he says, standing again. He waves at the window to the world outside. "You may not see it, but Gavin's using you…for something."

For a moment the air slips out of me. I can't breathe. Parker has scared the *what if* right back into me. I want to box my heart up and hand it over to Parker for safekeeping. What if he's right? What if this is just a minor detour on the road to heartbreak before I take the familiar path back to Parker? Or worse, what if I don't even get the chance to recover? Is Gavin using me? Is he planning to turn me in himself?

No. He would have done that already. Right? I try to bury my doubt, but it's like a rash that's spreading, an itch that won't go away. Gavin still has secrets, and I have no idea what they are. But they make me feel scared for myself, and for my friends.

"You don't know what you're talking about, Parker." My voice cracks.

"You're making a mistake. I wish you'd just see it." He sits next to me and runs his hands through his hair with such force I glance at his fingers to see if he's yanked out a clump. "I'll be watching him like a hawk. If he so much as makes you lose an eyelash," he punches his hand, "I'll pummel him."

Parker sounds so sure of himself—just like he was at the Center; it's hard not to smile a little on the inside. He always looked out for me. I should be grateful that part of him hasn't changed. But I'm uneasy and I'm not sure if it's because of what Parker said, or the fact that he made me question myself. Whatever it is, the lump sits firmly in the pit of my stomach.

Voices in the hall remind me we're not alone. The door flies open and the light kicks on before we can move.

"And here they are," Gavin says. He extends a hand to me and I take it, leaving Parker alone on the bed. Gavin pulls me close to him, like he's introducing me to an untamed dog, worried it will nip at me. "Dad, this is Tabitha."

The man beside him eyes me with wonder. His skin is slightly darker than Gavin's, his forehead broader. Still, there's a striking resemblance.

I glance back at Parker with a look that says, *See! I get to meet his dad.*

"Hello, sir." I shake the man's hand.

"Please, call me Bracken." He doesn't let go until Gavin clears his throat.

I don't have to turn to know Parker is on his feet. His body is so close I can feel the warmth on my back.

"And who's this?" Bracken asks.

"Tabitha's best friend," says Parker, ignoring the outstretched hand. Gavin's father drops his arm and his smile weakens.

"You must be quite an athlete," Bracken says, eyeing Parker's torso.

A twinge of pain crosses Gavin's face that makes me wonder what kind of compliments—if any—his dad has given him through the years.

"Like I explained, both of them are from the Center," says Gavin. "They trained daily."

"Well I'll be…" Bracken's eyes widen. "It's not just a rumor, then." He presses his lips together.

"Now that you've met them," Gavin says, "let's talk. Downstairs in the lab."

Bracken nods. "Help yourself to anything in the kitchen." He obediently follows Gavin down the hall.

Parker and I exchange a wary look.

What do they need to talk about? Alone?

As if he's thinking the same thing, Parker motions toward the door. "Let's get some fresh air." When we walk outside, I'm surprised how much easier it is to breathe. Then Parker grabs my arm.

"I think we should leave," he says, jerking the air out of me. I'm so stunned that he manages to drag me halfway toward the trees that surround the side of the property.

I slip out of his grip and he stops, glancing back at me with dread in his eyes.

"I'm not going anywhere, Parker. They're just talking."

"Yeah. In a lab. Doesn't that bother you?"

I ignore his question. "And just where are we supposed to go? We have no identification."

Parker grits his teeth and growls under his breath. "Why do you want to stay? Didn't you see his dad? How he looked at you? He's a scientist, you said so yourself. He probably wants to chop you up. Doesn't that freak you out?"

My insides feel like they're already being diced. What if Parker's right? I don't know anything about Gavin's dad other than his obsession with work—which happens to be for PharmPerfect.

"He was practically drooling when he saw you. He might as well pin you to a corkboard like a butterfly."

My instincts tell me to fight, or better yet, run. Then there's this steady little voice that keeps time with the beat of my heart, trying to convince me to wait. "Gavin hasn't given me any reason not to trust him."

"Well, I don't. And you shouldn't either." Parker climbs into Gavin's truck, pulling down the visor and checking the ignition. "If he left the keys, we can get out of here before he gets back."

I try to pull him out, but he shakes me off and I lose my hold, falling to the ground. I land with a thud and yelp in pain.

"Are you okay?" Parker hops down from the driver's seat. "I didn't mean for that to happen. I just want out of here. Something's not right."

My tailbone hurts, but not as much as Parker's words. They sting because there's truth to them. Being here with Gavin's dad makes me uncomfortable, trapped like a bug in a jar.

"It doesn't matter. We can't go anywhere. Even if he did leave the keys, it's not like you can drive. Face it; we *have* to trust Gavin. For now."

A manila folder sticks out of the door pocket behind Parker. It flaps in the breeze, waving me over. My eyes lock in and I stand. My feet seem to move on their own. It's the paperwork Gavin said was for his dad. Why is it still in the truck, then?

I open the file before I can talk myself out of it, and my jaw drops.

"What is it?" Parker leans in from the side.

"It's a letter…"

"Who's the guy in the picture?" Parker reads over my shoulder. "General Mitchell Rhodes, Special Forces." He hitches a breath. "Is that…"

I nod, and the horizon tilts. Parker catches my arm as I sway. "He—he's alive."

"It says he's a widow, that his wife and child died in a car accident."

I focus my eyes and scan the list of assignments he went on, countries he visited. One of the dates sticks out, and I point with a shaky finger. "This is the month and year they said my parents died. But my dad wasn't even in the country then, so how could this be right?" My stomach rolls.

"I don't know." Parker stands in front of me and lifts my chin. "But at least he's not dead."

Parker's right. I don't know what happened to my mom, but my dad is out there somewhere.

And Gavin knew. Why would he keep this from me?

My heart can't decide which way to break. Tears erupt and I fall into Parker's arms.

"Let's get out of here," he says. I nod into his shoulder.

# CHAPTER 24

We run across the main road into the dense forest. The under-
growth is thick, full of supersized ferns and decaying logs. Each
step is harder than the last. At this rate, it'll take us an hour to get
twenty yards.

"This is ridiculous," I say, so frustrated it almost comes out as
a laugh. I turn around to head back toward the sound of traffic.

"Where are you going?"

"I have a better idea." I stick my thumb out. "We're going to
hitchhike."

Parker smirks. "You're supposed to point your thumb at the
road, not the woods."

I switch hands. "It's not like I've ever done this before."

"Maybe I should try driving? At least we won't have to wait."

"Thanks, but I'm not ready to die yet."

Parker stands next to me and sticks his thumb out too. Cars
whiz by. One slows, but the driver changes his mind and takes off
as we jog toward it. Parker looks strong enough to lift a small car.
I don't blame people for not wanting to stop.

After several minutes, a semi truck slows, its brakes screech-
ing. When the trailer passes us, I spot Gavin on the other side of
the road.

He waves frantically as he calls out, "Tabitha!"

Parker grabs my hand and pulls, but my body doesn't move.
"Come on. He can't hurt you anymore."

He tugs again, hard enough for me to snap out of it. I tear my
eyes away from Gavin and we dart for the truck.

"Wait!" Gavin yells. "Come back!" Tires skid and a car blares its horn.

Parker reaches for the door handle, but before I can get in, Gavin grabs my shoulder.

"Let her go!" Parker lunges at Gavin, pinning his throat against the trailer with his forearm. Gavin gasps for air, clawing at Parker's hand.

As he struggles to free himself, our eyes lock. His words are barely audible. "Why…this…?"

"What's going on out there?" the truck driver hollers.

Parker pulls his arm back and motions for me to get in the cab. "Now's our chance."

But I can't leave. Not when I have so many questions. Why did Gavin keep my father a secret? And does he know what happened to my mom? Is she alive?

I shut the door. Parker groans as the truck drives away.

Between coughs, Gavin says, "What…the hell…was that about?"

I pull the paper from my pocket and shake the letter at him. "My father's alive. How could you keep this from me?" Parker's nod punctuates my anger.

"Oh my God, Tabitha…it's not what it looks like." He grips his head, eyes wide and full of something…fear? Remorse? "I didn't tell you because I haven't found him yet. I didn't want to get your hopes up."

Too late.

My eyes burn and Gavin reaches out like he wants to console me, but Parker is quick to block his hand.

"How do we know you weren't trying to keep her dad's existence a secret?" Parker sticks a finger in Gavin's face. "Maybe you never wanted her to find out. Maybe you and your dad had other plans for her." He pulls his arm back and pretends to slice his neck.

"W-what? No! My dad would never—" Gavin clenches his hand by his side, eyes flitting from Parker to me like he's afraid we're going to run if he blinks wrong. "Come back to the house.

I'll explain everything." He looks both ways, but Parker and I don't move when he steps out to cross the street.

"We can talk right here," says Parker.

Gavin comes back to the side of the road. He waits for a car to zoom by and takes a deep breath before he starts. "Chemical 31 is FDA approved, but it shouldn't be. It's so powerful they've had to dilute it so the regulators stay away. PharmPerfect wanted to find a way to make people tolerant to it."

"What's that have to do with Tabitha?" Parker snaps.

"I'm getting to that," Gavin says, keeping his eyes locked on mine. "My dad was on the research team. They spent millions on tests but failed miserably. So they moved my dad to a different project, incurable diseases. He worked with a redheaded patient whose spine was liquefying. That's when he discovered a gene variant, one that could handle some of the most powerful drugs without the damaging effects. A genetic loophole only in redheads that changed the way the woman could process drugs."

"Like me?" I ask, my voice small.

"Yes, but the gene isn't enough. A person also has to have a bacteria living in the intestines that can alter the chemical first. She didn't." Gavin's chin drops. "When the woman died, PharmPerfect devoted all its energy to finding that one in a million person that would have both the variant and the gut bacteria." Gavin steps closer. "Do you remember the first time we went to Dairy Land?" I can taste vanilla on my tongue, but the memory is bittersweet now. I manage a nod. "On the drive, you told me you were only six when they brought you to the Center. I would've been about seven. That was the first year I played little league, the year I met Ry. PharmPerfect put on this massive blood drive, they even can-celled practice one afternoon so parents could donate. The entire town got into it."

"*I Give,*" I say out loud, making sense of the sticker on my mom's polo shirt. Gavin wrinkles his forehead, but I motion for him to continue.

"According to the files Cherry stole for me, five people were flagged for cancer after the blood drive…including someone with the last name Rhodes. I'm assuming that was your mom."

"She had cancer? But why would they—"

"She didn't. It was a ploy to get people to submit to more tests. She had what they were looking for."

"My mom was kidnapped so your dad could study her?"

Gavin's hands go up in defense. "My dad was told the woman volunteered for the genetic study. I swear he knows nothing about what really happened."

My breath shudders. "What *did* happen to her?"

"My dad said the woman died before the research could begin."

A car speeds by and the air hits me like a shockwave. "They killed her?"

"I don't know…something must have gone wrong. I wish I knew."

There's a squeeze in my chest. All that matters is she's dead. The tiny bit of hope I clung to dies, and it's like I've lost her all over again. Tears prick my eyes.

"My dad," I say, voice shaky. "Why didn't he come for me? He just believed what they told him?"

"From what I gather, PharmPerfect waited until he was sent on a training mission, then they made their move, staging your deaths. There was even a funeral."

I wipe my face with the back of my hand. "Why? Why did they want us so bad?"

"To create a powerful new drug called Gideon. They want to grow the bacteria inside you then transfer the microorganisms into soldiers so they can take the drug without risk of liver failure. If they're successful, it'll land them a fat military contract."

"What's the drug supposed to do?" Parker asks as two motorcycles scream by.

"It uses the power of Clarity to improve decision making, Endurance so soldiers can work for days without needing to rest, and Power to make them stronger, faster—unstoppable. The doses are more than triple the legal limit. But if PharmPerfect can prove they're safe with this microorganism transfer, they'd have the government eating out of their hands. Our military has been surpassed by almost every nation—we're extremely vulnerable."

I can feel Parker's eyes on me. "This is why Kenny wanted me back so badly," I say lacing my fingers over my head, desperate for air.

Gavin nods. "You were the entire reason he buddied up with Cherry. He used us to get you out. All he had to do was say he infiltrated our group and brought you back." He paces along the side of the road, eyeing the driveway that leads to his house. "That military contract is within their grasp again unless we can keep you safe. Being out here in the open isn't a good idea."

"What if she agrees to let them make the bacteria in her?" Parker asks. "Will they stop chasing her?"

"That's not how it works," Gavin says. "She'll be kept alive, but sedated. They'll keep using her until the drug kills her."

"I thought you said I could process it?"

"You can. But in order to foster bacteria growth, you'd need to be given higher and higher concentrations of the drug. You can process it, but not forever. Not at the doses they'll end up giving you."

My stomach churns. "They'll never stop looking for me."

"Your dad might be able to help us if I can track him down," Gavin says, "That's what I've been trying to do. Finding him has been harder than I thought. Adrian's been trying to break into military networks." Gavin stops in front of us and reaches out. I stare at his hand, wondering if I should take it, but he drops it before I can decide. "I wanted to wait until we were on the mainland before I told you all of this. I'm sorry you had to find out this way. I was only trying to protect you."

I've lost my mom, but I have a second chance with my dad if Gavin can find him. The gust of air from a truck that rushes by makes my knees weak. I'm in shock, floating in the unthinkable fantasy that I might hug my dad again.

Gavin seizes the opportunity and reaches for my face, his

thumb caressing my jawline. Part of me melts, yearning for his warmth and safety. "We need to get back to my house, keep you hidden until we can catch the ferry."

"What ferry? And what's this talk about the mainland?" Parker asks, pulling Gavin's arm down.

"Let's get out of sight and we'll figure everything out," Gavin says, taking my hand and darting across the road. Parker obstinately follows.

"What about his dad?" Parker asks when he catches up to me. Anger radiates off of him. "How do we know he won't just turn you in—"

"Like I said, he didn't know she was being hunted down," Gavin says sharply. He looks at me, his voice softer. "He had no idea what they'd done to you and your mom until I told him. That's why I introduced you. He wants to help. PharmPerfect used him like they used you."

"That's hardly the same thing," Parker says.

"Look," Gavin says, taking a deep breath. "I know you don't like me. But you have to trust me. I want to keep her safe just as much as you do."

"Doubtful. Wherever she goes, I go."

Gavin rubs his face and gives Parker a subtle nod, as if he has no choice but to agree. He walks toward the house. When I try to follow, Parker's grip stops me. The front door shuts and Parker and I are surrounded by nothing but the hum of distant traffic and tall grass.

He moves in front of me. "You love him, don't you?"

The answer is convoluted. Yet the longer Parker stares at me, his eyes wide and glossy, the clearer the answer gets. I'd be lying if I said I didn't.

My throat is dry and I part my lips, deciding to nod at the last second.

"I don't get it." He shakes his head. "His dad works for the company that took everything from us. We have no future and no family—except each other." He throws his hands up, exasperated. "And yet you still trust this wacko?"

"Yes. I do." I glance at the house, half expecting Gavin or his dad to be peeking out the curtains, watching to see if we'll make a run for it again. I don't think it would matter if we did now. Gavin has told me everything I need to know. If PharmPerfect wants a fight, I'm going to give them one.

# CHAPTER 25

Inside, Gavin's dad is doing something I doubt he's done in decades: cleaning.

"Put those papers in the trash bag," Bracken says after Gavin shows him a stack he's holding.

"Are you sure?" Gavin asks.

"If I go through them one by one, we'll never make any progress."

Parker and I stand in the entryway, not sure what to make of the activity.

"We're getting rid of evidence," Gavin says, gesturing to his dad.

"It's the only way to keep you safe." Bracken's hands are trembling, his eyes glued to the paper in his hand. He stares at it like a picture that evokes a fond memory. Finally, his face tightens and he crumples it up, tossing it in the black bag. "Without the research papers, PharmPerfect will have to start over. They might not be able to transfer the microorganisms at all."

"Do you need help?" I ask.

Bracken motions for me to join, and a faint smile emerges, but it doesn't quite reach his eyes. Parker watches for a while before picking up a stack of papers.

"How do I know what to keep?" Parker asks.

"If it has numbers or a formula on it, throw it away," says Bracken.

"All of them?" I hold up a paper on PharmPerfect letterhead congratulating Dr. Stiles on his work with electrical signals and cells. It's even signed by the CEO himself, but Gavin gives me a firm nod. I glare at Trae Murphy's signature and the fancy gold company emblem underneath it before wadding the letter into a ball.

"My dad didn't keep his research on a computer. Everything's on paper or in his head." Gavin taps his temple. "Without the formula, they should have no reason to keep you."

"They'd stop looking?" The air seems easier to breathe.

Gavin holds his hand up as if he's trying to convince my enthusiasm to take a seat. "Maybe. Other scientists have reviewed my dad's work. They might have enough to work with. But it doesn't hurt to take precautions."

My joy isn't stifled. Even Parker wears a satisfied grin. I want to thank Gavin's dad, but instead I work faster, letting my hands say everything for me. I know how much this project, his life's work, meant to him. Now that he knows what it means to me, he's willing to throw it all away. Literally.

"We'll stuff the bags in the storage shed out back near the fire pit. I'll tell PharmPerfect an ember landed on the roof," Bracken says. His voice lacks confidence, but I have to believe this plan might work. I have to hold onto hope.

We work until the living room is empty, except for furniture and dust. Gavin vacuums with a machine that wheezes so loud it sounds like it's dying, and I polish the piano with a rag while Parker and Bracken haul the last couple of bags out.

I stroke the keys, hitting a few notes, enjoying the bliss that comes with each one.

"You play?" Gavin asks, unplugging the vacuum.

"It's starting to come back to me. All of it."

"No more headaches?"

"They're there. Just not as bad as when they first started."

Gavin moves across the room and stands behind me. I want so badly to turn around, to see his lips up close, to lose the distance between us.

"I don't expect you to forgive me," he whispers next to my ear. The hairs on my arms stand at attention, and my head leans slightly toward his mouth, like his lips are calling me. But his words push me away. "I'll do everything I can to keep you safe. That includes stepping aside."

My eyes follow him down the hall, watching him disappear into the office with the vacuum. I thought I needed to figure out how to forgive Gavin, but it won't matter. It's clear he isn't going to forgive himself.

• • •

We spend the next day cleaning the kitchen. It takes twice as long, but when all the dishes have been scrubbed and the fridge has been cleared of everything coated in mold, we sit at the table to eat the pizza Bracken picked up for lunch—per Parker's suggestion.

My hair is still wet from the post-cleanup shower, and even though my skin is clean, I'm a mess on the inside. My heart is cluttered with emotions that contradict one another. I want to take the next ferry out of Gladstone—to forget my life here. But I can't. I'm too attached to the people I grew up with and the new friends I've made. I wonder if Sasha's playing with Mary right now, if Paige and Ry are staying off Euphorium.

Gavin interrupts my musings when he sits on one end of the table looking deflated. He doesn't glance up as he takes a seat between Parker and his dad.

"There's a ferry tomorrow morning at six and another at eight. There'll be lots of cars on both runs, but I'd suggest getting on the earliest ride out," says Bracken.

"Why's that?" Parker asks.

"Everyone will be tired, in a hurry to get to work. Security guards will be trying to wake up. Your chances are better. But you'll need identification," Bracken says. "No one gets on or off the island without it. Now I know why." After a long pause, he clears his throat. "I have a friend at the lab…the paperwork won't be perfect, but it should get you to the mainland."

"Thank you," I say, reaching for a slice of pepperoni. "What's going to happen to you after we leave?"

Bracken shrugs as he rocks a little in his chair, like the idea of doing something risky is exciting. It's probably the first time in his life he's ever broken the rules. Parker kicks me under the table and shoots me a look that says *don't make him change his mind.*

"I've been spending too much time on that project anyway." Bracken dabs his mouth with a paper towel. "I've already given the company enough years. I don't intend to give them any more."

"Will you be fired?" I prod.

"More like, forced into early retirement," Bracken says. "When they hear a fire destroyed most of my work, I doubt they'll want to reinvest in me." He gives me a reticent smile.

"Can't they find something else for you to work on?"

"They need me for their war pill. Without you, I'm useless to them."

"I'm sorry." I mean it, and Bracken reaches for my hand.

"Why?" Parker's voice is brash, cutting through the sentiment. "Why do you care about this man's job? Your mom is dead and the company he works for is responsible."

"Parker!" I'm ashamed at his outburst, but also a little at myself. I should be angry. I *am* angry. But not at Gavin and his dad.

"It's all right." Bracken gives me an understanding pat on the hand and stands. "Identification won't make up for the years you've suffered, but it will at least help get you to some years you can enjoy. If you'll excuse me, I'd like to get to the office. I need to leave now if I'm going to get ID cards and birth certificates made."

Bracken grabs his keys and leaves us to finish eating. We polish off the rest of the pizza, thanks mainly to Parker, and clear the table.

Gavin carries over the plates and corners me by the kitchen sink. "I have something I need to show you. It's a surprise." Our eyes meet and there's a flash of excitement in his. I've missed that look, and it stirs something inside me. "Come with me." I follow him down the hall. I don't even notice Parker's not behind us until Gavin shuts the door and we're alone. My heart speeds up a little.

Gavin pulls a history book off his shelf. There's an envelope inside and he hands it to me.

I tear the seal carefully.

"It's not your original birth certificate," says Gavin, "but it *is* a certified copy."

All of the information is there: my birth weight, the hospital I was born in, my parents' names, Mr. and Mrs. Rhodes. Mitch and Ellen. I know her name now, and the realization makes my chest compress, uncertain of whether I'm about to cry or laugh.

"How'd you get this?" I ask, my hands shaking.

Gavin's standing in the shadow of his bookshelf, watching me read about my history. The darkness can't dull his smile. He knows how much this means to me.

"It wasn't easy. I had to jump through a lot of hoops. Whatever fake ID my dad comes up with will have to be what you go by until we can figure out what to do next. But at least you'll have this to remember who you were. Who you'll always be."

"Thank you." I hold the only piece of my past I'll probably ever own. The corner of Gavin's mouth turns up, and he stuffs his hands in his pockets like he's satisfied. A job well done.

"I'll find your dad. It'll just take some digging, and time."

That's all he's ever wanted. Time. I can't stay mad at him no matter how hard I try. I believe in him, trust him. My arms wrap around his neck, and I bring his mouth into mine. The birth certificate rustles near our faces as we kiss.

I can tell he's hesitant at first, but the longer our lips stay locked, the stronger he kisses back. I let the paper fall to the ground as Gavin tucks an arm behind my waist. He turns me so my back is to the wall. His mouth travels down my neck, bringing goose bumps to the surface of my arms.

"Does this mean you forgive me?" he whispers, his hot breath warming the sensitive spot behind my ear.

"For now," I say, and then his lips are back on mine.

I almost miss the rapping on the door until it grows loud enough that we can't ignore it. Parker peeks his head in. I don't try to hide the fact that I've forgiven Gavin.

"Your dad just called. It sounded important, but the machine cut him off."

Gavin gives my fingers a squeeze before he heads to the living room. Parker moves just enough to let Gavin by, stepping closer to me when we're alone.

"That's it, then?" Parker's eyes narrow as he studies my face.

"I can't shut off my feelings for him. It's not that easy."

"Trust me, I know."

I may have chosen my words badly, but I'm not going to let Parker guilt me away from Gavin.

The door swings open and I jump. Gavin has the truck keys in his hand.

"I have to go." He stands there for a moment, as if he has more to say, but his mouth snaps shut, and he leaves without so much as a goodbye.

"Where are you going?" I push past Parker, whose body is like a steel door. Gavin is already on the front steps when I catch up to him. "What's going on?" My voice is curt, hoping to get his attention.

He opens the truck door and reaches under the seat for a scrap of paper. Grabbing a pen from the side compartment, he scribbles something on the back of a receipt. When he turns to me his eyes are filled with anguish.

"If I don't come back in an hour, leave." He hands me the paper. "This is Adrian's number." He pulls me into him with a kiss that says it may be his last.

A kiss that scares me.

"Remember. One hour." He gets into the truck and tears out of the driveway.

I stand there long enough to watch the cloud of dust disappear. Parker is on the porch steps when I turn around.

"What did the message say?" I ask in a demanding voice.

"He said, 'They know her tracker's been removed. And they suspect I know where she is.' Then his voice cut out. The phone went dead."

I can tell by Parker's expression I'm not the only one who doesn't believe the call dropped by accident.

"If they haven't already, they'll figure out we're here." I glance at Adrian's number. "Gavin wants us to leave in an hour."

Parker's body tightens like he just finished lifting. "I say we leave now."

"We can't just leave. We have to help." The address from the letterhead flashes in my mind. "PharmPerfect's lab is on Addison Street."

"You can't just walk in there and demand they let Gavin's dad go. Why would they listen to us?"

"We won't give them a choice." I lead Parker into the kitchen, knowing this is my only option. "Gavin's dad has weapons in the lab." I point at the door to the basement. "There's a gun safe in the corner." Parker takes the bait.

I wait for him to make it all the way down the steps before I shout down to him. "I'm sorry! I'll send someone to get you out soon."

He stares up at me and his eyes grow wide. I slam the door shut. His feet pound up the stairs as I fumble with the padlock, nervously trying to get it to click tight. Parker beats the door with his fists.

"Open up! You'll get yourself killed!"

I cover my ears, trying to block him out.

"Tabitha! You're the one they want!"

"That's why I have to go. It's the only way to save the rest of you."

Parker pounds harder, enough to make the padlock bounce against the doorframe. "Tabitha!"

I can't say anything more without choking up, so I run down the hall to Gavin's room to retrieve the one thing that might help me pull this off.

Ms. Preen's little red pill.

# CHAPTER 26

I hide the key to the laboratory door under a garden gnome and head for the main road. Without Parker there to scare all the cars away, hitchhiking is a cinch.

I barely have my thumb out before a sporty black car pulls up. A man with eyebrows that look like they've been freshly trimmed lowers the passenger window.

"Need a lift?" He motions for me to get in. "I could use the company."

I hold the handle for a second, wondering if I'm making a mistake. But Gavin and Bracken risked their lives for me. I need to be brave.

The seat is soft, and my body melts into it. I have to lean forward to keep the sinking sensation at bay.

"Buckle up," he says, flashing a smile.

"I need to get to PharmPerfect," I say as we merge onto the road. "How far is it?"

Everything seems to slow down. The car. The music. The way he runs a hand through his wavy hair before answering. "We'll be there in about an hour."

That can't be right.

"Is there any way we can get there faster?"

"That depends. How fast do you need to get there?" He rubs my thigh, and I slap his hand away.

"Just let me out," I say, my voice shaky. "I'd rather walk."

He hits a button and I hear a click. My eyes flash to the door. His fingers slide down my arm and my body clenches. "I can pay you in cash or pills."

Pay me for *what*? Panic rips through me. His hand moves back to my thigh, and I roll my fist into a tight ball, connecting with his jaw.

The car swerves and I grab the handle, knocking the door with my shoulder. It doesn't budge. He growls, spitting out what looks like blood. He reaches for my leg again and I unlock the door. Flinging it open, I dive for the grassy shoulder.

I roll to a stop and lift my chin when I hear brakes squeal. The car's taillights shift from red to white. He's going to run me over!

I push myself up, crawling deeper into the grass as the car zooms toward me. There's a series of honks and the car stops. I look back at the fender, inches from hitting me. There's another vehicle in my periphery and the man throws his car in drive and takes off, spitting pebbles at me with his tires.

Shoes click against the paved road. "Are you all right?" a frightened voice asks. She sounds familiar…

I turn my head, my eyes settling on the pretty blonde. "Cherry?"

"Oh my God! It's you!" Her face goes white. "I saw you jump out of that car. Are you hurt?"

My hip feels bruised, and my hands and knees are embedded with rocks. I pick them out and wipe the blood on my shirt. "I'm fine." I try not to grimace when I press the lump on my head. "But Gavin's not."

I didn't think her skin could go whiter, but it does, and for a second I empathize with her. She cares about Gavin too, has history with him that can't be erased without a drug. I suspect she'll want to help, and when her eyes grow wide, I know I'm right.

"Get in." She gestures to her convertible. I drag myself to her car, feeling new body aches emerge. She pops the trunk and grabs a towel before I can sit down. "Use this." She covers the seat. "I don't want to get blood on the leather."

I collapse into the seat. It takes me twice as long to buckle, and she revs the engine impatiently.

"Where to?" she asks when the belt clicks.

"PharmPerfect. He's at the lab."

She smiles at me like I'm a small child. "Gavin's not in trouble. That's where his dad works. Didn't he tell you?"

"I know, Cherry," I say, exhaling. "But his dad went to the lab to…to get something. He ran into some trouble and Gavin left in a panic."

"If his dad's not home, then who's in the basement?"

I glance in the side mirror at the road Cherry had been traveling down, the road that leads away from Gavin's house. "Is that where you're coming from?"

She bristles. "Kenny asked me to stop by. See if anyone was home. He hasn't heard from Gavin lately. Who's in the basement?"

"No one you need to worry about right now. Just get us to the lab."

"Not until you tell me what's going on."

I don't trust her like Gavin does, but I need an ally right now and Cherry's the one who can get me where I need to go. "Fine. I'll tell you on the drive." She shifts the car into gear.

Her face stays taut as I explain everything—from Kenny's involvement, to the message on the machine. Her mouth finally relaxes when I finish. It seems that my selflessness has earned her respect. I am, after all, trying to save the man we both love. If I die, it'll be a bonus for her.

"I knew Kenny was lying," Cherry says under her breath.

"Then why are you helping him?"

"I'm not," she snaps. "I hate Kenny. He thinks he's better than everyone because his dad makes all the pills."

"But you went to Gavin's house." I gesture behind us.

"I was worried about Gavin. Kenny knew I'd come out here if he asked." Her voice is small, defeated. "I had to. It's Gavin."

I'm not sure what to say, but I nod to let her know I understand.

"Besides, I wasn't helping Kenny, I was helping Gavin. At least I thought I was," she continues. "Kenny started calling me a few months ago. He kept asking if I knew anything about this group that was going around stealing patients from the hospital. I pretended I didn't know what he was talking about, even when he told me he heard Ry was buying bodies in the Junkie District." She glances over and waits for me to meet her eyes. "Gavin told me not to say a word. He wanted to make sure I stayed safe."

"Why'd you open your mouth then?"

Her lips form a tight red line, just like her mom's. "Kenny tricked me into telling him. He made me think he had changed, that he really *cared* about people." She shakes her head in disgust. "Meanwhile Gavin was actually saving people—or at least trying to." She shoots me a sideways glare. "You weren't the one consoling him when he failed. It was destroying him inside…" Her wheel grip tightens. "I just wanted to help him…I should've known better than to trust Kenny." We're both silent for several seconds, then she wipes an eye and sits up. "So what's your plan?"

"I'm going to offer Kenny a trade. Me for both of them."

"You're going to give yourself up?" There's genuine concern in her voice.

"I think I know how I can get Kenny to let me go." I pull out the red pill.

She does a double take. "Where did you get that?"

"I found it." In your mom's purse, I want to add. "All I need to do is get him to take it."

"And how do you suppose you'll do that?"

I tuck the pill away. "I haven't figured that part out yet." The truth is I'm not sure I'll be able to pull this off. But I have to try.

My body tenses as we pull into PharmPerfect's parking lot. It's packed with cars, each trying to outshine the next. Cherry drives down the front row, and we eye the entry gate that leads to a garden area.

"That's where employees enter," she says as if it wasn't obvious.

My heart kicks into high speed when she parks. This is it. There's no going back now.

"He'll let you inside, right?" I ask.

"Absolutely." Cherry dabs on some lipstick. "Kenny still thinks we're friends." She smiles to herself.

"Tell Kenny he can have me if he lets Gavin and his dad go." She reaches for the handle and I grab her shoulder before she gets out. "I'll be in the bushes by the entrance."

"Bushes. Got it." She cracks the door.

"Wait." I struggle to keep my voice even. "Tell Gavin I'm at the house, locked in the lab. The key is under the gnome." She opens her mouth as if she wants to say something. Silence fills the air instead. "Whatever you do Cherry, don't let Gavin know I came with you. He has to believe I'm at the house or he won't leave."

She nods and gets out. I swear her hands are shaking as she walks toward the entrance, but maybe it's my vision because my heart is pounding so hard it's rattling my core.

When she's safely inside, I get out. I make a mad dash toward a shrub that isn't in view of the cameras and dive behind it. I take a calming breath and wipe my hands on my shirt.

Now all I can do is wait.

A few cars leave the lot and I hear chatter as people come and go. But no Cherry and no Gavin. Minutes tick by and I shiver, pulling my knees to my chest. Maybe this isn't such a good idea. What if Kenny doesn't want to negotiate? What if Cherry tells Kenny what I plan to do? Did I make a mistake trusting her?

A door slams against a wall, yanking me from my thoughts.

Three people rush by and I peek through the bush just in time to catch the back of Gavin's head.

"What's going on?" Gavin asks, grabbing Cherry's arm. They stop less than twenty feet away. "Why is he letting us go?"

"I blackmailed him," Cherry says. "I told him I recorded some of our conversations."

"Where's Tabitha? Is she safe?"

"She's at your house in the basement. I swear. She's the one who told me you were here." Gavin lets go of her arm and I fight back tears as they drive away.

Cherry fulfilled her mission. Now it's my turn.

The door opens and I hear someone walk a few feet, then stop. "You can come out now," Kenny says. He's sitting on a bench near the entrance. "You forgot about the window." Kenny points to the second story above me. "But at least I knew you weren't lying. That you were here."

"This is what you wanted, right?" I have to fight to keep my fists from clenching. Kenny needs to think I'm cooperating. I tuck my fear away and step out from behind the bush.

• • •

I follow him inside, wondering if this is the last time my feet will be in motion. The pharmaceutical company will have their test subject and my family is safe. A collection of people I care about. That's all a family is really. People you'd die for.

My knees shake as we reach a metal door. It has a vertical window that's covered in black film, making it impossible to see out. Kenny pushes me inside.

"Don't waste your time trying to get out. This glass is shatter-proof." He taps it with his knuckles. "I'll be back shortly."

The door clicks shut and my heart starts to tick off the seconds I have to attempt my own rescue. If I can pin Kenny down, maybe I can force him to take the pill. But how am I going to keep him from spitting it out? *Think, Tabitha.*

There has to be another way.

I survey the room. There's a medical bed and a counter lined with tongue depressors and cotton swabs. I rummage through the drawers. Then my eyes flash to the red hazard bin. I rip off the top, and my fingers tremble with excitement as I pull out a used syringe. I put the Fireball on the counter and jab the needle into it. Once the gel's extracted, I tuck the syringe carefully under my waistband.

A second later, the door handle turns.

Kenny has a man with him. He's older. The kind of man who would pose as the father in a young family on a magazine cover. He has Kenny's nose, his sense of confidence, and the same smelly cologne that screams *I'm rich and fancy.*

"Here she is." Kenny waves his hand like I'm a new car. "Don't let the brown hair fool you. She's the redhead you want."

"Wonderful," the man says. "I don't know how you pulled it off." His hand floats over Kenny's shoulder but doesn't drop. Kenny stands straighter, inching closer, as if the touch is confirmation of success.

"Should I alert the doctor?"

"Always thinking ahead, aren't you, son?"

As his father scans me over, my muscles tighten, like they're being shrink-wrapped around my bones. I cross my arms; afraid I might not be able to control myself. I want to rip this man to pieces for what he did to my mom, my friends, *me*.

"Sit." Mr. Murphy points at the hospital bed. When I don't obey, Kenny grabs my arm, jerking me toward it. "We've waited a long time for this." He adjusts his tie and gives me the same awful grin his son did earlier. "Think of it as doing a service for your country."

For a moment, I see scarlet in my vision. I hate them both.

"How could you do this to me? To everyone at the Center?"

"We all have to make sacrifices in life." He nods at Kenny as if it's their family motto. They probably have it embroidered on their couch pillows.

A loud ring makes me flinch. Mr. Murphy slides his phone out of the holder attached to his belt, and his brow furrows as he answers. "Yes…I see. Very well. We'll just have to speed things up then." When he hangs up, he snaps his fingers at Kenny. "Put her under so we can transport her to the hospital. I'm not going to delay this project any longer."

Kenny's body straightens and he turns to me. "Get up on the bed."

I wait for Mr. Murphy to leave before I lift myself onto the gurney, careful not to pierce my skin with the hidden syringe. The last thing I want to do is fall in love with Kenny before they dig through my intestines.

Kenny puts on some latex gloves, humming a cheery tune that

makes me want to stab him in the neck. I pull the syringe from my waistband, deciding that's exactly how I'm going to do it.

I hop down from the bed and Kenny looks up, face aghast as I jab the needle into his jugular, pushing the plunger down. I step back and he pulls it out, looking from the syringe to me and back again.

His eyes flash with fury. He steps toward me, but stumbles sideways, hitting the door.

"What...what...was in that?" His hand uncurls. The syringe drops to the floor and rolls under the gurney.

I grab his arm and lead him toward the bed. He swings at me like he's blind, his arms as limp as wet noodles. Finally, he sits down and grabs his head. I imagine the serotonin is flooding his brain right about now, the pleasure receptors kicking into high gear. According to Ry and what I read in Gavin's medical books, Fireball is strictly a pleasure drug, stripping people down to their primal instincts so that desire overrides rational thinking. I step away and blow out a breath of relief. Kenny looks around as if he has no idea where we are or what just happened. If this drug does what it's supposed to, maybe I'll walk out of here alive. He groans and brushes the hair out of his eyes, and when ours meet, he doesn't look dangerous anymore. His gaze drops to my chest and a smile spreads across his face.

"How are you feeling?" I ask, tentatively.

He hops off the gurney and staggers toward me. "I feel..." he unbuttons the top of his shirt, "good." Another button.

"No, no, no." I try to button his shirt, but he tickles me and I wiggle away. Bile creeps up into my throat when he licks his lips.

"Did you notice we're alone?" There's hunger in his eyes, like I'm a mouse he's hunting. He eyes the bed. "Shall we?"

Maybe this wasn't such a good idea.

I back up until my butt hits the gurney. In a heartbeat, Kenny grabs my face with both his hands. My insides twist at his touch. His breathing is heavy and he pulls me toward him. "You're so beautiful," he says, his voice sultry.

I jerk my head away before he can kiss me. "No. Not here." I press my hands against his chest. "Not like this."

He leans forward with a laugh and I nearly fall back onto the bed. My elbow catches the gurney in time. I prop myself up as he mashes his lips against my ear, his breath hot and moist. "We can do it right here."

My skin crawls. I shove more forcefully. "No."

He stumbles back and a flash of concern crosses his face.

"I-I mean, can't we go someplace quiet?" I say, sauntering closer. "We can take your car and climb into the back seat..." I can't believe I'm saying these things. It's hard to get the words out with a smile. I stare at my fingers as I run them along his arms, pretending it's Gavin, but my brain doesn't want to cooperate. My eyes meet his. "You'd do that for me. Right, Kenny?"

I lean in, kissing his jawline. My lips will never forgive me.

But it works.

"Of course," Kenny says, trying to force our lips together.

I grab his hand and lead him out. "Come on, let's hurry."

A woman at the front desk asks us where we're going, but we ignore her as we run out the door. Kenny's parked in the second to last row, but the drugs have clearly hindered his ability to focus and he struggles to find the right key.

"Come on, come on," I say. Two men come out the front door and look in our direction. I try to duck down, but they see us before I'm out of view. One of them shouts. Kenny starts the car and hoots in glee.

I hop in. "Go!"

He drives forward and hits the curb.

"Oops." He laughs as he backs up. This time he hits the car directly behind him, cracking the headlights.

The workers are running toward us when Kenny punches the accelerator, forcing one of the men to dive out of the way.

"Where to, my luscious vixen?" Kenny keeps his eyes fixed on me, waiting for an answer.

"The road!" He looks back in time to avoid hitting an oncoming car. I press a hand against my chest and blow out a breath.

"Getting anxious?" Kenny squeezes my side. When I push his hand away, he laughs like it's a game. He reaches his hand behind my head and leans over, pulling my mouth into his. His lips are slick and he tastes like scented oil.

I twist my body to get out of his grip, wiping my mouth on my arm.

"Baby, what's wrong?"

"I want privacy, that's all." I force myself to smile as I pet his shoulder. "I don't want to share you with anyone. We need to be hidden. We deserve to be alone."

"I don't know if I can wait." He stares at my lips, my breasts. I feel naked under his gaze, and every last inch of my skin crawls with disgust. "I know where we can go." He tears his eyes from me and presses the gas pedal harder.

"You need to slow down." The car snakes through the forest road, and tires squeal with each turn. Kenny puts his arm around me, nibbling on my ear. "Cut it out." I jab him with my elbow.

It only seems to fuel him though, and he runs a hand up my shirt. I deflect his arm and he tries again, but there's a bend in the road. He grabs the steering wheel and I suck in a breath.

We're not going to make it.

He hits the brakes and the car fishtails, gliding across the pavement like a puck on ice. The seatbelt digs into my chest as the car flies toward the ditch. A scream fills the air. Metal crunches. My head whips and there's a punch to my temple. Quiet surrounds me as it all fades to black.

• • •

Sirens sound as I come to. I look over at Kenny, amazed we're both alive. Blood drips from his nose onto the airbag, but he's smiling.

An emergency worker helps Kenny out of the car. There's glass everywhere. Shards glisten in the sun. Someone slides a brace behind me, strapping me down and securing my neck. They're taking me away. My breath quickens.

One of the emergency workers places a mask over my face.

I hear Kenny laughing. Maybe the drug wore off. Maybe it never worked. Maybe they'll say I died in a car accident. Again.

A worker secures my neck with foam blocks. I can't see anything but the sky now, and it's blurred with my tears. They load me into the back of a vehicle and shut the door. It's dark. And I'm alone.

I feel a prick in my arm and all the pain slips away. My head swims like it did when I was holding my breath underwater with Paige. When all I knew was the Center and all I wanted was a family.

And I got one. People, who would risk their lives for me, like Gavin.

I wish I could have told him goodbye.

# CHAPTER 27

"She's dead," a man says.

"W-what?" The woman's voice is panicked.

The man laughs. "I'm just kidding, Lizzie. Her pulse is normal."

My eyes flutter open as he removes his fingers from my wrist. He's facing a woman who sits near a computer against the wall. She bats his arm playfully and goes back to typing.

*Where am I?* Everything is hazy, like that halfway point between a dream and being awake. A machine next to my head beeps wildly, creating a series of jagged green mountains on the black screen. My brain is sluggish as I try to make sense of what's going on. It feels like we're moving, which means I must be in an ambulance. There's a mask secured to my face, feeding me crisp air. I pull in a lungful as I start to sit up, but there's a restraint holding down my arms, chest, and legs.

The man turns his attention back to me and smiles. "Look who's coming around." He lifts my eyelids, shining a light that practically blinds me. I wince and jerk my head to the side. "What's your name?"

"Tabitha Rhodes," I say, my voice muffled by the oxygen mask.

I hear typing and the woman calls out, "There's nothing in the system under that name."

The accident plays back in slow motion: The convertible skidding off the road. Kenny laughing manically. Red and blue lights flashing as I tried to stay conscious. Someone lifting me into the back of an ambulance, transporting me away from my goal. Away from safety.

Reality hits me and the words bubble up in my chest. "They erased my history!"

"Just relax." The man jots something on a clipboard. "You got lucky. Just a few minor lacerations, but they'll want to check you for a concussion."

My chest heaves, and suddenly I can't seem to get enough air. My brain screams at me to get up.

"Whoa! Whoa!" The woman jumps from her seat, tapping on the heart monitor. "Calm down. We're almost to the hospital. They're just going to look you over."

I shake my head. "No," I holler through the plastic. "Don't take me there!" My side burns, like it can already feel the scalpel.

"Have to," she says. "It's protocol."

I look around for a weapon. All I see are foam pads and cotton balls. The beeping speeds up and I manage to free a hand from the restraint. I rip the mask from my face and the woman's eyes grow wide. She pounces and grabs the hand that's loose.

"Easy there," she says. The ambulance turns and gravity pulls the room to the side. She loses her grip, and I tug on the strap across my chest while arching my body. White lights flicker in the edges of my vision and I wail as my back burns in pain.

"Hang on," the man says to his partner. He reaches for the shelf above his head.

The woman leans her body over me, pressing against my shoulders. "Hurry!"

"Got it!"

My eyes flash to the man's hands. He's holding a syringe. I flail, freeing one of my legs. I feel the stab of a needle as I start to swing my foot.

"It's in." The man pulls his hand back. My arm pulses and a warm current surges through me, making my toes tingle. I stare at the spot where he injected me, wishing I'd been stronger. Wishing I could think.

My breathing slows. The beeping settles into a leisurely cadence. And I smile.

"Better?" The man winks.

"Much," I mumble. His beard looks rough, but his face is kind. I decide to wink back, but I can't get my eyes to work separately. The more I try, the more it makes me laugh.

He chuckles. "Good. Now enjoy the ride. We'll be there shortly."

• • •

The EMTs unhook me from the oxygen machine and ease the gurney out of the ambulance. Two men in blue scrubs come out to greet us. They chat with the EMTs as I watch a bird fly over the building. I'm counting the windows when I hear a voice that makes my ears perk up. I turn my face toward a man in a business suit walking in my direction.

His eyes are a steely blue that makes me shiver. My heart races, and the euphoric feeling is replaced by a prickle of terror that climbs up my spine.

He leans over me with a sly smile. "You just missed my son."

Who's his son? *Think, Tabitha!* I know I was in an accident, but this man isn't a doctor. My jaw clenches as I try to make sense of what's going on.

"You'll be happy to know Kenny's going to be fine."

Kenny! My breath catches in my throat. The fog lifts and images of Meghan's bloody body flash in my mind like an alarm.

I reach for Mr. Murphy's tie with my free hand, grazing the silk fabric as he jerks his body back. When he wags a finger, I lift my head and spit, hitting his shirt.

Two nurses dash over as I twist back and forth, trying to wiggle out of the restraints. One nurse rams my shoulders down while the other straps my arm in place.

"Let me go!" They snap a new mask over my nose and mouth. There's no air being pumped this time, only my hot, recycled breaths that are heavy and full of fear.

When my limbs are cinched tight, Mr. Murphy steps forward,

a satisfied smirk on his face. "Don't worry. PharmPerfect uses only the best equipment." Someone hands him a clipboard, and he signs at the bottom, barely glancing at the paper. "I've assigned a team of top doctors to take care of you." He gestures at two men standing by the door and they nod obediently. "I'm going to see how my son is doing, but I'll come check on you later."

Mr. Murphy heads through the emergency entrance with an air of confidence, strutting like a peacock in full plumage. The doctors follow him. I whip my gaze around, searching for another escape. One of the nurses grabs the back of the gurney and shifts my feet toward the door. I rock my body, trying to tip myself over.

"Get me a needle," the nurse behind me calls out.

"No, don't drug me!" I plead through my mask. "I'll be good."

A woman approaches with a syringe, a drop of green liquid oozing from the needle's tip. My heart bangs wildly against my sternum. I suck in a breath, holding it while I make myself lie still. I lock eyes with the nurse pushing the gurney. "Please. No needle."

The nurse works a muscle in her jaw, her lips parted like she's about to give the order. Then, she gives the woman with the needle a slight shake of her head. My body unclenches.

The hospital buzzes with phones and intercoms as she wheels me past the reception desk and into the elevator. My head is positioned directly under the hatch where Gavin and I escaped after our botched rescue mission. My mind drifts back to that day, how close we came to getting caught. How awful it felt to lose Meghan.

I wonder if they'll wheel me to the same room to cut me open. I can almost smell the blood just thinking about it. My lip quivers and I bite down to punish it. I'm not dead yet. The Center taught me to be a fighter. I'll make them regret they did.

I inflate my chest, pressing against the straps, trying to loosen them. The elevator bings when we reach the fifth floor, and I continue my exercise as she pushes me through the foot traffic to a room on the end. She wheels me in and hits a button on the door when she leaves. The flashing red light by the entrance is my only company in the sterile room.

I give my torso a rest and strain my legs until my thighs feel like they'll spontaneously combust. Before I can try again, the door opens. A nurse rolls an IV bag hanging from a metal rod into the room. She shoves a needle into my hand and tapes it in place, hooking up the tube that will feed me the liquefied drugs.

She doesn't look at me; she works as if I'm already dead and leaves without a word.

I want to scream and cry and fight—anything but die. I grunt, urging my body to push harder before I'm too drugged up to care about survival. I watch the IV drip, teasing me like an hourglass. How many minutes do I have left before my body goes numb? Before I become a human incubator for organisms to make soldiers unstoppable? Then my muscles twitch like they've been shocked by an electric current. There's a fire in my veins. I flex, lifting against the pressure on my wrist.

Pop!

My right arm flies up. I stare at the strap dangling over the side of the bed, shocked. The IV drips faster, and I reach for the strap on my chest, tugging with all my might. It snaps like a rubber band.

That was too easy.

I sit up, examining my arms. They're red and splotchy and my muscles feel charged with power. My breathing is quick and shallow. Something's not right. I lift my right leg, and the strap comes off with ease. How is this possible? In the corner of my eye, another drop falls.

The IV's not putting me to sleep; it's making me stronger.

Why would they do that?

I hop off the bed. No time to worry about that right now. Giving the IV bag one last squeeze, I let my veins suck in the fuel before yanking out the needle and tube.

I'm prepared to try out my new strength on the door, but it's not locked. Odd. Then, I peek into the hallway. No guards.

The nurses and doctors must not be worried about me escaping. They probably think I'm halfway to dreamland by now. Did they mix up the IV bags by mistake?

I'll take all the luck I can get right now.

I ready myself to make a run for the exit, but hesitate when I see Kenny's dad exit a room three doors down. He stops to say something to a nurse and she laughs, throwing her head back and holding out a hand like she doesn't want him to leave. Eventually, he walks toward the elevator in assertive strides.

As soon as he's gone, I make my move. I don't stop until I make it to the third door.

I slip inside. Kenny's eyes bulge when he sees me and he bolts upright.

"Hello again," I say, my fists balled.

Kenny reaches for a remote on the bedside table and I swing my foot, kicking it out of the way. "Afraid to face me alone?"

"How did you get here?" Kenny's nose is bandaged, and there's a shiny glaze of cream under his eyes. He shifts uncomfortably, like he's debating whether he wants to make a dash for the door.

I inch closer.

"Why'd you do it, Kenny? Was there a reward? Or was it just for your daddy's approval?"

I grab his shirt, lifting him off the bed high enough to scare him. The fear travels from his eyes to his mouth as his lip bounces. "What the hell are you on?"

The door clicks and I drop him, ready to attack whomever steps inside. I freeze when I see it's Ry. I search his eyes, unsure what to think. His gaze flits to my arm muscles and I hitch a breath. "The IV bag. It was you."

"You weren't here to check on me," Kenny says angrily. "You were here to drug her!"

"I didn't lie," Ry says. "I came to check on my family." Ry gives me one of his perfect smiles. I want to hug him, but he gestures for the door. "Get out of here while you're strong enough."

Kenny's bed squeaks, and when I spin around he's barreling at me. My fist connects with the bandage on his nose. His head flies back and he groans in pain.

"I'll take care of Kenny," Ry says. "Go!"

"Thanks, Ry." I fling open the door.

An alarm sounds when I stick my head out and I glance toward my room. A nurse has her finger on a button on the wall. It's the nurse that wheeled me in, and when our eyes lock, she points at me. "That's her!"

I tear through the hall, my shoulders plowing into nurses and doctors like a battering ram. I head down the stairs. My feet hammer against the metal steps. The echo chases me until I reach the first floor and throw the door open.

I freeze when I see the gun pointed at my face.

# CHAPTER 28

The security guard motions for me to come out of the stairwell. I clasp my hands above my head, keeping my movements slow, non-threatening. I ease into the lobby, sliding my body along the wall, watching his eyes, waiting for my opportunity to take his weapon.

I'm about to make my move when there's a loud crash. The guard flinches as the ground shakes beneath us. Screams fill the room as people scatter, running from the truck protruding through the lobby door, jammed like it's stuck in a tunnel.

*Gavin!*

As my eyes search for him, something hard cracks me in the back of the skull. I drop to my knees, trying to blink away the spots in my vision. I turn my face as the guard lifts his gun again, the handle aimed at my forehead. I close my eyes, but I hear a pop and a thud and reopen them. The guard is crumpled on the ground. Gavin drops the tire iron and scoops me up. My body melts into his arms.

"You all right?" His mouth presses against my hair. I nod, clinging to his familiar scent. The smell of safety. "Hold on." He takes off down the hall toward the emergency exit. Outside, Craig's empty car is waiting for us.

We get in and the car squeals as Gavin backs up. He drives toward the exit, but it's blocked. Two security cruisers stand in the way of our freedom. I feel Gavin's stare and meet his eyes with a nod. This is our only way out, our only chance at freedom.

He floors it.

One of the guards waves at the other officer and crouches behind his vehicle. His head pops up, along with the barrel of his gun.

"Get down!" Gavin swerves, aiming for the cruiser on the left.

Bullets ping against my door. We plow past the police car, bouncing off its side, and the force makes my body lurch. I gasp as the seatbelt breaks my momentum. Gavin jerks the wheel. He struggles to regain control as our car bursts onto the main road.

Before my body can unclench, the back window shatters. Glass rains over us, and my hand flies up to cover my head. It's warm and sticky. My fingers tremble as I examine the blood.

"Are you hit?" Gavin asks, panic-stricken.

"My head…"

Gavin reaches for the spot and lets out a breath. "That's from the guard. You're going to be okay."

I feel the bump forming beneath the gash and know he's right. My heart slows.

The wind whistles behind me. I look over my shoulder, glancing through the hole. The buildings shrink as we merge onto the highway, away from the city center.

"How'd you find me?"

"Adrian tapped into the ambulance's communication link. They mentioned a girl without records." He wipes the sheen from his brow. "Cherry finally confessed what you'd done when we got to my house. But when we went back to PharmPerfect, Kenny's car was gone."

My spine straightens when I hear the faint sound of sirens, but Gavin doesn't seem to notice.

"I thought…" He grimaces. "I thought I was too late." He reaches for me, his hand warm over mine. There's suffering in his eyes, but a smile warms his face. His expression changes when the sirens grow louder. His lips form a tight line, and I whirl around to look out.

"Do you see them?"

My hair whips my face as we pass cars and trucks. "No, not yet." I face forward, pulling the strands away from my eyes. Gavin must be going twenty miles over the speed limit as he cuts through traffic to get around people.

Gavin blares his horn, muttering something about the driver in the far left lane.

"Where are we going?"

"Home base." He points and I lean forward, my hands on the dash. A thread of black rises up from a cluster of trees. It's so faint I have to squint to be sure it's really there.

"Is that smoke?"

He nods without taking his eyes off the road.

"But isn't that where—"

"The barn is," he finishes.

"We're going back? I thought it wasn't safe?"

"It's not. But that's the idea."

"That doesn't make sense." My questions stop when I see the flash of blue and red in the side mirror. "They're gaining on us."

Gavin curses and cuts across two lanes. "We need to throw them off." Tires screech and horns honk as he zigzags around cars. His eyes shuttle between the mirror and the road. "How many do you see?"

"Two. No. Make that three."

"I know where we can lose them." He wrenches the wheel, narrowly missing the exit sign as we leave the highway. There's a truck waiting for the light to turn green at the end of the off ramp. Gavin rides the shoulder to bypass it, turning right without so much as a pause.

We speed down a hill that takes us out of view from the exit and park behind a building that looks like it's been gutted—even the front door is missing.

Gavin kills the engine.

He reaches for my hand as the sirens grow louder. A bead of sweat trickles down my back. Neither of us moves or says a word, as if the sound of a single blink will give us away.

The wait lasts for no more than three minutes, but it feels like hours. When the sirens fade, I crack the window, forcing myself to breathe again. Gavin gets out of the car and picks up a large rock. He chips off the glass that still hangs from the rear window then we slip back onto the highway, driving the speed limit the rest of the way to keep the attention off of us.

When we reach the barn, the air reeks of smoke and loss. Any sense of relief I have goes up in flames. There's a plume of black rising from the building that once protected me. And in the spot Gavin's truck usually occupies, there's a white SUV.

"Don't worry," Gavin says as I jump out. "Everyone is safe."

I scan my surroundings, certain we're being watched. There aren't many places to hide. The barn looks skeletal. Orange flames are swallowing up the red siding. Embers float above our heads, and the smoky cloud looming over us feels ominous.

"But they're here." I point at the SUV.

"That's not them." Gavin grabs my hand. "That's us."

The blaze reflects in Gavin's eyes when I face him. The heat ripples the air and it's so dry I can barely swallow. "You mean everyone's here? Sasha? Mary?"

He nods. "Even Parker. My dad let him out." He nods toward the SUV. "That's his car. Our team's hiding out in the forest."

"But the barn? Why'd you destroy it?" It hurts to watch it burn.

"I'll show you." He leads me toward the shed. I hear shuffling inside and I rip my hand away from Gavin's in case I need to strike. Gavin pulls back the door and his dad drops a plastic container. It gives a slight bounce and lands on its side.

"You scared me," Bracken says.

"Sorry 'bout that." Gavin picks up the container, setting it on the shelf. I cover my nose, inhaling the strong smell of gasoline. "Are we good?" Gavin asks him.

Bracken peels off his long black gloves. "There should be plenty of fuel to keep it lit. I'll wait in the car. When they arrive, I'll take off like we planned."

"What's going on?" I say, a hint of desperation in my voice.

"He's going to try to get them to follow him. The plan is to make the cops think we've switched cars, met up with a getaway vehicle. If we time it right, at least one of the cruisers will follow my dad. That way if the signal doesn't work maybe we can get away…"

"What signal?" I feel dizzy from the smell and back up to the entryway. I'm trapped between heat and gas.

"I got a response. One of my messages must have made it through. The military heard us."

Now I really need air. When I step outside, I hear the faint sound of sirens.

The news and the fumes make my head spin. Gavin follows me out, gripping my arm as I waver. I focus on his eyes to steady my brain. "Adrian found a channel that worked."

"My dad…he responded?"

The sirens are fast approaching, and Bracken pushes us out of the way so he can shut the shed door. "Get her into the woods," he says, pulling the keys from his pocket.

Gavin tugs on my arm and we run. My legs feel like rubber, but we don't stop. We keep moving until we can't see the barn anymore. Gavin leans against a tree to catch his breath.

"What did my dad say?"

Gavin arches his back to stretch. When he relaxes, I see uncertainty in his eyes. "I don't know if it was him. They just asked some questions and I answered. I said I'd make a signal where they could find us. I don't know who got the message. For all I know, they think it's a prank, but it's a shot."

I try not to let my disappointment show, holding my chin up even though it wants to drop.

The sirens pierce the air and the hair on my neck stands up.

"They're here." Gavin cups his mouth and lets out a yipping noise, the kind a wild dog would make to find food or a pack to run with.

Someone answers the call and Gavin and I follow the sound. It takes several minutes for us to reach an uprooted tree. It lies on its side surrounded by mushrooms and decaying branches. A head pops up from behind the log and Mary waves, her grin stretching the width of her face.

I trip on a branch as I race to greet her. Everyone is here, and Mary's still hugging me as Paige sandwiches her between us.

"You made it." Paige grips my face as if she doesn't believe I'm real. Sasha's hug is quick, but she squeezes me hard enough to tell me she cares. Parker is the only one who doesn't greet me. I try to catch his eye, but all I get out of him is a nod.

The group bombards Gavin and me with questions, but their mouths clamp shut at the sound of a long blare.

Mary wraps herself around Craig's leg. "It's just a bullhorn," he says, smoothing her hair. "The bad guys are trying to get our attention. They want to know where we are."

"Is your dad supposed to call you when it's safe?" I ask Gavin.

Sasha doesn't wait for his answer. "Maybe we should head deeper into the woods." Craig argues against it, and the chatter starts up again, our voices lower this time.

All I hear is uncertainty and it triggers my own doubts. Would the military really come? What if they do, but it's not my dad? Maybe they'll agree with PharmPerfect's plan to make a super drug using my insides. I try to bury my pessimism, but when I glance over at Parker's gloomy face, it's hard.

Gavin and Adrian work to quell the group's fear while I slip away. I need to make things right with Parker. If we don't make it out of this alive, I at least want to have a clear conscience.

Parker doesn't look up as I approach. "Hey," he says, staring into the woods. His back is against the fallen log, and he's sitting several feet from the rest of the group, as if he got kicked off the team. Guilt punches me in the chest. It's a blow I probably deserve.

"I'm sorry I locked you in the basement." I sit next to him. "I didn't want you to get hurt."

He shakes his head. "Do you know how helpless I felt locked in there while you were running straight into danger? You had no right."

"Somebody has to stay alive if we're going to shut down the Center." I gesture to Mary, who's making a flower necklace while Gavin talks to the group. "She's still so young. So innocent." My voice breaks a little. "There aren't many of us that know the truth. I owed it to you to keep you safe. And to her."

A forgiving smile tugs at Parker's lips, but when he looks at me his eyes are sad. "It's not just that…of all the ways I imagined my life would be after the Center, this wasn't one of them." He pulls in a long breath, so deep it feels like he's sucking the air out of me. "My life's a joke."

"Parker, that's not true—"

"Of course it is. I mean, come on, I was raised to be a lab rat. Hell, on paper, I don't even exist." He tears at the grass between his feet, as if he's clawing his way to someplace else. Anywhere but here.

"Screw the Center, Parker." I rub his back. "They can hide our past, but they can't decide our future."

He meets my eyes again. "I hate what they did to us, what a nobody I am. Then you left me behind, trapped in that room." I cringe, my hand stopping on his shoulder blade. "That's not what I meant," he says quickly. "What I'm trying to say is, you could've died, and I realized my life would be worse without you in it." His lips press together when he pauses, his eyes flitting over to Gavin. "All I want is for you to be happy."

Tears brim my eyes. "I don't know what to say…" I squeeze his shoulder. "Except my life would be worse without you in it too."

My hand clamps down when we hear a pop pop!

I scramble to my feet at the sound of the agonizing yell that follows the noise.

"Noooooo!" Gavin wails, already halfway over the log. He's heading back toward the barn, and I bolt after him, ignoring Paige's plea for me to stop.

Gavin runs at full speed, but I'm quicker and cut the distance in less than twenty seconds.

"Stop!" I yell. "Don't go out there!"

When we reach the clearing, he brakes like he's hit a force field and laces his hands above his head. He groans at the scene. There are two police cruisers parked cockeyed in the drive and the SUV door is ajar. My eyes flash to the man lying on the ground, sprawled out as if he fell while trying to climb in. It takes a millisecond for me to piece it all together: Bracken's been shot.

# CHAPTER 29

"Dad!" Gavin darts through the field and I sprint after him, trying to snatch his arm. He growls at me to let go, dragging me a few feet. I try to tow him in the direction of the forest, but he's too strong and twists his torso to shake me off. I lose my footing and fall as Paige and Parker burst out of the woods. Paige points at me, but I clamor to my feet before either of them can help me up—or hold me back.

"Tabitha, wait!" Paige yells.

"I have to stop him!" I will my legs to run faster. Gavin's heading straight for his dad. Straight toward the man with the gun.

There's an officer behind the door of the police cruiser. He adjusts his stance and steadies his gun, pointing it at Gavin's chest. "Freeze!"

Gavin doesn't stop.

I hear the gun click and dive for Gavin's foot, stretching my fingers to catch his heel. He trips as the bullet whizzes by, and his body hits the ground with a *thud*. His groan is eclipsed by Paige's scream.

I roll over and sit up, expecting Paige to be running toward us. Instead, she has her hand around Parker's leg, his knee mangled like it's been turned inside out. I hurry to his side, helping Paige remove his shirt so we can stop the bleeding.

Parker curses as I cinch the fabric tight. "It burns!" He closes his eyes, gritting his teeth.

"Lie back. Try to slow your heart—" My advice is interrupted by the gravelly voice bellowing through a bullhorn.

"Put your hands above your head and walk this way." The

officer stands in the grass near Gavin, who's on his knees with his hands clasped over his head. The gun is on Gavin, but the officer's eyes are on us.

"He can't walk," Paige yells back. "You shot him!"

Tears streak her face. I try—and fail—to pinch back my own. Bracken looks dead, Parker's been shot, and Gavin has a gun to his head. My chest tightens like it's collapsing in on itself.

"Stay with Parker," I say, letting go. She shakes her head, and I wipe my face with my palm. "I have to, Paige. I'm not going to watch my friends die when I'm the one they want."

I walk toward the officer, picking up my pace when he presses the barrel against Gavin's temple. "I'm coming." I lift my hands above my head so he knows I'm surrendering. "You have me. Let him go."

The officer chuckles. "Get down and shut up." He motions with his gun and I drop to my knees next to Gavin.

"I'm sorry," Gavin says, lifting his chin. His eyes look sunburned, his face wrenched with guilt. But before I can tell him I understand, that he was afraid for his dad, we hear a soft moan. Gavin and I glance over at Bracken's body. He's not moving and the gravel is stained with blood, but the sound came from him, which means he's still alive—for now.

"Eyes forward." The officer waves the black barrel in my periphery.

"Hold your fire!" Another officer rounds the back of the SUV, his face flecked with ash, as if he's been sifting through the barn rubble looking for us. He props a foot up on the bumper and leans his ear toward the radio on his shoulder. "Don't shoot the girl." He gestures to me. "She's the one we need."

The officer with the gun grumbles and yanks me to my feet. He pulls my hands down to the small of my back and cuffs me as a sleek black car approaches. It parks behind Bracken's SUV, and when the door opens, Gavin yells out in desperation, "He needs a doctor!"

Gavin clamps his mouth shut when he sees who it is. Mr.

Murphy gives Bracken a quick once over and flicks his wrist. "We'll make sure he's taken care of."

"Murderer!" Gavin spits out the word. As if the barn is angry too, the wood begins to creak, and the roof collapses, sending a fresh puff of smoke and embers into the air.

The officer hauls Gavin away and I watch helplessly as he's slammed against the cruiser for a pat down. I turn back when I hear footsteps, swallowing hard when Mr. Murphy is close enough to count my freckles. Close enough to cut me here and now if he wanted to.

He looks out to the field. "How many are out there?"

"It's just the four of us." I drop my gaze to his lapel and try to control my breathing.

He must sense I'm lying because he makes a two-fingered gesture to Officer Ash Face. "Check the woods. My son said there were more of them. If they're in there, haul them out. Let's shut this operation down for good."

The first officer tosses Gavin into the back of one cruiser and comes back for me, tugging so hard the steel cuts into my wrists. "Let's go." He drags me toward Ash Face's patrol car.

"Easy now," says Mr. Murphy, walking alongside us. "I want this one unharmed." He smiles at me as if it's a shared joke between us. I wish he'd move in front of me so I could kick his teeth in.

"You have me. What more do you want?" The words taste acidic on my tongue, because I already know the answer. "Why don't you just let the rest of them go?" I look back at the field hoping that Paige and Parker have escaped. My heart sinks when I see they haven't moved.

Ash Face bypasses them and heads into the woods. Parker must be too injured to move, and Paige is too noble to leave him. Her top is splotched with red as she holds the blood-soaked shirt tight around Parker's knee.

Of course Mr. Murphy won't negotiate. He dissects children. I doubt he even has a heart of his own. Parker and Paige will either be shot or parted out, Bracken will bleed to death, Gavin's going to jail, and if the others don't get away...I don't want to imagine what they'll do to Mary.

I choke back my tears. "Please. You won. Isn't that enough?"

Mr. Murphy looks past me to the officer. "Take her away. I'll meet you at the hospital." Only then do his eyes land on me. "We have a lot of work to do." He disappears into his fancy car and the engine purrs contently when he starts it.

"You heard the man," the officer says, pushing down on my head. I stiffen my neck, fighting to keep my eyes above the hood of the cruiser. Even though I know this is the end, that once I'm locked behind this door I'll become PharmPerfect's science project, my fighting spirit refuses to make it easy on Mr. Murphy's team.

"Get in, you little—"

I shake my head from side to side and underneath the officer's curses, I catch the sound of gravel being chewed up by tires. The officer eases his grip and we both look over as two sedans pull into the driveway and grind to a stop in front of the exit.

The cars are almost identical to Mr. Murphy's. My friends are as good as dead—unless they got a head start.

"Get. In," the officer says, giving my head a firm shove. He may have muscle, but I have bite. I twist my face around, my mouth searching for the nearest clump of skin. I clamp down on his sweaty flesh and he lets out another explosion of expletives as his hand jerks back.

I ram him with my shoulder and take off for the woods. My body's unsteady without the balance of my arms and I'm barely ten feet when I feel a pinch in my back. A jolt of electricity courses through me. My limbs go rigid and I fall on my face, staring helplessly at the ground.

After several minutes, my muscles stop twitching. There's still a buzz between my ears when I hear a man's hardened voice say, "Get her up."

I'm hoisted to my feet. When I stop wobbling, I notice two men staring back at me with bulletproof vests that read SWAT across their chests. They flank a man in a military uniform. My brain snaps to attention and I look over my shoulder, searching for Gavin, who's still sitting in the back of a cruiser with his forehead pressed against the glass, his eyes wide. I can't tell if he's afraid or in shock. Probably both.

The military got Gavin's message, but it seems they decided to work with Mr. Murphy rather than reconnect me with my father.

Smoke and tears burn my eyes. I glance back at the soldier, his face rough and weathered, like he's been sleeping on a bed of sandpaper, or not sleeping at all. His hair looks like it's been colored in with a dull, gray crayon. When I meet the man's gaze, he scans my face, reading me with equal intensity.

"What's your name?" he asks.

"Tabitha Rhodes."

Shock flashes in the deep recesses of his eyes, like he doesn't believe me.

"Where did you grow up?"

"Gladstone…I think."

He frowns. "Where are your parents?"

"My mom died." I use my shoulder to motion toward Mr. Murphy's sedan. "That man used her for drug tests. The same tests he plans to do on me."

The man whispers something to one of the SWAT officers who immediately runs toward the newer sedans.

"And your father?"

I stare up at the sky, unsure how to answer. "He was on assignment when I was taken to the Center for Growth. That's all I know. I haven't seen my dad in ten years. I'm not even sure he's alive." I bring my gaze back to his and my lip quivers. "I don't know what Mr. Murphy's told you, but I'm not volunteering for the military's drug project, and neither are the kids he's raising for body parts."

The SWAT officer returns with a white box that looks like a first aid kit. "This is what we need," the soldier says then nods at Mr. Murphy's car. "Bring him out."

Mr. Murphy exits his vehicle with his eyebrows scrunched

together, as if he's been asked to spell the name of every ingredient in one of his drugs. My body tenses when he nears.

"This girl says her name is Tabitha Rhodes," says the soldier.

"That's impossible. She's been kidnapped by a group of kids who sell body parts on the black market. I'm sure her brain has been scrambled by the drugs they've given her."

Before I can object, the SWAT officer opens the white box and pulls out a syringe and a vial of purple liquid. He sticks it in and points the needle at me. "It's ready," he says, handing it to the soldier.

*So this is how it ends for me.*

I suck in a breath and there's a flash of amusement in the military man's eyes. He aims the needle at Mr. Murphy instead. "Let's try this again."

"Get that thing away from me." Mr. Murphy makes an X with his forearms and steps back. "What's the meaning of this?"

"Restrain him," the soldier says, his voice so sharp I flinch. One of the SWAT guys pulls Mr. Murphy's hands behind his back and I feel a small twinge of pleasure when the soldier punctures his neck. He drains the syringe and tosses it back in the white box. "Now. Be honest this time. What's this girl's name?"

Mr. Murphy's eyes gloss over and his face goes slack. "Tabitha Rhodes."

"What do you want with her?"

"To help the military, of course. You want stronger soldiers?" Mr. Murphy grins. His white teeth shine despite the cloud of smoke blocking most of the sun. "You need my help. And I," he nods at me, "need her."

"For a drug?" The man's voice is as stiff as his uniform.

"Not just *a* drug, *the* drug." Mr. Murphy leans forward and one of his hands slips free. He wags a finger in my direction. "We need her for Gideon. She's the incubator."

"How did you find her?"

"She was wandering the streets. Alone. A customer brought her in." Mr. Murphy beams. "She had the genes!"

"Genes like her mother?" The soldier's eyes are ablaze with anger and I shrink when his jaw tightens.

"Exactly!" Mr. Murphy tugs his other arm loose and claps his hands together with a single pop.

"So you admit she was raised for the experiment? And others," the military man gestures to Parker and Paige, "were raised for parts?"

"Yes! Business is booming. And with this girl, we'll be able to help our nation excel once again. Invincible soldiers." Mr. Murphy reaches for the man's shoulder, and in a flash, the soldier grabs his hand, twisting hard. Mr. Murphy wails and falls to one knee, his arm wound so tightly it looks like it will break with another half inch of torque.

"Before I'm through with you, you're going to give me the name of every doctor you work with, every person who's ever had any knowledge of this operation. Do I make myself clear?" The soldier lets go, and another man, one who looks like a SWAT officer without a vest, lifts Mr. Murphy to his feet and hauls him away.

People in dark, non-Gladstone police clothes materialize from the SUVs, armed with supplies and guns—ones that aren't pointed at our heads. They're talking on radios and moving so fast I can't figure out who's in charge or what's going on.

"We need medics, stat!" says a man behind me. I glance back to see him squatting next to Bracken.

I'm trying to absorb it all, to understand what this means—when the soldier barks orders at the Gladstone officer who Tased me. "Uncuff her," he says. The officer obeys and stands off to the side, cowering as if he's become a gazelle among lions. I flex my wrists and glare at him until SWAT finds a home for him in the back of one of the rigs.

"What now?" I ask, still unsure about the soldier, but convinced enough that I can drop my guard—at least a little.

"The FBI will talk to everyone who worked for Mr. Murphy to figure out who knew what, who took bribes—" He cuts himself off with a curt nod. "It's a long process. But I can assure you, no one else will be sold for parts."

"What will happen to all the foster kids?"

"We'll try to find them homes. Real homes," he says.

My eyes well up. "And the ones who are too old?"

"If they're eighteen, or want to live on their own, there'll be people who can help with the transition. They won't be left to fend for themselves just because the Centers close."

"What about PharmPerfect? That's shutting down, too, right?"

His jaw shifts like he's chewing on the answer. "They've been ordered to cease operations until the investigation is complete."

"W-what does that mean? Will they be able to open up again in a few weeks?"

"Certainly not the Centers. Those are shut down indefinitely and anyone associated in any way, shape, or form will be prosecuted. But the board of directors can claim they had no knowledge of what Mr. Murphy was doing, that he acted on his own. If investigators agree he's the one to blame, the board will fight to keep PharmPerfect up and running."

Before he can continue, I hear Gavin's voice behind me.

"Tabitha!"

I spin around and the knots in my stomach unravel. For a moment all the chaos around us falls silent. I let out a breath and Gavin jogs toward me, his smile widening with each step.

"Just a minute, sir," a female officer says, stepping into his path. She's wielding a notepad and he holds up a finger to me as she prattles off questions about the events leading up to today.

I turn back to the soldier and my breath catches when I see the way he's looking at me, examining me with eyes that look younger.

"I know it doesn't seem right that everyone isn't going to jail, but the folks at PharmPerfect won't come near you again," he says.

"How? How can you be so sure they're not going to continue—"

"I have contacts at the FBI who will update me if anything suspicious goes on while the board is being interrogated. You and your friends are all safe. You have my word."

"I don't even know who you are."

"I'm…I'm someone who has a personal interest in making sure you're okay."

I rub the sore spots on my wrists, but what I really want to do is rub my heart. It aches like it's waiting to be disappointed.

"What do you mean?"

"What I'm trying to say is," he steps closer, "I don't want you in foster care. I want you to stay with me." He reaches out, his finger grazing my cheek. "You can dye the hair, but not the freckles…"

I clutch my chest. "Does this mean…" My hands drop to my side. "Are we…?"

"We'll need a DNA test to prove it," he says, a gentle cadence to his voice. "But I have no doubts. Aside from the brown, you look just like your mother." His eyes brim with tears as he pulls me into his arms. I breathe in the smell of his uniform, making a mental note—a memory. *This is the smell of my father.*

I hold tight, trying to make up for a thousand lost embraces.

"You're really here." I laugh through my tears. "I can't believe you got the message."

"I thought one of the men in my battalion was playing a sick joke." My dad loosens his grip. "Who's Gavin?"

I pull back enough to point. Gavin's still caught up with answering questions, but he catches my eye and gives my dad a respectful nod. "He's part of the rescue group that saved kids from the Center. We were living here." I wave at the nearly nonexistent barn.

"No one needs to hide anymore. We'll find everyone a place to call home."

I smile at the thought. "That's all any of us ever wanted." I wipe my eyes when we let go, but he keeps an arm around me, as if he's afraid he'll lose me in the mix of people running around.

In the corner of my eye, I see two officers lifting Parker, carrying him to an ambulance that's just arrived. "Where are they taking him? Is he going to be all right?"

"Don't worry, they'll transport him to a hospital on the mainland. The doctors will repair any damage."

"Can I say goodbye?" My dad nods, and I hurry before they can load him.

"Parker!"

He looks up with a strained smile. Although he's clearly in a lot of pain, I see relief in his eyes.

"That's him, isn't it?"

"Yep. That's my dad." I rock on my heels. I have a surge of energy, so pumped I could blast off. "He's real. Can you believe it?"

"That's great," Parker says, but when he purses his lips, part of my happiness fades.

"They're going to find us homes. All of us."

"I'm eighteen. It's a little late." The medic averts her eyes as Parker's voice wavers.

"They can still help." Parker looks doubtful and I go on. "Don't you see? This is your chance to start over, be whoever you want. You could join the military or FBI, work to stop guys like Mr. Murphy." His mouth spreads into a slow smile. "Let's make a pact." I hold out my hand for him to shake. "Once you get better, we'll work together to make sure PharmPerfect pays for what they did to us."

He quirks an eyebrow. "I guess I can agree to that." He shakes. I hug him before the medic radios in that they're on their way. Then the door closes and I watch Parker leave, feeling like part of me is going with him.

Paige is waiting nearby, and I walk with her back to my dad, who's in a deep conversation with Gavin. They look up when we approach.

"Is Bracken going to be okay?" I ask Gavin, torn between throwing my arms around him and hugging my dad again. Gavin nods and opens his arms for a brief second before shoving his hands in his pockets. I smile, thinking this must be what normal feels like, what girls with protective fathers get to experience.

"He'll be all right." Gavin struggles to keep his hands tucked away. "He's lost a lot of blood, but they said no major organs were hit." Finally, he can't resist and his arms stretch wide, curling around my body. I lean toward him just as Paige hollers.

"There are the others!" She takes off for the woods, like she's trying to beat someone in a race. Like Meghan would have.

"Others?" My dad narrows his eyes, squinting at the figures popping out from behind the trees.

"Our team." I share a look with Gavin.

Paige twirls Mary around in the field before setting her down to greet the rest of the crew. Mary runs at Mary-speed—half skipping, half prancing—until she reaches Gavin's arms, and we squeeze her between us. Gavin's arms are long enough to envelop us both. It's the best Mary sandwich yet.

"She's from the Center, too?" My dad rubs his eyes as if he's coming out of a daze.

I let go of Mary and Gavin, taking my dad's hand. Our fingers lace naturally, like they were always meant to fit together.

"Come on." I tug him toward the trees. "I want to introduce you to the rest of my family."

# ACKNOWLEDGMENTS

As solitary as the act of writing is, it takes a team to turn a manuscript into a book. Luckily, I have an incredible village of people willing to read my crappy first drafts and cheer me on when revisions threaten my sanity.

This book wouldn't be here today without my fabulous critique partners. Cindy Wilson, who works at cheetah-like speeds and shines a spotlight on ways to add tension and depth to each scene—thank you for letting me call you in a panic when I can't fix a plot hole or just need to talk out the end of a scene! And J D Abbas, who's a grammar whiz and loves my characters as much as I do. Drinks on me for our next dinner date! (Thanks for putting your skills to work editing my acknowledgments too! ☺)

My unstoppable agent, Whitley Abell, who has such great insight to make my novels better. I am always excited (and a little terrified) to send you new material because your notes are spot on. This has been an incredible ride, and I can't wait for our next book journey together!

To my wonderful beta readers who see past the early errors and still ask for more chapters even when they suck—thank you! In no particular order (because they're all great): Denise Mealy, Barb Schatz, Marilee Eerkes, Danette Cap, Vanesa Cruz-Montaño, Shawna Haag, Jessica Schultz, Jaime Mahoney, Joan Mauk, Nancy Chott, Wali Martin, and Amy Halfmoon. There are also dozens more who read a few test chapters—and I am so grateful for the direction each of them provided!

My dear friend and reader, Marnaé Collins, who let me use her childrens' names and then kill one of them in the novel. ☺ Forever and always, I love you, F.S!

Tina Saey who helped me with the scientific elements in the story. Thank you for letting me bug you on Christmas Eve. You were more helpful than you'll ever know!

I'm forever grateful to the wonderful team at Diversion Books who believed in me and my story. Each of you have been instrumental in making my book dreams come true! Eliza Kirby, Sarah Masterson Hally, Erin Mitchell, and all the staff working behind the scenes to make this happen—thank you!

To the folks at Chandler Reach Vineyards—your wine is the salve that helps me get through revisions.

Wendy Poteet, Katie Nelson, and Shelbey Sawyer—thank you all for being so eager to support me with launch parties!

I can't forget my online writing family—Michelle Hauck who encourages and supports writers with her contests; and Colleen Oefelein who hosted my book cover reveal and creates such beautiful banners and images for me to use.

The amazing Juny Soukhavong who can wave a hand over a computer and create an eye-catching website and powerful book trailer. And Josh Kandle for his gorgeous work on my marketing material.

And of course the lovely staff at the Mid-Columbia Libraries (especially the Prosser branch)—thank you for standing behind local writers and your genuine interest and support of my work.

To the great team at the Pacific Northwest National Writers Association who care so much about writers and helping them find success, thank you!

You the reader, of course, for letting my characters run free in your head!

And to Matt, who is probably wondering why his name is at the bottom. It's because you're the most important. Thank you for working so hard to allow me to stay home so I can do what I love: write. You're the best husband a girl could ask for. If it weren't for you, I wouldn't have my babies: Soleil, Autry, and Tatum. And I wouldn't have my book baby either. See, we have four kiddos! Now we're good! ☺

JESSICA KAPP always thought her penmanship would improve with age. She even wished for it on her eleventh birthday. But after having a hard time deciphering her own writing, she hijacked her grandma's typewriter—a really cool one with white correction tape—and  started creating fictional worlds. She loves to imagine the what-ifs of life as she writes contemporary and speculative fiction for young adults.

Jessica lives with her husband and children on a small farm in Washington with far too many goats and the occasional cow.

Connect with her at **www.jessicakapp.com**,
**www.facebook.com/authorjessicakapp**,
or on Twitter at **@JessKapp**.

CPSIA information can be obtained
at www.ICGtesting.com
Printed in the USA
BVOW09s0005110717

489027BV00002B/2/P